Unraveling

Emily

ANNA REZES

ISBN: 978-1-950657-01-8 (paperback)
ISBN: 978-1-950657-05-6 (hardcover)

Library of Congress Control Number: 2019904872

This is a work of fiction. Names, characters,
places, and incidents are either a product of the
author's imagination or are used fictitiously. Any
resemblance to actual persons, living or dead,
events, or locales is entirely coincidental.

Cover design by German Creative

First Edition: June 2019

Words Imagined
Hilliard, OH

www.annarezes.com

To everyone who encouraged me.

prologue ~

A life built on lies has a shaky foundation, one destined to crumble when deadly truths are brought to light, revealing this life has been an elaborate façade. For the last five years I've been piecing together this puzzle I call my life. Now that the jagged edges are in place, I want to tear them apart and set them on fire, anything to help erase the picture of what I am destined to become. Though my life has not been normal for a long time, I never expected it to come to this.

Desperate and out of options, I cling to hope which feels tragic because it cannot save me. Hope is a trick. It's intangible, like grasping air during a free fall. I should accept my fate, but so long as I'm breathing, I will latch on to hope, knowing the consequences could destroy me.

As I reflect on my mistakes, the chill from the cement floor bleeds into the marrow of my bones. Through the bars of my cell, I watch the unsteady rise and fall of his chest. The man I love most in this world has been unconscious for a while now, and I'm painfully aware that his precious life is draining away before my eyes. If only I could reach him, he might have a chance.

I stretch my arms through the barricade, pushing until the iron cuts into my skin. Then I push harder, enduring the pain in my shoulder. I cannot reach him. I don't even come close, but I try. He's dying right in front of me, and I'm powerless to do anything, but watch.

"I'm so sorry," I whisper. "It's all my fault."

I hit the bars between us as my lips quiver, and the moisture in my eyes overflows. Crying, though it resolves nothing, is my only option as guilt consumes my heart.

one ~

I gaze out the oversized window wondering how much longer this will take. I shift, sitting sideways on my silk cushioned seat to thoroughly avoid my reflection in the wall of mirrors hanging before me. A love song drones on in the background. It does nothing to mask the uncomfortable, yet inevitable silence between myself and the lady next to me. We are amicably ignoring one another, yet I can't help but feel insecure.

I glance at myself in the enormous mirrors to see my black flats peeking out from under my nicest pair of dark jeans. I hadn't realized they were frayed until forced in front of this reflective wall for the last two hours. The brightness of the track lighting overhead emphasizes my pale complexion and dull blond hair that falls past my shoulders in desperate need of a trim. I straighten my posture, looking every bit as uncomfortable as I feel.

"Oh wow, I love this one!" the familiar voice chimes. I turn to find my sister's glowing face. Her smile is radiant. She's beautiful, even without the white satin dress draping her curves and flowing out in a tangle of tulle trailing behind her. The dress is not my taste, but no one could deny the stunning young woman on the pedestal.

The elusive woman sitting next to me springs from her chair, wiping tears from her eyes. She rushes forward to hug my sister. "Oh darling, you look beautiful! This is the one!"

As they embrace, I focus on their relationship. It looks so natural, like they could be mother and daughter. I'm happy my sister will have a mother again, even if she is a mother-in-law. The petite middle-aged woman is well put together, from her dark red nail polish matching her silk blouse, down to her pressed black slacks and patent leather heels. Her bronze skin screams tanning bed, and her makeup looks professionally done. Her artificial air intimidates me, but I cannot deny she loves my sister and is just the kind of woman Sam would admire.

They break apart to begin a close inspection of every pearl and sparkling bead. The familiar pain of grief and loss weighs on my mind as I think of our own mother. The mother who will never see her daughter get married.

Sam's impatient sigh breaks my trance. I realize I'm staring at them with my thoughts miles away. My brain commands my tongue to form words, but I feel lost in the reality of my sister getting married.

My sister spins on the pedestal to stare expectantly. "Emily, what do you think?"

I muster a big smile and stand from my chair. "Sam, you look . . . like a princess."

She has always been a princess, and the spectacle of a dress makes it official. Her eyes light up as she turns around to admire her reflection. She touches her waist caressing the dress.

"I do?" she whispers.

Dressed in black, the saleslady, Monica, walks around the corner with a bundle of tulle in one hand and a sparkling silver comb in the other. Without saying a word, Sam kneels when Monica approaches the pedestal to fasten the new accessories in her hair. Monica is wearing a real smile instead of the fake plastered-on smile she'd been sporting all morning. Sam is sweet but tends to make a production out of everything. It can be exhausting trying to please her, and this dress is the last of twenty my sister has modeled, but none of the others had this reaction.

My sister's wavy mahogany hair falls to the small of her back. Half is swept up into a makeshift up-do, and the comb slides easily into place. A fluff of tulle sits on top leaving the veil to drape over her shoulders and out past the sweeping train. Sam begins crying. It's an odd reaction to a piece of tulle, although, I might cry too if someone put that ball of fluff on top of my head.

Sam wipes tears from her flawless golden skin. "Judy, do you think your son will like it?"

Her soon to be mother-in-law answers in a choked voice, also wiping tears, "Of course. He will love it! Sweetheart, you could wear a burlap sack and still be the most beautiful woman in the world to him."

Tears spill down her cheeks and Monica brings tissues. Is this normal? Should I be crying too? I smile to cover my discomfort. It's not out of Sam's nature to cry, but I've never been able to make sense of her reactions, so I remain silent, eager to escape.

The sunshine is calling my name from outside the bridal shop windows, and I need it more than ever after sitting next to "Miss Tanning-bed" for two hours. I need the sun, I need fresh air, and I need to get out of here before Sam makes me try on bridesmaid dresses.

"Is this the one?" Monica asks, before giving a spiel about ordering, time frames and so on. I stop listening and mindlessly count the number of beaded tiaras in the case beside the mirror.

They set their wedding date for New Year's Eve and it is sure to be an extravagant occasion. Sam's wealthy in-laws insist upon paying for the entire event, dress included.

Once Sam finishes with the sizing, a perfect size two, she walks with me to the bridesmaid dresses while Judy and Monica complete the paperwork. We browse the endless assortment of colorful and shockingly expensive dresses. The time, money, and planning that goes into one day is absurd. I make a mental note to elope if I ever get married.

"So, I was thinking of getting all the bridesmaids together to try on dresses next Thursday," Sam says, as she pulls out a bright yellow tulle dress. My eyes widen in horror, and she catches my reaction before I can hide it.

"Oh, come on, I have better taste than this!" She holds up the yellow fluff and then shoves it back on the rack. "But if it's what I wanted, then I'd expect you to wear it. I know you're young and can't understand—"

"I'll be eighteen in a few weeks." As the words come out of my mouth, I realize how juvenile they sound and wish I could take them back. I hate when she pulls the age card. For most of my life, I have been more responsible, more reliable, and more adult than Sam has ever wanted to be. So, what does it matter that she's four years older? I came to this appointment to support her. I sat through dress after dress next to a woman who at the very least dislikes me. I smiled and said encouraging words because she's my sister and because I love her, but I hate when she treats me like a child. "You know I'll wear whatever you choose," I promise, trying to defuse the situation.

"Meaning you'll suck it up and wear whatever God-awful thing I pick. Gee, thanks, Emily!" She's taking her anger out on the rack of dresses, and I'm hoping they don't have a you break it, you buy it policy. "I bet you don't even want to be in the wedding!" she accuses, giving up on the rack to glare at me. "You could use my help with style, you know." She gestures to my wrinkled shirt and tattered jeans.

I knew I hadn't dressed cute enough today, despite my effort. Sam is a few inches taller standing in her stiletto heels. I come just past her shoulder making it hard not to feel like a child while she's lecturing me.

"I'll make you look good and, of course, you'll just pout the whole time," she says, full of valley girl attitude.

I give her a look that says, "Really?" because we both know she's the one who pouts her way through life. With her big brown eyes and full luscious lips, she always gets whatever she wants. Her face has a baby doll quality, and when she smiles, she has perfect dimples in both cheeks.

We look nothing alike. She received her height, features, and golden complexion from our dad while I'm a dulled down version of our mom. While Mom had piercing emerald eyes, mine are more grey than green, and while she had shining blond waves, my straight hair falls somewhere between light brown and dishwater blond. Dishwater blond. Who came up with that anyway?

I take a deep breath. I don't want to fight with her. "Samantha, I love you. And I want to be a part of your big day." I've heard several people call it that. "I want you to dress me up like Barbie." I cringe at the thought. "I'm happy you found Dan. He really is perfect for you." This part is true. He knows how to handle Samantha and all of her drama. And there is a lot of drama.

"Oh Emily, I love you." She pulls me in for a quick hug. She's one of the few who can get away with hugging me.

As she releases me from her grip, I ask, "Did you decide on your other bridesmaids?"

She takes a deep breath and releases a sigh before she begins, "Well, Dan only wants his three closest guy friends and his brother and cousin." The intensity in her voice is classic Samantha. "As for bridesmaids . . . well, you of course, and I have to have Leah." I can barely keep from scowling. "Then there is Rochelle." She starts tallying us on her fingers. "Eva and Alison. I wanted to ask Jenny, but Mia will be mad that Alison is in it and . . ."

I am trying to pay attention, but she's lost me. As she continues to ramble on, complaining about someone named Amber, I think of the list she's given me. I've always liked Rochelle, Samantha's old college dorm-mate. They are opposites in almost every way, and in all honesty, she's probably the only real friend my sister has. The others are a mixture of superficial high school friends and sorority sisters, except for one.

Leah.

As much as I like Dan, I hate his younger sister, Leah, who graduated with me this year. I had hoped never to see her again, but apparently, fate is playing a cruel joke on me. She was unbelievably nasty to me, dishing out Emily Burk gossip and making my life a living hell. The only satisfaction I'm getting out of being stuck with her is she's stuck with me. I wish I could've seen the look on her face when she found out.

"Okay girls, the order is complete," Judy says, interrupting Sam. "I thought we would do lunch before the cake tasting."

"I should probably leave straight from here, so I'm not late for class." I fake disappointment. "I would be happy to try bridesmaid dresses next Thursday as long as we start early."

"Perfect! I'll see you the same time next Thursday!" Sam says, wrapping me in another hug.

After an awkward nod to Judy, I make a run for it. I take a deep breath of fresh air as I walk out into the sunshine. It's a warm Ohio day with a subtle breeze in the June air. I walk to my car, undoubtedly the oldest and most battered vehicle in the parking lot. The faded green paint and accents of rust complement the missing passenger side door handle. My weathered Toyota Avalon is embarrassingly loud, but she runs well despite the two-hundred-fifty-thousand miles on her.

I bought the car just before my sixteenth birthday with the money I saved up from babysitting and mowing the neighbor's lawn. My deafening muffler catches the attention of two women going into the bridal salon. They pause their conversation to gawk as I drive away.

I started taking summer classes at the community college after graduating from high school two weeks ago. I still don't know what I want to do with my life, but I know community college is all I can afford. To fill in my downtime I work thirty hours a week at the pet supply store, but it's not enough to fill the void my friends left behind.

Morgan was the only girl I really clicked with in high school, and she went off to college a year ago. For my senior year, I had only my three best guy friends. They were like brothers to me. Alec is cheerful, with an inappropriate sense of humor that makes him lovable despite his player tendencies. Gavin is smart; he's the level head to Alec's free spirit. Then there is Ben who is the glue that holds the three of them together. He can be the life of the party—allowing Alec to talk him into ridiculous situations—and other times he's pensive but not in a brooding way. I feel most at ease with Ben, perhaps, because he's comfortable with silence, and most of the time I have nothing to say. The four of us had a good thing going. They formed their own opinions, unswayed by the gossip. The guys didn't pry or want to talk about feelings like girls tend to do. Alec liked to remark about his latest female conquest, and that was as serious as it got—until Gavin told me about his feelings for me.

Gavin liked me all along, and I think I knew it. I just wanted him to keep his feelings to himself. After years of friendship, I began to wonder if the other guys only allowed me to hang out with them because of Gavin. I didn't want to lose him, so when he professed his interest in me, I made the wrong decision and tried to force my feelings. As my boyfriend, everything he did annoyed me. It didn't last long, and the one kiss we shared was terrible. I broke up with him on his birthday. I didn't mean to. I planned to wait at least a few days, but I kept feeling sick about leading him on.

They were my best friends, but I silently accepted the blame for making the last weeks of our senior year awkward. I was angry with myself, and the guys tried to pretend everything was normal, but I'd seen how they treated ex-girlfriends, so I've avoided them since graduation. It turns out; I miss them more than I expected.

Lost in thought, I almost miss my exit. Merging lanes at the last minute, I barely make it, slowing as I loop the exit ramp curve. I round the corner to find a woman standing in the middle of the road wearing nothing but a nightgown and snow boots. Slamming on my breaks, the crazy-haired woman doesn't move. She appears calm, looking right at me as my car is about to plow into her. My tires screech and my heart leaps at the moment of impact. I want to squeeze my eyes shut, but I can't look away, so I witness the collision, but there is no impact. Instead, my car passes through her. I follow her crystal blue eyes until she is right next to me inside the car. She reaches out, and I feel her hand on my face, the chilling caress of a ghost as her hand passes through my body. "It is you." I hear her whisper.

My car comes to a stop, and the woman disappears. I turn around to look for her, only to be met with the blare of angry car horns. I hit the gas, accelerating away from whatever the hell that was. I check my rearview mirror as I go, but the woman vanished as if she had never existed at all.

Reeling, I pull into the campus parking lot and pull up the dash cam footage on my phone. I've never been so grateful for my dad insisting on the stupid dash cam despite me thinking it was a waste of money.

I watch the moment I got off the exit, and this time there is no woman. There is just me, slamming on my breaks for no conceivable reason. I shake my head, clearing my thoughts. My mother's psychiatrist once told me that post-traumatic stress could cause hallucinations. Maybe that's all this is. It's been a while since I allowed myself to think of my mother, but with Samantha getting married, I've been thinking about her a lot. She is always a trigger for me, reminding me of the worst time in my life. That has to be what this is, stress manifesting itself in the most bizarre way. I tell my heart to calm down as I exit the car.

two ~

Arriving on campus, I realize I have an hour to spare before class. I was so desperate to escape the wedding planning that I didn't realize how early I would be for my lecture. In an attempt to distract myself, I walk around campus before settling on a bench. I try to enjoy the perfect weather, but my mind keeps wandering back to the hallucination, so I dig out my phone for something to do. I have no one to call or text, and after years of bullying and harassment, I deleted all social media. I put my phone down and search my backpack for a granola bar.

"Hey, Em."

Looking up, I recognize the tall, broad-shouldered guy wearing his usual jeans and t-shirt. He looks like an athlete, though he never played any sports in high school. Between his muscular build, his natural bronzed skin, and dark spiky hair, he has broken a lot of hearts over the years, mostly because he ignored the incessant teen stalkers. I've always respected him for that, and right now I'm surprised he didn't ignore me, after all, he is Gavin's best friend.

Caught off guard, I set my phone down and stutter, "Oh! H . . . hey, Ben. I didn't know you were taking summer classes."

"I'm not an overachiever like you, I'm just checking it out," he says, acting like nothing is wrong.

"Oh," I say, feeling self-conscious. "So, what do you think?"

He smiles but shakes his head. "I'm still undecided. My parents want me to go to a university out of state, but I think this would be a better fit."

"I didn't know you were applying out of state. Isn't it too late to get in anywhere? The deadlines were months ago."

He shrugs, saying, "I'm not too worried about it. I don't think taking a year off will destroy my life. My parents disagree, so they plan to have me move to the East Coast to start classes at the end of August. We'll see about that."

"East Coast? What School?"

Again, he shrugs. "Like I said, I'm undecided."

I don't want him to move away, but I always knew he would go places. Still, I'll miss him. I already miss him in the month we haven't talked. Shame comes flooding back, and I look away trying to ignore the tension between us.

He settles next to me, his face reflecting my worry, even as his big brown eyes comfort me. "You disappeared after graduation or really even before that."

"I'm sorry," I say because I'm not exactly sure what he's asking for, but sorry pretty much covers it all.

He begins, "This thing between you and Gavin—"

I cut him off. "Listen, I know I hurt Gavin. I don't need you to remind me. Honestly, I'm surprised you even said hi. I'm not gonna bug you, or Alec, or Gavin. I'm sorry. I didn't mean to mess it all up." I stand, wanting to get as far away as possible. I turn to pick up my bag, but it's still unzipped, and in my haste, I fumble with the zipper.

He catches my hand. "Emily, what are you talking about? You didn't mess anything up. You and Gavin gave it a shot. It didn't work. So what? We're still friends."

My eyes narrow with doubt.

He looks amused. "Emily, we've been friends since sixth grade. Do you think we can't be friends because of this?"

I point out, "You've been friends with Gavin longer."

"It's not an either/or kind of situation. It's simple. Do you want to be my friend, Em?"

I was friends with boys to avoid this kind of conversation. After overhearing my sister fight with her girlfriends, I decided early in life that most girls were just too intense for me and now here I am acting like a girl.

Ben's face turns serious. "Em?"

"Of course, I want to be friends."

He grins, reminding me why so many girls throw themselves at him. I'm not immune to his good looks, but I've built up a tolerance over the years. He's my friend, and I've never wanted or expected more.

He moves his hand from mine to pat the bench, waiting for me to sit down before he says, "Glad we figured this thing out."

"I broke up with him on his birthday," I remind him, in case he forgot and that might change his mind.

He snickers, "Yeah, about that. I thought you were into him."

"I tried to be into him, I mean, I like Gavin. He's just . . ." I shrug my shoulders. "I don't know. It felt weird. You guys are like brothers to me."

"Oh," he says, before going introspective on me. He does that sometimes. I don't force conversation. I know he'll start talking again once he's sorted everything out in his head. Sometimes, I wish I could crawl in there with him to see what's so important.

In the silence, I gaze across campus. A blond guy leaning against a tree averts his gaze making it obvious he had been watching me. I observe him back. It's only fair. Summer looks good on him with his sun-kissed complexion and short blond locks. I peer down at my pale arms and can't remember the last time I had a good tan. I glance back, and he's looking straight at me, sending a shiver through my body. Instead of looking away, I watch as he runs a hand through his messy blond hair. It looks soft, and I feel an urge to touch it. That's strange. I'll pretend I didn't just want to touch a stranger's hair.

Embarrassed, I stare at my feet waiting for Ben to say something.

"Are you busy tomorrow night?" Ben asks.

"I work until eight."

"Let's hang out. I'll pick you up after work, and we can grab a bite."

"I assume you'll want to take my car," I say with a smirk.

He laughs. "No, no, I'll drive," he insists.

Ben hates my car. He's tried to persuade me to let him work on it, but I've seen the work he's done to his own car, and I don't want an extravagant sound system or custom rims. I don't want to boost my engine, whatever that means. I like my car as it is.

"What? You wouldn't want to be caught in my—what do you call it? Scrap metal?" I tease.

"Well, I figured if we took your car, we'd spend most of the night waiting for a tow."

"Hey, she's got a lot of life left in her."

"That's very optimistic of you!" he says between chuckles.

"I've become quite attached to my hunk of scrap metal."

"It makes sense. You've always gravitated towards broken things. Take your dog, for instance."

"You're right. I mean, why else would we be friends?"

"Touché," he says, standing to leave. "Now that you've wounded my ego, I'm gonna go enjoy summer while you waste away in class. See you tomorrow, Em."

I watch him leave before I resume searching for my granola bar. I pull out a few books, and just as I thought, I find my snack smashed at the bottom of my bag. I eat it anyway. It's exceedingly messy despite my careful bites, and I'm covered in crumbs by the time I finish. I stand to wipe the crumbs from my clothes.

I hear laughter and look up. Under that same tree, the blond guy is shaking with amusement. His eyes lock with mine before he glances down to where I'm brushing crumbs from my shirt. He's laughing at me. Heat touches my cheeks as embarrassment floods my body. Turning my back to him, I gather my things, desperate to escape. I don't need to look to know he's still watching me. It's as if I can feel his eyes following my movements.

I turn to leave, catching his unabashed smile as he looks me in the eye with blatant curiosity. I stare back at him, finding myself mesmerized by his bright eyes and breathtaking grin. I don't smile back, but I can't look away. I panic as he moves toward me. I tell myself to look elsewhere, but something about him pulls me a step closer.

Though he looks to be in his early twenties, he doesn't fit here, standing out like a shiny quarter in a jar of pennies. He would be more suited as a model for a runway in Paris than a simple community college. Nevertheless, here he is striding toward me, stealing my breath and filling me with an overwhelming urge to run. His sexy smirk gives me the impression he knows all my secrets.

Get a grip, Emily. He's just a guy!

But even as I scold myself, his bright blue eyes wash through me, paralyzing me, leaving me captivated. He's about to walk right up to me, but I can't let that happen. If this is how I react to him at a distance, what effect will he have up close?

Annoyed he's affecting me this way, I pry my eyes from him, pull out my phone, and pretend to answer a call. When I peek through my lashes, he's still coming my way.

I take a deep breath and watch him pass by. He's near enough to touch, near enough to smell his sweet masculine scent. Unexpected disappointment crashes over me as I watch him walk away. I expect him to turn around or look back, but instead, he rounds a corner moving out of sight. I stand, unable to move, completely hypnotized by this mysterious blond guy. I shake myself out of my weird trance. Brushing off the strange encounter, I head to class.

Humanities class is held in the largest lecture hall on campus which is nonessential with such a small summer class. Students are sprawled out through the enormous room. I find a seat halfway down the aisle and sit to the far right making sure to avoid my fellow students. I pull my phone from my pocket and play games until the elderly professor limps up to the podium at the front of the room. He looks like he should have retired at least ten years ago, but once I experience the way he teaches with enthusiasm and passion, I'm grateful he's still teaching. He makes the class feel like story time. His lecture goes on for two hours before he dismisses the class late, with apologies.

Tardy for my next class, I jump out of my seat, flinging my book bag around, so it drapes the front of me. I load my books as I rush to the exit. I am barely paying attention when I approach the door and almost run into the back of another student. Startled, I look up, stopping just in time to avoid plowing into *him*. I smell the familiar scent before I recognize the expensive clothing. The blood drains from my face as I stare up at the mysterious blond guy from earlier.

He's laughing at me again. "You're terribly clumsy, aren't you?" he says in a deep silky voice. "It's rather endearing to find such a beautiful woman whose movements completely contradict the elegance a body like yours suggests."

Unsure how to respond to such an inappropriate comment, I try to move around him, but he steps in my way. "Allow me," he says, pushing the door open. He stands in the doorway, holding it open for me.

Even after I look away, I feel the intensity of his stare. I squeeze by him, speeding out the door without a word when I hear him murmur, "Until we meet again."

I half run to my next class. When I enter the classroom, the professor doesn't even notice me taking a seat in the back. Of course, now I'm winded and focus on slowing my rapid breathing.

It's only an hour, but despite coming in ten minutes late the remaining fifty minutes feel like an eternity. The freshman orientation class is required, so even though it's a joke, everyone is forced to take it. I tune out the teacher as she rambles on about all the library has to offer.

I use my time to mull over the strange situation with the alluring blond guy. I have humanities lecture with him, so I will most definitely see him again. I am good at ignoring people, so I don't know why I'm letting him get to me. Why was it so hard for me to look away from him? Never in my life have I been one to swoon over a guy, but the attraction was intense, and I hate the small part of me that looks forward to seeing him again, especially after he laughed at me and called me clumsy.

After class, I drive home. I pull up to our ranch style house built back in the seventies. My parents purchased it ten years ago, thinking this little suburb outside of Columbus would be a safe place. They had the intention of fixing it up. I remember my mom digging out big bushes in front of the porch, leaving large holes in the flowerbed. She told me I could pick out my favorite flowers and we'd plant them together.

That was nine years ago, just before she left. I look down at the big holes of dried dirt covered with weeds as I step onto the porch, reminding me of one of the many broken promises. I walk through the front door, leaving the constant reminder behind.

Maggie is standing in the front room with her tail nub wagging excitedly, taking her hips along for the ride. "Hey, Mags!" I lean over to pet her head. "Ben doesn't know what he's talking about. You're perfect," I say to her.

Three summers ago, the young Doberman Pincher showed up on our front porch. When I found her curled up on our doorstep, her ears were clipped, her tail docked, and she was bleeding, broken, and severely malnourished. She took to me immediately, but when Dad came to look, she snapped at him. He wanted to take her to the pound, but I knew they would likely put her to sleep. It was obvious she wasn't taken care of, and I felt she deserved a second chance. I persuaded Dad to let me keep her with the understanding if she ever tried to bite me, the pound would be her fate. He couldn't deny how gentle she was with me and eventually, she stopped growling at him.

Dad's keys are on the rack, and I realize he must've parked in the garage.

"Em?" he calls from the kitchen.

I walk into the small outdated kitchen and drop my bag on one of the tattered wooden chairs. "Hey, Dad."

My dad is tall with dark hair and olive skin. He's standing next to the sink fiddling with something. There are a couple of plates on the yellowing laminate counter next to him. I look up at the clock. It's five-thirty. He usually doesn't make it home until after six-thirty.

"You're early," I comment.

"Between projects," he says.

Dad's job is important, but I still can't understand what exactly it is he does. He's some kind of IT system analyst, and apparently, that requires working a lot of overtime.

"I talked to Samantha," he says. His eyes always light up whenever he talks about Sam. She will always be his little princess.

"Oh, you know she found the perfect Cinderella dress today."

"Yes," Dad says, "she told me I couldn't see it until the wedding." I can tell he wants to be more involved with the wedding plans, but he doesn't know how. "Your turn to shop next, huh?"

"Yeah," I groan, "bridesmaids next Thursday."

Understanding my animosity toward shopping, he encourages, "Be patient with your sister. This is a big deal for her."

"I know, she's been planning this day since she was in the womb. I don't get it, but I'll be supportive."

"I know you will," he says, as he motions toward the back door. "You hungry?"

I look out through the window and see the grill already smoking on the porch. It's out of the ordinary for him to be home for dinner and usually, when he is, we order pizza.

"Yeah, what're you making?"

"Burgers." He grins, picking up a plate of ground beef molded into thick lumps.

"I'm always hungry for burgers."

three ~

The next morning, I arrive at work a few minutes before ten. I park my car next to Ashley's old yellow Mustang. I like working with Ashley because there is never a dull moment. She's tall and thin with hair so bleached it looks white. Her blue work t-shirts are always way too tight, yet she still insists on knotting the back of the shirts, so her stomach shows. She turned twenty-one a few weeks ago and occasionally comes to work hungover. She gets away with it because she's the owner's daughter. It irritates some of the other employees, but I think she's entertaining.

I walk through the door, and Ashley's face pops around the corner with a horrified expression. "Oh my God, Emily! I'm so glad you're here!" She comes at me in a panic. "So, I'm like totally freaking out!" She grabs me by the arm and hauls me toward the row of fish tanks. "I don't know who left the lid off, but they are like, everywhere!"

We round the corner. "Oh!" Crickets are scattered everywhere.

Ashley's face is ghost white. "You know I hate bugs!"

I crack a half smile. "You know they won't hurt you, right?" She rolls her eyes at me, but I see a shiver run through her and know she needs me to do this for her. "I'll get 'em. Don't worry."

21

She claps her hands together. "I am so glad you're here. I thought I was like, gonna die." I see another chill go through her.

"Go!" I order her away.

"Thank you. I'll owe you forever!" she says, hurrying back toward the registers.

It takes me most of the morning to gather the crickets, and we get busy with customers in the afternoon which makes the day go quickly.

"So, you're almost eighteen," Ashley says, as she locks the front doors at the end of the day.

"Yep, July third." I sweep a pile of bird seed from the floor.

"Do you have plans?"

"No," I answer, immediately wishing I could take it back.

"You should totally come to my party!" She is hell-bent on corrupting me. I enjoy hearing her crazy stories, but I have no desire to become one.

"Well . . ." I try to think of a way around this.

"Come on! You need some fun in your life." She jumps up to sit on the counter. "When's the last time you hung out with friends?"

I regret telling her what happened with the guys. She knows too much for me to lie.

"Well, actually I'm meeting a friend tonight."

"Oh? And who is this friend of yours?"

"Ben. I ran into him yesterday."

"I thought you said they all hated you," she says, crossing her legs in a very Sam kind of fashion.

"Guess I was wrong." I shrug.

She rolls her eyes and shakes her head. "How come I've never met any of these guys before?"

My phone vibrates in my pocket and instead of responding to her question, I answer, "Hey Ben."

"I'm outside," Ben says,

I turn to look out the big windows and see his shiny black Corvette parked right out front. "Okay, I'm just gonna be a few minutes."

Ashley catches on and squints through the window. "Tell him to come in!" she shouts, already waving him in.

"Umm," he makes a questioning sound.

I sigh, "So, how about you come in for a minute?"

His headlights turn off. "See ya in a sec."

I hang up and walk to the trash can to empty the overflowing dustpan.

Ashley looks confused. "So, he's like picking you up?"

"Yeah." I dump the bird seed in the trash.

"Like, it's just the two of you?"

"Yeah."

Looking frustrated, she says, "Like a date?"

"It's not a date!" I shake my head and walk to the door.

She slides off the counter and says, "So what are you guys doing tonight?"

"We'll probably just get some food and hang out."

"Hum," she sighs, shaking her head. "I don't know what I'm gonna do with you."

I'm glaring at Ashley as I open the door for Ben. Ashley's eyes widen as he walks through the door. She's seeing what every girl sees when they meet him.

"Hey," I greet, noting his ripped jeans and t-shirt. Nothing fancy. Nothing date-like.

Ashley is smiling like a school girl as she steps forward to shake his hand. "You must be Ben. I'm Ashley. I've heard so much about you!"

I give her a look of disbelief, while Ben questions, "You have?"

Ashley ignores his question and asks her own. "So, what are you guys doing tonight?"

"I don't know," he shrugs and looks at me with a smile. "Where do you wanna go?"

"I don't care," I answer, realizing this is going to be weird. The two of us have never hung out without Alec or Gavin. They always came up with the plan. Now it's just the two of us, and Ashley is putting ideas in my head. I try to console myself. We are just friends. He's like a brother. It'll be fine.

"So, you have a nice car. What year is it?" Ashley pries.

Ben stands up a little straighter. He loves talking about his car. "85 Corvette. She's taken a lot of work."

"So, do you work on cars?" She tilts her head to the side, definitely flirting.

"I tinker," he answers in a macho tone.

I laugh out loud at his statement. He looks down at me, offended. "Hey, I can do a lot more than you can, Miss No-muffler!"

"Yeah, like install a shiny new gas pedal. And how exactly would that fix my problem?"

"Your solution is easy! It's called a junkyard."

"My car is twenty years newer than yours, and she's a lux-ury vehicle!"

"Maybe she was fifteen years ago. You just don't understand cars."

Ashley is biting her bottom lip like she's barely able to contain her excitement. "I'll finish up here. You two have fun on your date!"

"It's not a date," I correct.

She looks at me. "Honestly, Emily, I'd take his car."

Ben says, "Eh, I need to run to the bathroom before we go."

I point to the back corner. "It's right back there."

As soon as we hear the bathroom door close, Ashley exclaims, "Oh my God! He's totally hot! And tall! He's like, what? Six three! Seriously, you've been holding out on me. And he's so got a thing for you!"

"We're just friends."

"Bullshit! The way he looks at you—" She fans herself. "Why can't he be older?" She grabs my shoulders and shakes me. "Are you blind! He's a catch with his sexy car, dark eyes, and muscles that beg to be touched. You've got tall, dark, and gorgeous falling at your feet, honey."

"Ashley! I know what he looks like! But I'm telling you, he's just one of the guys."

"Is it because you don't think you're hot enough? Cause you're totally hot! I know you don't see it, but you've got the flirty green eyes and hair I'd die for. You're a bit pale, but your skin is fantastic. Your shape . . ." Ashley takes a step back, observing me. "That shirt doesn't do anything for you." She reaches forward and grabs at my shirt, trying to pull it tighter.

I shoo her hands away, complaining, "Stop it! What are you doing?"

"You've got a cute little figure. You need to show it off. I mean, you are crazy not to go for him!"

I look down at my blue work t-shirt and khaki pants feeling inadequate, until I remember who we're talking about. "Ashley, you're missing the point. Ben doesn't care what I'm wearing, and neither do I. I'm just glad to have my friend back. I'm not trying to win him over. We're friends. Stop reading into it."

"Sure, cause you're so good at reading guys, right? What was the other one's name? Was he tall, dark, and dreamy too? I wish I knew what was going on in that pretty little head of yours."

"Sorry to disappoint you."

"Three years isn't that much younger," she whispers, as the bathroom door creaks open. "Let me know if it doesn't work. I'd be happy to take him off your hands." Ashley jumps onto the counter twirling a lock of her bleach blond hair.

I'm standing with my hand on the door by the time Ben comes around the corner.

"Ready?" he asks.

I nod. "Lock the door behind us," I say to Ashley.

"Nice to meet you, Ashley," Ben says.

"Oh, it was very nice to meet you and—"

"Ashley," I cut her off, pulling Ben out the door. "Make sure you double check all the lids before you leave. We wouldn't want any more crickets escaping." She shudders, and I let the door close between us.

Ben looks amused.

"What?" I ask as we walk to his car.

"You were being mean."

"No, I wasn't."

"You just threatened her with crickets so she wouldn't call this a date again."

"I didn't threaten her, and I already told her this wasn't a date. You're hot, so she just assumes every girl wants a piece of you."

He stops walking and says, "Wait, you don't? Eh, I guess we should call it a night."

I whack him with the back of my arm. "Shut up!"

"What? Do you think I might have a shot with Ashley?" he points back to the store and then takes a few steps back. "Should I go back and see?"

"Oh, it's gonna be like that?"

Ben laughs, moving forward. "Well, if you're gonna be a baby about it, I guess I'm stuck with you. So, what'll it be? Do you want to go eat, get takeout, or check out movie times?"

Dinner and a movie feels too much like a date. Then again, a sit-down restaurant is date material also. "Why don't we grab a pizza and go back to my house?"

Ben nods as we continue to his car only for me to pause, again. "Wait, what about my car?"

"We'll come back later. Or if we're lucky, it will get towed, and we'll go car shopping this weekend," he says with a smirk.

"Hardy-har."

We pick up a pizza and go to my house. All the lights are off which means Dad is working late as usual.

"Will Maggie bite me or do you think she's used to me yet?" Ben asks, as he grabs the pizza and we head inside.

"I'm not sure if she's even used to my dad yet. She could use another chew toy though." Opening the front door, I grab Maggie's collar. "I'm gonna take her out." I flip on the light and open the back door, thankful for my neighbor, Opal, who takes care of Maggie when we're not home.

When Maggie and I walk into the living room, her hair stands up and a deep growl rumbles in her throat. "Leave it," I command. She relaxes next to me but doesn't look away from Ben.

"Wow," Ben says. "That's quite an improvement, but she's still scary as shit."

I join Ben on the couch and Maggie lies at my feet. The pizza box is already open, and he has a slice in hand. It feels so good to have him here. I want to tell him how much I've missed him, but instead, I grab the remote and start flipping channels.

"Wait, go back to the commercial," Ben says.

I flip the channel and turn to Ben in question.

"Watch," he points to the TV.

A man is playing fetch with his dog; only the dog isn't the least bit interested. The man rubs the dogs head saying, "Spike, what's wrong buddy?"

Sighing, the dog flops to the floor, turning its mopey head to the side. The man opens the bag of Zappy dog food and the once depressed dog springs to life, running to the open bag. Now the dog can catch anything, even the cat from next door.

The man turns to the camera and shrugs, "Well, my dog's happy!" Then a tacky jingle starts, "When there's no fun to be had. We can make your puppy glad. Treat your canine to whole food Zappy. We guarantee your dog will be happy."

Ben is laughing, and I say, "What's so funny about that?"

"It's Zoloft for dogs," he says, tossing a piece of crust to Maggie. She growls and dodges the treat. "She clearly needs some Zappy."

"Pretty sure even antidepressant dog food wouldn't help her like you."

As it turns out, it's easy to be with Ben without the other guys. We sit for hours talking and cracking up over everything. I laugh so hard my stomach hurts.

The garage door opens around eleven-thirty, and my dad walks in through the kitchen looking exhausted. His hair is a mess and his shirttail is hanging out.

"Rough day?" I ask.

He sighs, "It's been a long one." He eyes the pizza box and then Ben. "Hey, Ben."

"Hey, Mark."

"What are you kids doing?"

Ben and I share a look, and I say, "We're just hanging out."

"Where's your car?" Dad asks.

"I completely forgot about my car. Ben picked me up from work."

"I can take you to go get it," Ben says, standing up to grab his keys from the table.

Walking back into the kitchen, Dad says, "That's okay, I'll take you to work in the morning. I have to go back to the office anyway, and it's pouring out there."

I look at Ben. "Maybe you'll get lucky and my car will wash away by morning."

His good mood dissolves and his smile looks forced. "I guess I should go."

I feel like I'm losing him, but I don't know what to say. "I'll give you an umbrella," is my pathetic response.

"I won't melt." He makes his way to the door.

"I'm not kicking you out."

"I know, but you have to work in the morning, and I'm kind of tired anyway."

He's lying. Maybe he's worried what the guys will say about him spending time with me.

"See you tomorrow," I say in a weak attempt to get anything from him.

"Yep, see ya."

He walks out the door, down the steps, and into the sweeping rain. He gets in his car, closes the door and lowers his head to the steering wheel for a moment. Finally, his headlights come on, and he's driving away. I want to know what's bothering him. Maybe I'll ask him tomorrow.

Dad raises an eyebrow as I enter the kitchen "Alone? In the house with a boy?"

"What? I've had the guys here before, and you didn't mind."

"Yeah but . . . don't you have any girlfriends?"

"Yeah," I laugh, thinking about Ashley, "And trust me, I'm better off hanging out with Ben."

"Just the two of you? What if . . . ." He can't finish his thought. And I don't want him to.

"Dad, it's just Ben and really do you think you have to worry about a guy getting near me with Maggie-the-man-eater guarding me?"

"I can't argue with that." He bends down to pet Maggie sitting at my feet. Maggie doesn't look like she's enjoying his affection, but she allows him to rub her head for a moment before backing out of his reach.

"Anyway, you better get used to it, because I'm hanging out with Ben after work tomorrow."

"Just Ben?"

"Yes, just Ben. He's my friend."

He shakes his head. "If you say so. Goodnight, Em."

"Night, Dad."

four ~

I work until four o'clock on Saturday and thankfully Ashley isn't there to ask me a bazillion questions about my time with Ben. After work, I go home and take care of Maggie while I wait for Ben. His car pulls up out front and I climb in.

"Hey," he calls, as I slouch into the passenger seat.

"Hey," I say, closing the door. "So, where are we going?"

"My house."

Groaning, I ask, "Are you gonna make me sit and watch you work on your car all night? I'm not Alec or Gavin. You know I get bored with car stuff."

He laughs at my expression. "Well, you could learn a few things. But no, believe it or not, there's an actual house beyond the garage."

"Ooo, how mysterious! Am I actually going to be allowed to enter Benjamin Cetrone's mansion?" I joke, although, mansion isn't far off. The house is huge and the family is small. It's just Ben, his fifteen-year-old sister, Molly, and their parents. The guys use Ben's garage because it fits not only their three cars but also his dad's drool-worthy, cherry red Ferrari. When I visit, I park on the street, so the oil from my hunk of scrap metal doesn't leak on their custom stone driveway.

"Only if the doorman will let us pass," he says with sarcasm. Seeing my look, he clarifies, "My parents are out of town. They're looking at a house in Florida."

Dread surges through me. "So, even if you don't go to the East Coast for school, you're moving to Florida?"

Amused and a little smug, he laughs. "No, they're looking for a vacation home. We've had a condo there for years, but they want a house. I think they want to move down there once Molly graduates."

"When do they come back?"

"Tomorrow night. I have to pick them up at six from the airport."

He doesn't talk much about his family, and I'm suddenly very curious. "Why didn't you go with them?"

"Because they drive me crazy. It's bad enough my parents are making me go on this stupid vacation over the Fourth of July."

"You don't want to go on vacation?" I can't understand how it could be so bad. They have all the money in the world and have gone to some of the most beautiful places on earth.

He glares at me. "It's not a vacation. That's what they call it, but it's Hell. My mom takes my sister shopping while my dad disappears for hours, only to reappear just in time to shower before they get back. It doesn't fool anyone. The smell of alcohol and cheap perfume linger. My mom pretends everything's fine and she puts on her robe and slippers and goes off to the spa for a 'special' massage." He makes quotations with his fingers. "They cheat on each other all the time and expect my sister and I not to catch on. I hate it. And it keeps getting worse. I spend most of my time on the beach to get away from them."

I don't know what to say. This is the most I've ever heard him talk about his family and it's very revealing. I can see why he doesn't mention them, and I have no idea how to respond.

"Spending all your time on the beach must suck," I say with sarcasm, cringing to myself and hoping he'll accept what I can offer.

"I guess I sound like a spoiled rich kid."

"Ben, you are a spoiled rich kid."

His brows flinch, and he swallows the lump in his throat.

"Not that you act spoiled. Ignore me. I just mean your family is wealthy. I'm no good at giving advice, especially when it comes to family. My mom was crazy, remember? I guess we all have our own brand of family dysfunction."

"Guess so," he mumbles.

There are no railroad tracks running through town, but if there were, I would've grown up on the wrong side. Not saying I ever needed for anything in life, but most of the kids I went to school with came from exceedingly wealthy families. Our school could afford the most advanced equipment and the best teachers. The student parking lot was filled with brand new cars, kids wore the best brands, and everyone who was anyone had the latest accessories. If I had to judge solely by the way Ben acted, I would say he grew up on my side of the tracks, but I've been to his house and have seen enough to know differently.

Ben's house looks elegant with its pristine flowerbeds and white stone pillars. The house is built on a slope backing up to a golf course. Although I've never been inside the house, I imagine it's just as regal as the exterior.

We pull into the stone driveway and Ben parks in his usual spot in the cavernous garage. Shaking his head, he mumbles, "Sorry I unloaded on you."

"It sounds like your parents kinda suck," I say, stepping out of the car.

"Yeah, they do," he says, walking around the car to meet me by the door. "Are you ready?" He rubs his hands together. "We could go around to the front entrance if you'd rather."

"Just go," I sigh, nudging him through the side entrance.

We enter into a luxurious foyer with more sparkling marble than a museum. The creamy white wallpaper has an intricate, lavish design that probably costs a fortune. I stand frozen, amazed by the opulence. Ben tugs my arm to move me along. We pass under a chandelier dripping with crystals and into an open room. I'm already feeling underprivileged. I know he's watching me, so I try to hide my astonishment. The house looks huge from the outside, but the inside is more enormous than I'd ever imagined. Mansion may have been an understatement. Just how wealthy is this family?

He takes me into a massive office with vaulted ceilings, a behemoth fireplace and plush maroon velvet drapes over the windows.

"This is my dad's study."

"Is he in the mob?" I question, looking at all the leather.

"This is why I don't let people in my house," Ben says.

"You don't let people? I thought . . . we all thought it was your parents who wouldn't let us in."

"I know. It's easier to blame them." Placing his hand on my back, he says, "Come on." He ushers me to the next room across the hall. It's just as tremendous with black glistening stone floors, wispy white curtains, and a wall of mirrors with a horizontal bar running down the middle.

"It's my mom's dance studio," Ben explains. "Before she married my dad, she was a world-renowned ballet dancer."

"Wow, I never knew," I say, tucking a strand of hair behind my ear. I try to conceal my thoughts, afraid he won't show me anymore.

We wander into the living room where the floors are made up of grey shining stone. In the center is a plush white area rug with a cluster of beautiful white furniture. Windows cover the entire length of the room with French doors leading out to a balcony overlooking the golf course. As impressive as this room is, there's no way I could feel comfortable here. It's too white, too cold, and everything is too expensive.

My eyes are drawn to the big brown fluff of fur on the floor in front of the fireplace. It's the only dark object in the room. I wonder if it's a bear skin rug until it moves. I jump, thinking my eyes are playing tricks on me.

"He's more pleasant than Maggie," Ben notes.

"That's a dog?"

The brown beast lumbers toward us with his tail wagging, looking like an overgrown puppy. His pink tongue hangs from his mouth and drool is dripping, leaving puddles on the spotless floor.

"You knew I had a dog. Well, technically he's my sister's dog. This is Max." The dog comes right up to me, his head at my waist. I rub his furry head as he licks me, drooling a huge gob of saliva down my arm.

"Awe, he's a gentle giant," I say, as I stroke his neck. "You're just a giant teddy bear, aren't you?"

"He's a Newfoundland," Ben explains. "One-hundred-eighty pounds. He drools and sheds, a lot. Come on; we can wipe that off."

I'm not bothered by the drool, but I'm surprised his parents would allow such a slobbery, hairy mammoth in their immaculate white house.

The dog follows as we leave the room. Ben points to a stairway that leads to one of the kitchens. I wonder how many kitchens one house needs. We reach the bottom of a spiral staircase to find another spacious living room with a kitchenette at the far end.

Ben leads me through a door then closes it behind us. I'm greeted with grey carpet and old posters hanging randomly on the arctic blue walls. Ben's scent wraps around me, and I grin knowing without a doubt this is his room. Navy curtains hang floor to ceiling along the back of the room most likely hiding the view of the golf course. Although it's nothing compared to the rest of the house, his bedroom is still half the size of my house.

"This is your room, huh?"

"Yep. This is where I hide out whenever I'm home," he says, looking embarrassed.

I turn to explore the spacious room while he walks through a half-open door and flips on the light.

"Of course, you have your own bathroom." I enter behind him. "Wow, I stand corrected. You have your own spa! A walk-in shower, jacuzzi, and a separate room for your toilet! Ben, your bathroom is bigger than my bedroom!"

Ben laughs uncomfortably, as he pulls a towel off the rack and dampens it before wiping the drool off my arm. "See why I don't let people in here?" He tosses the towel on the counter, and we leave the bathroom.

"What? You don't want us to break your stuff?"

"Seriously, Em. Look at this place. People would look at me differently."

"People already look at you differently."

He scowls at me and walks over to the wall of curtains. "Down the hall, there's a movie theater next to the heated indoor pool and sauna." He's not bragging as he shoves the curtains aside. "And right outside there is another pool and hot tub."

The doors open up to a private retreat. A patio surrounds an in-ground pool complete with a diving board, spiral slide, and a waterfall. The pristine golf course makes for a perfect backdrop to this mini paradise.

"And don't forget about that football stadium you call a foyer," I tease.

Ben doesn't smile. I know all of this makes him uncomfortable, so I switch tactics.

"Honestly, I'm not impressed. My private pool is at least twice as big as yours and you've been lucky enough to experience the extravagance of my personal movie theater."

His eyes light up. "You got me there."

I continue, "This place is a dollhouse compared to my digs."

"This dollhouse is eleven thousand square feet with six bedrooms and nine bathrooms. Nine! Who the hell needs nine bathrooms?"

"Benjamin Isaac Cetrone, you only have nine bathrooms? You're practically underprivileged." I stride away from the doors pretending to be bored with the view and look around for any new surprises. That's when I spot an acoustic guitar. Bingo.

"Do you play?" I pick up the guitar and spin around. "Don't lie to me, now."

He mumbles, "Yeah, I play."

"Are you good?"

"I'm okay," he admits.

"I hope that's not the equivalent to the way you 'tinker' with cars. Come on. I want the truth." I push, for some reason knowing he's more than okay.

"I'm pretty good," he concedes with a sly grin and coy eyes.

I take a breath and steady myself. It's frustrating how attractive he is right now. "Will you play something for me?" I beg, "Please?"

He takes the guitar, but only because I'm shoving it at him.

"I've never played in front of anyone except my little sister. And she doesn't count."

I have never seen him look so shy. I lift the guitar into his arms, encouraging him. "I don't count either. Just pretend I'm not here."

He shoots me a doubtful look, and I shrug, determined not to budge. We continue our staring match, but eventually, he wraps the strap around his shoulder, settles the guitar in his arms, and begins strumming. I watch his fingers caress the strings as the soothing sound turns into a mellow song. It's something I recognize; one of the classics, but it melts into a different tune as he picks up the pace. His fingers pluck their way up the neck of the guitar so quickly I can't possibly follow their movements. I hear him tapping the base of the guitar, using it as a drum. I've never heard anything like it before.

When he stops, I have to catch my breath. "What was that?"

"Music."

"I've never heard the guitar sound that way!"

"It's an integrated percussive technique."

"It's amazing! Where did you learn to play like that?"

"I've been playing since I was ten." He raises an eyebrow. "It's amazing what you can learn on the internet."

"You're really good!"

"Says the girl who knows nothing about guitars."

It's true, but I can't imagine I'm wrong about his level of talent. He starts to lift the guitar strap from his shoulder, but I stop him.

"No! I want to hear more!"

"I'll play as long as you don't mention this to anyone."

"Deal."

He starts playing again and it appears effortless. His fingers speed across the strings, yet a gentle song comes to life. He sits on the corner of his bed as I lower myself to the floor. Max, the gargantuan dog, comes and lies next to me, resting his head in my lap.

I am enthralled by Ben's talent and how relaxed he looks while playing. With his music, he creates a warm, soothing ambiance inside an otherwise cold empty mansion. I've seen a whole new side of him today. I try not to speculate on why he's decided to reveal so much of himself to me because I'm grateful. I want to know everything about him.

five ~

During my hour break between classes on Tuesday, I go to the campus café where I'm safe from the miserable heat.

"Emily."

I stop before I reach the sliding glass door of the brick building. I turn to look for the person who called my name, but I see no one. I shrug it off and walk into the lobby to get lunch. I grab a pub table and hike myself up on the chair. I'm unwrapping my sandwich when I hear it again.

"Emily."

I gaze around the room. Everyone is busy. People are coming and going, but no one is paying attention to me. I finish my sandwich and dig around inside my book bag.

"Emily," the deep voice calls again.

I'm unnerved. I check my phone expecting to see I've pocket dialed someone, but no one is there. Emily is a fairly common name, and it's obvious this Emily isn't me, so I stave off my curiosity and ignore the voice.

I pull a crumpled yellow paper out of my bag and try to smooth out the accordion pleats so I can read about the performance I need to attend for my humanities class.

"Hey, Emily."

I look up, surprised to find Morgan's light blue eyes beaming at me. She's smiling, and her summer freckles are already sprinkled across her suntanned cheeks. Her long dark hair has grown even longer since I've seen her last. She was my only girlfriend from school and the last I heard she was in Florida.

"Morgan, what are you doing here?"

"I came home this spring. Florida just wasn't my thing."

She's never been good at hiding her emotions. Her facial expressions give her away and judging by the look on her face; whatever happened in Florida must have been terrible.

"So, are you here to stay?" I smile, selfishly hoping she's not going anywhere.

"That's what it looks like. I got into the nursing program at the university. I start this fall, but I scheduled some classes here to make sure I'm all caught up." She looks hopeful. She's wanted to be a nurse from the time she was five.

"That's great!"

She looks down at my mess of crumpled papers on the table. "I'm glad I ran into you. Did you just start classes?"

"Yeah," I say, clearing a spot for her. "Here, do you want to sit with me?"

"Actually," she hesitates, looking behind me toward the café counter. "My cousin is with me. We're having lunch together." By her tone, she sounds as if she would rather sit down with me.

"We can catch up later," I offer.

Just as I say this, someone walks up from behind to stand by Morgan's side. My mouth gapes as I look into the face of the mysterious blond guy, the one I almost trampled running out of my humanities lecture. He's the one with the perfect skin, stunning blue eyes, and a body belonging to a male model. And he's Morgan's cousin!

"Emily, this is my cousin, Patrick," she introduces and then turns to her cousin, explaining, "Emily is my good friend from high school."

So, this peculiar guy who had me so flustered last week has a name. Patrick. The guy whose gaze I could not escape, whose eyes pierced right into my soul and left me mesmerized. The guy I was so desperate to escape and stop thinking about is now standing in front of me doing it all over again.

Holding out his hand, he speaks in his deep silky voice, "Nice to meet you, Emily."

I haven't regained control of myself. I don't want to be rude, but I hate him for having this power over me. I close my mouth in a frustrated grimace and place my hand in his. I look up and immediately regret it. I find his sapphire eyes and instantly drown in them. His skin is smooth around his iron jaw, and I stare at his round, supple lips wondering how they would feel on mine. Oh my God! What's wrong with me?

His strong hand lets mine fall after we shake, and I regain a fraction of my footing on the situation. I cannot look away from him as I struggle to put my thoughts together, let alone a sentence.

"You!" It comes out harsher than I planned, and I try to correct myself, but like projectile vomit, I spew without grace. "You *laughed* at me and called me clumsy!"

Teeth show through his parted lips. "I see you remember me," he coos.

"Yeah, I remember."

His smile grows as he suppresses a laugh. Relieved our eye contact is broken, I look to a perplexed Morgan. Her scrutinizing gaze settles on Patrick.

"Well, that's new," Morgan mumbles.

"We have a class together," Patrick says. "To a degree, we met last week."

Morgan's worried eyes land on me before she glares at Patrick. "Go on outside. I'll meet you in a minute."

"Emily, it's so nice to see you again." Patrick's hand grazes my arm, but I'm afraid to look at him. Still, I watch as he saunters to the door where he turns to wink at me before leaving the building.

"I'm sorry," I say.

"That's the first time I've ever seen anyone openly upset with him."

"I didn't mean to—"

Morgan interrupts, "You don't need to apologize, Emily." Her eyes fill with concern. "Can I ask what happened?"

"I just told you. He laughed at me!"

"Did he hurt you?"

"What? No! He watched me eat and laughed. He stared me down, told me I'm clumsy and almost made me run into him . . ." I stop when I realize how stupid it all sounds. I'm being irrational, and now I've made it uncomfortable. I look down trying to remember why I was so angry with him.

Morgan laughs to herself. "You've gotta come to our Fourth of July cookout. We can celebrate your birthday and catch up. I've really missed you." I can tell she wants to hug me, but she resists, knowing I am not a hugger.

"Is *he* gonna be there?" I say, sounding like a petulant child.

"Yeah," she says with a smile.

"You just saw how well we get along, right?"

"I mean it when I say you are the first person I've ever seen angry with him. And for nothing," she laughs. "It's refreshing. Patrick has a way with people. Even when I want to be mad at him, I can't."

"Morgan, I'd love to spend time with you. I just—"

"Just consider it."

"Okay."

"Great, I'll call you. I have to go catch up to him. I thought he . . ." She stops herself. "I'm just glad you're okay."

What? I'm reeling on the inside! What did she think he did to me? She's glad I'm okay. What would he have done? What has he done? If he's capable of terrible things, why is she having lunch with him? And why would she invite me to spend more time with him?

"Hope to see you at the cookout, Emily," she says, breaking my train of thought.

"It was great to see you, Morgan."

During my next two classes, my mind keeps wandering back to Patrick. I feel little relief in knowing his name. Every time I think about his beautiful eyes and perfect lips, I remind myself even his cousin thinks something is wrong with him. I refuse to be a girl smitten by a guy based on his looks. I've seen the way girls look at Ben; the way Ashley eyed him up and down and her reasons for liking him were superficial. All she saw was a hot car and a hot body when she knows nothing about him. This makes me angry. Isn't it the small things about someone that makes them who they are? And still, I sit through class daydreaming about Patrick, who is shattering everything I thought strong about myself—everything separating me from becoming a shallow teenage girl.

Still, I can't help but feel there is something special about him—not just his looks, but something deeper, something mysterious, something familiar. I put my head down on my desk in frustration. I had forgotten about him over the weekend. And here I am back to where I was last Thursday. I don't want to see him again. I can't allow myself to flounder in his gaze ever again.

I call Ben when I get out of class

"Hey, Em."

"Hey, wanna hang out?" I ask.

"Yeah."

"Are you busy now?" I ask, desperate to find a distraction from Patrick.

"I'm just at my house working on my car. I'll be done in a few minutes."

"Okay, I'll meet you there."

On my drive, I blast the music to drown out my lingering thoughts. I am exhausted with myself by the time I arrive at Ben's house. He's in the driveway "tinkering" with his car when I pull up. He meets me at the end of the driveway.

"Are you kidding me? As hot as it is and you're outside working on your car?"

He laughs and looks me over. "Well, Em, at least I'm dressed for summer." He motions to his shorts and what's left of his t-shirt. His sleeves have been cut off so drastically the shirt barely covers any of his chest.

I gesture to his homemade muscle shirt. "Really?"

He points at me. "It's ninety-eight degrees out, and you decide to wear jeans and long sleeves?"

"I'm not wearing long sleeves! It's a t-shirt, just like yours was before you mutilated it."

"Okay, but my sleeves never came to my elbows," he defends.

"So, it's a big t-shirt."

I roll up my sleeves and follow him back to his car.

"We don't have to stay out here anyway," he says. "Come on; get in the car."

He pulls off what's left of his shirt as he walks to his side of the car. His body has a slight sheen from working in the heat, and I can't take my eyes off his defined muscles glistening in the sun. He grabs a fresh shirt from behind the seat and pulls it over his head before getting in.

He's already backing out of the driveway before I think to ask, "Where are we going?"

"To a movie."

"I thought you had a built-in movie theater here?"

"I do," he answers, looking at me like I'm missing something. "I don't want to spend my evening with Renee and Everett." He speaks his parent's names like they are curse words.

"Okay, but—"

He puts his finger up to stop me. "Look at you. You're hot, and you get cranky when you're hot." I open my mouth to argue and again he cuts me off. "You'll be happier once we're in air conditioning."

I can't argue with him. He knows me too well. The car ride is too quiet, though, so my mind keeps drifting back to Patrick. I become more and more angry with myself and my complete lack of control over my thoughts.

"Do you wanna talk about it?" Ben finally asks when we pull into the theater parking lot.

"About what?"

He glances my way. "About whatever you've been mulling over for the last twenty minutes."

"Umm, no." I'm surprised it's that obvious. Maybe I'm like Morgan in the way I can't hide what I'm thinking.

"K, just thought I'd give you the option."

I do want to talk about it. I just don't know what to say without sounding pathetic. He pulls into a parking space and before he can bring it up again, I jump out of the car and start walking toward the theater. He hurries to catch up with me.

"What are we gonna see?" I finally think to ask.

"I guess we'll see whatever's playing at eight."

We find a comedy that's starting soon and buy tickets. Before going into the theater, Ben stops for popcorn. The evening is better than I anticipated. Ben is still just one of the guys, no weirdness. I've missed my guys. I wish they all could've been here, even Alec with his vulgar language and severely inappropriate sense of humor.

When we walk out of the theater, the sky is dark, but warm air lingers from the afternoon sun. A cool breeze tickles my skin and spreads goosebumps down my arms.

"Emily!" A voice calls from across the parking lot. We turn to look.

Ben squints through the dark. "Is that Morgan?"

"I think it is." We start walking in her direction. "I ran into her on campus today. She just moved back from Florida." I was so preoccupied with Patrick that I forgot to mention Morgan being back.

"That's cool."

"She . . . um . . ." The blood drains from my face and I come to a halt as I recognize the unmistakable man walking next to Morgan. Patrick is cool and confident as he strides toward us wearing a smug smile.

Ben turns to check on me, following my gaze, he asks, "Do you know him?"

"Sort of," I answer, "Morgan introduced us today."

"Ben?" Morgan calls, as she approaches.

Ben turns and throws his arms around Morgan in a bear hug. Patrick is a few steps behind, so I keep my distance. When Ben and Morgan step back from their embrace, Ben scrutinizes Patrick.

Patrick offers his hand to Ben. "Hi, I'm Patrick, Morgan's cousin."

Ben looks reluctant as he takes Patrick's hand. "Ben," he offers in response.

Morgan looks from Ben to me and raises an eyebrow. I sense an awkward moment coming so before she asks aloud, I rush to clear the air.

"Ben is really into romantic comedies these days. He couldn't talk the other guys into coming, so here I am. What are you guys seeing?"

"We were just on our way to catch the new Marvel movie," Morgan says. "What are Alec and Gavin up to these days?"

I feel a pang of guilt and exchange a look with Ben before answering, "Um."

Ben laughs, taking me by surprise. "Gavin finally got the balls to tell her."

"Oh!" Morgan understands immediately and shakes her head.

"It didn't end well," Ben mumbles under his breath.

I lower my head in shame.

"Emily," Morgan soothes. "It's not your problem. I told Gavin it would be over if he told you. It's his fault, not yours. You can't help how you feel."

And maybe that would've been true if I didn't try to force it and break up with him on his birthday. My embarrassment keeps me silent.

Ben breaks the awkward silence. "I know you guys have a movie to catch, but we'll have to hang out soon."

I look up straight into the eyes of the enemy, but unlike earlier, Patrick's overwhelming blue gaze now fills me with a strange sense of calm. Something is different about him. His whole face is softer, gentler somehow. I choose to stare at him knowing I can look away this time. He's almost a complete stranger, yet something about him is strangely familiar, almost comforting.

Morgan is talking to Ben, saying, "My family is having a cookout on the fourth. I invited Emily earlier. Ben, you should come too."

"Emily," a deep voice whispers just inside my ear. It's the same voice from earlier. Patrick's lips aren't moving, and Ben just opened his mouth to answer Morgan.

He says, "We're going on vacation next week. We won't be back until Friday."

"Sweet, naive Emily," the voice in my head murmurs.

I turn in a circle searching for the source of the words. No one is there. It's evident no one else is hearing what I'm hearing, probably because I'm going mental. My panic must be apparent because Patrick is giving me a strange look like he's wondering what I'm doing. Geez, I'm wondering what I'm doing, too.

"It's okay, love," the voice whispers in my ear.

My mom was almost thirty before she started hearing voices and seeing things. If I'm going nuts, is this it?

As if I didn't have enough proof, the woman I thought I hit with my car appears behind Patrick. She's wearing regular clothes this time, but her hair is still a frizzy mess. She speaks, and her voice resonates inside my head, *Bred to be orphaned, pursued but not found. The weak build the strong to find light underground. Rising from nothing to fight for a cause. A victim, a killer, an innocent one.*

Patrick turns to look behind him. Seeing nothing, he spins back with a look of concern. The woman fades away, and I blink, shaking my head. I knew it might happen someday, but I'm not even eighteen. Morgan says something to Ben, but I don't hear it. The two exchange another hug. Morgan touches my shoulder before she and Patrick walk away. Did they say goodbye?

"Bye," I whisper too late.

It takes me a moment to recognize Ben just said something to me.

My eyes jerk to him. "What?"

"You okay?" he repeats, taking in my expression. "What's wrong?"

Exhaling the breath I didn't know I was holding; I realize there are no words to explain.

"Do you need to sit down?" Ben asks, placing a hand on my back. "Are you having a panic attack?"

I can't breathe. I'm hearing voices! I'm going crazy, and I'm terrified.

"Emily, why don't you sit down."

"What? No. I'm fine. It's . . . nothing. I'm . . . I'm tired."

It's a blatant lie, but he doesn't question me. He simply buries his hands in his front pockets and we head back to the car.

We drive in silence for about ten minutes before he tries again. "You know you can talk to me, right? If it was a panic attack, it's nothing to—"

"It wasn't a panic attack!"

"Then what happened? Was it her cousin that put you in a bad mood?"

"I'm not in a bad mood!"

"Really?"

I stay silent.

"Is he what was bothering you earlier?" he asks.

"No."

"Okay, so what did he do?"

"What? He didn't do anything. It's not about him." This time I'm not lying. No longer am I thinking about the mysterious guy I've wished I could get out of my head. Wish granted! Now all I can think about are the voices in my head. This wasn't how I saw things going. I'll be committed to a psychiatric hospital by eighteen—if I make it to my birthday.

Ben groans.

"What?" I ask, turning to him. I look at him for the first time since we got in the car. His knuckles are tight on the steering wheel, and he looks miserable. I forget my question and ignore my problems to focus on Ben. I hate seeing him like this.

"Ben?" I reach a hand out to touch him.

Jaw tightly clenched, he shakes his head without diverting his eyes from the road ahead.

I pull my hand back. "Ben, what's wrong?"

His eyes lock on the road ahead of us, but I see his bewildered anger. "Are you serious, Emily! You are blind!" His voice is too loud in the small car, and I know his leg would be bouncing if he wasn't driving.

"What are you talking about?" I say with a shaky voice.

Ben throws his head back on the headrest and continues to stare at the road. I don't know what to expect. There could be another outburst, but that's not like him. He pulls the car over to the side of the road. He still won't look at me. I keep waiting for him to say something. The minutes tick by. Just as I am about to speak, he turns to me.

"Emily, it's like this big part of you died with your mom. I saw what you went through when she was committed. Even though you'll never admit it, I know you're still mad at your dad for hospitalizing you after her death. I've defended you when the assholes at school talked shit. That suspension my junior year was because Michael and Duncan wrote that shit on your locker. They were laughing about it! I couldn't let them keep laughing. I ditched Gavin and Alec to hang out with you tonight because . . . because it's you, it'll always be you. I won't go off to school and leave you behind." His eyes lift to mine slowly like he's afraid to see my reaction. "I can't give up on you, which makes no sense because you can't even be honest with me."

I'm in shock. My whole body hurts from his words. A sharp, familiar stab of ice trickles down my spine. When I realize I'm not breathing, I force myself to inhale. Then my mind goes numb, rejecting the pain as my brain kicks into autopilot.

I jerk the door handle, and I'm out of the car in an instant. I'm walking down the country road without direction. It isn't long before he is catching up to me. He steps in front of me grabbing my shoulders. "Where are you going?"

I push his hands off and brush past him. "Go Away!"

"Emily, I'm not leaving you out here."

"Stop following me!"

"Then stop!" he pleads.

"I can't!" My anger keeps me walking. Being my friend has cost him way too much. Why didn't he walk away years ago or at the very least after graduation? That would have been a clean break. I never meant to be a burden. Why would he think he can't leave me? I swing around to face him.

"At least let me take you back to your car," he begs, looking exhausted. "We don't have to talk."

"You have feelings for me!" I brush the windblown hair from my face. "Why? Why me?" He stays silent, so I continue, "You know more than enough to be frightened away, but I never asked anything of you. You're one of my only friends, Ben. I never wanted you to suffer because of me. I never wanted to be a burden. Why didn't you just walk away?"

His expression turns to anguish as he averts his eyes. Too afraid to hear his answer, I head back to the car.

"Wait, Emily," he pleads, and I turn toward him. His face is tortured by what he doesn't want to say, "I couldn't walk away, just like I can't walk away now." He reaches out as if to touch me but thinks better of it. "You're not a burden. I've known you for thirteen years. I know where you've come from, so I know you've spent most of your life shutting people out. Sometimes I think you're screaming inside, waiting for it to be over." He tucks a strand of hair behind my ear. Then in almost a whisper, he continues, "I never said anything before because I didn't want to lose you. You're always so ready to run, and I didn't want to give you a reason."

I can't breathe. I feel so raw, and my body trembles. Ben sees me for what I am. Damaged! Why would anyone want to hold onto that?

"I don't run from everything," I defend.

"You're running away from me right now. Whenever things get hard you either run or—"

"WHEN THINGS GET HARD!" I explode. "When has it ever been easy, Ben?"

"This, Emily." He motions between us. "This is easy. You just don't let anyone close enough. Not since your mom . . ."

I look down, but he raises my chin and our eyes lock. "I'm not Gavin."

"Exactly, Ben. You're not Gavin. You're . . . it's you." I stare at him, hoping he can grasp what I mean.

"I'm your friend no matter what," he continues.

"Maybe guys and girls can't be friends," I think aloud, my voice shaking.

He wraps his arms around me and pulls me into him. I let it happen. Closing my eyes, I allow myself to lean into him. It feels so good to be in his arms, but it's going to hurt that much more when he's not there—when he realizes I am too much, and he can't be burdened by me anymore. I witnessed it with my parents. I watched my dad hold on to a broken woman for so long it nearly destroyed him. But for right now, at this moment, I shut out the ugly image and wrap my arms around him, savoring the feeling of us holding each other.

As we linger in our embrace, he says, "Nothing will change how I feel about you, Em."

I smile into his shoulder and say, "Okay, Ben. Let's go home." We walk shoulder to shoulder back to the car.

Ben says, "I don't want you to feel awkward around me. I know you think of me like a brother."

"I don't. I mean . . . I thought you understood. Alec and Gavin are like annoying brothers who I like despite their flaws, but you . . . you and I are good together and I . . . I can't risk losing you, not again . . . friends?"

"Friends," he promises.

In my head, I continue my thoughts. *And when you realize I'm too great a burden, I will absolve you of your promise and walk away a better person having known you.*

six ~

On my way to work the next day, I find myself obsessing over Ben. I haven't stopped thinking about him since he dropped me off at my car last night. He agreed we were still friends, but I'm not sure about anything anymore.

I think about calling him but drop the idea. Haven't I screwed up enough of his life? I teased him when he got suspended for fighting. I had no idea it was because of me. How stupid of him. How utterly ridiculous, senseless, macho, and . . . well, sweet. Maybe we don't need to go back to being friends. Perhaps we can be more.

"No," I say aloud. I can't allow my mind to wander down the path of what-ifs. I won't be responsible for destroying him. I heard voices yesterday, and it's just a matter of time before my life unravels, ruining everything in its wake. I should distance myself now so no one will mourn my loss once my dad is forced to commit me for good this time.

The pet supply store is busy when I arrive, so I'm safe from Ashley's questions, at least for a little while. At first, I think she may have forgotten about Ben. Of course, that's not the case.

"So," she says in a leading voice when she gets a break between customers. "Tell me everything." I give her a tired look, and she huffs, "Come on. My week has been awful! Give me some good news."

"It's not good news."

"What?" she shrieks.

"I don't know if he'll want to see me anymore."

"What? Why? What did you do?"

"Nothing, but he's too good for me, Ashley."

Her eyes are wide with outrage. "Did he say that?"

"No, but it's the truth," I say, turning to walk away.

I open my eyes in a fog, unable to figure out what's beeping. I look at my alarm, baffled for a moment before I remember how to turn it off. It's only eight o'clock.

"Oh no!" I let my head plummet back to the pillow. I have bridesmaid shopping this morning. I roll out of my warm, cozy bed and my bare feet hit the cold hardwood floor. I hate this day already.

I take a shower, making sure to shave my legs. I stand in front of my closet far too long, as my search for something to wear takes forever. The light pink summer dress I've only worn once will do the trick. I dig through the pile of shoes at the bottom of the closet and find a pair of pink flats that look dressy enough. Crap, I should've painted my nails.

Digging through bathroom drawers that used to belong to my sister, I find soft pink nail polish. Applying the polish, I fumble like a two-year-old trying to color inside the lines. I remove the smudged polish, but the cotton ball sticks to my nail and smears the paint. I wipe the entire nail and start over. I do this four times before I realize I'll be late if I continue. I leave the smeared polish and rush to apply makeup and straighten my hair.

Somehow, I manage to arrive at the dress store a few minutes early. Parked a few spaces down is a black Mercedes which means Judy and her daughter, Leah, my high school bully, are here. I don't want to spend any more time with Leah than I have to, so I wait in my car pretending to be busy.

At ten o'clock sharp Judy and Leah walk into the store and two minutes later my sister and Rochelle pull into the parking lot. Sam looks stressed as we say our hellos and make our way inside to meet up with Judy and Leah. It is just as uncomfortable as I imagined. My sister is unaware of the burning hatred Leah and I have for each other, and I plan to keep it that way.

Monica, the same woman Samantha bought her wedding dress from is helping us again today. Once we have our dresses selected, Monica leads us back to the fitting rooms. We take turns trying on different colors and styles. I'm relieved to be sharing a dressing room with Rochelle instead of Leah. Alison, another bridesmaid, arrives as we step onto pedestals to model our dresses. Alison is loud and bossy for such a petite girl, and she immediately begins ordering us around like she's running the show.

My sister and Alison have Monica standing on her head by the time they narrow the dresses down to three options. I'm not a fan of any of them, but I am happy the dress will be a simple, classic black. I smile and pretend to like them all.

I stand on the pedestal wearing a floor-length gown with a plunging halter, while Leah is in a super short strapless and Rochelle is wearing a knee-length with ruffles and sequins. My sister, Judy, and Alison are staring between the three of us.

"Emily, your boobs look fantastic in that one!" Sam announces, gesturing to my cleavage. It makes me want to hide in the dressing room. Instead, I plaster on a smile and stay put.

"Leah, your legs are fabulous in that one and Rochelle, that dress is amazing on you!" Samantha sighs, exhausted. "What do you girls think?"

Alison is the first to speak; although, I'm not sure she ever stopped. "I think you should stay with long. It's elegant and the wedding is on New Year's Eve. It'll be cold."

I can't imagine the sheer fabric of the dress I'm wearing could keep anyone warm from the cold winter air, but I keep my smile in place and think positive thoughts.

"Turn around," my sister orders me.

I spin, almost tripping over the length of the dress.

"I love how it dips in the back," Alison continues. "I mean we probably won't be able to wear much as far as undergarments go, but you have the perfect bridesmaids to do this. All of us are thin and we'll all be dieting for the wedding anyway. If Emily looks good in it, then I'm sure it'll look good on all of us."

I swallow hard to keep from choking on her statement. The only reason Alison isn't in a dress is that her size zero frame was "too petite and perfect"—her words, not mine—to try any of these dresses, which she made very clear, many, many times. I look to Rochelle, and she reciprocates my look of annoyance.

Monica speaks up, "That is true. Most bridal parties couldn't pull off this style of dress. Now, I know we're missing a bridesmaid today. Would she—"

"Oh, Eva is my size; she'll look great," Alison interrupts.

"Great!" Monica says. "What do you think Samantha?"

"I love it! Alison's right! You girls are going to look phenomenal!"

"Then it's settled," Judy announces. "Let me grab my camera. I want a picture of the dress." She bends over to get her camera from her purse.

I am mortified that I will be the one in the picture. I feel so exposed up top and wish I could be in any other place at this moment. "Do you want someone else to try it on before we get pictures?" I say, hoping it will allow me to escape.

"No, you look the best in it. The dress looks like it's probably your size," Judy says.

"Yeah, just a foot too long," Leah chimes. "And we should probably make sure we all get mani-pedis before the wedding. We wouldn't want Emily painting her own nails." She draws everyone's attention to my botched paint job. Alison and Judy chuckle while my sister is oblivious, but Rochelle's look of concern bothers me the most. She's feeling sorry for me and I hate that look. I am strong enough to deal with a little razing; I don't need sympathy.

I continue my fake but pleasant smile. After all, Leah's comment was tame, a kitten compared to the ravenous tiger I know her to be. Deep down I'm furious Leah will be Samantha's sister-in-law. I don't want her venom anywhere near my sister.

Judy starts snapping pictures of the dress as I try to rein in my fury. One by one we are measured and sized. Alison is the hardest to fit. She orders the smallest size, knowing the dress will need to be taken in. I can't believe she made the dieting comment about herself. I'm sure it was intended for me, but I am thin enough and not about to diet to make her happy. Maybe I'll put on a few pounds; that would piss her off.

They're still in the middle of ordering Leah's dress, but I'm going to be late, so I give my sister a quick hug before leaving for class.

I arrive in the parking lot with a few minutes to spare. When I enter the lecture hall early, I remember to look for Patrick so I can strategically sit far away from him, but I don't see him anywhere. The professor is hobbling on his cane toward the podium as I take the same seat as the week before. I remove a notebook and pen from my bag as the professor begins his lecture.

A few minutes into class, I'm already cold. My book bag covers my legs, but the cold air is blowing directly from above. It becomes increasingly more frigid as the lecture progresses. Feeling the hair on my arms and legs rise, I check my phone only to discover a mere ten minutes have passed.

I do my best to focus on the lecture, but my mind wanders back to Ben. I can't figure out what I'm going to do. Can we really stay friends if there are other feelings involved? Maybe it will be easier if we stay away from each other. He can get his life back on track and go off to that East Coast school his parents have been pushing for and I . . . I haven't heard any voices since Tuesday. Hardly something in which to feel relief. It is just a matter of time.

"Hey, love," I hear a sultry voice in my ear.

I freeze. I can't believe it. The voices are back just like that.

"Didn't mean to startle you." It's a whisper.

Warm breath grazes my shoulder, and I flinch, spinning to see Patrick has taken the seat right next to me. He's leaning precariously close. His beautiful eyes are watching me. I was too enthralled in my thoughts to notice him arrive. At least I'm not making it up in my head. Wait, what did he say?

"Hey, love," he whispers. I watch his lips move. Why would he call me that? I'm not his love, and it's not okay for him to sit next to me. He gently strokes his hand down my arm. "Are you cold?"

I jerk my arm away and whisper, "No!"

He's doing it again, making me feel entirely mesmerized and irritated at the same time. I look back to the professor, remembering I'm in a classroom. A cold chill runs through me and I shiver.

"I'm only trying to be nice to you, you know."

I shoot him an offensive look and turn to write in my notebook.

Shhh! In case you haven't noticed, we're in class!

Annoying me even further, he takes the notebook and pen. I stare at the professor, not hearing a word. After a moment, Patrick hands the notebook back for me to read.

I know you think I'm rude, but I know you better than you realize. I hope you'll come over on the fourth. There are so many things we need to discuss. You look stunning today. I didn't peg you for a pink dress kind of girl, but there are so many things about you I have yet to discover. You are beautiful, love. I hope you are well. I know you're cold. I have a sweater in my bag. I would be delighted to lend it to you.

I turn to him as he offers the sweater. I decline, and Patrick snatches the notebook back and starts scribbling. He thinks he knows me. The thought is laughable. He hands it back.

If you put the sweater on, I won't bother you again during class.

I deliberate for a moment and without looking I reach out. Instead of placing the sweater in my hand, he wraps it around my shoulders. I leave the sweater on, but I try to ignore him and stare toward the podium.

I take notes, but my mind is anywhere but on this lecture. As much as I hate that the sweater belongs to him, I am grateful to be warm. Eventually, I put my arms through the sleeves, hating how wonderful it smells. As his aroma surrounds me, I look down at my notebook and reread what he wrote.

He doesn't know anything about me, and I don't think I want him to. Is he hitting on me? Maybe, I need to be blunt with him, after all even Morgan is leery of his behavior.

"Do you want to stay here all day?"

I can't believe he's talking out loud during class, especially after he promised not to bother me again. I take in the room, realizing the students are making their way to the door. I was too caught up in my thoughts to notice class was over.

"He let us go a half hour early, love."

"Don't call me that!"

"Whoa." He holds his hands up in surrender. "Sorry, Emily."

"Thanks for the sweater," I say, as I stand. I shrug out of it, hand it back to him, and grab my bag. "And really, you have no business calling me love."

He smirks. "Fair enough. I'll try my best to refrain."

"Thank you," I say, as I hurry past him and walk up the aisle toward the back of the room. Just as I reach the door, a smile slides across my face because all things considered this has been our most pleasant encounter.

"Wait, love, you forgot your notebook," Patrick says, breaking my confident stride. He's right at my ear. I hadn't heard him come up behind me. The smile slips from my face, angry he couldn't refrain from the little nickname for more than ten measly seconds. I turn to face him; only, he isn't there.

Perplexed, I search the empty room. Patrick is still in his chair halfway down the lecture hall. My jaw drops. He's not even facing me, yet I heard him so clearly. It wasn't a shout, just a whisper. I take an involuntary step in his direction, wanting to know how this is possible. And the revelation hits me. It's his voice I've been hearing. I don't understand how he's doing it, but it has to be him. I should've figured it out sooner. No one ever calls me love. No one, but him. But his mouth was unmoving when I heard the voice at the theater. A ventriloquist is the first thing that comes to mind, but he's clear across the room from me, and it was a whisper.

I glide foolishly back down the aisle, stopping at his row. "What the hell?" I breathe, almost inaudible.

His smirk is gone. His lips don't move, but I hear him whisper in my ear as if he's inside my head. *I told you I know you better than you realize.*

Too freaked out to stand, I stagger into the seat at the end of the row. How is this possible? How am I hearing him inside my head? When he reaches for me, I push up from my seat to escape, but he catches my hand wheeling me around to face him.

He says, "I didn't mean to frighten you."

Stunned, I gawk at him for a second before responding, "I think that's exactly what you wanted, to frighten and shock me. I don't care why. I want to know how. How are you doing that?"

"You'll understand soon, and then we can talk," he says aloud.

"Tell me how, Patrick. How the hell are you doing this?"

He scoffs. "Honestly, love, I don't understand how you're not aware of your capabilities."

Now I'm really pissed. "My what?"

"You're oblivious. You have so much to learn."

"Then explain it to me!"

"I wish I could, love, but that's not my responsibility, and I don't want to step on anyone's toes."

I don't know what he means, but he's genuinely scaring me. "You don't want to step on anyone's toes, yet you're more than happy to screw with my head." I try to rip my hand from his iron grip. "I'm not enjoying this little game of yours. I want you to stay away from me."

"Liar," he smirks. "You're cute when you lie, but you're terrible at it. We'll need to work on that."

"Listen, you're freaking me out, and I don't know what you think is going on here, but you're wrong. Just leave me alone."

He smiles. *"I can't do that, love,"* his voice rumbles in my head.

"Don't! Don't do that. I have to go to class," I say firmly, trying to remove his grip on my hand.

"I'll give you some time," he says, releasing me.

It takes a moment before my legs remember how to move. I walk out of the lecture hall wondering what the hell just happened.

I try to compose myself as my mind reels with unanswered questions. I debate going back in to get an explanation, but I can't. Running is my safer option, so I forget about my next class and drop my assignment in my teacher's mailbox.

I drive home to change clothes and pick up Maggie to take her to the park. As soon as we're on the trail, I unhook her leash. We hike ten miles through forest and shallow creeks before the sun begins to sink in the sky. The trees cast long shadows warning me of approaching darkness. My shoes are soaked through with water and dirt covers my legs from slipping down a steep hill. I'm sticky with sweat and I know it's time to go home.

Dad is on the couch watching television when Maggie and I arrive home. He appraises me as I walk through the door and his expression turns to concern.

He sets his beer down. "Was shopping really that bad?"

I totally forgot about shopping, but I'm exhausted and don't feel like explaining, so I nod.

"Where were you, Em? You look awful."

"We went to the park and hiked one of the trails," I explain.

"Looks like you fell off one of the trails."

"That too."

"I ordered a pizza," he says, changing the subject.

"Okay, I'm just gonna go jump in the shower."

After a long steamy shower, I slip into comfy pajamas and feed the dog. By the time I get to the living room, the pizza has arrived, and Dad is on his second slice. I grab a piece and take a big bite. As the pizza hits my tongue, nausea stabs through me making it difficult to swallow. I usually love this pizza, but between my worries over Ben and my confusion with Patrick, I've lost my appetite.

Dad's watching a shoot'm up, explosive detective movie. Once the first movie ends, we watch the sequel. It's brainless entertainment which is just what I need.

Dad clicks off the television, turns to me and says, "So what's going on?"

"Huh?" I question.

"Come on, when is the last time you sat down and watched a movie with your dad?"

I think about it for a moment. "People are difficult," I reply vaguely.

"This about Ben?"

"Not exactly, I just always thought guys were easy to understand, and now I don't know what to think."

"Is there another guy?" he asks.

"No, what do you mean another guy?"

"Well, you know your mom always had guys chasing her. It looks like she passed that on to you." Then offhand, he says, "So your birthday is next week."

He rarely mentions Mom, and now he has blown right past it like it's nothing. He keeps talking when I don't say anything.

"I figured you would be busy with your friends on your birthday, but I'd like to spend a little time with you, just the two of us."

I nod, shaking off my surprise. "I'm going shopping Tuesday morning with Sam, but I should be home in the afternoon. Then I'm free the rest of the day."

"Aren't you hanging out with Ben?" he asks.

"He'll be in Florida."

"Okay, so the two of us on Tuesday," he recaps, as he stands from the couch. He walks into the kitchen and calls for Maggie as he opens the back door.

I head to my room and am almost asleep by the time Maggie curls up at my feet. That's the last thing I remember before my alarm startles me awake the next morning.

seven ~

Like every Friday, I work with Ashley all day. The morning creeps by, and I think Ashley's mad at me for not giving her more details the other day. She's still talking to me and pretending everything is fine, but she's huffier and more impatient than usual. It's a slow day, so I listen to her prattle on about the new guy she's dating. He sounds like a jerk, which is precisely the type of guy she falls for. She describes him as hot, artsy, and mysterious. The more she talks about him, the more I get the impression he barely knows she exists; yet, for today he's the center of her universe.

At three o'clock, the store is empty. I am stocking shelves down aisle three when I hear Ashley gasp. A second later she calls to me from the register in front.

"I thought he said you weren't good enough?"

I know immediately she's referring to Ben. I put down the box of dog treats and start walking toward the front of the store.

"No, I said I wasn't good enough," I correct her.

"He must not believe that."

I round the corner of the aisle. "Why?"

She's standing, leaning against the counter with her back to me. Her arms are crossed in front of her as she stares out the windows.

"Because," she says, turning to face me. "He's here."

I look out the window and see Ben walking toward the door. I feel a flood of relief as soon as I see him. Then I see the worried expression he's wearing and feel a brick drop in my stomach. Everything has shifted since our conversation on the side of the road. Now I'll find out how much it altered our friendship.

Ashley offers, "Do you want me to be mean to him?"

What a strange question! I can't imagine being cruel to Ben. "No," I say without hesitation.

As Ben enters the store, his eyes zero in on me, and I can't seem to catch my breath. I am eager for his friendship but scared I've already ruined us.

"Hey," he greets with a smile.

"Hey," I echo, as the brick in my stomach starts melting. We stare at each other for a moment, both unsure what to say.

Ashley grabs a bin from under the register and breaks the silence. "I'm just gonna take this to the back room and sort it."

I look at her with gratitude, and she nods her understanding. She scurries around the counter sweeping past us, and she's out of sight.

Ben steps forward closing the gap. He motions between us with his hand. "This is gonna be awkward, isn't it?"

"I don't want it to be."

"You're avoiding me," he accuses.

"No, I'm not," I lie, looking down at my feet.

"Yes, you are."

"Well, I didn't know if you would want to hear from me," I admit, peeking up at him.

"I told you we're friends no matter what, Em."

"I know, but—"

"You're ridiculous," he says.

So, it appears he hasn't realized that he's too good to be my friend and that makes me happy. Happier than it should.

He pulls me into a hug even though he knows my aversion, but I don't fight him. Not today, maybe not ever. I bury my face in his chest, close my eyes, and wrap my arms around him. He smells amazing, and I feel the tug to be closer to him. I pull away before he becomes more of a temptation.

"So, I thought you were going to Florida?" I question, thinking he should be on a plane by now. Maybe he finagled his way out of the trip. God, I hope so.

"I told my parents I'd meet them at the airport. Our flight leaves at five, but I couldn't leave before we settled this." He buries his hands in his pockets.

"It's really good to see you."

"I'm gonna miss your birthday," he says with regret.

"It's not a big deal, and I'm gonna be busy with my family anyway."

"I'll still call you."

"Forget about it. Go soak up the sun because who wouldn't want to spend July in sunny, hot, humid Florida," I tease.

"You know I'd rather stay here."

"You'll be back next Friday. It's only a week."

"Already counting down the hours until I come back from Hell, I mean vacation." He gives me a grim smile. "We have a late flight on Friday, so maybe we can get together next Saturday."

"Sure, now go before you miss your flight."

"Yeah, that would be just awful."

"Come on, Ben." I tug him toward the door.

I hear Ashley's footsteps behind me. She sets the bin on the counter. "Nice to see you again, Ben," she chimes. The box is still a mess, clearly untouched.

"Good to see you," Ben says, glancing in her direction.

"Have a good flight to Hell," I say, wondering what it's like to fly first class. I wouldn't be surprised if they have their own private jet.

"Sure, it'll be great," he says with sarcasm and walks out the door.

"Damn, look at that hottie!" Ashley says.

I spin around to see her staring out the window. I follow her gaze and realize she's not gawking at Ben. I feel the heat touch my cheeks. *CRAP!* Ben gives Patrick a curt nod as they pass each other. Patrick is heading toward the door. How did he know where to find me? I've decided to actively avoid him rather than confronting him with my many questions. I turn to hide from him, but it's too late. He's already in the door.

I make it a couple of steps before I hear his deep voice, "Emily."

I freeze in place, squeezing my eyes shut as if that'll make him go away, but it doesn't work. Ashley's jaw drops, and she looks at me in disbelief. I give her a worried look filled with screams for help. A look that says, *"Be mean to this one!"* She doesn't catch on.

Patrick grips my shoulder and spins me around.

"What do you want, Patrick?"

"I have questions for you, love."

I glare at his perfect sapphire eyes and hard jaw. He runs a hand through his blond hair as he watches me.

"Questions?" I ask, annoyed when he brushes a wisp of hair from my face.

"I'd like to know how old you are."

Instead of answering him, I ask, "How did you find me here?"

"You're easy for me to find, love."

"Don't call me that!" I jab a finger against his chest.

"Sorry. I didn't mean to offend you." He backs up a step. "I asked Morgan where you work."

"Why didn't you just ask her how old I was?" I say, crossing my arms.

"I guess it was an excuse to see you again."

"You said you'd give me some time."

"Twenty-four hours is time," he states. "Now if you would be so kind as to tell me your age."

"How old are you?" I ask, more out of spite than curiosity.

"Twenty. You didn't answer my question."

I raise an eyebrow and remain silent.

"You think you're clever, but I'm happy to stay here all day." He mimics me by crossing his arms.

"I'm almost eighteen."

"Eighteen?" He looks puzzled. "When is your birthday?"

"When's yours?"

"August sixth."

"Mine too. Now, what are the odds?"

"Are you always so evasive, love, or is it just with me?"

"Are you always so inquisitive, or is it just with people you're currently stalking?"

"Why, are you jealous?" He leans forward. "When did you say your birthday was?"

"You need to leave. I have work to do."

He spins in a circle looking around the vacant store. His eyes, full of humor, land on me. "I can tell you're swamped."

I glare at him. "It's July third. Now, will you please leave?"

"When can I see you again?" he asks with a sense of urgency.

"I don't want to see you again. And if you don't leave, I'll call the police."

"That sounds like fun." He laughs at my threat.

"Seriously, I don't want to see you."

"You pretending you don't want to see me is cute." He's scrutinizing my every move, making me uneasy. "Don't you have questions for me?"

"No," I lie. I have questions, but I don't trust him.

"Really?"

"Yes, really."

His tone turns serious, "If I told you your life depended on it, would you believe me?"

"No."

"It's adorable that you're still trying to lie to me." He's suppressing a smile as he leans forward. "Listen, we are going to get together again. It's simple, really, either we set a mutually beneficial date, or I will show up whenever I feel like it. It's your decision. Take your time, love; I've got all day."

As I stand seething, Patrick turns to move next to Ashley. "Hello," he says in a seductive voice.

"Hi," she breathes, wilting on her feet.

She is mesmerized by him. He reaches out to take her hand, and she happily obliges. He leans forward, touching his lips to her fingers. She looks like she might faint.

"My name is Patrick. It's a pleasure to meet you . . ." He pauses for her name.

"Ashley," she exhales, fluttering her eyelashes.

"Ashley," he repeats in his deep sensual voice.

Does everyone react to Patrick this way? She's acting as helpless as I feel around him. If not for my mistrust, I might also surrender to his irresistible charm.

"Stop!" I yell.

Ashley jumps.

"Stop what?" Patrick feigns innocence, but his smirk gives him away.

"You know what you're doing," I scold.

He turns to Ashley once more, "Well, it was a pleasure to meet you. It looks like she is the jealous type after all. I think it's time for me to go."

"You don't have to go," Ashley pleads. "You should stay."

"I'll see you again soon, Ashley," he promises.

I can't stand it anymore, so I blurt, "If I agree to meet you, will you leave Ashley alone?"

"Yes, that's excellent. When is your next day off?"

"Monday."

"Great. I'll meet you on Monday at your place. Shall we say, one o'clock? That should give you time enough to sleep in."

"You know where I live?"

"I'll find you," he says with confidence.

"Of course, you will."

He pulls my hand from my hip. His moist lips graze my knuckles, and I jerk away, slapping his angelic face. It's out of character for me, but I can't help myself. Ashley gasps. Patrick looks momentarily stunned. I hold my breath. He blinks once before he throws his head back with a burst of laughter.

"I can't wait to know you, Emily Burk!"

My jaw drops and I simmer with anger. I clench my fists and my palm stings from the contact with Patrick's face. He turns away laughing and opens the door to allow a little old lady and her flat-nosed pug to enter the store.

He's still shaking with laughter as he walks to his car. Ashley doesn't say anything, looking too stunned for words. I return to stocking shelves while Ashley remains behind the register twirling her hair, deep in thought. Once she locks the door at closing, she unloads on me.

"Emily, what the hell?" she scolds, without giving me a chance to explain. "You have not one, but two gorgeous hotties chasing you! You force one to get on a plane to Florida, and you slap the other one in the face! What's wrong with you?"

"It's way more complicated than you make it sound, Ashley. Patrick isn't even a friend. He's a nuisance that won't go away, and Ben is my best friend. I don't want to ruin that."

"So, like, you're what? Just gonna remain friends?" She pauses before she starts her next rant. "I mean did you see his designer shorts. I bet those cost him three hundred bucks! He's rich, he's super-hot, and he's willing to be just friends with you. That's crazy, Emily! And then there's Patrick, Oh My God! He's perfect! And the way he looks at you, I'd kill to have him look at me like that."

My words come quickly. "Okay, but when they find my body chopped up in a basement somewhere then maybe you'll understand why Patrick is dangerous. And Ben can do whatever he wants. I want him to be happy."

"You're an idiot! He'd be happy with you! And I'll take Patrick, basement and all," she adds.

Ashley goes on and on about Patrick. He's become her new obsession. I bet she can't even remember the guy's name she'd been obsessing over this morning. She's so fickle when it comes to men. When I see Patrick again, I don't care what it takes; I'm going to make sure he stays away from her.

Ashley and I close up the store, and I think about calling Morgan to find out what's wrong with her crazy cousin, but I wouldn't know where to start. The last time I tried, I'm the one who sounded crazy. Maybe I am, but at least I haven't heard any voices since I told Patrick to stop.

The weekend goes by in a haze. I set a personal record for consecutive times hitting the snooze button, and despite all the rest, my eyes still have trouble staying open at work. The sleep must be contagious because I'm back in bed by seven on Sunday night.

eight ~

I wake on Monday with sunlight flooding my room. The alarm is buzzing, and I wave my hand around blindly until it finds the button to squelch the noise. My eyes begin to focus, and I see the clock. It's noon and Patrick will be here in an hour. I can't believe how long I've slept and I'm still tired. I cover my head with the blanket wishing for more shut-eye, but my bladder protests. I groan as I toss the sheets aside and stumble to the bathroom. I pass my reflection in the mirror and shudder. My hair has fallen out of its ponytail and hangs in tangled knots. Red creases imprint the side of my face and my eyes are bloodshot. My only option is to shower.

Once I'm out of the shower, I'm suddenly freezing. I blow-dry my long tangles on the warmest setting, hoping to ease the chill, but the warmth of the dryer almost puts me back to sleep.

I finally make my way into the kitchen. I don't like coffee, but I need something to wake me up. I've often made coffee for Dad, so I'm familiar with the routine. Before the coffee finishes brewing, I hear a knock on the front door and Maggie lets out a warning bark. Good, my scary guard dog will protect me from Patrick. As

I open the front door Maggie's nub tail begins wagging as she nudges between my legs. She sniffs and nuzzles up to him.

"Unbelievable!" I gasp. She only has this reaction to one other person in the world and that's me!

Patrick is composed and charming as always. "Hello," he greets. "May I come in?"

"Why ask? You'll just do it anyway," I mumble, moving aside for him to enter.

Once inside, he kneels down to Maggie and strokes the sides of her neck. She's like butter in his hands.

"Maggie, not you too," I moan.

Patrick caresses the scars down her side where her fur never fully grew in. "How'd she get these marks?"

"I don't know, but I'm pretty sure a man caused them. She hates men. I expected her to be at your throat, but of course, you're the exception."

"Dogs like me," he says, coming to a stand. "Does that make you uncomfortable?"

"Everything about you makes me uncomfortable."

"If it helps, Morgan is aware of my presence here."

"Your presence here? Who talks like that?" I sigh, too tired to argue. "Whatever." I turn and move back into the kitchen with Maggie and Patrick on my heels.

The coffee finishes brewing, and I have a mug ready with a heap of sugar. From over my shoulder, Patrick laughs. "Are you going to have some coffee with your sugar?"

Too exhausted to come up with anything witty, I mumble, "I don't like coffee."

"So why drink it?"

While stirring my drink to dissolve the sugar, my eyes droop, and I complain, "I'm tired."

"Haven't you been sleeping?"

"All weekend."

"Interesting." He rests his hand on the small of my back. "Why don't you sit down?"

He removes the hot mug from my hands and leads me to sit at the kitchen table. Leaning my arms on the table, I prop my head in my hands. In a small voice, I say, "If I go to sleep, will you leave? I think I'm getting sick. Maybe I have mono. I feel like I've been in a coma all weekend."

"It won't last much longer," Patrick says gently.

I'm irritated by his comment, but almost immediately my irritation floats away. I feel like I'm submerged underwater. I feel . . . peaceful. Everything is distant, dark, muffled.

Startled, I open my eyes to find Patrick shaking me. "Emily, you just fell asleep! Here, take a drink of your coffee." He pushes the cup into my hands. I make a face as I sip the bittersweet concoction.

"Where is your mom?" he asks. He doesn't know talking about my mom is taboo.

"Dead," I whisper the painful truth. My eyelids become too heavy and I close them for a moment.

"How long?"

"Five years."

"And where is your dad?"

"Work, always working."

I'm strangely subdued, walking a fine line between wakefulness and sleep. The truth seems to pour out like tap water, so I ask the question I really want to know. "How do you talk to me without moving those lips?"

Only as my fingers graze his mouth am I conscious of my hand out in front of me. What am I doing? I pull back and fold my arms. I try to pull myself together, but it's too hard to form a coherent thought. I imagine this is what it would feel like to be drunk, very,

very drunk. I have no control over my thoughts, my words, or my movements. Did I just touch him? I giggle. I try to concentrate on my breathing. In and out. In and out. And once more I am back in the dark muffled water.

Disoriented, I open my eyes and search the room for something familiar. I blink at the white ceiling above recognizing the dark wooden blades of the ceiling fan in my living room. I feel the worn texture of the old couch I'm lying on, but I don't know how I got here. The television is on mute and it's dark outside the window. I feel something move at my feet.

Patrick is watching from the end of the couch while holding my feet in his lap. I yank my legs up, curling them to my chest. I wrap my arms around my knees and stare at him, trying to piece together my last lucid memory. "How did I get here?"

"You almost fell out of your chair when you dozed off. I thought the couch was a safer option."

"Did you carry me in here?"

"Yes."

I narrow my eyes. "What time is it? Why are you still here?"

"It's nine-thirty, and we still haven't talked."

"You've been here for over eight hours!"

"Not the whole time. I picked up Chinese." He motions to the collection of white paper boxes on the coffee table. "I didn't know what you liked to eat, so I got a little of everything. I knew you would be hungry when you woke."

The food was a nice gesture, but I'm still disoriented.

"Where is my dad?"

"He's working late. He left you a message."

"How do you know he's working late? Did you listen to my voicemail?"

He smirks. "Your password was easy to figure out."

"You're kidding, right?"

"One, two, three, four was my first guess." I'm ready to rip him a new one when he says, "Your dad is going to explain everything tomorrow."

I'm thrown. "Explain what?"

"The truth. I'm baffled why he would wait so long, but I suppose he did his best with what your mom left him."

"Excuse me!" I bolt upright. "You can stalk me, corner me, hack my phone, but you won't say another word about my mother! Do you understand me?"

"Emi—"

"Not another word!" I shout, trembling. I can't remember the last time I was this angry.

Patrick watches me like one would watch a screaming toddler. He's patiently waiting out my tantrum. And I realize, I'm not finished.

"You are trouble! I can't even keep my thoughts straight when you're around! What are you still doing here? Get out! And stay the hell away from Ashley and me!" I demand.

Calmly, he soothes, "Emily, I'm not the problem. I know you're confused, but you'll understand soon."

"Understand what, Patrick?"

He looks apologetic, as he answers, "The truth about your mom and about you."

I let out the breath I didn't know I was holding. My anger crumbles and I sit down on the edge of the couch hiding my face in my hands. I rub my temples trying to dissolve the coming headache.

"How could you know anything about my mom?"

Moving closer, he answers softly, "Please understand there are so many things I want to tell you, but you have to talk to your dad first."

I feel his eyes burning into my skin before I look up to meet his gaze. "Why are you here? Why did you wait eight hours to tell me to talk to my dad? Why didn't you just leave?"

"I've never met anyone like you, Emily. You are fascinating," he says with reverence.

"You're only interested in me because I don't melt like butter when you're around."

He chuckles as he says, "That is intriguing, but it's more than that. You completely captivate me."

I wonder if he's patronizing me, but his full lips are smiling seductively. His sun-kissed skin, strong jawline, and angled cheekbones are too perfect. His bright eyes gaze into mine and I'm mesmerized. He really is beautiful! He touches my knee and my pulse quickens. He leans into me and I can't look away. I inch forward, enjoying his masculine scent. His lips are so close. If I lean in a little more . . .

I blink, breaking the trance. "You!" I croak, as I brush his hand away. I clear my throat and start again. "You should leave!"

"You should eat."

Looking at the food, I remember how hungry I am, but I turn to argue instead.

"Save your breath, love. I'm not going anywhere. I do have one question though. Where are all the pictures?"

"What pictures?"

"You have no pictures on your walls. Don't you think that's a little strange?"

"Really? You're calling me strange?"

It's true. It is strange not to have any pictures. I didn't realize how odd it was until the guys pointed it out to me my junior year. My sister used to cover her walls with snapshots of her friends. I have one picture of my mom sitting on my nightstand, but as far as family albums go; those are kept hidden away on computer flash drives somewhere. I guess photos of our once perfect family are too painful for Dad to have sitting around, but I don't tell Patrick this. In fact, I don't say much of anything for the next hour with the exception of asking him to leave.

Patrick refuses to go. He is cordial. I might even go so far as saying he's nice. He serves me food and tries to make pleasant conversation. It's beyond strange. All of his actions are generous and sincere, but it's a wasted effort on me. His unwelcome presence makes me feel like a hostage in my own home.

Patrick, the prison warden, is currently sitting at the opposite end of the couch ignoring my dad as he enters the kitchen from the garage.

I stand to face him as he walks into the living room. I call, "Hey, Dad."

"Hey Em." His eyes zero in on Patrick and then he looks to me for an explanation.

"This is Patrick. He's Morgan's cousin. He brought me Chinese."

Dad eyes the open food containers spread across the coffee table and smiles at the tremendous assortment. "That's a lot of food for the two of you." His smile fades as he scrutinizes Patrick who is sitting with his back to us.

When Patrick stands, his whole demeanor changes from pleasant and attentive to cold and distant. I've never seen Patrick look like this before. Though he appears calm, I feel anger burning within him as he saunters around the couch and across the room to stand toe to toe with my dad.

"Patrick?" I question.

"It's okay, love. Stay where you are." Patrick's soothing words are spoken directly into my mind, but when he speaks aloud to my dad, his tone is aggressive and frightening. "If you love her, how

could you keep it from her? I don't know how you've suppressed it for so long, but she's already changing."

He brushes past my dad on his way toward the front door. Hand on the knob, he turns to look at me. Unsure where to look, my gaze oscillates between the two of them before settling on Patrick. The concern I find in the depth of his blue eyes unnerves me, and I wonder how much he sees when he looks at me.

My fear evaporates as he no longer feels like a threat. I'm aware we're staring too long, but I can't tear my eyes away, and I sense a connection building between us. The door opens and a cool breeze fills the room.

"Happy Birthday, Emily," Patrick says before he exits.

I'm left standing in the middle of the room staring at the door, as I try to piece together what just happened. There is silence for a long moment before I hear Dad approach me. I try to break my gaze from the door, but I'm frozen in place, lost in thoughts that threaten to drown me until I feel Dad's arms wrap around my shoulders.

"Now I understand what's going on." His tone is weary. "Some boys are more difficult than others."

I pull away watching his expression turn to guilt. Patrick told me there are things he's keeping from me, but I didn't believe him until now. "What's going on, Dad? What did he mean, I'm already changing?"

He glances at the jumble of open food containers. "Let's clean up this mess and then we'll talk."

I shake my head. "Dad, I need to know what's going on. Please."

He opens his mouth to speak, but it falls closed, and he purses his lips. His eyes are heavy with secrets, and his body is tense. I watch a dozen emotions pass through him. Minutes tick by before either of us speaks.

"Okay," he concedes, releasing a deep breath. "Emily, your mom wasn't ill. She was . . ." He gives me a wary look, pausing too long. I wait in silence as he puts his thoughts together. "She was never sick. She wasn't crazy. We were trying to protect you."

Needing the extra support, I lean on the chair behind me. I'm deeply concerned and wondering if my father is in denial about his crazy dead wife. "Dad, she was unstable. She heard voices. You, you're the one who had her committed."

"She made me, but she wasn't sick. She was special."

"Dad, I miss her too, but she was sick. She killed herself, remember?" As much as I hate what I'm saying, it's the truth. And he knows it.

"Emily, it's not true. She's dead, but it wasn't suicide, and she was never sick. Please try to understand. We had to protect you."

"Dad—"

"I'm so sorry to keep it from you for so long. There is so much to talk about, but the first thing you need to understand is your mother was gifted. She had certain abilities. She could hear things, see things, feel things, and people loved her because of her alluring, mysterious ways. She captivated everyone around her."

He's lost, sadness oozing from every pour and I'm helpless to stop it. He's mourning her all over again, and I cannot go through this one more time. I have to distance myself. I turn to leave, and he speaks my name. With a broken heart, he pleads for me to stay. Reluctantly, I turn to face him.

"It's in you, Emily. She never wanted you to know. She was trying to find a way to stop it. She left so you'd be safe, and I know it hurt, but we did everything we could to keep you safe." His eyes fill with tears. "But it's happening. And that boy is right." He glares at the door before turning to me and grabbing both of my shoulders. "There's nothing I can do to stop it. You . . . you are changing."

Pushing my emotions back, I blink at my dad. He looks so grave and a sliver of uncertainty slips through my mind. I try to make sense of what he just told me. Everything about him tells me he's speaking the truth, yet his story is flawed and inconceivable.

I shake my head, trying to clear it. "I'm sorry. What?"

"The lies were to protect you. Everything we did was to protect you," he exhales, looking away, shame heavy on his features.

His arms fall from my shoulders as I take a step back. I look to the front windows. Just beyond the porch, there are holes in the flowerbed where no flowers were ever planted. Then I look around the room at bare, picture-less walls. There are no family keepsakes or homey decor, just the bare essentials, just enough to make it a livable space. No wonder Samantha didn't spend any time at home. We've lived in a shell of a house for years, and it's been obvious to everyone except for me.

"Everything you did was to protect me? I don't understand. You committed me after mom died. Are you saying that was to protect me?"

"Yes," he says, taking a step forward.

I step back, just out of his reach, my composure cracking like the eggshells I've been walking on since the day my mother died. "Then you failed. Miserably. Those were the worst weeks of my life and you made me think I was mentally ill."

"I promise you; there was a reason for all of it. You see, these capabilities—"

Shaking my head, I cut him off. "I can't. I can't wrap my head around this. If what you're saying is true and Mom wasn't sick, then how dare you lock her away from me. How dare you make me think she took her own life."

He's giving me the look I hate. It's the "Poor Emily Burke, her mom committed suicide," only he's saying it was a lie.

"What could you possibly be protecting me from that's worse than what I've been through? I needed her! Do you even know what my life has been like?" I shake my head, not giving him a chance to answer. "No! No, because you're never around!"

"Emily, I don't think you're grasping the severity of the situation. If I'm not around, it's because I'm protecting this family. Your mother had to do unimaginable things to keep us safe."

"Like what? Live in a mental institution!" I accuse, loudly.

"Emily," he says, trying to reason with me.

"What happened to Mom? If she didn't commit suicide, what happened to her?"

He blinks slowly before answering, "She wasn't mentally ill, but death had been stalking her for a long time. Eventually, it caught up to her and she made me promise to keep you away, you and Sam. She didn't want either of you to witness her death or suffer because of it."

I shake my head. "That can't be . . . it just . . . None of this makes sense."

"She was—"

"No," I breathe. "I don't . . . I can't handle this. I can't be here right now." On instinct, my body is moving without my conscious permission. A second later my hand is on the doorknob, and I feel the rush of cool air as I make my escape into the night.

I'm running. Running from the deception. Running from the pain. Running from the things I cannot escape.

nine ~

I have so many questions, but they feel trivial compared to the magnitude of betrayal I feel from my dad. So, I run, just like Ben says I always do. Maggie follows me out the door. We jump in my car and soon find ourselves in the park. We hike a trail in the nearly pitch-black forest which proves treacherous, leaving me with gashes and bruises. Each time I stumble, Maggie loyally sticks by my side, licking my face and silently encouraging me to pick myself up and continue.

When we arrive back home around four in the morning, Dad is in the living room waiting for me. He jumps out of his seat when we walk through the door. "Emily, my God! I wasn't prepared to have this conversation tonight. Let me explain."

I hold a hand out, motioning for him to stop. "I need some time, Dad. I can't deal with this tonight."

"Sure, I understand. We can talk in the morning. I'm relieved you came home safe, Emily."

I go straight to my room without any intention of speaking to him in the morning. I lock the door behind me and change out of my filthy clothes before getting into bed. I stare at my ceiling until the sun creeps up outside my window. Lying beside me, Maggie rests her head on my chest. She lets out an exhausted sigh, and I wrap my arms around her wondering what I'm going to say to Dad the next time I see him.

I think back to our conversation.

"Your mother was gifted. She had certain abilities. She could hear things, see things, feel things, and people loved her because of her alluring, mysterious ways. She captivated everyone around her."

I go over it a hundred times in my head trying but failing to make sense of it. He's trying to convince me that the worst events of my life were to protect me. From what? My life has been a cruel web of pain and humiliation. Whispers plagued me in the school halls. Rumors spread like wildfire across social media forcing me to seclude myself from normal teenage activities. Bitterness boils up, spiraling into burning anger deep in my veins.

Family members are the people you're supposed to count on to be honest and have your back. Dad has destroyed my trust, and I wonder if Sam is aware of the deception. But I know Sam wouldn't keep that secret—not from me.

I don't remember falling asleep, but my phone vibrating on the nightstand startles me awake.

"Hello," I answer with a raspy voice.

"Happy Birthday!"

"Thanks, Sam."

"Are we still on for three?"

Shopping is my sister's favorite thing to do, and every year for my birthday she loves to drag me along and treat me like her own personal Barbie. The clock tells me it's two in the afternoon and I'm still covered in dirt and dried blood from the night before.

"Three is perfect."

"Yay, can't wait. I'll see you soon, Em. Bye."

I struggle to sit as I gather my thoughts. Yesterday feels like a bad dream which I might believe, except for my sore, aching muscles and the mud-crusted clothes piled on the floor. On my way to the shower, I search the house only to discover my father is absent. Typical. Work is still his top priority.

Once I'm finished getting ready, I leave the house, unable to stand being inside for one more second. As I crouch to sit on the porch step, my phone vibrates, and I find a new text from Dad.

Happy Birthday. I know it's a lot to take in. Please let me explain. Love you.

My phone is clasped in my hand as I contemplate my response. He had years to explain, but he waited until he was backed into a corner to talk to me. I feel betrayed, and I'm not ready to accept an explanation.

Let me have my birthday. We can talk another time.

My phone vibrates again, but this time it's Ben calling. I think about letting it go to voicemail, but our friendship is already strained, so I hit the button and lift the phone to my ear.

I try to rally a cheerful voice. "Hey, Ben!"

"Happy Birthday!"

"Thanks."

"What's wrong?" he asks.

I guess I'm not very good at faking happy. "I had a fight with my dad. It's nothing."

"Since when do you fight with your dad?"

Dad and I have never had a normal father-daughter relationship. I don't get in trouble, my homework is finished on time, my grades are good, and on top of that, I've held a steady job since I was thirteen. I'm responsible and don't give him any reason not to trust me.

"Ben, let's not talk about this right now. Tell me about Florida."

"Let's not talk about that either," he says with irritation.

We are both silent until a car pulls up to the curb and I jump to my feet. "I have to go. My sister just got here."

"K, talk to you later."

Before I can say goodbye, Ben is hanging up.

When Sam gets us to the mall, I let her drag me into all of her favorite shops. Her Barbie Doll obsession over me becomes a needed distraction. Her infectious giddiness has a way of cheering me up. With all the wedding planning I realize now how much I miss having my sister to myself.

It's seven o'clock by the time we leave the mall, and I wish I could hang out with Ben. Being around him makes me feel relaxed and secure.

"Oops, you had plans with Dad, didn't you?" Sam says, looking at the time.

"No, we did our thing last night."

"In that case, do you want to have dinner with Dan and me? We're going to his parent's house."

I go with the first excuse that pops in my head. "Morgan is back in town, and we've been meaning to catch up." At that very moment my phone rings. "Speak of the devil," I say, before answering, "Hey, Morgan."

"Happy Birthday, Emily!"

"Thanks. Are you free to hang out tonight?"

"Yeah," Morgan says, "I'm at home right now if you'd want to come over."

"Great, let me swing by my house and grab my car. I'll see you in a few."

Dad's truck is in the garage as we pull up. I take a deep breath and turn to hug my sister. Hugs from Sam are one of the few comforting constants left in my life.

"Thanks for a great day, Sam."

"It was my pleasure. I'm flying out tomorrow to the beach house with Dan and his family. I won't be back until next week, so have a great Fourth of July."

Retrieving my brightly colored shopping bags from the back seat, I say, "You too. Love you."

"Love you," she says before I close the door.

I'm relieved Sam doesn't come in the house. I shove my goodies in my car before going inside. I head straight for my room and pull an overnight bag from the closet. After packing, I fling it over my shoulder and head out. Maggie watches me longingly. I don't want to leave her behind, but I can't take her with me. I bend down, kiss the top of her head and whisper, "I'm sorry."

"Where are you going?" Dad catches me before I'm out the door.

"I'm staying with Morgan tonight."

"Emily," he says my name the way parents do when they're about to lecture.

"Dad, I can't," I say, as I turn and walk out the door.

ten ~

I pull off the country road onto the long gravel driveway that leads to Morgan's house. It sits on several acres with a private lake. I park behind a very expensive white BMW that looks like it belongs in Ben's garage next to his dad's Ferrari.

I leave my things and walk to the porch. The frosted glass front doors are encased in a crimson border. The rest of the old Victorian style house is a variation of creamy colors, adding to the character of the intricate woodwork.

Morgan rushes out to embrace me. "Happy birthday, Emily! We have so much catching up to do. Come on."

I fight my initial reaction to push her away and instead hug her back.

We venture upstairs, and it appears we're the only people in the house. Once in her room, we get comfy on her big fluffy bed. She looks like she's going to burst. "So, what's going on with you and Ben?"

I should've expected it or at least been prepared for the subject, but I've had other things occupying my mind. My head falls into my hands. "I'm not sure it even matters anymore. The truth is; I really like him, but everything is so complicated. He called me earlier to wish me a happy birthday, but we were both upset because Ben is stuck in Florida with his family and I just got into a fight with my dad."

Morgan's face shows concern. "You got in a fight with your dad? That never happens. What can I do?"

"Actually, can I stay with you tonight?" I ask feeling guilty for inviting myself.

"Of course, you're always welcome here. I hope you know that," she says, and then more quietly she asks, "Are things really that bad?"

I nod yes, shake my head no, and finally shrug, irked I can't explain. She's too kind to push me further on the dad subject and instead offers, "So wait a while with Ben. If it's meant to happen, it will."

"I don't think anything can happen, but ever since he told me how he feels, I can't help but notice parts of him I've never noticed before. And it's crazy how he's always been there for me, more than I ever knew. I mean, he got suspended for defending me, and he's put college on hold. But I wonder what will happen when he realizes it's too much. I'm too much." I roll to my side and prop my head on my hand.

"Wow, there is a lot there we need to discuss. I've never seen you like this."

We continue talking and catching up. I find out why she left college. Morgan's roommate went out one night leaving the door unlocked. Morgan went to sleep early because of finals the next morning. In the middle of the night two drunk guys stumbled into her room. They overpowered her, held her down, stripped off her clothes, and covered her mouth to muffle her screams. Her roommate came back just in time. Even though she wasn't raped, she was violated and never felt safe after that. The two guys got away with a slap on the wrist, making Morgan feel additional betrayal by the lack of consequence.

While I am a pessimist—expecting bad from people—Morgan is genuinely optimistic. She sees the best in people and situations. Optimism can be very annoying, but with Morgan, it is part of who she is. Even with her faith in humanity rattled, she is eager to carry on with her life. Her motto, everything happens for a reason, is still holding strong.

I tell her about my year, leaving out my recent discoveries. After everything that's happened to me recently and after hearing her story, I feel childish for worrying about Gavin. We reminisce over stories from our past, and I feel a pang of guilt realizing if I hadn't accidentally run into Morgan on campus, I wouldn't be here now. It's so easy to drift apart. We went different directions and almost lost each other in just a year. I promise myself I won't let it happen again. Even if she moves to Antarctica, I'll make an effort to hold onto such a gem in my life.

"I'd better get my stuff out of the car," I say, standing.

"Okay. I'll follow you down. I'm thinking about making a pizza. Are you hungry?"

Opening her bedroom door, I shrug. "I could eat."

Morgan makes her way to the kitchen while I head to the car. The wraparound porch is brightly lit, but the country sky is pitch black without city lights. As I open the back door, the interior light blinds me for a second. I stuff my shopping bags into my overnight duffle and pass the BMW on my way back. I meet Morgan in the kitchen, drop my bag on a chair, and hike myself up on a stool at the counter.

Leaning toward me, Morgan asks, "Pepperoni pizza okay?"

"Sounds good. Are your parents' home?"

"No, they're out getting fireworks for tomorrow."

Morgan's family has a firework display every year. It's their Fourth of July tradition.

"So, whose car is out there?"

She scoffs, "That's Patrick's car, of course. Leave it to him to end up with a ridiculously expensive car."

"Patrick?" I swallow nervously. "Is he here?"

"He's around here somewhere. Probably in his room."

"What do you mean . . . in his room?"

She cocks her head as if I'm missing something obvious. "He lives here. You know that, right?"

"I . . . didn't know that, no."

"He didn't tell you?"

I shake my head wondering first why she thought he would've told me and second why didn't he tell me? Shrugging, I suggest, "It must have slipped his mind."

"So, what's going on between the two of you anyway?"

"Nothing." I burst into nervous laughter having no idea what's going on when it comes to Patrick.

Her brows furrow. "Are you at least sort of friends?"

"I don't think so."

"I think we get along quite beautifully, myself," Patrick contends from the doorway, his tall stature leaning against the door frame. His arms are folded across his chest, and his blond hair is messier than usual. He is smiling from ear to ear, and his bright eyes are searching mine from across the room. His once white button-down shirt is filthy and missing buttons. His jeans are caked in mud while dark smudges stain his lovely features.

"What happened to you?" Morgan snickers.

He doesn't break my eye contact as he answers her. "Setting up the fireworks. Someone has to do the dirty work so the rest of you can relax and enjoy the show."

His gaze is seductive. I look to Morgan who is gawking apprehensively between Patrick and me. The oven buzzer rings letting us know it's finished preheating. Morgan shifts her weight and turns to put the pizza in the oven.

"I thought my parents were out picking up the fireworks," Morgan says, as she closes the oven door and turns back around.

His stare shifts from me to Morgan. While his gaze is otherwise occupied, I view him unrestrained for the first time since we met. The two of them are talking, but the words are a blur. His alluring baritone becomes music to my ears.

Even as disheveled as he is; he looks impossibly fresh. My nostrils fill with his sweet masculine scent, causing my eyes to close involuntarily. A hint of mud and sweat mixes with his alluring musk. His dark jeans fit like they were specially tailored for him. His open shirt reveals a chest so enticing I can't look away. Warmth spreads through my body—building—getting hotter by the second. I'm barely holding myself together, finding no flaw, no imperfection. I want him to look my way, and as he turns in my direction, I am imprisoned by the ocean behind his magnificent blue eyes. I hold my breath, feeling as flimsy as a school girl with a crush. I understand now why Ashley and every other girl I've seen find him irresistible.

"Emily!" I hear Morgan cry, effectively capturing my attention.

Snapping my head around, I break out of my pathetic stupor. "What?"

"Didn't you hear me? I asked you three times."

"No, I'm sorry. I guess . . . I zoned out."

She's quick to forgive. "Did you bring your bathing suit?"

"No." What have I missed? How long have I been staring? I hate that I lose myself when Patrick is around.

"Well, I have a few that might work," Morgan says, unaffected by my mood.

Patrick leaves the room to travel up the stairs. I find myself trying to follow his quiet footsteps above, so I won't be taken off guard next time.

When we finish eating our pizza, we make our way up to Morgan's room. I hear the shower in her adjoining Jack and Jill bathroom, so I figure Patrick must be staying in the room opposite hers.

Morgan and I watch a movie we've already seen a dozen times over the years. It quickly becomes background noise as the two of us continue to catch up. I learn about Morgan's new job working nights at the local hospital. She's hoping to stay there and get a job as a nurse once she's finished with school.

Morgan has been back for a month and she already has her life back on track moving steadily straight ahead. I have no idea what I'm doing with mine. I wish I had a strong desire to be something or an ambition to strive for, but what I have is a very uncertain feeling about almost everything.

I'm keenly aware of the shower turning off in the next room. I listen intently, but can't hear a thing, so I assume he goes back to his bedroom. I wonder what Patrick is going to school for and how he can afford such a nice car.

It's almost midnight when Morgan's mom taps on the door. Julie peeks her head in to say hi. She and Tom have just returned from somewhere, and she says her quick goodnight. Morgan and I crawl into her queen size bed, and she's out in a flash.

I lie watching the shadows on the ceiling for an hour without finding sleep. The more I struggle to get comfortable, the further awake I become. To avoid waking Morgan, I quietly make my way to the bathroom and close the door before turning on the light. I flip the switch and stifle a scream. Patrick is leaning against the sink as if waiting for me.

"What are you doing? You scared me," I breathe, putting a hand to my heaving chest.

"It's nothing in comparison to what you do to me," he purrs seductively.

My mouth hangs open until I find my voice. "W . . . what?"

His confident eyes stare into mine. Those eyes are toxic for my otherwise infallible constraint. My legs waver under me. He is ruinous to my composure—disastrous to my self-control. He steps toward me, and I slink back farther into the door I'm already pinned against. He takes another step and reaches for me. I'm frozen and desperately fighting to keep my thoughts coherent. If I let him touch me, I won't be able to break his spell.

His eyes trail from my shoulders down my arms as his hands follow. Every hair on my body stands on end at his touch. He gently pulls my hands from my chest examining all the scrapes and bruises I acquired on my clumsy hike the night before. The look of disapproval appears to consume him, but with my injuries being mild, I wonder about the level of concern etched in his face.

"I'm afraid you've had a terrible birthday, love."

I shrug, unable to speak. It hasn't been my best birthday, but I was lucky enough to spend a good part of the day with my sister and Morgan which makes today better than most.

"Come with me."

I have no time to question him. He's already pulling me through the adjoining door into his bedroom. Although everything rational in me screams not to go into a dark room alone with Patrick, he's taken away my choice. My nervousness turns to full-fledged anxiety as he closes the bathroom door with his foot, his hands never leaving my wrists.

We're alone in his bedroom with the doors shut, and the curtains hanging heavily over the moonlit windows. The only glow of light comes from under the bathroom door. I barely contain my inner turmoil as we stand linked in the darkness.

"Emily, you have no reason to be frightened by me."

A new sensation trickles up my arms, and I wonder where the sudden heat comes from.

"Patrick, what is that?" I can't help the subtle quiver in my voice.

He remains unruffled. "Just a minute more and I promise I'll turn on the lights. You are very special. I know it's hard for you to understand and your dad did a terrible job explaining, but Emily, this is not a bad thing. I know it seems that way to you but—"

"How do you know?"

I'm tired of being in the dark, but my thoughts are less clouded now that I can't see him. Dad's explanation was vague, but I still don't understand how Patrick could have any answers.

My frustration builds at his continued silence, and the warm sensation begins to burn as it spreads through my body like fire. "Ouch, Patrick, what are you doing?"

"Just a second," he says, unfazed by my irritation.

A painful moan escapes as I attempt to wiggle away from the heat, but Patrick's grip remains firm, and I still can't see a thing. "Let go, Patrick!" I twist my arms in another attempt to pull away.

"Almost done . . ." he says, holding tight. "There!"

In one fell swoop, the heat departs, and his hands release my wrists. I tuck my arms against my body and retreat several steps. Just as I am able to distinguish his outline in the shadows, he moves away. When he turns on the light, I am momentarily blinded.

Despite my apprehension, Patrick appears unphased. An easy smile lights his face as he glides back to me. "Look," he says, reaching forward.

I back away, afraid of his touch. Glancing at my arms, I gasp and hold them out in front of me flipping them over. The scratches disappeared, along with the bruising. As a matter of fact, my muscles are no longer aching either. "How . . . How did you . . . I mean . . ." I lift my gaze to stare at him in question.

"I told you it's not all bad."

"Patrick, how is this possible? How is any of this possible?"

His smile fades and his tone becomes serious. "Are you ready for the answers?"

I look around his room to find I'm only a step away from his bed. I back up to settle my body on the corner of the king-sized bed. "I've been ready for answers. You're the one refusing to give them to me."

"Very well. What would you like to know?"

"I want to know all of it! Like what the hell is going on and how you can talk to me without talking and what the hell did you just do?"

He snickers under his breath as he joins me on his bed. What was I thinking? I'm alone with Patrick. In his room. On his bed! I want to run while I have the chance, but these answers are too important, so I pivot to face him.

His back rests against the dark leather headboard while his legs stretch out in front of him crossing at the ankles. Even with the space between us, he feels a little too close, and he looks too smug.

"You aren't going to answer me, are you? You're just toying with me again. This is stupid," I say, moving to get off the bed.

"You inherited your gifts from your mother just as I inherited my gifts from my mother. I know this because only women can pass along these traits," he explains, and I settle back down.

"Okay," I say with hesitation.

"I'll tell you the story I was told. Do you think you can hold your questions until the end?" He watches me with one eyebrow raised in challenge.

"I'll try."

He jumps right in. "It started about five-hundred years ago with a pregnant queen on her deathbed."

I have to try harder than I thought to stay quiet, while I internally shake my head and roll my eyes with disapproval.

He continues, "All the medicine and healing practices were failing, so in the wicked king's desperation he called upon a magical healer from a faraway land."

"And bippity boppity boo, she was all better, right?" I say, unable to restrain myself. He gives me a dirty look, making me feel childish. And to my surprise, he doesn't continue his story. "Okay, I'm sorry. I'll be quiet," I promise.

He stares me down, and I wonder what he's thinking. He moves closer to me on the bed which causes an immediate increase in my pulse. He sits cross-legged just before me with his knees touching mine. When he reaches out, I shy away. His open palm caresses my cheek. My body is tense and a thrilling warmth spreads through my body. I tilt my face away from his palm, but his other hand is already there to catch my other cheek. He guides my head forward to meet his gaze. I know I should pull away, but part of me wonders what a kiss from Patrick would feel like.

"Let me show you, love."

"Show me what?" I mumble through my fog.

"Do you trust me?"

"No."

His grin emphasizes how close his lips are. "I'm going to show you anyway."

At first, I think he's going to kiss me, but just like that bippity boppity boo bullshit, Patrick's room dissolves into a lavish bedroom from medieval times. A woman is lying on an enormous bed. The guilted quilt is pulled down to her thighs, revealing a round belly under her regal gown. Though she appears to be on her deathbed, a sparkling crown adorns her intricately woven blond tresses. Four maiden women are tending to the ill queen.

How I could be seeing the pregnant queen from Patrick's story is beyond my comprehension, but those thoughts escape my mind as a burly man barges into the room. He's dressed in an elaborate garment with animal fur draped over his shoulder. He wears a golden crown atop his head with gemstones sparkling from every finger.

The queen and her maidens cower at his presence. The king doesn't appear cruel, but seeing how others react to him, I sense he's someone to fear. An ancient woman follows him into the room. Her skin is dark and wrinkled as crepe paper. Her hollow cheeks, white eyes, and silver hair peek out from beneath her embroidered hooded cloak. She is small and hunched but moves with grace as she halts the king with a gesture. Her bony hand sweeps out from behind her cloak revealing her ring-laden fingers as she points him toward the door. A violent look flashes across his face but is replaced with a blank stare as he makes eye contact with the old woman. The king leaves without a word.

Once the king is gone, the old woman moves urgently toward the Queen. She drops her cloak and beneath she wears a simple dress revealing her tiny frame adorned with jewels and medallions.

The picture blurs then fades away, and before I know it, I'm back in Patrick's room staring into his eyes. Patrick pulls away, removing his hands from my face, but he can't go far because somewhere along the line I must have grabbed onto his t-shirt. My hands are fisted in the flimsy fabric.

"Now will you let me finish my story?"

Releasing his shirt, I nod, afraid my voice will crack if I try to speak. I need him to keep talking so I can pull myself together enough to ask him what just happened.

"When the shaman arrived, she kicked the king out for she knew he was a loveless, abusive man who only married the young woman so she could bear his sons. The king threatened the shaman's life if she didn't save his unborn son, yet he didn't care about the life of his beautiful bride. The shaman spoke silently to the queen's spirit bringing her back from the brink of death by laying hands on her pregnant belly while uttering incantations. A dense fog covered the castle for days while they communicated.

"When anyone came near the healer, they would forget their purpose and be frightened away by a single glance from the glazed eyes of the old woman. She could bury thoughts deep into the minds of others without them knowing the ideas were not their own.

"When the queen was ready to give birth, the elderly shaman helped deliver three daughters. The third child was stillborn. The queen demanded to hold her dead infant. The grief-stricken queen cradled her precious daughter placing a gentle kiss on her forehead. The baby took her first breath and exhaled with a life-inducing cry. The queen died immediately after the kiss, choosing to trade her life for her child.

"The king was beyond furious. He would've sacrificed all three daughters and the queen for one son. He threatened the old woman and she, in turn, cursed him with a spell of sterility and vowed to protect the girls from him. She gifted the girls with her inherent powers of the shaman and threatened the king with death should he ever raise a hand to his daughters.

"The shaman cared for the princesses, teaching and instilling them with magical gifts. The king feared the shaman and gave orders to kill the elderly woman. None of the assassins were successful, and the shaman died of natural causes on the girls' fifteenth birthday, leaving the girls alone before they had fully grown into their sacred gifts.

"The princesses kept developing and maturing their abilities on their own. They spoke to each other without words, read emotions, held the power of persuasion, and were bestowed the gift of healing. However, it was the third born—the miracle brought to life by the sacrifice of the queen—who had the most potent powers. Maybe it was because she owed her life to magic or because she was favored by the elderly healer; whatever the reason, she learned how to take complete control over others. When she inflicted her mind on someone, she could induce whatever emotions she chose, and it would result in a physical response. With any passing emotion she experienced, those around her would feel it as well.

"One evening the king struck one of her sisters, and as a result the third princess went to bed angry, dreaming of revenge. She woke to the sound of screaming knowing immediately that her nightmare was real and discovered her sisters had killed the king. It was her fault because it was in her dream and in her mind. She killed her father using her sisters as the weapon. Once the king was dead, the girls were thought of as black witches and were forced to leave their home.

"Eventually, each sister bore children and discovered their offspring inherited their gifts. While both male and female children manifested their gifts around the age of sixteen, only females passed their gifts to their offspring.

"And there you have it," Patrick draws to a close.

Silence fills the room. I stare down at my newly healed arms. I don't want to believe any of this, but there are things in my life I can't explain. Patrick can speak to me without talking, so maybe the voices in my mom's head were real. I remember Dad's words. *"Your mother was gifted. She had certain abilities. She could hear things, see things, feel things, and people loved her because of her alluring, mysterious ways. She captivated everyone around her."*

My head is shaking, and a burst of hysterical laughter fills the room.

In the next instant, Patrick is on me, tackling me to the bed with his hand flush against my mouth. "It's two in the morning. What are you thinking? Do you want them to find you in here?"

I swallow my laughter with a gulp, finding it impossible to breathe while he's lying on top of me. His face is just inches from mine, and his hand captures the small breaths that manage to escape me. Pressed so close, I'm sure he can feel my erratic heartbeat. When he's certain I'll be quiet, he pulls his hand away and lies on his side next to me.

"It's all ludicrous," I whisper, scooting onto my side in an attempt to put more space between us. It doesn't work. Just as I move to prop my head in my hand, he maneuvers so his face is level with mine.

"Give it time to sink in," he whispers.

My first reaction is to make a sarcastic comment, but I have no words. Dropping my face into my hands, I try to wipe away the images, but I can't. In my bewilderment, I say, "A shaman, an evil king, and princesses? Sounds like a fairytale, Patrick."

"Perhaps our life is a fairytale, love, but you can't deny the gifts we're capable of."

"If we both have these 'gifts' as you call them—which I'm not buying—and it's passed down from our mothers, then are we related? Is that why you're so familiar?"

His lips twitch, fighting a smile. "Those sisters lived over five-hundred years ago. I have an excellent knowledge of my family tree and you, love, are not even in the same forest. It would be over twenty generations before we could trace our lineage back to 'fairytale' princesses. Technically, you're more closely related to . . . Let's say . . . Ben. As for being familiar, perhaps it's my abilities that are familiar to you."

I think about that for a moment, doing my best to understand the lineage. "I'm still not buying that story. It's ridiculous."

"Sometimes the truth is more ridiculous than the lie."

"Did you heal me?" I ask.

He nods reaching out to take my free hand in his.

"How?"

"It's one of our gifts," he says.

"How did I see the queen?"

"We have the ability to share our thoughts, like the way I spoke to you the other day. The vision I showed you tonight is the same concept but with images. It's more involved, so many never successfully learn the art. I'd predict only a handful have actually mastered the skill."

"Wait, there are others?"

"Yeah," he says like duh, "but not as many as there used to be."

I'm waiting for him to laugh and tell me the jokes on me. Instead, he stares back with eyes filled to the brim with the knowledge that I'm too much a coward to believe.

"I don't believe it," I say.

"Don't or won't?" he challenges.

I shake my head and try to pull my hand from his, but he holds tight pulling our linked hands to his chest. My heart leaps at the contact, and I relax into him allowing him to maneuver me, feeling unable to control my thoughts.

"I just want to test something," he whispers.

Just like that, any remaining anxiety washes away. I'm captivated by his brilliant blue eyes. I am enraptured by his infinite calm as if he's breathing it directly into me. I close my eyes and sink slowly into the deep, blissful ocean called sleep.

eleven ~

I open my eyes to find myself stretched out on Morgan's bed. She appears to be gone and judging by the light coming through the window; I've overslept. I hop out of bed and rush to the door. As I enter the hallway, I run into a solid figure. I stumble back and arms shoot out to steady me.

"Good morning," Patrick says, pulling me closer. His lips are stretched into a wide smile as his eyes find mine.

I place my hands against him, his flimsy t-shirt doing nothing to hide his muscular chest from my touch. As I push away from him, all the previous night's events fill my head, and I grab his shirt and pull him into Morgan's room.

Shutting the door, I glare at him. "What did you do to me?"

"Relax, I didn't do anything inappropriate. I helped you sleep and carried you to bed. You don't need to overreact."

"Overreact! You put me to sleep with your mind! How else should I react?"

"Less like a victim for starters," he snaps, before calming himself. "I wouldn't have done it without your permission, but if you recall you allowed me to help you."

"From now on, I want you to stay out of my head."

"Well, then maybe you should do the same." His tranquil mood is giving way to frustration.

"What does that mean? You think I'm getting in your head?"

"Ha!" He laughs without humor. "That's exactly what I mean. Yesterday in the kitchen with Morgan, if you'd been listening to the conversation, you would have known I was barely coherent myself, what with you drooling over me."

"Drooling!" It's barely less than a shout. I quiet myself before I continue. "What are you talking about?" Embarrassment creeps up my neck. Had he noticed me gawking at him?

"You're just lucky Morgan was there or . . ."

"Or what?" I demand, letting my hands ball into fists.

He shakes his head. "You still don't get it."

"Maybe if you would talk to me like a normal human being, I could understand. You continue to give me riddles and fairytales!"

His voice assaults my head from the inside. All I can do is cringe and close my eyes to the intrusion. *"Emily, do you not understand that your mood swings are driving me crazy! Your every emotion plagues me. I'm barely holding my own with you constantly talking into my mind, yet you get mad when I speak into yours. You asked for the truth, so I gave it to you, whether you believe it or not. You have these special abilities that you obviously have no control over. It might be news to you, but I am only trying to help."*

When I open my eyes to look at him, something feels different. My mind is racing to figure out what it all means and why he thinks I'm in his head.

"You are," he replies out loud.

My eyes widen with horror. If Patrick can hear my thoughts, then he is the one intruding.

"I wish that were true, but you are in here." He points to his head. "And I can't seem to block you out."

I test him.

"Seven, zero, two, six," he says, without skipping a beat.

Realization dawns as I think back to the incident in the kitchen with new awareness. My breath catches in my throat as I begin to comprehend what this means. Embarrassment floods me, and I want to crawl under the bed.

"I can't say I didn't enjoy it." He takes a deliberate step toward me. I move back in response and collide with the wall. He continues taking methodically slow steps until he's only inches away. His eyes meet mine before he ducks his head down to whisper in my ear.

"You think I'm irresistible," he taunts. He closes the little space between us until the warmth of his body presses against mine. My arms hang powerless as I feel his soft breath against my neck. "But nothing is more enticing than you, love."

My attempt at pushing him away is stilted by the urges racing through my body, but when his lips graze my neck, only one impulse remains. It's a visceral reaction, one I certainly hadn't expected.

My hand grips his throat, reacting so automatically that I'm shocked by my own behavior. I catch a glimpse of fear before his mask of unfettered calm melts back into place.

My whole body—wired with tension—fights to control my tightening grasp around his neck. I try to let go, but my hand has a mind of its own. His face becomes flushed from the restriction of blood and oxygen, and his eyes search my face.

His hand casually wraps around my wrist, and he moves my hand away from his throat speaking softly as he releases my arm and steps away. "As I said, you've had a lot of mood swings lately, and that's because this is all so new to you. I should have known better. I seem to . . . intensify your emotions."

Intensify? He somehow has a way of overriding my logic. I don't know where my violent reaction came from. Sure, it makes me angry he can hear my private thoughts, but a large part of me wanted him to kiss me. I have no idea how those feelings translated into strangling him.

I take a step forward. "I need you to teach me how to control this, so you don't hear anything unless I want you to."

"It will take time, Emily. We'll work on it but now is not the right time. Morgan is already waiting for you."

I glare at him for a moment before a smile stretches across my face, an idea taking form. "Fine, suit yourself." I rush downstairs to search for Morgan, worried he still listening to my thoughts.

I find her down in the kitchen sitting at the counter talking to her mom. The two are snacking on a fruit tray, and Morgan is dressed for the day with her bikini strap peeking out of her shirt. I'm surprised it's already afternoon.

"Hey, I was about to come wake you," Morgan says brightly.

"Sorry I slept so long." I take the seat next to her, attempting to look as though my mind is not preoccupied.

"Don't worry about it. You needed the rest."

Julie says, "You girls have fun. I'm going to help your father with the boat." She leaves through the back door, and the outside heat wafts through the room before the door closes.

"It's already ninety-five degrees out," Morgan says. "I figured we'd go swimming. I think I have a bikini that'll fit you."

I nod with fake enthusiasm. I already feel exposed, knowing my thoughts are not my own. Now my body will be on display as well. At least Morgan and I are about the same size and tiny string bikinis aren't her thing either.

"Are you hungry? We're having a cookout this afternoon, but I figured you would want something to hold you over."

I grab a hand full of grapes and begin to munch. "This should hold me until later," I reassure Morgan with a full mouth, not wanting to hold her up any longer. She eyes me skeptically.

"I'm not much of a breakfast person. You know that."

She nods and stands from her seat. "Let me show you the suit."

I follow her to her room where she pulls a royal blue bikini and black board shorts from her dresser. She tosses them to me, and I spot the tag hanging off the shorts.

"Have you ever worn any of this?"

"No, I washed the bathing suit, but haven't worn it and the shorts, well, obviously I haven't worn those. You can have them if you like. I thought I'd be on the beach all summer, so I went overboard buying bathing suits when I was in Florida." Sadness seems to creep over her, but she pushes it away and smiles. I admire her attitude, her ambition, and her confidence, especially after the situation she went through.

"I'll try them on," I say with as much spirit as I can muster.

Before changing, I make sure both bathroom doors are locked. Once I'm certain I'm alone, I slip into the suit. It's a sporty, halter bikini top with thick straps hooking behind my neck and back. I have a little more cleavage than I'm comfortable with, but I have that in every bathing suit. The royal blue bottoms narrow almost to strings at the sides, but the black board shorts make up for the skimpy bottoms. I walk out of the bathroom with a smile.

"Oh good, it fits!" Morgan exclaims from across the room. "What do you think?"

"It's perfect."

She grabs the beach towels folded on her bed and starts for the door. Reality rings like an alarm in my head. I turn to look at my bag as if I can see my phone through the canvas.

"Morgan, go ahead. I need to call my dad. He's probably worried."

"Sure, I'll wait for you downstairs." She shuts the door behind her on her way out.

I have two missed calls and a new voicemail. It's from Dad. "Emily, I understand you're angry with me. I hope you'll let me explain. Patrick called me . . ." Dad's message continues, but I stop listening, caught by the mention of Patrick. No, it wasn't just the mention of Patrick; it was the idea of him calling Dad. Their last interaction was hostile, and I'm confused why he would contact my dad at all.

I've reached the end of the message and a female voice chimes in with options. I replay the message. ". . . Patrick called me tonight to let me know you'll be staying with Morgan until Thursday. I hope you come home soon. I love you." There is a heavy sigh before the line goes dead. I am not ready to talk to him yet because I can't forget his deception. Although I feel a little guilty, he knows I'm safe and won't be gone forever.

I meet up with Morgan on the back porch. "Are things okay?"

"Yeah, things are fine," I lie.

"Good."

A hundred feet from the back door the yard becomes a small beach which opens into a serene lake, heavily wooded on the far side. The rest of the lake is bordered by steep slopes of untamed grass among scattered trees. To the right of the beach is a small dock securing a wooden rowboat with two oars. It's the only way to travel across the lake. The clear water becomes cloudy a few feet below the surface and in that murky water hides randomly scattered boulders. To avoid the hazards, Morgan's parents designated a safe swimming area years ago.

Streams feed the lake which keeps fresh water circulating. There is one distant peek across the lake where the water stands still in a quiet cove surrounded by trees. Cattails and lily pads grow wild there. A few brave stragglers grow along the outskirts, and occasionally a lily pad will detach from its stem and drift over to the swimming area.

I've forgotten how much I love this lake. Although I've never been close with the rest of Morgan's family, they've always welcomed me. I think it's odd I've spent so much time here and never heard of Patrick before. I wonder why he's living with them now.

We're just to the edge of the beach when Morgan yells over her shoulder to someone behind me. "Do you need help?"

I turn to see Morgan's dad and Patrick coming from the driveway. The two of them are carrying opposite ends of a wooden boat. It looks identical to the rowboat sitting in the water, only newer and freshly polished. Morgan's mom follows behind with an oar in each hand.

"We've got it," Tom calls. They make their way down to the small dock and slide the boat into the water. We wander closer to the dock, watching them work.

"Isn't it perfect?" Julie exclaims, dropping the oars in the boat.

"It is perfect!" Morgan agrees.

I feel Patrick staring at me before I make eye contact. He's wearing that overconfident half-smile. I look away as I begin singing an annoying ditty from a car commercial in my head. If what he told me is true, he won't be able to block it out. I look up just long enough to see him cock his head to the side looking curious. I'm not sure how all this works. In his story, he described it as speaking without words. I continue singing in my head and anyway what's the harm?

Tom, Julie, and Patrick return to the house while Morgan and I swim and boat for the next few hours. I don't know how close Patrick needs to be to hear my thoughts, so I continue to sing in my mind. I'm surprised how easy it is to come up with a variety of irritating jingles. I'm not getting all the words right, but the idea is to annoy him enough to persuade him to teach me how to keep my thoughts to myself. I take breaks to have conversations with

Morgan, but I unintentionally get the catchy melodies stuck in my head, so I can't stop even if I wanted.

Patrick comes to get us when the food is ready. He informs us Morgan's sister, Nellie and her boyfriend, Noah, have arrived. He grins like he's enjoying an inside joke. I don't let my guard down, continuing the arrangement of terrible ditties in my head just in case.

Morgan and I air-dry as we sit at the picnic table on the open back porch with everyone. The smell of the barbecue chicken wafting through the summer air is enticing even in the heat of the day. The table is set with all my summer favorites including freshly squeezed lemonade.

I eat too quickly, stuffing myself to the brim. Ready for a nap, Morgan and I relax in lawn chairs until the heat becomes too much and we venture back out into the water. This time Nellie, Noah, and Patrick join us. I look away when Patrick takes off his shirt and continue the stupid jingles in my head as I swim away.

I casually avoid him for the next few hours by spending most of my time in the lawn chair. Miserably hot, I continue telling Morgan I need to work on my tan. When she isn't looking, I apply another layer of sunscreen. I know I'll be a pretty shade of lobster-red after spending most of the day in the sun, but it's worth it to avoid him.

Late in the afternoon Nellie and Noah take a boat out onto the lake. After they leave, Morgan and Patrick board the other one. I sigh in relief knowing I can finally cool down in the water while they're gone. My relief is short-lived because as soon as I stand from my seat, they invite me along. I try to convince them I'm fine on shore, but they're relentless. Finally, seeing no use in fighting, I give up and get in the stupid boat with the two of them.

Morgan sits facing Patrick who is in the middle. That leaves me to sit behind Patrick who is flaunting his half-naked physique.

I chide myself for looking and for not wanting to look away. When did I become this girl?

I'm trying to refrain from gawking, but not even the chatter in my head is any good against my relentless desire. His muscles tense and flex as each stroke of the oar emphasizes his perfect body. I distract myself by focusing on the water rippling and dripping with each stroke of the oars. I continue singing in my head, ignoring Patrick and all the questions weighing heavily on my mind.

"Uh oh," Morgan groans. "I have to pee."

"I'll turn us around," Patrick says.

"That's okay," she says, jumping overboard. We're not far from the dock, so the beach is close. Her head pops up out of the water as she swims toward the shore.

"You guys go ahead," she calls over her shoulder.

"We'll wait for you," I offer, feeling ready to jump ship myself.

"Nah, go ahead. Sorry guys," she replies, moving quickly through the water.

I don't know what to say. This is more than a coincidence, more like a ruse to leave me stranded with Patrick. Maybe this was Morgan's plan to force us together. I don't know what Patrick will do and am surprised when he begins to row away from the shore.

"What are you doing?" I demand.

"What? She told us to go ahead."

"That's rude. We should wait for her."

"Silly girl. Do you think she really has to pee? You know just as well as I do, this is her way of bringing us together."

"Morgan wouldn't do that. She's not that pushy. You made her do it, didn't you?"

"You mean did I bribe or compel her? Now, love, that's rude."

I am not happy with this turn of events. I'm nervous about being alone with him because I have this inexplicable attraction to him, leaving me feeling vulnerable, but Patrick is the one with the answers, and I need clarity.

twelve ~

The soft breeze prickles against my sensitive skin as he propels us smoothly through the water. He probably knows I'm debating jumping overboard. I look back at the passing water finding us further from the shore and further from Noah and Nellie's boat. It's quiet aside from the repetitive songs I'm humming in my mind.

"I'm surprised you haven't tried the Zappy jingle yet. If there's no fun to be had, we can make your puppy glad." Patrick laughs over his shoulder.

My eyes burn into his back, wishing I could irritate him as much as he does me. My singing has only entertained him. It's the opposite of what I intended. I stop the incessant jingles and sigh at the quiet, admitting, "I kind of like the Zappy commercial."

It reminds me of good memories with Ben like the night in my living room. The thought brings a wistful smile to my face. If only Ben didn't have to go to Florida, he would be spending the day with us, and it'd be the two of us on this boat instead of Patrick and me.

Patrick's shoulders tense. I don't just see his irritation; I sense it radiating from him. His emotions hang in the air like fog, and it takes me a minute to truly understand the connotation behind his thoughts.

"You're jealous!" I snort. It's not something I would've picked up on a few days ago, and it makes it harder to deny the strange abilities Patrick calls gifts.

He lowers the oars and swings toward me on his bench. My eyes wander down his chest, over his stupid sculpted shoulders and chiseled abs. His body is the equivalent of bringing a gun to a knife fight. His eyebrow arches after the thought appears in my head, and his smug half-smile returns. I scold myself for having the idea, however unintentional it may have been. I use the only arsenal I have by switching my thoughts back to Ben.

"You don't fight fair," Patrick says through a sexy smirk.

"And you do?" I reply, gesturing a hand to his half-naked body.

I'm horrified when I realize his eyes are raking over me just as amorously as mine had done to him. Feeling naked in my new bikini and shorts, I barely resist the urge to cover myself with my arms. As heat from my embarrassment touches my cheeks, I feel another emotion radiating from him. Desire.

His eyes rest on mine without trying to hide his lust. The tension between us builds until I can't stand it and look away.

"You're starting to understand your abilities," Patrick says.

"I thought I told you to get out of my head."

"I'll teach you how to keep your thoughts to yourself, but first I need you to come sit over here where Morgan was sitting so I can see you while I row."

Keeping my body low to save us from tipping, I maneuver over his seat with a little help from him and sit on the other side of the boat. He turns to face me, and I watch as he picks up the oars and once again the boat is moving.

Patrick says, "I believe you have a few questions for me."

"Why did you call my dad?"

"You were upset. He was worried, so I let him know you were safe."

"That wasn't your decision to make, Patrick!"

"You can't possibly be angry with me for letting him know you're safe. You're going to forgive him if you haven't already. It's one less thing for you to worry about, love."

"It's still not up to you. Why are you even here? You know, with Morgan and her family. I've never heard them talk about you before."

"I grew up several hours away but moved here to be closer to the city for an internship. You probably haven't heard about me because my mom and Morgan's dad had a falling out before I was born. When my aunt heard I'd be in town, she invited me to stay."

"An internship?"

"Yes, a business internship for the summer."

"Is it a paid internship?"

"That's somewhat personal, don't you think?"

"I think you breezed right past personal when you started listening to my thoughts."

"Touché," he says, looking far too pleased with himself.

"Is it a paid internship?" I ask again, not actually caring, but hoping to make him uncomfortable.

"Not exactly, but it does have its perks."

"What do you mean?"

"The car, for starters."

I roll my eyes. "They let you drive that ridiculous car?"

"No," he raises an eyebrow, "they gave me that ridiculous car."

"That's a pretty expensive perk for a summer internship."

"Incentive to stay with the company on a more permanent basis."

"Somehow, I doubt they offer that to all of their interns."

"No, they don't."

"I'm not surprised." I frown, asking, "Are you going to stay?"

"I don't think I want the job."

"Why?"

"Are these the questions you want to ask?"

"Yes," I say defiantly, but at his pointed stare, I relent. "Look, you know way too much about me and I know next to nothing about you. So, consider this leveling the playing field. Tell me why you don't want the job."

He considers it for a moment before saying, "I would spend a considerable amount of my time traveling, not that I have anything against travel per se."

"So, what's the problem? Is it the company? The people? The money can't be bad if they buy cars for their interns."

"It's an excellent company, my coworkers respect me, and money would never be an issue."

"I keep waiting for the *but*. Like, it's a great company, *but* the job sucks."

He secures the oars inside the boat to let us drift. He closes his eyes and takes a deep breath. When he opens them, I see nothing but serene calm. It's not as noticeable as the jealousy or the desire I felt earlier, but it hangs like a fine aura framing him.

"There are complications with every big decision," he says, dismissing the actual question.

"That's a non-answer," I complain. "Let's try another. If Morgan is a part of your family, why isn't she affected by any of this?"

"My mom and Morgan's dad were both born with the magic in them. My uncle's gifts will die with him just as my gifts will die with me. Only a woman can genetically pass it along. So, my mom passed it on to me just like your mom passed it on to you. When you have children, you will pass the gifts on to them."

I laugh, "I am never having kids, so it'll die with me."

"That's your decision, but I hope you reconsider one day. I should warn you; Tom tries his best not to use his gifts, so he's not thrilled I'm staying here, Morgan, Nellie, and my Aunt Julie know nothing about our lineage or gifts. There is a reason my uncle put distance between himself and my mother."

I have trouble envisioning Tom as anything other than normal. "Wait, Tom doesn't want you staying here?"

"No, though he's too polite to say it aloud. I threaten his way of life. He doesn't want his family finding out about either of us."

"Does he know about me?"

"Yes, but it's unlikely he knew before you started changing. Now there's no denying it." He takes a deep breath. "I did warn him about you so—"

I throw a hand out to stop him. "You warned him about me?"

"Of course."

Since my mom's death, people tend to view me one of two ways. Most often I get the sympathetic gaze like they just found out I have cancer, but every once in a while, I get the harsh glare like they found out I am cancer. And right now, I feel like the unwanted disease. I never meant to put Tom in this situation. Then another thought occurs.

"What about my sister?" I inquire. "Our mom must have passed it to both of us. Is Sam lying to me too? Nellie and Sam were on the same volleyball team. Did Tom notice her?"

"I'd venture to say your sister is oblivious."

"Why?"

"That is a good question. One I could only speculate upon, because I don't have all the details. For a definitive answer, you should ask your father."

"And that's the second question you haven't answered," I note, spotting a stray lily pad. I still have a lot of questions. Like, wouldn't it be easier for Patrick not to worry about insignificant me with all my baggage? His eyes are glued to me when I look up.

"Emily, nothing about you is insignificant. You are rare and special."

I roll my eyes.

He continues, "The first time I laid eyes on you, I was mesmerized." He wavers for a moment. "Your voice was so clear in my mind. You had me magnetized by your adorably self-conscious, yet genuinely oblivious nature."

"That sounds like an insult," I say, but he talks right over me.

"When I came up to meet you, you weren't the soft-spoken woman I expected. You were strong, determined, and angry. It took me off guard and knocked me off my game."

I know he's referring to our first bizarre encounter on campus and it's strange to hear it from his perspective because I was the one hypnotized by the mysterious blond guy. Is this some sort of game he's playing?

"That!" He points a finger toward me, accusingly. "Right there! That's what gets me. Whenever someone compliments you, you belittle it and think they're trying to get one over on you."

"Oblivious!" I laugh. "Is that a compliment?"

"Yes, it is! I also recall telling you how you fascinate me, and you thought I was patronizing you. You're doing an excellent job pretending to be a normal, happy girl, but you're so guarded. I understand people haven't always been pleasant to you, but I'm trying to help. I know your world has been flipped upside down and arguing with your father troubles you tremendously. You don't have to pretend with me."

"Troubles you tremendously? Who talks like that? And everyone fights with their parents."

"Assuming that's true, you have reasons to be upset with him. There were more advantageous ways to handle the situation."

"Since you seem to know it all, how do you think he should've handled it?"

"With honesty from the very beginning."

His sincerity softens my response. "Dad said he was protecting me," I reply, feeling the need to protect my father's decisions even though I may not agree with him.

Patrick lifts an eyebrow. "If his goal was to protect you then he should've been teaching you, not keeping you in the dark."

"Ever heard ignorance is bliss? Maybe he wanted me to be oblivious."

"Then he succeeded!"

"My dad is a smart man. I'm sure he had his reasons. Why did you tell him I would be home tomorrow? Why not tonight? I mean, especially if I'm not welcome here."

"Emily, you are welcome here. I'm the one who isn't welcome, but until he comes out and tells me to leave, I'm staying. Besides, I was hoping to spend a little more time with you." He grins. "And don't you want to stay for the fireworks?"

"You're not going to kiss me again, are you?"

"And lose my head? No thank you, love."

"It's just . . . I didn't mean to have such an extreme reaction. I tried to let go, but I couldn't."

"You have powerfully conflicting emotions about me," Patrick says. "Part of you understands you need me, but you are hell-bent on hating me."

I huff, pushing back the pieces of my wayward hair as it blows in the breeze. I don't need him.

"Part of you thinks you do," he chuckles, ticking me off even further.

"It's convenient you're here to answer my questions, but I don't need you, Patrick."

"Oblivious and stubborn," he mutters under his breath.

As the sun sinks in the sky, the heat continues to warm my already baked skin. I'm overexposed both physically and mentally.

My gaze slides to the water to observe the growing collection of lily pads. "What are you doing, Patrick? The boat will get stuck in the shallow water!"

We enter the mouth of the cove and Patrick gestures around at the beauty surrounding us. "This is your favorite spot, isn't it?" It's posed as a question, but he already knows the answer.

"We'll get stuck."

"Don't worry your pretty little head, love. I got this. We won't get stuck."

His swagger threatens to gag me. Deciding it is better to ignore him, we sit in silence as the boat drifts down the middle of the snake-like stream. While Patrick gently steers, I watch frogs jump across lily pads and plummet into the water. The ravine continues back further than I thought possible. I've never been back this far, and it looks like we're headed straight toward a thick wall of grass standing tall out of the water. My eyes go wide as I brace myself for the collision, but Patrick calmly pushes aside the grass with an oar and guides the boat through the thick strands. The towering grass gathers back together behind us, concealing us from everything else. Just as I begin feeling claustrophobic, the grass opens ahead of us revealing a small round pond.

I gasp at the beauty. It's a scene from a fairytale. The edge of the private pond surrounds us with wildflowers and weeping willows. The whimsical paradise is perfectly hidden, a well-kept secret belonging only to us and the sun which finds its way through the branches to glisten on the gentle water. Birds hiding within the cattails at the water's edge sing a lovely song. The limbs of a nearby weeping willow blow lazily in the soft breeze. The leaves act like fingers stirring the water's surface. Unable to resist the beautiful serenity, I graze my hand across the water.

The boat drifts toward a willow tree, and Patrick uses his arm to open the leaves that hang over the water like a curtain. The branches drape closed behind us further hiding us from the world. The shade is soothing relief to my pink seared skin. I look to the twisted trunk standing at the water's edge and gaze up through the tangled branches.

"This is so beautiful," I breathe. "I'm starting to believe we might actually be in a fairytale, but if the birds start braiding my hair, I'm outta here."

Patrick chuckles under his breath. "This is my favorite place. It might not be a fairytale, but it is easier to believe in magic when I'm out here."

"I've never been back this far. I didn't even know this was here. How on earth did you find it?"

The boat settles in a stationary position, and Patrick looks up at the tree. "I guess I have a knack for uncovering invaluable treasures."

I cock an eyebrow. "Whatever you say. Thanks for sharing your paradise."

"My pleasure."

Birdsongs and hushed movements of wildlife are music to my ears. My gaze wanders around the small picturesque place until it falls back on Patrick who is staring at me. I narrow my eyes trying to keep my guard up, trying to talk sense into myself. Maybe this was all just a ploy to soften me up.

"There you go again." He grins, amused by my private thoughts. "Always thinking I'm out to get you."

I cross my arms in frustration. "You said you'd teach me how to keep my thoughts to myself."

"I will."

"So, teach me!"

He sighs, "It will take time."

"How long?" I ask, a wave of concern washing over me as I remember the overwhelming emotions I felt from Patrick a few

125

minutes ago. If he can't control himself after years of practice, then how long will it take me?

"Emily, I was sixteen when I got my abilities. For nearly four years I've had perfect control; however, you tend to bring out the worst in me. Normally, I'm flawless."

"Normally? So why does Morgan think you're dangerous?"

"She doesn't view me as dangerous. She just sees the way girls, well, most girls throw themselves at me. She was worried you had succumbed to my charm and I dismissed you. She was proud of you when she saw how you reacted to me."

"About that charm of yours. Besides the obvious, why do you have that effect on everyone?"

"The obvious?"

"Oh, come on, Patrick, don't act ignorant. We both know you don't have a modest bone in your body."

"Are you undressing me with your eyes again?" There is laughter in his eyes.

"I get it now. God made you beautiful to cover up how unbelievably obnoxious you are."

Cue Patrick's deep rumbling laughter. The sound reverberates inside of me, touching me somewhere so deep, a place I didn't know existed until this moment. For once I think he may be as carefree as he pretends to be.

Once he pulls himself together and wipes away a tear, he says, "The pull I have on everyone is part of my skill."

"Skill? Are you kidding me?"

"It's part of my abilities. You'll have them as well. You will be able to be whomever you want to be; do whatever you want to do. You possess a magnetic pull that will only strengthen with time and practice," Patrick assures me.

This is why I'm so drawn to him, because of the magnetic pull he's mastered.

"So, what do you do when girls throw themselves at you? Keeping in mind, they only throw themselves at you because you don't give them a choice."

"That depends on how much time I have," he says with a suggestive smile.

"You manipulate them! Don't you feel guilty?"

"Manipulate?" Aghast, he places a hand against his chest. "Hardly, I'm simply living my life."

"Really? You don't feel like you're taking advantage?"

"Absolutely not," he says with a sly grin, "I'm an attractive option, and I can assure you I have never once done anything to anyone against their will."

I give him a look of disgust. "Only because you take away their willpower!"

"Perhaps." He shrugs with a dark gaze. "Nevertheless, I give people options they didn't have before. Besides, what would you have me do? Nothing? That would be a waste. People have no idea what's good for them."

I blink slowly thinking there's no way I could have heard him right. "Oh, and you think you know what's good for them?"

"Yes." He smirks, and I realize he may be a sociopath.

"Are you kidding me?" I whisper, as the part of me that loathes him resurfaces. "I will never be like you."

His chin dips, but his eyes train on me with stubborn perseverance. I feel an undercurrent of emotions barreling up from inside of me. I don't care if he knows. I want him to know he repulses me.

"Emily," his voice is deep and executed with precise measure. "Love, you really ought to be able to control your emotions better than this."

Irritated to my core, I can't believe his arrogance. He smiles at my reproach because he has no conscience. Is this why Tom doesn't want him here? Is this what I will become? Is this how my mom was? My anger turns to fear. Dad said my mom did unimaginable things. What did he mean? Did she manipulate people without a moral sense of right and wrong? Will I manipulate people to get whatever I want without restriction like Patrick does? Will I lose my moral code? I know my feelings are becoming irrational, and I try to snap out of it, but I am drowning in confusion. Each devastating crash of emotion washes over me like waves of an angry ocean. They engulf and consume me until I can no longer control my thoughts.

In some sense I know I'm sitting in the boat across from Patrick, but my mind feels lost within my body. The lucid part of me ducks my head between my legs while I hyperventilate. I've had a panic attack before, but this is something entirely different. I close my eyes, and there is no boat, no pond, no Patrick. Everything is altered, and I'm submerged in an ocean during a violent storm. Dark waves roll over me one after the other, pushing me deeper under the cascading water. My lungs burn as I gasp for breath, inhaling the salty water. Darkness surrounds me and my chest is on fire. I am drowning.

Just as my hope fades, I discover a life force nearby and sense Patrick with me. I cannot see him, yet I feel him—not physically—but somehow, I know he's there.

His calming emotions envelop me, and I welcome them like air. It's a life raft rescuing me from drowning. The more I breathe in, the more I feel Patrick pulling away. He's toying with me, showing me what I want—what I need—only to rip it away. I draw it to myself and cradle it like something precious. I let the calm sink in and take a staggering breath. He's fighting me, but it doesn't matter. Holding onto this piece of him without great effort, I have no intention of giving it back. Maybe he will see what it's like to be taken advantage of.

More than just the serene calm, I feel surges of overwhelming pleasure. I'm no longer drowning under the current of the waves or sailing in the life raft. I'm soaring atop the crushing waves, controlling and directing them. I am the driving force behind each monstrous crash and I'm excited by the frenzy. I hold my hands out in front of me and feel the dominance radiating from them. It's an immense thrill that electrifies me, and I crave more of this power. I need it!

"Emily," Patrick's voice is muffled, distant, and strained. I look around and don't see him here. I don't understand where his voice is coming from, or where he is. Then I realize I don't know where I am. None of this makes sense. Am I dreaming?

"Emily, please."

It's barely audible. Where did he go? He sounds so far away. I follow his voice.

I fight to regain control of my body. When I successfully open my eyes, I realize Patrick is very close. Too close. I am crouching over him holding his perfect face between my hands. I release him immediately and scurry back to sit on the floor farthest from him.

When I look up, Patrick is hunched over and gasping for air. He's looking at the floor with his arms outstretched holding tight to the sides of the boat. He looks exhausted, weak, vulnerable like he's just been beaten. I don't know what happened, but I know I just did something awful to him.

My head is shaking involuntarily, too overwhelmed for words. Witnessing Patrick looking so defeated unnerves me. His head slowly rises out of its stupor. His skin is pale, and there is something eerie about his eyes. His usual sapphire orbs are a milky blue.

"What happened?" I whisper, slumped against the side of the boat, my hands gripping the edge.

He closes his eyes to steady himself and his body trembles as his breath comes rapidly. He needs time to recover, so I wait. His breathing eventually slows, and I see a glimpse of his calm returning, but it takes a long time for his eyes to reopen, and the paleness in them scares me.

I'm out of my mind frightened, not of Patrick, but myself. "What did I do? Please, tell me what happened!"

Neither his weary tone nor his words comfort me. "You stopped."

"I don't understand."

His voice is sorrowful, and with a heavy sigh, he says, "I underestimated you, Emily. You're much more powerful than I could've known, love."

It's the first time I'm happy to hear his nickname for me. He looks nervous being so close and I see the fear he's failing to hide.

"Patrick, what exactly did I do?" I'm desperate for the truth but terrified of the answer.

"I wanted you to experience your power and at the same time block my power over you, but . . . you saw what you wanted, and you took it." He hesitates, absorbed with his thoughts. "You didn't realize what you were taking."

"What was I taking? I don't even understand where I was. I thought I was drowning."

He takes a breath and I brace myself. His voice is deep and smooth, "You were taking parts of me."

A crude laugh springs from me, adding to the strangling tension. "What?"

Looking at me as if I had grown a second head, Patrick leans forward. "Emily, you were taking my gifts . . . my spirit . . . my life."

I gasp. "Is that possible?"

"Yes."

"Oh my God." I slump back.

He releases his grip on the boat. "Only those with incredible power can take the power of another the way you just did."

"But I stopped, right, you said it yourself. I stopped."

"Which only makes it more unbelievable. You should've killed me. I should be dead."

"You're saying I almost killed you?"

"Yes."

"With my mind?"

"Yes."

"I'm not a killer, Patrick."

"No, I guess not. What stopped you?"

"What stopped me? You . . . you did. I didn't know where I was and then I heard you and you . . . you pulled me out of it."

"You heard my voice?"

I nod and move up onto the seat.

"You shouldn't have been able to hear me," he says in a solemn tone.

"Why not?"

"You just shouldn't have." He lifts the oars ready to row. "Let's talk about this later. We need to get back."

He rows us toward the curtain of leaves hanging from the willow. The bow of the boat splits the fine branches to make an opening. My fingers trail the soft leaves as we glide through the willow into the pond. The dipping sun feels warm against my skin as we near the wall of grass that will lead us back to the open lake.

"Patrick," I feel an urgency to ask him as many questions as I can before we're back with the others. My insides are shaking, but I try to keep the fear out of my voice when I ask, "What am I?"

He tilts his head to the side and with a velvet voice, he croons, "You're Emily."

I give him an exhausted look, feeling the tall reeds of grass tickling my arms, but I don't break his stare. "You know what I mean. What are we?"

"We're human. Just like everyone."

"Humans can't do the things we can do."

"We are humans who have extra abilities."

"Patrick?" I know he's drawing this out.

With a sigh, he explains, "I've heard different names for what we are, but I prefer to be called human. We have human blood pumping through our human veins with all of our human parts. My mom always told me it was good to humanize ourselves; otherwise, we may think we're superior. We could lose our humanity and become monsters if we take what we want because we can—because we think we deserve it."

I know he's speaking from the heart and I like what he's saying. It sounds right, but he's completely contradicting everything he said earlier.

"But . . ."

"I was pushing you," he interjects. "I was trying to irritate you, not that I have to try."

"I don't understand," I say, watching the open lake reappear behind Patrick.

He continues rowing us into the vastness of the lake as he explains, "I had to push you to your breaking point so you could begin training your mind."

"You meant for that to happen?"

He shakes his head. "It wasn't supposed to go down that way."

"So, what went wrong?"

"It was too much. The emotions overtook you. You felt as if you were drowning and truly in your mind you were. You felt my presence, and you latched onto me. You didn't realize what you were doing. That power in your hands . . . You wanted it. You could've completely taken it, but you stopped. You stopped when you heard my voice."

"It was barely a whisper."

"It seemed that way to you because you were so deep within my mind."

"I was what?"

"Let's not worry about this now," he says like I didn't just try to kill him. "The sun is almost down, and they will be waiting for us. Calm down the best you can. I don't want you to look amiss. They'll wonder what I did to you."

"Or what I did to you!"

"It's nothing for us to worry about now, love," he soothes. "Let's just breathe and regroup."

It's as if I'm seeing him for the first time. He's different, and I have a feeling I'm looking at the real Patrick right now. Starting at his bare feet, my gaze slides up his long powerful legs and over his chiseled abdomen. His chest and shoulder muscles tense and flex as he rows. His heartbeat thrums in his neck as his wavy blond locks blow gently in the breeze. There's so much more to this handsome, peculiar man than I could ever have imagined. But his eyes are foreign to me, a stranger behind the faded misty-blue. I want his bright eyes back.

"What happened to your eyes?"

"What are you talking about?"

"You don't know? They're light blue instead of their usual sapphire. I'm surprised you haven't heard it in my mind.

"You are more difficult for me to hear now," he answers with a melancholy tone.

I'm surprised by my unexpected sadness that he can't hear my thoughts even though I was sure that was what I wanted. "It sounds like your plan worked . . . sort of."

I hear his deep voice inside my head. *"You can still speak to me whenever you like."*

"I thought you couldn't hear me?" I say aloud.

"I said it was more difficult."

I try to speak into his mind, feeling incredibly stupid as I shout in my head, *"Thanks for the ride!"*

His body stiffens. "A whisper would suffice."

"I'm still learning," I excuse myself. We've already made it into the deep end of the swimming area. The other boat is tied at the dock and Morgan is sitting on the beach laughing with her sister and Noah.

"Thank you for joining me," Patrick says politely.

His form has become a silhouette to the setting sun, and I watch as Morgan gets up from her chair on the beach. I realize our time together is slipping through my fingers like sand through an hourglass. I'm not ready for our trip to end. I still have more questions, and as much as I hate to admit it, I'm still shaken from our bizarre encounter and not ready to leave him.

As the boat drifts toward the dock, I panic, "Patrick!"

"Yes?"

"Can we talk later?"

"Of course."

"Tonight?" I ask, hoping I don't sound too desperate.

"Tonight is perfect," he reassures, gently guiding the boat alongside the small wooden dock as Morgan approaches.

Patrick leaps onto the dock with animal grace and turns to offer me his hand. I feel the electric tingle between us as we touch. I look him over one more time—sensing a connection—feeling a comfort I hadn't understood before. I reluctantly let go and force myself to walk the small dock while he ties the boat.

I stop and turn, unable to resist asking, "One last question?"

He finishes tying the rope and stands to face me. "Sure."

"The job? What's the complication?" I ask as Morgan walks to my side.

He sighs and stares at me with tender eyes. He whispers into my mind, *"You. You're making me question everything."* He looks to the ground, a shy characteristic very unlike him. He steps around me and strolls away.

I am a statue. It reminds me of the first time we met. I feel hypnotized by him. Does he feel the same?

"Patrick?" Morgan calls after him in frustration. She doesn't know I got my answer. He doesn't even acknowledge her complaint as he strolls off into the evening.

I put my hand on Morgan's shoulder. "It's okay. I've been interrogating him all evening."

With one hand on her hip, she says, "Speaking of the evening. Where did you guys go?"

"We were in the lily pad cove. Don't worry; nothing happened."

It's a lie. Everything changed in the course of a single boat ride. I know Morgan wants to know what happened between us, but Patrick made it clear she isn't to know anything.

As Patrick meets up with Tom in the middle of the yard, Tom turns to stare at me with a look of apprehension. I can't help seeing him in a new light with the knowledge of his secret.

"You guys were gone for two hours!" Morgan complains, drawing my attention back to her.

"Are you serious?"

"Yeah, it's almost nine o'clock."

"Wow, Morgan, I'm sorry. I didn't know we were gone so long."

"It's okay. I got to catch up with my sister. I guess her boyfriend isn't so bad."

We walk back to the house having almost an hour before the fireworks begin. Morgan has already taken a shower while she waited for us to return. I take a cool shower afraid to put too much heat against my tender skin. Once finished, I slip into my new jean shorts and a tank top. The straps press painfully against the sunburn on my shoulders, but aside from going nude, there is nothing I can do. I run a brush through my wet hair and grab a sweater. Slipping on my sandals, I run downstairs to meet Morgan.

"Mmm, that smells delicious!"

Morgan is heating some leftovers from the barbecue. "I thought you'd be hungry, so I heated enough for both of us."

thirteen ~

The dim lawn is flickering with hundreds of fireflies tempting the child within to chase and catch the lightning bugs instead of joining the others on the beach. Unable to resist, I grab a flash of light as we walk. I open my hand just as the bulb glows on my palm and in a second, it's airborne again. The dusk is turning to dark, but the sky is clear, and the glowing moon shows us the way to Nellie, Noah, and Julie already gathered on the beach. They welcome us as we arrive.

A wave of apprehension flows through me as Tom walks toward us through the dark. I feel like an intruder in his midst.

"Don't worry about it, love. They want you here," Patrick's voice croons in my ear, startling me.

I gasp, and Morgan looks at me in surprise. I shake my head and wave away a pretend bug to nullify her concern. We settle down on the blanket spread out across the ground. When Tom joins us, he gives me a welcoming smile, and I feel an enormous comfort from the small gesture.

"It will be a treat to sit back and watch," Tom says, as he sits down next to his wife. "I'm so glad Patrick offered to do them this year."

An explosion of sound erupts, and I'm awed by the brilliant kaleidoscope of colors filling the sky over the lake. We all enjoy the spectacular show with a round of applause after the big finale. Once the clapping subsides, the silence is deafening as we adjust to the stillness. The smell of smoke drifts through the air, reminding me of past years remembered. I'm staring over the water when his voice manifests in my head again, this time not as startling.

"So, what did you think?" Patrick's voice is so arrogant I can practically hear his smirk.

I answer silently, feigning disinterest, *"I guess it was okay."*

"Ouch," he replies.

I smile, proud of myself. I hope I knocked him down a peg or at the very least wiped the cocky grin from his face. I look up and realize Tom is watching me with curiosity. My smile dies as I wonder if he too is able to hear my thoughts.

The conversation begins to pick up around me, but I'm caught up worrying about all the things in my life that are out of my control. I keep my eyes on the water until I hear the smooth voice from behind me.

"So, what did you guys think?" Patrick says.

"It was amazing! It was so professional! I loved it!" They all shout at once. I'm the only one to remain silent. I look up and am surprised to see he doesn't look smug at all. Instead, he's wearing a big toothy grin. He looks younger, innocent, and genuinely excited."

It's heartwarming to discover I'm in the middle of a happy family moment belonging in a frame on a wall—the kind that hasn't existed in my life for far too long. I glance around this loving family, and the smile slips from my face. The pain of what I've been missing all these years threatens to strangle me. I don't belong here. I feel more alone here surrounded by people than if

I were actually alone. I want to go home. I have to get away from here.

"Hey, I'm gonna go back to the house for a minute," I say to Morgan. She gives a questioning look. "Bathroom," I say, as an explanation.

She nods in understanding. "Do you want me to walk with you?"

"Nope, I'll be right back."

There is a chill in the breeze, or maybe it's the chills emanating from my sunburn. I put on my sweater as I walk past Patrick and Noah.

Though the house isn't far, the trip seems to take forever. Chatter and roaring laughter from the group by the lake fills the air. The sound sends an aching so deep within my heart; I swear I hear it crack and fear I'm bleeding internally. As I enter the house, I immediately shut the door behind me blocking out the noise.

It's silent in the house except for the low hum of the air conditioner. I take a deep breath, but the pain I feel is debilitating. I hide in the bathroom around the corner. As soon as the door closes, my knees buckle, and I slide down the wall onto the floor. I want to cry, but no tears come. No tears ever come. I squeeze my eyes tight willing away this all-consuming grief.

Morgan's family is too much of a reminder of what my family should look like—what it would look like if my mom wouldn't have left all those years ago. I always blamed her sickness for the splintering of our family, but now I don't know what to believe. Dad's explanation has shattered everything I thought I knew. Should I feel responsible for the absence of my mom? Was I the reason for all of the pain and suffering?

My sister is the only one who escaped the tragedy in one piece. I know our dad loves us, but he never really recovered. That's why he buries himself in his work. All the late nights and business trips are an excuse to put off coming home to the house that reminds him of everything he lost. On top of that, I know he hasn't forgiven himself for committing me to the psych ward after my mom's death. And maybe it's petty, but I've never been able to forgive him either. It's another taboo we never discuss.

My only crime was grieving like any child who lost her mother. I cried and sobbed until my tears dried up and I became detached—unable to comprehend the loss—but feeling sad and alone. I never want to go back to that place, so I learned to hide my emotions, bottling my sadness up so tight I didn't know how to cry anymore.

So that leaves me here, locked in a friend's bathroom, crumpled on the floor feeling altogether despondent and unable even to weep. I haven't shed a tear since I cried myself to sleep that first night at the hospital five years ago.

I take breaths to calm myself in the midst of my panic attack, fighting my innate urge to run. Tomorrow I will have to go home and face my dad. I need to understand why he lied to me. It's killing me to be angry with him, but I feel so betrayed.

I know I can't stay locked in this bathroom all evening, so I scrape myself up off the floor. I splash water on my face and it stings against my cheeks. The mirror reflects the extent of sunburn painted across my face and chest. My hair is a shade lighter from today's sun exposure, and my eyes are a brighter shade of green against the redness of my skin.

I step out of the bathroom and stumble when I see Patrick sitting in a wingback chair in the corner of the room. He's leaning forward with his elbows resting on his knees and his fingers steepled. I look around but don't see or hear anyone else. He looks at me with his dark blue eyes overflowing with worry.

I take a tentative step into the room, asking, "What are you doing in here?"

"I was worried about you "

"Why?"

"I felt your pain," he says, as he rises from the chair.

"I'm fine."

He's not buying it. "You're not fine. Like I told you before, you're great at fooling everyone else, but you cannot deceive me."

As he drifts towards me, I hear myself say, "Everyone's so happy. I didn't want to infect them."

He closes the distance between us, wraps his arms around me, and pulls me into him. I attempt to push away, but he holds me tight. It doesn't take long for me to stop pretending that I don't want him close. I need the closeness, so I hug him back, and his head comes down to rest on mine.

He whispers, "I'm so sorry, Emily."

I take a staggering breath and my knees tremble. If not for his arms holding me together, I would fall to the floor and shatter like a china doll. I hold him tighter allowing his calm to envelop me. His warmth sends heat radiating into my body. It feels especially hot against my sunburn. We stay this way for several long moments before I gain enough strength to stand on my own.

Feeling enormously grateful, I give him a genuine smile once we separate. Breaking the silence, I say, "Your eyes are back to normal."

"Yes, and yours are looking fairly bright as well."

"You mean next to my burning red flesh," I laugh.

He shakes his head. "You're not burnt."

"Maybe your eyes aren't back to normal," I tease.

"Look." He gestures to my body.

The red on my legs has faded into a golden brown. I rush to the bathroom to look in the mirror. My face is a little pink, but the parts of me that were red moments ago have now darkened into a beautiful tan. I remove my sweater and bring down the strap on my tank top where the burn was the worst. The searing pain is gone.

I gawk at Patrick standing in the doorway. He looks pleased and a little entertained. I'm completely blown away. He reaches over to caress my exposed shoulder.

"Forgive me," Patrick apologizes. "I had to make sure you still looked a little pink so the others wouldn't ask questions."

"Forgive you?" I'm breathless. "Thank you! I didn't think I would be able to sleep tonight because it hurt so much."

He gives me a brilliant white smile and then it fades into a tender grin. I know the look. I feel the longing. I have a hard time believing this is the same Patrick from this morning. I watch his lips wondering what they would feel like against my own. He steps closer to place a hand on my cheek waiting for my response. My breathing escalates, and I brace myself against the wall behind me.

"Emily, I know I said I wouldn't, but I'm going to kiss you now."

I nod permission as he cups my face in his hands and tilts my chin. I close my eyes just before his supple lips meet mine. He kisses me gently as if he's afraid I'll break. His lips linger coaxing mine for the second kiss. By the third kiss, I am butter and have completely melted. He pulls away leaving one hand to remain on my cheek. My eyes flutter open.

With a devilish grin and a low voice, he suggests, "That wasn't so bad, was it?"

I mumble, "Mmm."

He loops his arm through mine. "Let's go."

I don't argue, but when I take a step forward my legs turn to jelly and I stumble into him. He catches me and gives me a second to right myself. With that same devilish grin, he leads the way back to the beach.

I'm happy for the little walk. It gives me enough time to put my head back on my shoulders where it belongs. The group has moved across the beach to roast marshmallows over a fire. I tear away from Patrick's arm before anyone can see the two of us linked. I give him a look of apology, but I think he understands.

We stay out by the lake for another hour before Tom and Julie retreat inside, leaving the five of us to hang out on the beach. The rest of the evening is full of fun and laughter. Whenever a wave of panic threatens, Patrick magically appears at my side to envelop me in his calming presence.

As Morgan and I head back to the house, I stop. Turning to her, I say, "Thank you, Morgan. Really, thank you for everything."

"You don't need to thank me, Emily. Honestly, I'm glad you're here."

I step in to give her the hug she's holding back. It takes her by surprise, but she doesn't say anything, she just squeezes me tight.

fourteen ~

I wake early the next morning still wearing the shorts and tank top I wore the night before. At some point in the night, Morgan must have thrown a blanket over me. I move carefully out of bed to keep from waking her. I hurry to her bathroom door, but it's locked. Before I can make a decision to knock or use the other bathroom, the door slides open. Patrick stands in the doorway looking powerful in his business suit and tie.

"Good morning." His words gently caress the inside of my skull, wiping away any remaining cobwebs of sleep.

"Well, aren't you overdressed!" I return silently, unconsciously drifting toward him.

He looks pleased by my involuntary movement and just when I decide to back away, his arm reaches for me. He pulls me into the bathroom and closes the door. The smell of aftershave or body wash or whatever it is that makes Patrick smell so delicious fills my senses.

"Where are you going?" I ask, trying to be inconspicuous about my reaction to him.

He gives me his half-smile. At the same moment, I spot my reflection in the mirror and cringe. We're definitely not in a fairytale because I certainly don't wake up looking like sleeping beauty. No, I wake with my hair in knots, my clothes askew, my eyes puffy, and my cheeks flushed. I certainly don't understand his fervent gaze.

"I don't know if I'm going anywhere, anymore," he says, moving closer.

Goosebumps emblazon my arms at his simple touch.

I repeat, "Where are you going?"

"My internship. You've been very distracting. I always forget how hard it is to leave you." And with that, he picks me up like I weigh nothing and swings me around to sit me on the counter. He plants himself between my legs and comes in for a kiss, but I turn away on reflex. Patrick flinches, singed by my inherent rejection.

I explain, "We just started getting along. Do you really want to risk messing that up?"

His palm glides across my cheek resting two tempting fingers on my lips. He stares longingly, effectively answering my question and I'm not sure why I'm resisting.

"You feel it too," he whispers, just inches from my face. "Damn it." He shakes his head avoiding my eyes, as he lifts me from the counter. He places a chaste kiss on my forehead, releases me, and retreats to his room. Before closing the door between us, he says, "Have a good morning, love. I'll see you in class."

"Uh-huh," I muster before the door closes.

I arrive on campus early to find a comfortable spot to catch up on my assignments. After lounging under a tree reading for hours, I wander down the sidewalk toward my class and find Patrick lying on the stone wall next to the sidewalk. His hands are tucked under his head, and his chest is exposed, his shirt laying forgotten in the grass. I stop and lean over him to block the sun from his face.

"Hello, love," he drawls, his eyes remaining closed as a cocky grin spreads across his face.

"Really?" I say, moving out of his sun and sitting down next to him. "Look what you're doing to all these poor helpless girls."

His smile widens. "Is it working on all of the girls?" he asks in a sultry tone, peering up to unleash his hypnotizing eyes.

Attempting to ignore the effect he has on me; I turn my head and change the subject. "Have you gone anywhere for your humanities project?"

He sits up. "There is a play tomorrow evening if you would like to accompany me."

I look over and my eyes automatically drop to his bare chest. Realizing my mistake, I roll my eyes and say, "Will you please put on your shirt? It's distracting."

"I'll put my shirt on when you agree to go with me," he says with a smirk. "It's just two blocks from here, tomorrow at eight."

"I have to work."

"They can let you off a little early. You work with Ashley, right? I'll come talk to her."

His words hit a nerve, feeling ever so slightly like a threat because I remember how Ashley reacted to him the last time. "I don't want you around Ashley."

"Why?" he questions, "You think I would compel her?"

"You wouldn't have to. She already thinks you're a God."

He places his hand over mine on the stone wall as he quietly gazes at me. I get lost in his eyes, and my mind drifts. When he speaks, his words feel like silk against my ear. "Emily, you know you want to get this assignment out of the way."

I yank my hand away from him, separating from his thoughts. "Don't you dare use that on me!"

"Just seeing if I could," he shrugs, unrepentant. "I had you for a second."

"And that's the longest you'll ever have me."

He nudges my shoulder. "We'll just have to see how our date goes tomorrow."

Red lights are flashing in my mind, and though I don't completely understand my apprehension, I know this doesn't feel like the Patrick who held me together the night before. I stand up to put more distance between us, saying, "I'll meet you here on campus tomorrow night since it's only two blocks away."

He's looking at me funny. "Okay, I'll meet you here." He observes the distance I put between us and questions, "Are you suddenly frightened by me?"

"No," I say, sounding defensive.

He slips his shirt over his shoulders and says, "Will you do me a favor? Pay attention to the people around you as you go to class. I'll be right behind you."

I shake my head. "Okay, whatever," I say, walking away.

There are more people on campus than usual, or maybe it's just because I'm paying attention. I haven't gone twenty feet when a guy holding a frisbee approaches me.

"Hey, I'm Tucker," he offers, forwardly.

I continue walking.

"Are you on your way to class?"

"Yeah, why?"

"It sucks you have to sit inside on such a beautiful day," he says. "What class do you have?"

"Humanities."

"Ah, I just finished my last Humanities class. Do you have that old man with the cane? I can't believe they let that senile old man teach."

"I like that senile old man." I walk faster trying to brush him off, but he sticks to me like a leech.

"Are you busy after class or maybe you could skip class and come hang out with me."

"No."

"Well, maybe we can hang out another time." His shameless advances keep coming. Other than Patrick, I've never had anyone openly hit on me. It's irritating, and he's not getting the hint.

"No!" I say, but he continues.

"What about later tonight?" he says, crowding my space. "Just give me your number and we'll work it out." He pulls his phone from his pocket. "You can stop by my apartment. Do you live close?"

I stop and turn ready to give him hell, but a masculine voice comes from behind me. "Is this boy bothering you?"

My frisbee-playing stalker backs away. "I'll see you around," he says, before fleeing the scene.

I turn to face my rescuer. He must be at least ten years my senior, and I see why the other guy didn't stay to argue. His cut-off shirt boasts massive tattooed biceps, while his clean-shaven head reveals a fully tattooed scalp. I mean to thank him, but I'm intimidated by his presence.

"Look at you. You're a hot piece." He wraps an arm around me, and I get a whiff of alcohol as he talks.

Attempting to move out of his grip, I pull my words together. "Umm, I'm late for class."

"Let's take that sweet ass somewhere more private." He slides his hand over my butt, saying, "Don't worry baby, I'll teach you things they don't teach in class."

He's intimidating, but I can't help but laugh at his ridiculous line. He scowls and pulls me closer, pinning me up against him so tightly that his hold becomes painful.

"Let go of me!"

"I'll take her," Patrick's gentle voice floats to my side.

This menacing man must have five inches and at least a hundred pounds on Patrick. They engage in a silent stare-down, unaware of my presence.

"Patrick, what are you doing?" I ask, wordlessly.

In true Patrick style, his unblinking stare incapacitates the unwelcome intruder. The silent tension between them ends as abruptly as it started, and the man releases me from his grip. He appears confused as he turns to stomp away.

A sigh of relief escapes me, but I flinch when Patrick touches me.

"I could've handled it," I say, with misplaced anger.

"Yeah, I'm sure you had it under control," he mocks.

"What was that all about anyway? Did you get what you wanted?" I demand, feeling violated. "Was that your plan? Were you trying to be my knight in shining armor, because I don't believe in that!" I turn and hurry away.

"Are you kidding me?" He walks after me. "You're kidding me, right? Why would I ever purposely put you in the hands of a man like that?"

Spinning around, I throw my hands out to my sides, "I just told you why!"

"You think I have white knight syndrome?" he mocks. "I wanted to show you how irresistible you are to those around you. You attract a lot of attention to yourself—another thing we'll have to work on."

"*We* don't have to work on anything!"

"You can't deny those guys were hitting on you!"

I shake my head. "For all I know, you manipulated them into doing it."

"I certainly did not. Emily, you have no idea how powerful you've become. Everyone is drawn to you. Look around, love, it's not just frat boys and alcoholics that are watching you."

I don't like the way his words are filled with conviction. I think about what he's telling me and let my eyes wander to the people around us. Both girls and boys, young and old are watching with intense curiosity. I see, and worse I feel the blind interest behind their stares. It's not the desire I feel from Patrick, but more of an inquisitive compliance, an aberration to the standard way of thinking. I feel an undeserved reverence radiating from the minds of these unknowing strangers.

Overwhelmed by my own ability, I duck my head and grab Patrick's arm to pull him into the lecture hall with me. I whisper, "How do I make it stop?"

"You can't. Your pull on them is only going to get stronger, so you need to learn how to control it so it's not so overwhelming."

We make our way down to our seats in silence, but as soon as we sit, I'm quick to ask, "But why is this happening now?"

"It's been happening. You just haven't been paying attention. This change should've happened at least a year ago. With the amount of power you have, I can't believe it didn't happen sooner."

"I just want it to stop."

"Emily, you need to embrace it. It's a gift."

"Maybe it is to you!"

I sense a brief backlash of emotion in his mind before he hides it from me. He doesn't continue the conversation; in fact, we don't talk for the remainder of the class. I try to listen to the adorable old professor, but I can't focus.

After class, Patrick and I part without a word. I go to my next class and he goes . . . well, the truth is, I have no idea where Patrick goes. I don't know what other classes he takes. I know so little about him because our conversations are so limited in their subject matter. And even though Patrick appears to be honest with me, he's evasive, making it difficult to read his true self.

While I'm miserably suffering through my freshman orientation class, I focus on the things I can and cannot control. It sparks an idea, and I turn my attention toward my teacher who I usually tune out. I'm surprised how easy it is to get into her head. She's fresh out of college and anxious about her first-year teaching. She's overly worried about what the students think of her, and she's got a secret crush on the cute guy in the front row.

I merge my thoughts with hers, my instincts kicking in to make it nearly effortless as my thoughts easily resound in her mind. I envision the warmth of the sun, the fresh air, and the students' excitement over being dismissed early. I know I'm manipulating her and even though I yelled at Patrick for doing just that, it doesn't stop me.

The teacher announces, "Why don't we leave the rest of this for next week. Enjoy your day. No homework!"

The class is silent and unmoving for a moment.

"Go!" she says again. The class lifts with excitement. I hurry to gather my things and escape, afraid my manipulation will wear off.

I've never felt so alive as I walk out of the building. The sun has never been quite so exhilarating, and I don't remember the last time I felt so liberated. I walk a little taller and feel a little brighter as I venture out to the parking lot, but my confidence falters when I recognize the lean body propped against my car.

Moment crushed. "I thought you weren't talking to me."

"Yes, well I thought you didn't want any of this," Patrick says, unmoving from his position against my driver side door.

"I haven't changed my mind."

"Really?" he questions bitterly.

"Really."

"Then shouldn't you be attending class?"

"We got out early."

"Oh, I know." His laugh is condescending. "I have experienced precisely how persuasive you can be."

"Are you stalking me?"

"I could feel you using your gifts."

"It's a stupid class."

"You made it irrefutably clear you didn't want *any* of this, yet you're so quick to use it to your advantage."

I throw my hands out to the sides. "I didn't think it would actually work."

He looks to the sky, his hands gripping his hair. He lowers his arms, taking a frustrated breath before his eyes level with mine. "So, you thought you would just experiment with a human mind. Let me get this straight, you're allowed to use your gifts haphazardly, but you scold me for not allowing that man to rape you."

My hands land on my hips. "You're being over-dramatic. I had that under control."

"Really?" he accuses.

"Really!"

He leans forward with a smug grin. "I told you it's not all bad."

"I wouldn't have felt so desperate to leave my class if you hadn't filled my head with all this . . . this insanity!" I fold my arms across my chest, determined to stand my ground.

"It's okay, I know you're excited to go home and talk to Daddy," he says with spite. He takes a step to the side and opens my door. With a hand gesture, he invites me inside.

As I climb into the car, I feel the venom roll off my tongue, "Don't pretend to be a gentleman, you jackass."

"Don't pretend to be a victim!" He slams the door in my face, nearly hitting me.

I'm shocked by the hostility. Stunned into silence, I blink a few times as I watch him disappear. I've only seen glimpses of his anger, but I know it's something I shouldn't invite.

fifteen ~

Arriving home, I take a worrisome breath, attempting to collect myself before walking through the front door. Maggie is right there to welcome me home with a wagging tail nub and lots of kisses. When I bend down to greet her, something catches my attention. Dad is fidgeting nervously by the couch. As if sensing the tension, Maggie lets out a low growl. I straighten and put myself between the two.

"Hi," I say.

As soon as I speak, he's crossing the room and doesn't stop until he's hugging me.

"I was worried you wouldn't come home today," he says, pulling away.

He looks like he hasn't slept in days. Feeling guilty, I avoid his eyes and look past him to find an intricately carved wooden box the size of a child's lunch box resting on the coffee table. Curious, my body carries me forward. The closer I get to the object, the more afraid I become. Afraid of a wooden box? That's ridiculous. Pushing past the fear, I reach to touch the skeleton key laying on top.

"Wait, don't touch it," Dad warns, pushing my hand away. "I need to prepare you for what you might see or remember when

154

you make contact. This box is linked to a memory. I don't expect you to understand but trust me this once."

I don't question him because after what I've witnessed in the last two days, anything seems possible.

"What do you remember from the day your mother died?" he questions.

I delve into the past. I was in seventh grade. It's a day I'll never forget. I was living in a cloud of humiliation because I had passed out earlier in the day. I had no memory of my blackout aside from making a big scene. I thought my life couldn't get any worse. Then later that day a teacher came to pull me out of my seventh-period class to explain there had been an accident. She escorted me to the office where Opal Williams, my seventy-year-old widowed neighbor, sat waiting for me. I was given no further explanation, so I knew it must be very bad.

The car ride with Opal was disheartening, and when we arrived at the house, no one was there to greet us. My sister showed up a few minutes later, having driven herself home from high school. Tears were streaming down her face as she ran to embrace me. She had no idea what had happened and was just as worried as I was.

Dad was the last to enter. His desolate expression was painful to watch as his haggard body crossed the living room. His skin was ashen. His eyes drained of hope. He cleared his throat to speak, and I wanted to stop him. Perhaps if he didn't speak it aloud, it wouldn't be true. But I couldn't stop him, just like I couldn't stop my mother from dying. A sob escaped my lips as he relayed the devastating news that our mother was dead.

I blink, bringing myself back to the present. My eyes blur as I stare at the box in front of me. I blink again to adjust my focus and something wet drips down my face. I touch my cheek, inspecting the glistening moisture on my fingertips. I'm crying.

"I don't want to remember that day," I conclude.

Dad looks at me lovingly and says, "How much did Patrick explain?"

"You know about Patrick?"

"Yes, he told me, though, he didn't need to. I could feel him trying to get into my head the moment we met. When you marry an Olvasho, you learn to recognize when they get into your head."

"Marry a what?"

He looks confused. "I thought Patrick explained."

"He didn't mention anything about an Old-vash-oh?" I voice, testing the neologism.

"Ol-va-show," he articulates. "It's what most individuals like you and Patrick call yourselves. It's what your mom was. You are descendants from the original Olvasho sisters."

"So, there is a name for us. Patrick called us human." I feel odd to include myself in a group with Patrick.

"That's true, you are human, but you're capable of more than a normal human. I'm not sure what you've discovered so far."

I knew this would be a difficult conversation but having him sound so comfortable about this topic—like we are talking about the weather instead of special powers—is hard to wrap my head around.

"What am I capable of?"

"You have the ability to read minds and see into souls. You can communicate with people and animals on a profound level. You have heightened senses which allows you to experience those around you with more intensity. Someday you may be able to put your thoughts into another's mind; although, it can be quite invasive." Dad points to the table in front of us. "Do you remember this box?"

I rub my temples, willing away my oncoming headache. "No . . . Eh, yes . . . It's so hazy, I can't remember."

"You said Mom told you about it when you blacked out that day. She came to you with her last words. You didn't remember right away. You woke up one night shortly after your mom died and asked me about this box. I pulled it out for you. Inside, we found papers written in the Olvasho language that I'm unable to decipher. You became inconsolable as you read the information. Something about it triggered the memories from the time you blacked out. I never want you to experience that kind of pain again, but it seems inevitable. I've kept it from you as long as I could. Now it's time for you to remember."

He reluctantly hands me the skeleton key and images begin to emerge. I delve deeper into the hazy memories. Events come into focus, and I gasp as I relive the past all over again, as if it's happening for the first time.

I'm in seventh grade sitting at my desk surrounded by students chattering all around me. The girl to my left is leaning over her desk talking to me about her mega crush on Jason Fowler. I'm listening intently when the whole room disappears into blackness. My mother's face appears directly before me in the dark. I'm submerged in panic when I see the grief in her eyes.

"Emily, my love, take care of yourself. I'm so sorry." She places a kiss on my forehead, leaving me feeling faint before she disappears.

I search the darkness in confusion before the classroom solidifies around me. My focus is anywhere but on the girl talking animatedly beside me. I'm searching the room for my mother. It feels like there is a constricting noose around my neck making it impossible to breathe. A piercing agony rips through my chest and I let out a shriek, collapsing onto the floor.

Tears erupt from my eyes, and I ignore the attention I've captured. I only want one individual's attention, and she's gone. I close my eyes as the teacher rushes to my aid. The darkness behind my eyelids recedes, and my mother's terror-ridden face emerges from the nothingness. I barely make out her raspy whisper, "The box . . ." Blood sputters from her mouth as she struggles to stay on her feet. She grabs for the nearby wall but collapses mid-reach. She breathes one shallow breath before the life behind her beautiful emerald eyes is snuffed out.

Forced out of the darkness, I open my eyes to see my teacher crouched over me. My peers stare at me with curiosity, and I notice Ben's worried expression despite the tears clouding my vision. My seventh-grade mind tries to make sense of it, but it's already fading. The images disappeared from my mind as quickly as they came, leaving me with no memory of my blackout. I was left confused and drowning in humiliation at my outburst.

I blink and I'm back in my living room sitting next to Dad with the unopened box before us. Vivid memories illuminate my mind.

"She was murdered!" I jerk up from the couch as if I can pull away from the memory. "Mom was murdered," I repeat quietly, mostly to myself, trying to unwind the messy tangle of lost memories. Now I understand why I was inconsolable when I was twelve. The images are haunting. Mom came to me mentally to say goodbye. I was not meant to follow her after she said goodbye, but I went back into her mind and found her—something I shouldn't have been able to do at twelve-years-old.

How could I have forgotten the look of terror on her face as she realized I was with her? How did I forget the knife? It was jagged and long with a carved bone handle. How is it possible I forgot such a gruesome scene? And why don't I remember the pain? Her pain seared itself inside my head. I felt everything she felt. I remember the blood sputtering from her lips. I was with her as she spoke her last words and breathed her last breath. I suffered her death as if it was my own. And then, almost immediately, I forgot it all because my abilities weren't developed enough for my brain to process the experience. But I retained the memory in my subconscious mind, where I had tucked it away until I could comprehend all that had happened.

Bile rises in my throat. I lose my footing and Dad lunges forward to catch me as I take a dive. The wooden floorboards disappear beneath me as darkness takes hold.

I wake on the couch in a daze. I sit up too quickly and feel another wave of dizziness and nausea.

"You okay?" Dad says from the chair next to me. "You passed out."

Bracing my head in my hands, I say, "I changed when I was twelve, didn't I?"

His voice sounds broken and apologetic. "Yes, all of the Olvasho powers hit you at once and you couldn't control them. Anyone who came near you would instantly feel your pain like it was their own—like they had just watched their mother die in front of them."

"That's why you committed me?" I ask with realization.

"Not exactly," he shakes his head. "I called your mother's friend to help you. She was able to suspend your powers from manifesting temporarily. It's comparable to shoving the cork back into a bottle of champagne. We weren't sure if it would work or how long it would last. We knew it could burst open anytime and we had to find a safe place for you. The group of Olvasho who killed your mom was looking for you. We didn't know how much they knew, so we had to be careful. Before we took you to the hospital, your mom's friend altered some of your . . . Eh . . . memories. It was done to calm you, but you didn't understand. You were confused and felt I had betrayed you, but the truth is, I had to keep you safe."

He's pleading with me to understand now since I couldn't before. His expression breaks my heart. I was deeply hurt at the time, and I never quite recovered. I was angry with him for causing me more pain. He's right. I felt betrayed. Now I begin to see the glimmer of reality in the dark memory. I'm starting to recall the lost moments, the ones that were altered, the ones my mom's friend stole from me.

I remember the screaming. The jostling around in other's heads. The confusion—so much confusion. I remember Dad sending Samantha to the neighbor's and calling my mother's friend. I remember the secretive woman coming to our house. She helped confine the power inside my body and the pain overwhelmed me like an overfilled balloon ready to explode.

I remember being in the car on the way to the hospital as the extraordinary woman cupped my head between her hands. Staring into her mesmerizing sapphire eyes, I watched as they faded from bright blue to an eerie milky color. My memories shifted, changed and ultimately disappeared. I remember it all now, except the secretive woman. She's an outline, a shadow, all except for her spooky blue eyes.

"Who was she, Dad?"

"She only let me remember enough to explain it to you when the time was right. She could knock on our door today and I wouldn't recognize her, but she was the only one your mom trusted. Once she finished with your memories, she worked on my mind, putting in place a sort of protection and alarm system in case an Olvasho found me. I would be alerted—my mind protected—making it nearly impossible for them to compel or get information out of me. Only the woman knew how to unlock my mind."

"If she was so trustworthy, why did she erase your memories?"

"She was cautious. If she had been caught helping your mother, they would've killed her too."

"What did Mom do? Why would anyone want to kill her?"

160

His eyes drift to the coffee table. "Because of her Valla blood," he whispers, as he taps his finger on the wooden box. "Look in here. It will explain better than I can."

I look at the carvings on the box and then back to him. "What's Valla blood?"

"Look in the box."

He doesn't stay to explain; instead, he walks into the kitchen. I place the key in the lock and open the lid to find red velvet lining. Papers scatter the interior. I don't know what I was expecting, but I envisioned it being more climactic.

I examine a slip of paper with a foreign script. It appears to be written in a language I've never seen before. I examine it anyway. The swirling connected letters are intriguing. They twist and whirl around the paper in an alluring cursive. I follow the lines to the very bottom of the page and return to the beginning discovering words and sentences out of the scrolling lines. I don't know how my mind can process the alien language, but the message is brief and informative. It explains it is written in the Olvasho language and to a normal human, it would look like scribbles on a page.

I place the scrap of paper to the side, and my interest turns to a pink envelope. I recognize my name scrolled across the front written in the odd language. I retrieve a folded letter from inside. Even though the letters may be in the foreign script, the handwriting is all too familiar. It belonged to my mother and somehow the words become clear.

My darling Emily,

I'm sorry I have to leave. I love you so much, more than you can fathom. I hope you will never need to read this letter, but if you are, then I was unsuccessful. First, I want to tell you just how special you are despite what anyone might say. You have abilities others can't begin to comprehend. You will be the one to stop this feud. It only makes sense it would be you.

You have the blood of Valla. It is a beautiful gift, a powerful weapon, and a deadly curse. There is a war going on, and they will come for you. You must be prepared, stay focused, and wield your weapon judiciously. If you run, they will follow. Know you don't have to go it alone. There are those who will fight alongside you. Trust wisely, my strong, beautiful girl. You have a delicate heart, keep it guarded, but not hidden for its beauty will bring unconditional loyalty. Most importantly, don't let them decide who you are. Only you have the power to choose your actions, and I believe you have an extraordinary destiny ahead of you.

I love you more than you know,
Mom
P.S. Read the leather-bound book and draw strength from the names. You are the last Valla blood.

I wipe the tears from my eyes as I find the leather book and begin reading, hoping to obtain more answers. It must be a hundred pages, and it starts very similar to the story Patrick told me, only it paints a much darker picture than the fairytale version Patrick described. This story gives the name of the old shaman woman, Reyshen, as well as the names of the three princesses, Isa, Leona, and Valla.

Valla was the stillborn sister with the strongest powers. The death of their father, the king, was not the extent of their story. The very next paragraph paints a gruesome picture of towns destroyed and a vast pool of death in Valla's wake. Reluctantly, I read on realizing she must have lost her moral compass along the way. Valla not only learned to control her immense powers with precision, but she also mastered manipulation, mind control, and murder. She was the puppet master, using people. Most of her subjects went insane long before she tossed them aside.

Valla had a favorite man, Jonathan, she held onto for a long while. She eventually moved on, but because of his importance to her, she couldn't bring herself to destroy him like she had the others. When Jonathan woke from the trance she had held him under, he remembered every detail from his life with her. He was one of the few who had not lost his mind, but he was traumatized, nonetheless. Jonathan had heard tales of the powers of Valla's sisters, Isa and Leona, and he believed they were his only hope.

He searched for years, and when he finally found her sisters, he told them of the devastation Valla left behind and begged them to stop her. It took five long years to find and kill Valla. Her death was gruesome but not nearly as disturbing as what the sisters did next. They murdered Valla's four healthy, innocent children for fear of what they might become, believing them to be demon spawns. There had been rumors of a fifth child born to Valla, but there was no proof to support the claims. This is where the story ends. I flip through the book finding empty pages bringing me no closure, no answers to my many questions.

I remind myself this happened a long time ago, yet it's completely unnerving. I get to the last page and find a tattered note shoved into the binding. I open it carefully, afraid it might crumble. I read the unfamiliar handwriting.

The note states that the alleged fifth child was not only real but went on to have children and grandchildren of her own, one of which wrote this note. She states she's one of the last of the Valla blood and goes on to explain her great-grandmother was the fifth child and for generations they've been hunted, leaving only the author of this note and her sister alive.

I am haunted by the long list of names below the small scribbled message. Each name is different, but they all have three things in common; each is female, each is labeled as a descendant of Valla, and each has a little mark to signify their death. The dates are listed beside the names, documenting their birth and death. The first name was dated nearly two hundred years ago. I read down the list and am surprised to find most of them close to my age when they died. They were all running for their lives. They were all hunted by their own kind. There is only one name on the list that is not marked as deceased; Selma Konig, a descendant of Valla, January 27, 1979 -.

I place my fingers over my mother's name. I might get sick. I know what I'm supposed to do, but I cannot put the finality of death next to my mother's name. And I refuse to sign my name on this list of victims. I feel the urge to run. I need to get away from this. I shove the tattered list into the binding and throw the book across the room.

"I won't do it!" I shout. "I can't do it!" I sob, the tears streaming down my face.

I hear Dad's footsteps before I see him. He picks up the discarded book and embraces me in a comforting hug.

"I can't do it, Dad," I sob into his shoulder.

"It's okay, Emily. You don't have to do anything. I've got you, kiddo. I've got you."

"Dad, they're all dead," I say, pulling from his embrace. I grab the book and remove the note from the binding, shoving it into his hands.

"Honey, I can't read this," he says, handing it back.

"It's a list of death. They're all dead. Most of them never reached their twenties." I point to Mom's name. "Mom did. Mom survived so much longer than most of them, but I can't . . . I can't do this. Dad, am I some kind of demon? Is that why they want me dead?"

"No sweetheart, no." He pulls me into his chest where I continue to weep.

When my tears run dry and the trembling stops, I pull away to ask, "Dad, are they after me?"

"Yes," he says, with grave concern. The silence between us stretches until he continues, "They've been looking for you for years, but your mother and I implemented procedures to assure your safety. Your mother was legally committed to the institute, so if anyone went looking, they would find a woman there by the name of Selma. We changed all of her identification to match the woman posing as your mom. Selma stopped by the institute only when we came to visit. The rest of the time she was out taking them down. The Olvasho she hunted were influential people who had mansions and compounds all over the world.

While your mother was wiping out their compound in St. Louis, things went awry. She hacked into their security feed and was sending me information. I saw them coming, but my warning came too late. I witnessed the moment they caught her and eh-" He clears his throat. "There were protocols put in place at the institute in case of your mother's death. We made sure nothing could lead them back to us. On her death certificate, her time of death was marked three days prior to the actual date, making it more difficult for anyone to make the connection to grieving families. I've worked diligently for our protection, and they haven't been able to find us. Still, I continue to send out enough false information to keep them off our trail."

I fall back onto the couch, thinking about everything he's telling me. All of his late nights at work were not because he dreaded coming home, but because he was working to keep us safe. He's spent his life protecting me and I was totally unaware.

"What about Sam?" I look up at him. "Is she in danger? She must have these abilities. How could she keep this from me?"

He takes a seat next to me on the couch before he answers, "Anyone close to us could potentially be in danger, but Samantha doesn't know anything about this. She doesn't have Olvasho abilities."

"But it's passed along to all Olvasho children. How did it skip Sam?"

"Samantha was not born from an Olvasho," he emphasizes the last word and the puzzle pieces begin to click into place. I feel foolish for not realizing it sooner.

He goes on to explain, "Samantha was a baby when her mother died."

"Sam is my half-sister?" The words don't feel right on my tongue. Nothing about this feels right. Sure, Samantha and I look nothing alike, and we act nothing alike, but I will never think of her as anything less than my sister. "I mean, to be honest, I'm relieved Sam doesn't share my Valla blood, but why didn't you ever tell us?"

"Because of Samantha. I don't want her to know the truth. I didn't realize Samantha's mother was an addict until she was pregnant. She failed to stay clean through the pregnancy. I took full custody of Samantha the second she was born while her mother went to rehab over and over. It never took. She never even wanted to meet our baby girl, and she never got to because she overdosed when Sam was only two-months-old.

"Selma came into my life when I was a single father trying to raise a three-week-old crack-baby. She helped me with Sam's doctor appointments and medications. Selma was my angel and kept me sane through the worst of it. Samantha made huge improvements, reaching milestones the doctors told us she never would. I didn't know about your mother's abilities back then, but she saved Samantha. She saved us both. We got married within that first year and I never felt the need to explain to your sister that Selma wasn't her biological mother. I wanted to save her the horrors of her first year." He fights back the tears.

"I won't say anything to her, but when did you find out about Mom?"

"A couple of years after we married, your mother disappeared in the night. It wasn't like her, so I filed a police report, but honestly, I was worried she'd left me. She always seemed too good to be true.

"The next couple of days I began hearing her voice in my head. I thought I was crazy, but I listened to the voices because it was all I had left of her. It didn't take long to discover something bizarre was happening. I left Samantha with a friend and followed your mother's voice. It took weeks for her to lead me to Chicago where she was being held captive in a hotel. The Olvasho group holding your mother underestimated her brilliance and our connection to one another. It was the only reason we were able to escape."

His gaze becomes unfocused as he reflects in silence. I'm sure he's telling me the PG version of the story, and I understand why he kept the mysteries of my life hidden, and why he never wanted to talk about these secrets.

His expression darkens as he continues, "Capturing your mother wasn't their only objective. Their goal was to obtain a child they could mold and manipulate; someone loyal who they could use as a weapon. They chose your mother because of the strength of her Valla blood and because she was pregnant with you."

I stare in horror. "They wanted mom because of me?"

"You were the only reason they didn't kill her eighteen years ago," he says, trying to comfort me. "When she escaped, she twisted their minds into believing the pregnancy failed, so they thought you were dead. We were lucky to get away with you. She always said as long as I kept you safe, they would believe the Valla bloodline died with her.

"We picked up Samantha from our friend, but we never returned home. We were on the run until we changed our identities and found a permanent home here."

My mind is a whirlwind of emotion. I'm running through a revolving door of guilt, grief, fear, and anger. I'm barely paying attention as Dad continues, "They started on her trail when you were five. By the time you were nine, Selma could feel them closing in. That's when she left. She hated the idea of putting us in danger, so she said I should raise you alone while she hunted them."

The revolving door of my brain comes to a screeching halt.

"Hunted them?" I'm shocked by the thought of my soft-spoken, beautiful mother hunting anyone. "But . . . but we visited her at the facility."

"Yeah, she wanted to keep the illusion."

"The illusion that she was crazy? Why?"

"She didn't want you to think she had abandoned you. This way we could visit her in a neutral location when she came to town, but she spent most of her time tracking them."

"That was a terrible plan, Dad! Did she at least find them?" I cry, angry I couldn't spend more time with her, angry they couldn't have come up with a better plan, and angry they had to lie in the first place.

"Yeah, she found some of them."

"Did she kill them?" It comes out as a whisper.

"Do you really want that answer?"

I shake my head, not wanting to know, but knowing just the same. My parents built me a life filled with fabrications and white lies, and each revealed secret becomes a piece that clicks into this disturbing puzzle of my broken life.

In a small voice, I say, "Thank you for telling me the truth."

His eyes crease, and he gives me a sad smile. "I'm sorry, Em."

"I ruined Mom's plan." I slump back into the couch, letting my head rest against the cushion behind me. "They know about me because they felt my presence when she was dying. They discovered my existence. That's why she looked so scared. She died, knowing they'd come looking for me."

Dad nods in agreement. "It's been nearly impossible for them to track you without you having your abilities. Now you'll need to be very careful."

"I don't have to use these abilities, do I? Can't I turn them off?"

"It doesn't work like that. You can't flip your gifts on and off with a switch."

"We did it when I was twelve."

He's shaking his head even before I finish. "I'm sorry Emily, but it won't work. I'm surprised it's taken this long for them to show up again. There is no getting rid of them this time."

"Why are my abilities showing up now?"

"My best guess would be because of Patrick. Having another of your kind near must have brought your abilities to the surface."

"Patrick? Do you trust him?"

"He hasn't given me any reason not to trust him. He hasn't made any move to compel me or get information. With that said, I would stay cautious, but I trust him enough for now. For all he knows you're an Olvasho just like him."

"But he said I was special and powerful."

"Though Valla's blood is the strongest of the three lines, there are varying levels of strength for all Olvasho. Even with your power, most wouldn't conclude you are Valla's descendant. Most Olvasho don't know the Valla bloodline still exists. I'm not worried about Patrick right now; I did an extensive background check on him."

Leaning forward, with my hands on my knees, I ask, "Should we move? I mean, would it help to move around?"

"If we were to move now, we would become easier targets. I haven't detected any immediate danger, but I've put contingencies in place here just in case."

"Contingencies?"

"Just simple precautions to keep you safe. I'm probably being paranoid." He stands from his seat and turns to face me. "Anyway, I know it comes at a bad time, but I have to fly to New York tomorrow night for work. And while I'm there, I'll continue to lead the Olvasho on a wild goose chase."

I feel a tightening in my gut. I don't want him to leave me, and I worry there could be men in black armed and ready to burst through our door at any moment.

As he moves toward the kitchen, he says, "Your mom could check the intentions of others simply by being near them. I know she had a lot more experience, but it wouldn't hurt to try reading Patrick."

He doesn't know I've already been inside Patrick's mind. The only thing I learned from the incident was I frighten myself. I'm more powerful than Patrick, but why wouldn't I be? After all, I'm from the evil Valla lineage. According to the book, I have Valla's demon blood running through my veins. I don't want to think of the book, but worse things come to my mind. My mother's death haunts me no matter how much I wish to block the horrific images.

My perception of life is changing and I need time to catch up. I've always felt I never quite fit into this world. Now I know why. After everything I have learned in the last forty-eight hours, I know I'll never be naive or innocent again. The dark reality of truth has tainted my life.

I hear the back door open and flinch. I jump off the couch and join Dad in the kitchen to find he's only letting Maggie out. I don't want to admit it, but it's obvious I'm afraid.

"Do you want some food? You must be hungry," Dad says.

"I don't feel like eating."

"I know Em, but you should try anyway."

I shuffle toward the cabinets pretending my world hasn't been flipped on its side.

Sitting at our small kitchen table, I twist my spoon around in the soggy cereal. I really try to eat, but after a few bites, I feel it clawing its way back up my throat. In my mind, I rearrange the fractured pieces of my life, but no matter where the pieces fall, the puzzle never comes together quite the way I want. How do I pretend to be normal when every part of me has been deemed unorthodox?

I'm feeling sorry for myself when a noise from the other room pricks at my ears. Before I can turn to search for Dad, my mind reaches out to connect with his. I feel a strange sensation just before his thoughts and emotions assault me. I experience the pain and sorrow he's endured, the worry he feels for me every day, and his resolve and determination to continue fighting to keep me safe. He's stronger than I gave him credit for. He's a soldier who has been fighting for me since before I was born.

"Emily?" he calls from the living room as he nears the kitchen. I sense his movements in my mind but sever my connection with his thoughts.

"Was that you?" he asks, when he reaches the kitchen door.

I waver for a moment before I understand what he's asking. "You could feel that?" I ask in disbelief.

He nods. "Do you know how to control it?"

"Umm, not very well."

"It took your mom years to do what you just did and if I didn't have this protection over my mind, then I wouldn't have had any idea. Have you done that before?"

"Yeah," I confess.

He smiles as he pulls out a seat and sits next to me. I push my cereal away as he leans toward me in anticipation. I don't know what he's doing, but sensing his excitement makes me nervous.

"Do it again," he instructs.

"Umm . . ."

"Go on; do exactly what you just did."

I take a breath and concentrate on him. It's difficult now that I'm conscious of what I'm trying to do. My teacher earlier today was easy, maybe because I didn't believe I could do it. Now I know. The idea scares me. What if I hurt him like I did Patrick?

I cut our connection, sitting a little straighter in my seat. "No, it's too dangerous. I hurt Patrick."

He looks stunned. "You got into Patrick's mind?" He sounds impressed.

"Yeah, but it was a mistake. I didn't know what I was doing and I almost . . . I had no control. I could've killed him!"

"Wow!" he says, looking ten years younger. "I didn't know you'd be such a natural. Who knew it'd come to you so quickly, especially after everything that happened when you were twelve?"

"A natural? I hurt him! I totally lost control."

"If you lost control then Patrick wouldn't be alive," he justifies, having far too much faith in me. "But you regained control and didn't kill him. Now come on and try again."

I lie in bed, hugging Maggie. Every last bit of energy has drained out of me, yet I can't sleep. Each little house creak or gust of wind startles me. My eyelids become so heavy that I can't keep them open. When they do close, I get a glimpse of soothing oblivion before my mind betrays me by revisiting my mother's last seconds.

I turn over in bed and stare at the picture of my mother on my nightstand. Picking up the framed photo, I bring it to my chest, wrapping my arms around it. It's a senseless thing to do, but it eases a little of the pain. The reminder of good memories must be enough because this time when I close my eyes, my mother is smiling.

sixteen ~

My mind wakes slowly, and I curse the dreadful sound emanating from my alarm clock. Grumbling, I hit the snooze button on the little torture device and turn over on my pillow. Dozing off, I tease myself with a few extra minutes of sleep. What I want is a few extra hours of peaceful morning slumber.

Soon the alarm sounds again forcing me out of bed. I watch as Maggie stretches and pulls the front half of her body to the floor before leisurely dragging the bottom half along. I laugh at her morning routine, surprising myself. I hadn't expected to start my day with laughter after everything that happened yesterday.

Last night Dad encouraged me to practice reading his mind. He tried his best to teach me how to control my extra senses. He explained how to shield my mind, but without a test, there is no way to know if it actually worked.

Today is my first day back to work since I turned eighteen and that means I get to open the store by myself. It's something I used to look forward to, but now that it's here I hate the idea. It means more time alone to think about the very real threat of being hunted.

When I realize Dad has already left for work, my paranoia hits an all-time high. I find myself checking over my shoulder, frightened by my own shadow. I peek around the shower curtain every few seconds to make sure I'm alone. Once I'm out of the shower, I hurry to get dressed in case men in black suits barge in. At least I'll have clothes on as they drag me from my home.

I wipe the steam away from the mirror and freeze as I catch my mother's emerald eyes staring back at me. It only takes a second to realize they aren't my mother's eyes, but my own. When did my dull grey-green eyes turn into emeralds? They are mesmerizing, just as mesmerizing as Patrick's, making me all the more conscious of how I am different.

Ominous clouds hang heavy in the sky matching my mood as I drive to work. I brighten up once I'm there. Whether it's the fluorescent lighting eliminating shadows, the upbeat tune on the radio, or just the normalcy of being at work, I'm grateful for the reprieve.

Only two customers venture in within the first hour, so I spend most of my time stocking shelves and feeding fish. Ashley was due to arrive at eleven, but ten minutes after, there's no sign of her. I text her, but there's no response.

At eleven-twenty she still hasn't shown. I'm worried something has happened. I try to call her this time, but it goes straight to voicemail. I keep myself busy, so my mind doesn't have time to create the worst-case scenario, but I'm running out of things to do.

Standing at the front counter, I look out the big windows. The clouds block the sun, and there is a heaviness in the air. Then I see them. A pair of headlights pull into the parking lot. The yellow Mustang rounds the corner beaming like a ray of sunshine on this bleak day. A sigh escapes me as relief sinks in. Thank God she's okay!

She's barely parked her car before her door swings open, and she's running toward the store. She makes it to the entrance as fat raindrops plummet from the sky. As she rushes in, her thoughts overwhelm me. The loud, unwelcome intrusion causes me to stumble back a step before figuring out how to block it.

"I'm so sorry, Emily!" she says in a hurry. "I got really wasted last night and somehow, I, like, totally lost my phone."

As she rambles on, the last few days seem to melt away like they never happened. Just like that, I feel like my life goes back to normal. I feel like Emily Burk, a regular teenager with a normal screwed up life.

"Why are you smiling?" Ashley asks.

I try to hide my grin.

"Oh my God! Something's different about you!"

My smile vanishes. How could she know? She eyes me with curiosity, trying to figure out my secret. She can't really tell, can she?

"Oh!" she gasps, throwing a hand over her mouth. "You had sex!"

"What?" I say, experiencing relief and shock simultaneously.

"You did! Look at you, you're glowing!"

"N . . . no . . ."

"Don't deny it! Who was he?" she asks, without waiting for an answer. "Ben is still out of town, isn't he? OH MY GOD! It was the other one! That perfect specimen of a man!"

I'm shaking my head, but she doesn't notice.

"Emily, come on! Spill! Tell me everything!"

"There is nothing to tell. Nothing happened."

Even as relentless as she is, I'm grateful for her interrogation. I'd much rather think of ways to dodge her questions and listen to her invent theories on my love life than to think about the real issues threatening my life. After ten minutes of denying her accusations, a customer enters the store interrupting our conversation.

Mid-afternoon the clouds let loose, and it pours. No one needs pet supplies badly enough to fight the storm, so the store remains vacant for an hour. In the meantime, Ashley drags as much information out of me as she can. I tell her about my time with Morgan and Patrick, yet she's only interested in talking about Patrick.

"So, did you at least make out?" she probes.

"No! We talked, went on a little boat ride, made s'mores, you know, stuff that friends do, nothing crazy."

"And he didn't kiss you?" She sounds utterly disbelieving.

I choose my words carefully. I don't want to lie, but if I tell her about our kiss, I'll never hear the end of it, and I still don't know how I feel about that kiss. "Ashley, I'm not sure how I feel about him. He kind of drives me crazy."

"He's supposed to drive you crazy! That's how you know you really like him," she answers emphatically, reminding me not to take relationship advice from her.

"We fight every time we try to have a conversation."

"Then stop talking! There are other things you could spend your time doing!"

"But I like Ben." I shock myself, as I say it aloud.

"You can like more than one guy," she justifies.

"I don't trust Patrick."

"It's not like you're marrying him! You don't have to trust him to have a little fun," she sighs. "Look at you. You're smitten!"

"I am not smitten!"

"Whatever you have to tell yourself. I just can't believe Patrick didn't kiss you. Of course, you probably would've given him a black eye for trying."

"You would love his car," I say, attempting to change the subject.

"So, he has a nice car, too?"

We spend the next half-hour talking about his car, and that's pretty impressive seeing how I know very little about cars. Either way, it makes her happy.

I change into jeans and a black button-down shirt before heading out the door. Ashley gives me a look of disapproval before I go, offended I didn't wear the low-cut halter top she offered. I leave work early enough to give myself time to drive to campus and meet Patrick.

I arrive on campus unsure exactly where we're meeting, so I walk toward the central courtyard. The rain has stopped, but the sky has me wishing I had brought my umbrella.

My phone vibrates in my pocket.

Pulling it out, I answer, "Hey, Dad."

"Where are you?" he asks.

"At school."

"Why?" He sounds anxious.

"I'm going to a performance for class."

"Okay," he says, as his voice settles.

"Is everything okay?" I ask as I scope out my surroundings for anything out of the ordinary.

"Everything is fine. Just wanted to make sure you're okay."

"I'm fine," I tell him. And I was fine, until this talk with him.

"Good," he says. "I wanted to let you know I'm getting on the plane soon so my phone will be off."

"Okay."

"Will you be all right at the house alone?"

"Yes, I am an adult." And I will be hiding under the covers like a little girl.

"Okay. My phone should be back on in a couple of hours. Call me if you need anything."

"Like to check my closet for the boogie man who wants to kill me. Really, Dad, I'll be fine."

"I wouldn't leave if I didn't think you were safe," he reminds me.

"I know."

"I love you, honey."

"Love you too."

After we disconnect, I see a shadow from the corner of my eye. As I turn, I flinch, realizing it's not just a shadow, but a person.

"Oh my God, Patrick!" I grab my chest, trying to calm my galloping heart.

"Didn't mean to startle you, love."

Crap! And I thought I was careful.

"You seem a bit on edge. Is everything okay?" Concern touches his eyes, and I wonder if he's trying to listen to my thoughts.

"I'm fine," I huff.

He nods as if it's an acceptable answer. "Shall we?" he asks, offering his arm.

I hesitate, so he lowers his arm and says, "All right, let's go."

The silence is heavy as we reach the edge of campus. His hand wraps tightly around mine, and before I can object, he confesses, "Just let me hold your hand, Emily. I feel better when I can touch you."

The feeling of tranquility begins trickling through my fingers, creeping up my arms, radiating through my chest until it fills every part of me. I close my eyes as the blissful serenity takes over.

Abruptly, Patrick drops my hand, ripping away the harmony like a heavy curtain pulled to reveal a blinding sun in a dark room. With the absence of Patrick's touch, anxiety fills every cell, leaving no room for peace. I am alert and on guard as my panic returns, threatening to collapse me from the weight of its resounding pain.

"Sorry, love, let's wait until you're sitting down to try that," Patrick sincerely apologizes. "You're more drained than I realized."

I nod, barely hearing him as I attempt to reject the ache in my gut. Was it this bad before? My surroundings become muffled and foggy, and I wonder if he notices I'm gripping my stomach like it might burst. I can barely keep up with his unwavering pace. The small theatre up ahead becomes a beacon. The sooner we're inside, the sooner I can sit and catch my breath.

Inside the theatre an old Hollywood theme surrounds us. The theatre floor slopes until it reaches the elevated stage. The aged wooden floor squeaks as we progress down the aisle. Rows of red velvet seats are packed tightly together like pages in a book. Patrick guides me to the back row where I fall into the plush cushioned seat. He settles beside me, sliding my hand into his. The tranquil sheet of serenity is pulled over me once more. I lean into him, lapping it up. I am distantly aware of my head resting on his shoulder, but it's too soothing to resist.

I find myself diving into the depths of a clear blue ocean, lounging in peaceful oblivion. Sleep finds me here in this sapphire abyss. The water swirls and shifts around me until all of the color fades from the ocean. I look around to see where all the bright pigment has gone, only to discover a mermaid swimming toward me in the clear water. I get lost in her cerulean eyes, unearthing all the brightness of the sea captured there. I gasp, temporarily forgetting that I can't breathe underwater. As I choke, the mythical creature before me wraps her arms around my waist, and we float toward the sun.

Once we reach dry land, the mermaid's fins become legs, and the ocean dissipates around us like a mist. The dazzling blue eyes of the mermaid belong now to a woman with long blond hair pulled into a loose braid draping over her shoulder. She looks angelic in her white flowing dress. She appears confident, but worry lines etch her face. Before I can ask who she is, she turns to look at her six-year-old child. His blond hair matches hers, and he has beautiful delicate features and long lashes surrounding dull blue eyes.

An unfamiliar room solidifies around us. Cheap frames decorate the walls while toys scatter the scratched wooden floor. A tired sofa, with torn cushions, sits in front of a small television atop a shoddy table. The only light shines through dirty, cracked windows. I look back to the woman and her son. She kneels in front of her weeping child, wipes his tears, and kisses his forehead, calming him with her soft voice.

A brawny man enters the room. He appears to be yelling, but I can't hear him. I conveniently find a remote in the palm of my hand. I tap the volume button until I hear the commotion.

He sounds frantic. "They're here! You must go! Now!"

Before the angelic woman can speak, he puts a finger to her lips and shakes his head. "Go! Now, while you can." He shifts his eyes toward the boy. "For him, you must."

She nods in understanding but is reluctant to leave. The young boy is sobbing as she picks him up, balancing him on her hip. The man shoves a backpack in her hand before kissing them both. Tears well in her eyes as the burly man envelops the woman and child, proclaiming his love for them.

"Go!" he orders.

As the woman retreats out the door, her son screams, "Daddy!"

The picture before me cracks into shattered pieces that fall to the floor. I stare at a giant humming television. The channel is scrambled. I must have lost reception, and I want to change this station. I look to my palm for the remote, but it's not there. Instead, I find my phone. I don't remember dialing anyone, but I hear it ringing. As I put the phone to my ear, I hear Patrick's voice.

"Emily." He sounds angry. I don't like when he's angry. It scares me.

"Emily," he repeats.

I open my mouth to respond, but I can't find my voice. I look over my shoulder to see a man dressed in black rushing toward me with a knife in his hand. I attempt to scream, but no sound escapes my lips. I try to run but my legs are heavy, and my coordination is all wrong as if I'm running through quicksand. The man in black is gaining on me, and the only sound I hear is the terrifying footsteps behind me.

"Emily!"

I open my eyes and jerk my head to look behind me. The man in black is gone, replaced by a dimly lit theatre. I turn back to find Patrick's dark glare upon me. Leftover tension from my dream swirls through my body. Bewildered, I straighten my shoulders trying to orient myself. People on stage are acting out a scene I don't understand. A few patrons are scattered through the theatre, but the seats close to us are vacant. I feel a nudge, and when I look up, Patrick is still glaring at me.

"Out!" he insists, pointing toward the door.

I scoot out of my seat and make my way quietly to the door with him on my heels. The sky is darker now than when we entered, and I wonder how long I was sleeping. As soon as we exit, Patrick's hand closes tight on my shoulder. He whips me around so quickly, I stumble.

"What the . . ." I start but am silenced by his clenched jaw and furious eyes. Anger shines between the cracks of his typical infallible poise.

"Your blood is poison," he breathes.

"What?" I swallow, instinctively moving away.

He grabs my wrist and drags me back toward campus. I have no idea what brought on his volatile temperament. I attempt to pull away from him as he pulls me along, but his grip is unforgiving. Finally, he brings us to a halt on an isolated path next to campus parking. He drops my wrist and looms over me, so I have to tilt my chin up to see him.

"You are Valla blood. I always thought the Olvasho exaggerated the stories of Valla's descendants, but they're true, aren't they?"

"No." My breath catches in my throat and I look away. "I don't understand what you're saying." I feign ignorance, but my heart plummets in my chest. I concentrate on keeping him out of my mind while simultaneously looking unaffected by his startling accusation.

He cups my chin in his hand and tilts my face up to his. "Look at those emerald-green eyes." His words are feather soft, almost a purr, giving the illusion of seduction, but his purr has the grace of a ravenous lion. His fingers tighten painfully on my jaw before he drops my face and turns his back to me. "That power you hold is unimaginable." He takes a leisurely step away. I think he's fighting to regain his composure. "Furthermore, your mother died five years ago," he says in a deceivingly smooth voice. "The last Valla died five years ago. I doubt that's a coincidence."

I swallow my fear allowing anger to take its place. At the same time, Patrick's veil of pristine calm slips, showing real emotion as his hands clench into fists.

"Are you going to hit me?" I take a step toward him, daring him to swing.

He pivots, and I get a glimpse of confusion before his hands relax. "Why ever would I hit you, love?" His voice is a lethal combination of sugary disgust. "If I were to hit you, well, if you are truly what they say then you would execute my entire extended family as retribution, because that's just the sort of thing Valla blood would do."

"You're acting like you don't even know me, Patrick. You just spent days combing through my head. I don't know what brought this on, but I haven't done anything to warrant this reaction!"

"Yet! You haven't done anything, yet," he says, "but you will. It's only a matter of time."

I throw my arms out to the sides. "What exactly are you accusing me of, Patrick?"

"I'm not accusing you of anything. We're simply reviewing the facts. If you're the last Valla, then you'll kill everyone you love. That's who you are. It's in your Valla nature." There is an internal struggle going on behind those eyes. "I really didn't want it to be true."

"How dare you! I am not a killer, Patrick! And I love the people in my life too much to hurt them!"

"I loved the people in my life, too," he says with sadness, looking down for a moment. When his eyes lift to mine, hatred burns in their depths. "That was the last time I saw my dad, or did you already know that?"

I've lost track of the conversation. His dad? Then it clicks, and I say, "My dream?"

"Don't play stupid!"

"I honestly don't know why you're so upset with me."

"Let me in!" He raises an eyebrow and explains, "In your head. Let me in."

"No!" I shake my head, baffled he'd even ask.

"Let me in, so I can see if you're lying."

"How stupid do you think I am? Honestly, Patrick?"

"I'll get the information regardless. I'm asking more as a courtesy than a request."

Acting out confidence I don't feel, I take a step toward him, but he doesn't back away. "I almost took you out on that boat," I remind him.

"You could've killed me in the boat, but you didn't. You should've killed me in the boat. Go ahead, try to kill me now." He steps even closer.

I want to prove I'm not weak, that I can defeat him, but then I remember him hollow and broken in the boat, and I know there is no way I would hurt him. I'm not the monster he thinks I am.

"Patrick, I'm not going to hurt you. Why would I?" I whisper at a loss, letting go of my false bravado and showing him a vulnerability, I hope I won't regret.

"Damn it!" he shouts, startling me, all swagger washed away. "You're a Valla. That's why!"

"Whatever you think you know about Valla blood is wrong! I'm not who you think I am."

"You are!"

"Fine!" As soon as the word is out of my mouth, I feel my mind open to him. I will prove to him that I am not a monster. A shiver runs down my spine. Maybe it's stupid to trust him.

"It's stupid to trust anyone," he says bitterly, already reading my thoughts.

"It can be lonely not to," I whisper.

"Why were you prying through my mind?"

"I wasn't prying. It was a dream."

He laughs as realization dawns on him. "You really don't know. I don't know what to do with you. I don't know whether to be frightened, angry, or turned on." His fingers grip through his hair as he silently deliberates. "That wasn't just a dream you had," he says, letting go of his hair and dropping his arms. "It's the last memory I have of my father."

I recall the beautiful little boy in my dream screaming for his daddy. My stomach churns as I make the connection.

Patrick continues, "That's a part of me I don't let anyone see, ever. I've worked hard to conceal that memory." He steps closer to me. "Yet you slipped right in. And you didn't even mean to. You didn't even know what you were doing."

"I'm sorry," I say, as his fingers glide over my cheek.

"Nobody but a Valla could've done what you've done to me. Twice! Nobody but a Valla has those green eyes . . ."

"Lots of people have green eyes," I say when his sentence falls, but he's not listening.

"Nobody who wants to live helps a Valla," he finishes in a whisper, dropping his head to avoid my eyes.

"I'm not a killer, Patrick.

His fingers press into my lips, his anger entirely gone, replaced by a look filled with sympathy and acceptance. "You will be."

I take a step back, offended he's calling me a killer, yet more disturbed he's speaking as if resigned to the idea like he would expect nothing less from me, a Valla blood.

"My mother died," he says suddenly.

"So, you know what it's like to lose someone you love."

"I lost everyone. My dad disappeared and my mother died in my arms." He turns his face to the dark sky.

"I'm sorry," I empathize, reliving my own painful memory. I hold my breath, waiting for him to say something, anything. I feel my future hanging in the balance.

He's perfectly still, but eventually, his blue eyes find mine, and he breaks the excruciating silence by accusing, "You don't know how dangerous you are."

"I do know, and it scares me knowing what I could become, knowing others will fear me. But nobody gets to tell me who I am! Only I decide that and all I know for sure is that I'm a human being with human blood pumping through my human veins with all of my human parts. Isn't that what you said? Anyone can be dangerous given the right circumstances. I don't want to be a monster like the people who hunted my mom or the dozens before her just because of a name. Those who hunt and kill us are evil, yet they label us as the demon spawn. How do they justify slaughtering innocent lives because of a label they invented?"

He winces.

"I am Emily Burk, and the only thing you do by adding Valla to my name is put me in danger." My emotions come bubbling to the surface, and I turn to leave before I cry in front of him. I head back toward the parking lot.

"You can't walk away from me! Especially now!"

I stop mid-stride and turn. "Why? My instincts were right! You are trouble. I knew it the second I laid eyes on you."

"I'm your best chance. I can protect you."

"You think I'm a killer!" I throw my hands out. "Why would I trust you, Patrick?"

He steps forward. "Have I done anything to harm you? I've done nothing but help you, love. I even gambled my life to help you discover who you are. Does that sound like someone who wants to hurt you?"

I recall the boat ride, the night around the fire and the closeness. He held me together when I was falling apart, yet I don't think it's enough.

"I don't want your help, Patrick."

"You do if you want to remain yourself."

"What does that even mean? No, you know, I'm fine. You should walk away. Protect yourself. I'm dangerous! Remember?" I turn away and begin walking in the direction of my car.

"I'm not leaving," he says, only a few steps behind.

"You said yourself, those who help Valla blood end up dead." I remind him, without looking back.

"Emily, if you don't stop them, they will kill you."

"I know!" I shout, spinning around. "I've read the list of death! But I don't see any attainable solution other than hiding, which I was doing a damn good job of before you strolled into town! So what do you expect me to do? Call said individuals hell-bent on killing me and say hey, please stop slaughtering my bloodline. We're not monsters, and we don't actually have demon blood."

"You're being juvenile, and besides, there's no reasoning with them. The only way to stop them is to kill them."

"So that's it? Kill or be killed. Those are my only options?"

"It might not be tonight or tomorrow, but if you don't stop them by force then someday they will track you down."

Carefully, I step closer to him. "How do you know?"

His fingers tangle in his already knotted hair. "I know more than I should."

"How?"

"My mom worked for them."

My heart stops. "What?"

"They're the reason she's dead."

Once my heart starts back up and I remember how to breathe, I ask, "Do you work with them? These monsters!"

He drags his hands down his face and shakes his head. "How could you even think . . ." He releases a breath and his eyes connect with mine. "When my mom realized what was really going on, she went rogue, and they murdered her for it. They also abducted my father and, in all likelihood, eliminated him too. How could you think I'd work with them, Emily? Do you think I'd let anyone use me?"

"I have no idea what you're capable of."

"That's an insult. You know me, Emily." He reaches for me, but I take a step back.

"What else are you keeping from me, Patrick?"

"I'm not keeping anything from you. I usually don't discuss my past because it's irrelevant and nobody needs to hear another sob story. Your denial is what's making this more difficult. Those monsters who killed your mother are aware of your existence. They are searching for you, Emily. It's only a matter of time before they find you."

The hairs on the back of my neck stand on end as a chill travels through my body.

"Let me protect you," he pleads, taking advantage of my temporary paralysis by moving closer until he's standing right in front of me.

I look up into those beautiful, sad eyes of his. "We are not friends, Patrick. Look at us; we spend most of our time fighting and the rest of the time, we're . . . er . . ."

He tilts my chin up and his lips fall on mine. It's a loaded kiss like he's trying to make me understand. I don't like the possessive undertone as he holds me to him. I push away mid-kiss and lower my head onto his chest. He thinks he needs me. I felt it in his kiss, I hear it in his mind, and I see it in the wounded expression he wears. I find my emerald eyes reflected in his. My eyes may as well be demon-red because they give me away, screaming, I am Valla, the last of the "demon blood."

He thinks he can protect me and maybe he can, but Patrick is a conundrum to me. His Jekyll and Hyde act is too hard for me to follow. His intensity is scary even when he's being sweet. He muddles my thoughts and stirs things up in me, but the idea of needing him in any capacity is too much. I may trust Patrick enough not to hurt me, but I can't afford to need him. Dad, on the other hand, has always had my back and kept me safe.

"Please, Patrick, I need you to leave me alone," I whisper. I move away before I lose the tears I'm holding back.

"I can't," he says with an ache in his voice. "You're Valla—"

"Isn't that enough reason to leave me alone?" I say over my shoulder.

He catches my wrist. "I'll keep you safe. You can trust me."

I look down at his hand on my wrist. "Then. Let. Go."

He releases me, appearing genuinely betrayed.

I jump in my car, shove the key in the ignition, and throw the car into drive. I maneuver out of the parking lot and press the gas pedal to the floor. My car shoots forward only for me to slam on my breaks at a red light. My eyes fill to the brim with unshed tears, and I want to be as far away from him as possible before they spill over the edge. Rain sprinkles down on my windshield, and that's all it takes for the warm droplets to trickle down my face. I ignore them and clench my jaw tighter. I am not ready to fall apart. Not yet.

The light turns green and I floor it. I speed through the next set of lights, turn the corner to get onto the highway and merge into traffic. Rain falls heavily from the dark sky, and I flip on my windshield wipers. Even with the relief from the wipers, the road appears blurry through my tears. I wipe at my eyes with no relief as new tears continue to rain down my face. The dam that held them back for the past five years has collapsed, and now there's no stopping the flood.

Merging again, I take the next exit. With trembling hands, I pull into an empty gravel lot and turn off the engine. I sit and listen to the rain beating against the car roof. I droop over the steering wheel and sob.

My body convulses with each vibrating breath. Tears soak my lap as fear takes hold, crawling over my skin to burrow into the marrow of my bones. The only time I cried this hard was when my mom died, and that experience landed me in a psych ward. My tears increase as my mind unwillingly wanders down memory lane.

It feels like hours pass before I calm myself enough to be rational. The tears have subsided, but the pain lingers. I turn the key in the ignition, but my car refuses to come to life. I try it again with the same result. I check to make sure the vehicle is in park. I know I'm not out of gas. I try to start the car one more time and get nothing.

Unbelievable!

seventeen ~

It's eleven o'clock and I'm stranded. Dad should be in New York by now, but when I call his cell phone it goes straight to voicemail, so I leave him a message about my car breaking down. I contemplate who else to call. My sister is at the beach with Dan. Morgan is working at the hospital. Ben is in Florida until Friday. Oh wait, today is Friday. He said he had a late flight, but maybe . . . I already have my phone to my ear before I know I've made the decision.

"Hey," Ben answers on the second ring.

"Umm. Hi." My voice is hoarse.

"What's wrong?"

I clear my throat. "My car won't start."

"Where are you?"

I look around without seeing anything familiar. So stupid, I can't even tell him where I am. "Umm, an exit off the highway. There's a shady gas station and an old mattress factory."

"Okay, I'll be there in a few minutes," he says, before hanging up.

I can't believe he knows where I am, but I'm relieved he's on his way. He didn't even comment on the fact that my car is dead.

I drop the phone in my lap wishing I could forget the last week, wishing for it to simply fade away like a bad dream. Maybe ignorance is bliss. I close my eyes, but my mom's death is beneath my eyelids, her whisper is in my ear, and her kiss on my forehead. I open my eyes with a gasp. My heart sinks and my breath staggers. I don't want to see or relive these memories. The tears return and soon I'm sobbing all over again.

The buzzing phone pulls me back to the present. Ben's face lights up the small screen. I don't want him to find me like this, so I toss it onto the passenger seat and let it ring. I clear my tears and straighten in my seat. My sobs soften, barely audible above the torrential downpour.

Headlights pull into the gravel lot and shine through my windshield. When the lights turn off, I see Ben's face behind the steering wheel. I lose all composure, buckling into myself, crying like a little girl.

Ben is out of his car attempting to get my passenger-side door open. There is no handle, so he knocks on the window, the heavy rain already weaving through his dark hair. It drips down his handsome face and has already soaked his t-shirt. I reach to open the door, but he's already crawling into the back seat.

"Damn door," he mumbles, as his muscular body settles onto the worn leather of my back seat. He closes the door and leans forward to study me closely.

Embarrassed he's seeing me like this, I turn my head toward the windshield. My hair becomes a curtain to shield me from his inquiring eyes.

Leaning forward over the console, squeezing up next to me, he brushes my hair aside. He gently whispers, "Emily? What can I do?"

I shake my head as my voice catches in my throat. "I just wanna go home."

I unbuckle my seat belt, determined to go, but his hand catches my wrist before I reach the handle.

"Emily?" he says, his words a caress. He watches me for a moment before taking a deep breath. He reaches both arms under my body and effortlessly lifts me into the back seat next to him.

His hand grazes my cheek, sliding down my jaw to tilt my chin up. I forget I'm upset. The only thing that matters now is Ben and his warm brown eyes welcoming me into his soul.

"Thanks for coming," I whisper, placing my hand on his knee, greedy for the intimacy of another person. No, not just another person. I'm greedy for him.

Noticing my hand on his knee, he whispers, "I'm happy to be back."

"You don't look happy. I'm sorry to drag you out here."

His hand covers mine. "Why are you sorry? You have nothing to be sorry for. I was only gone a week, Em. What the hell happened to you?"

I shake my head, unsure how to explain.

His thumb strokes the back of my hand and I adore his soft touch on my skin. The electric sensation trickles through me. He rests his forehead against mine and the closeness makes it impossible to think. I fall into him. He gathers my body against his chest and his warmth is overwhelming. I feel his breath exhale as he presses soft kisses against my head. I snuggle into him and hear the thrumming of his heartbeat. His powerful arms hold me close, and I get the bizarre and beautiful sense of home.

"Ben," I whisper.

He lifts his head and pulls away from me. I lose my words feeling the cool wetness of my shirt for the first time without the presence of his heat.

His jaw clenches as he averts his gaze to the dark window. "I know you're seeing him," he says, in a low growl. "I just . . . I can't." He rubs a hand over his forehead before covering his mouth in frustration.

"Seeing who? You mean Patrick?" His eyes shift, so I assume I'm right. "I'm not seeing him. At least not for the reason you think."

I don't know how he knew. I want to tell him everything, but how can I possibly explain.

"Ben, I missed you. It's probably not right how much I missed you. I don't want you to leave me again." My palm caresses his cheek stubble. His eyes close at my touch. My heart flutters as his hand cups mine and pulls it to his lips. He's struggling for control right along with me.

My chest heaves and the words gush forward, "Ben, you're my best friend and me . . . I have so many problems, and you know I'm not good enough for you—"

"Emily, that's ridiculous. I love you exactly as you are."

The significance behind his words and his gentle smile have me tossing all of my reservations out the window. I feel the urgency build between us and can't hold back any longer. I slide my hand around the back of his neck just as his supple lips press into mine. One of his hands glides down to the small of my back while his other finds the nape of my neck. His fingers weave into my hair as his tongue caresses every part of my mouth, pushing me to the edge, and a moan escapes my lips. He responds with a growl while his fingers grip me tighter as his restraint slips away. We mold our bodies together as our mouths move in harmony. The tender passion grows desperate and frenzied, feeling undeniably right.

He pulls away to trail kisses down my neck, and I forget to breathe. My hands caress his broad shoulders, gliding along defined arms, and wrapping around his muscular back. Any semblance of control I once had is now entirely gone. In its place is a living, breathing fire responding directly to Ben's actions.

As his tongue lingers on my neck, the inferno grows hotter, my breathing more rapid, and my urge to feel more of him consumes me. Desire overwhelms my senses, enhancing every touch, every sound. Wanting him desperately, I push my fingers under the rim of his shirt greedy to feel his skin. I run my hands up his spine exploring the smooth contours.

He pivots me so gently that I'm barely aware we've moved until I feel the cool leather against my back. His body rests against mine with his arms supporting his weight. Our passionate kisses continue. Lost in my desire to feel as much skin as possible, I tug his shirt up.

His lips stop moving and he rests his forehead against mine. I urge him to continue, but he doesn't budge.

With a deep sigh, he says, "This is wrong. I've wanted you for so long. But not like this."

The fear of his rejection extinguishes the inferno building inside me. I drop my hands. "How can you say this is wrong? Isn't this what you want?"

He lifts his head to look at me. "Yeah, but do you?"

When I don't respond, he lowers his mouth to whisper in my ear, "I'm in love with you, Emily Burk. I think I have been since seventh grade. Don't try to hide from me. Talk to me."

"You're not allowed to be in love with me. You can't."

"Yeah, Emily, I'm pretty sure I can and why wouldn't I be? You're brave and beautiful, resilient and selfless, and God you make me laugh. You think you're broken because of all the terrible things that have happened to you, but you're wrong. They've made you softer and stronger at the same time. You have a depth that most people can't comprehend, let alone possess. And I wouldn't have you any other way. To me, you are perfect."

With his face just inches from mine, I'm lost in his sincere dark eyes. My arms twist around his neck and I press my lips to his. I kiss him eagerly, and he returns my kiss just as amorously while pressing his body into mine. I tug his rain-soaked shirt up, and thank God; he doesn't fight me this time. His face separates from mine as he whips it over his head and immediately his lips return to mine.

The feel of our skin touching sends searing desire through me. Temptation boils as my fingers graze the top of his boxers peeking out of his khakis. I've never done anything like this before, but I want him so completely. I reach for the button on his shorts.

"No," he repeats in a rough whisper. "Not like this."

"Why are you stopping?"

"Because the last we spoke you said you only wanted to be friends and you're clearly upset about something." He brushes the hair off my cheek. "I want you to be sure. And I don't want to do this in a car."

"I *am* sure. I want you, Ben. I can't think of anything I want more."

"God Em, you're killin' me! I've gotta move now before I can't," he says, without moving.

"Just to be clear, you're turning me down?"

"I'm not turning you down. I'm postponing."

"But why?"

"Because you just spent every day for the last five years pushing me away, so I need to know this isn't just a reaction to whatever has you so upset."

"I get it. I just don't like it."

"I don't like it either," he says, kissing the tip of my nose. "I've gotta move now."

"You said that already."

He shakes his head, "It's harder than I thought it'd be."

"That's what she said."

He laughs as he shifts his weight, letting me free of his restraint as he sits up. "Did you really just make a that's what she said joke?"

"Sure did, Mr. Sexy-pants."

He bites his lip and offers me his hand. He pulls me up so I'm sitting with my knees bridged across his lap and my head on his shoulder.

"Oh no!" I groan. "I think you might be my white knight."

He laughs aloud, startling me.

"What?" I question seriously, but the contagion of his laugh spreads a smile across my face.

"No offense Em, but you're not the type to be rescued."

"Offense taken," I say, although I'm not sure why it offends me. Hadn't I been the one to say that to Patrick just yesterday? "I made you drive out here in the middle of the night to come and get me."

"Yeah and I'll always come, but you'll never be the damsel in distress waiting on prince charming to rescue you. If I showed up here tonight professing to be your knight in shining armor, you'd be walking home in the middle of this thunderstorm."

"You might be right." I shrug as my hand caresses his exposed chest. "You have a nice tan. You must have spent the whole trip on the beach avoiding your family."

"Molly and I spent a lot of time on the beach together. At least our parents are fighting now instead of pretending everything's okay."

I take in the new information, leaving the patter of rain to fill the silence between us.

Ben breaks the quiet with a hesitant question. "Em, how did you end up here in the middle of the night?"

My face falls as I think back on everything that's happened in the last week.

Ben continues, "You don't need to explain. I've just never seen you so upset. At least not since . . . well, you know."

"Ben, I want to tell you, but it's complicated, and I'm afraid you'll think I'm, umm . . . You might not want to see me anymore. In fact, you really should get back in your car and drive away now to save yourself the trouble."

"That's not gonna happen."

After seeing his determination, I ask, "What do you know about my mom?"

His body freezes because he knows this topic is forbidden. The last time he spoke of my mom, I ran.

I continue when he doesn't say anything. "She started hearing voices and acting strange, so my dad committed her, and three years later she killed herself."

"I've heard the stories. I've just never heard you talk about her."

"My mom wasn't crazy. I . . . Eh . . ." He waits patiently, and when I gather my thoughts and pull my head up to speak, my words disappear. His beautiful, caring, chocolate eyes are desperate for the truth—a truth that would pull him into my chaotic world and lock him into a dark secret.

"Emily, you can talk to me."

I shake my head. "As much as I want to tell you, it wouldn't be right." A tear escapes the rim of my eye, betraying me. "I can't do this to you."

Ben follows the tear as it trickles down my cheek. "You can," he encourages.

I want to believe him. I want to wrap my arms around him and never let go, but I don't want him to suffer the way my dad suffered because of my mom. Defeat settles in, finding a home in my heart.

"Emily, look at me."

I lift my head and before I can interpret his look, his lips crash into mine. I don't think. I respond, kissing him back with everything I have. My arms snake around him as he twines his hands through my hair. His body presses into mine. I remind myself to breathe when his lips break away. I arch into him, my head falling back as his tongue lingers on my neck. He places tantalizing kisses down to my throat and my nails grip the contours of his back as he teases his way to my cleavage.

Ben's fingers find the top button on my shirt. He pauses as if asking for permission.

"Please," I moan, needing to feel more of him against me.

His hands make quick work of unfastening my top. I bite my lip nervously when he pulls away to study the progress. His sensual look sends goosebumps over my skin and my heart feels like it's going to gallop right out of my chest. His lips find mine and his breathing is just as erratic as my own.

"Emily," Patrick whispers in my head.

I gasp, frozen by the intrusion. Ben pulls away. He doesn't say anything, but he knows something's wrong.

"Damn it, Patrick! Get out of my head!" I scream internally, while Ben waits patiently for me to make the next move. I cradle Ben's face in my hands before lifting my lips up to kiss him.

"Think about what this will mean for him," Patrick echoes in my ear.

Talk about killing the mood. I want to ignore Patrick's warning, but he brings reasoning back to my incoherent thoughts. If I love Ben, I should let him go, but I don't want to let him go. I want to be naive and young, and I want him to keep kissing me into a blissful ignorance.

The only sound inside the car is our ragged breathing. Even the drumming of rain against the roof has slowed. I quiet my breath, quiet my anger, quiet the boiling lust of the moment, but when all is calm, I hear Ben's thoughts. It's a low rumbling noise, a tangled network of ideas too interwoven to comprehend. Like a jumbled ball of yarn, it would take time to unravel and separate each strand. I open my eyes and all at once the strings unravel and his thoughts come together as one.

"I pushed her too far. She's gonna run," Ben thinks. In his mind, he doesn't see me as broken at all. He thinks I'm strong, capable, and in a way, he sees me as his white knight. He believes I've already saved him somehow, but he's blind to the potential devastation.

I like knowing what he's thinking, but it's an intimate invasion of privacy, so I pry my mind away from his. After touching his thoughts, I don't know how I'm supposed to leave him. I should run so he'll be safe. I know I should. But I can't. I won't. Instead of listening to the unappealing logic, I follow my heart.

"Ben," I whisper, tenderly touching his face. "I'm sorry. You're wrong. I'm selfish. I'm selfish enough to drag you into my mess of a life and I don't want to let you go."

"Good." He gives me a little smile.

"Will you take me home?"

He nods, hovering above me. He lowers his face and kisses my neck one last time, inhaling deeply before he moves away.

The rain has dwindled to a drizzle. It may be the only chance we get before the downpour begins again, so we collect my things and head to Ben's Corvette. As Ben buckles his seatbelt, he catches me watching. Beneath thick lashes, his eyes are smoldering. I pull him in for a simple kiss that quickly becomes heated. When our lips separate, Ben throws the car in gear and the tires spin in the gravel.

I ask, "Do you think my car will be okay here?"

"Yeah, I'll come back in the morning to work on her."

"I can only imagine how excited you'll be if she gets stolen."

"Any other time you'd be right, but after tonight I have a whole new appreciation for that beautiful hunk of scrap metal."

"Of course you'd start appreciating her after she breaks down."

"Are you sure you need to go home?" Ben asks.

"Yeah, my dad's out of town, so I need to let Maggie out."

"We can swing by and let her out, or you can bring her with you to my house."

"Your house? And where exactly would we put Maggie in this car?" I look around the tiny Corvette.

He shrugs. "It was just an idea."

"Or, you could stay with me," I say, surprising both of us.

eighteen ~

It's a quiet fifteen-minute ride to my house. I find myself wondering if Patrick is near. Is he stalking me? Shifting from mind to mind until he locates me? Or did he ever really leave my mind? I don't sense his presence. I can't hear his thoughts, but it's unsettling to know he's been keeping tabs.

The rain picks back up as we make our way to my front door. I shuffle for my keys before finding the one I need. I open the door to Maggie's warm welcome into the dark room. I flip the switch. With a quick pop, the lightbulb flashes and the room goes dark. I'm tempted to call it an omen and walk right back out the door, but I push the fear aside and write it off as a fluke. I tread carefully through the darkness to the lamp on the side table. I flip the switch and dim light floods the room.

I sigh, glancing around. It looks just how I left it. No one is crouched in a corner waiting to pounce. As soon as the tension begins to fade, I feel a sudden vibration and let out a small squeal. Ben suppresses his laughter as I reach into my pocket for my phone.

"Hey, Dad," I say.

"My flight was delayed, and my phone was acting up. Are you okay? What happened to your car?"

"I'm fine," I assure him. "On my way home, my car broke down and Ben came to pick me up."

"Ben? What happened to Patrick? Weren't you meeting him tonight?"

"Yeah, I met him, but I left early."

"Are you okay?"

It's such an open-ended question, and I don't know how to answer honestly. I'm not okay, not in the slightest. "Umm," I hold a finger up to Ben, motioning that I'll be just a minute. I venture down the hall into my bedroom, flipping on the light.

"Dad, Patrick knows." I shut the door behind me. "I didn't tell him, but I accidentally got in his head and saw things I wasn't supposed to see. He was so angry. He knows I'm Valla blood. He said my green eyes should've given me away." He's quiet on the other end of the phone, and I try to wait for him to tell me what to do, but his silence is deafening. "Dad?"

"What exactly did Patrick say?"

I do my best to explain our conversation; from Patrick's sleek anger to his accusation that I'm a killer, to his mother's involvement and death, and his father's disappearance. I tell him about Patrick's offer to help protect me even knowing I'm the last Valla blood. The only thing I omit is the kiss.

Dad sighs. "It's my fault. I should've prepared you. I just wanted you to have as much of a normal life as possible."

"What do I do, Dad?"

"Where is he now?"

"I told him to back off and leave me alone."

"What?" He sounds bewildered. "He knows who you are. He knows the danger. He offered to protect you and you told him to leave you alone?"

"Yeah! Dad, he said I'm a killer! He seemed to accept me as this murderous monster. You said most people didn't know I exist. He definitely knows. How can I trust him?"

"Well, it's better to keep him close. I wonder what he was thinking. Was his offer sincere? Did you check his thoughts?"

I hesitate to answer, realizing I don't know Patrick's true intentions, but feeling his emotions during our kiss, I don't think he plans to harm me.

"I'll take that as a no," Dad says, breaking the silence.

"I don't think he'll hurt me. I'm pretty sure his offer was sincere, but Dad—"

"Does Ben know what's going on?"

"No." I close my eyes as guilt weighs on me.

"Keep it that way. I'll be home as soon as I can. I'll have to look at flight times, but I should be back by tomorrow afternoon at the latest. If you ever need something and you can't reach me, call my office and Chris will take care of you." With a worried sigh, he asks, "Where are you right now?"

"At home."

"Make sure all the windows are locked, please."

His comment is unsettling. I can't remember the last time I opened my windows and last night I made perfectly sure they were bolted shut. I walk away from my windows feeling like someone might be watching me.

"The windows are fine, Dad," I say, unwilling to make myself an easier target. I sneak up beside one of the windows and quickly pull the curtain closed.

"Okay, I love you, Emily. I'll call you in the morning. And just so you know, Olvasho usually have blue eyes and light hair. While the Isa and Leona bloodlines produce male and female offspring, the Valla bloodline is strictly female. Green eyes are a common trait for Valla lineage. I suppose your hair will begin to lighten now that your abilities have arrived." He sighs. "I'll make sure I don't miss your next call."

I hang up and lean against my bedroom door pondering my newest discovery. I look at the ends of my dull blondish-brown hair. It's a fraction lighter, but I blame that on the sun. I glare at my windows, feeling unsafe. I hate feeling vulnerable in my own home. I turn off the light and spin around to leave my room.

I find Ben leaning against the back of the sofa. I slip my phone back into my pocket as I walk to him.

"I'd rather not stay here tonight," I whisper.

"You don't have to. You can stay with me."

"What about your parents?"

"They have their own wing of the house. They won't even know you're there."

"You sure it's okay?"

"You go get your things. I'll let Maggie out," he says.

Feeling safer knowing I won't be staying here tonight, I flip on the light as I reenter my room. I head straight for my closet, unbuttoning my wet shirt on the way. I pull a dry one from its hanger as I let my shirt fall from my shoulders. I'm about to drop it in the hamper when I notice movement across the room. I spin to find a lean figure lying across my bed with his hands tucked casually under his head. I pull my shirt across my chest to cover my bra.

"Patrick, what are you doing here?"

"Admiring the view," he says, unabashed.

"Get out!"

He moves to sit on the side of the bed untouched by my anger. "You're beautiful, but I suppose you know that." He stands and takes a few steps forward. "That boy can't protect you, but I suppose you know that, too." His words are bitter as he comes toe to toe with me. "I don't understand why you're angry with me.

I'm the only one who seems to value your life what with your dad leaving you untrained and alone and you being careless in a moment of lust."

He reaches around me to pluck my phone from my back pocket. While he's fidgeting with my phone, I attempt to pry into his mind to read his intentions. He shoots me an intrigued look, and when I fail to get in, he laughs at my failure.

"You do a better job in your sleep," he coos with delight. "You're trying to force it. You have to let it come naturally, love."

"First you stalk me, then you break into my house, and now you're giving me advice? I'm supposed to be this big, bad, ugly monster, but I can't do a single thing right."

"I wasn't stalking you. I wasn't even nearby when out of nowhere your thoughts assaulted me. Tell me, love, why is it when you're making out with someone else, your thoughts reach for me?"

"You're a liar!"

"Am I?"

I take a deep breath to rein in my anger. "How far away do I have to be for my thoughts to be my own?"

A smile crawls across his face. "You don't want my answer."

"Patrick!"

"Thirty feet is my normal reach to get into someone's mind. Apparently, your reach far exceeds my own. It's probably a Valla thing." He hands me my phone and leans forward. "Go ahead, ask me. Ask me where I was."

"I'm not playing this game, Patrick."

"Twenty miles, Emily! I was at my uncle's when you reached for me."

I don't know whether or not to believe him. "I never reached for you, Patrick. You weren't even a whisper in my subconscious and that kills you, doesn't it?"

"What kills me is watching you make a fool out of yourself. At some point, you're going to realize your boyfriend and your dad can't help you. Call me. I won't be far, but in the meantime keep your thoughts to yourself." He looks toward the door right before Ben walks around the corner.

Patrick is standing too close to me while I hold my shirt across my chest. Ben's look of confusion turns to anger. He stands a little taller, making his already broad shoulders more daunting. Patrick is unaffected and leans in to kiss my cheek. Furious, I want to slap him, but he's to the door before I can pull my thoughts together. Watching me closely, Ben parks a hand on Patrick's chest halting him from leaving. It would intimidate anyone else, but Patrick just cocks an eyebrow.

"Em?" Ben questions, as he stands toe to toe with Patrick.

"Patrick," I say into his mind. *"I'm not a monster."*

"It's not me you need to convince," he responds into my thoughts. *"But you're a Valla. You'll never be safe, especially when you're being . . ."* his eyes flick to Ben, *"careless."*

His tone is cold as he speaks aloud, "When you change your mind, you have my number."

Ben is fuming as he blocks Patrick's way.

"Let him go," I say, avoiding the potential fight.

Patrick snickers. Ben gives me an incredulous look but reluctantly moves to the side.

"As if he had a choice," Patrick says, voice full of arrogance as he walks out.

I feel Ben's disapproval, but I don't want to know what he's thinking right now.

"Are you okay?" he asks.

I nod.

"Do you want me to give you a minute to change?"

I nod again, so he closes the door behind him. I throw on a new shirt before packing a few things in a bag and heading out to meet Ben. I say goodbye to Maggie and we're out the door.

Once we're back in Ben's car, he asks, "What the hell was that?"

"What, Patrick?"

"Yeah Patrick. What's with Patrick? How did he . . . when did he—why was he at your house?"

"I don't know. He doesn't have any boundaries."

"I'll take care of that," he offers, sounding more than a little eager.

"No, I'm sure Morgan wouldn't like that."

"Morgan thinks something is going on between you and Patrick, and I can see why."

"What?"

"Well, what was that back there?"

"It's complicated."

"Complicated my ass! Something is off about him," he spits, barely containing his anger.

"Ben, please, can we not talk about this right now. I'm exhausted and just want this day to end."

He falls silent with a frustrated sigh.

We pull into Ben's gigantic garage a few minutes later. I'm still worried we'll run into Ben's parents, but instead of walking through the stadium size foyer, we go down a simple spiral staircase. Once we reach the bottom, we walk down a hallway lined with closed doors and take one that leads into the family room outside of Ben's bedroom. We enter his room without seeing anyone. I set my bag down on the floor as he closes the door.

I'm instantly nervous. I know our relationship has changed, but I don't know where to go from here. I feel completely drained from the day and suppress the urge to cry.

"You never told me what was wrong," Ben says, cocooning my face in his hands.

I'm relieved he left his anger in the car. "Can we talk about it in the morning? I'm exhausted."

"In the morning then," he agrees, pulling me into his chest where I willingly surrender. He guides us toward the bed. Our eyes lock and I'm faced with the intensity of his desire. It's more than just his look; it's an aura surrounding him. I remind myself the closer I get to him, the more it's going to hurt when it all falls apart, but as he leans in for a kiss, I quickly abandon my logic.

We collapse onto his king-sized bed. Hands frantic with impatience, we race to undress each other breathless with desire when we are interrupted by a knock on the door.

"Damn it," Ben breathes, as we gather ourselves and straighten our clothing.

"Should I hide?" I whisper, smoothing my wayward hair.

He grins before going to his door. "No, just stay there."

As soon as Ben turns the knob, the door flies open, and he stumbles back. Max, the oversized puppy, bounds through the door eager for my attention. I rub his head as saliva dribbles from his mouth.

A teenage girl with dark ringlet curls hanging past her shoulders stands in the doorway. I recognize Ben's fifteen-year-old sister, Molly, from her photos. She's petite and shares Ben's beautiful tan skin and big chocolate colored eyes, but Ben has never given me the cold glare she's sending me now. She crosses her arms and tilts her hip, openly appraising me. I feel insulted and self-conscious. Ben pulls Molly into the room and shuts the door behind her.

"What do you want?" Ben says with irritation.

She looks insulted by his tone. "I don't know," she huffs. "Max was going crazy. I thought he needed to go outside, but he ran to your room." She looks back at me. "Maybe because you have company," she says in a snobby voice. "So, what's she doing here?" she asks as if I'm not right in front of her. "Doesn't she have a boyfriend?"

"Emily is staying here tonight," he says.

She continues to glare at me like I'm something disgusting she found on her shoe. "Is she really worth it?"

"Molly!" Ben scolds.

I look to Max who is drooling and wagging his tail oblivious to the confrontation.

"Just sayin', how many times does she have to screw you over before you get it?"

"Get out!" Ben demands, opening the door for her.

She looks shocked. "Somebody has to look out for you," she tells him.

"Get. Out."

"Whatever, I still think you're better off with Natalia. Max!" she calls, but the dog doesn't move from my side. Molly glares at me as if it's my fault.

"Come!" she demands, but the dog doesn't budge.

"Go," I whisper, and the dog turns to follow her.

Ben closes the door and comes to sit next to me on the bed. "Sorry, my sister is kind of a bitch."

"She's a fifteen-year-old girl who's trying to look out for her brother," I say, brushing it off.

"I don't need my little sister looking out for me." He leans into me playfully.

I sigh, "Everybody needs somebody. Anyway, I really need to get some sleep. I'm supposed to work tomorrow. Where should I sleep?"

He looks puzzled and says, "The bed." He must sense my reluctance, because he adds, "I'll sleep on the couch." He motions to the opposite side of the room.

"I doubt you'll fit; besides, I'm not taking your bed. I'll sleep on the couch." I grab my bag and walk into the luxurious bathroom. "I'm off to the spa."

He gives me a weak laugh as I close the door between us, feeling second-rate. As Molly so eloquently pointed out I've complicated Ben's life. With girls lining up to be with him, I feel stupid for not realizing there might be someone else, someone better.

When I come out of the bathroom, I'm ready for bed in my t-shirt and shorts. Ben has the sofa pulled out into a bed. He's changed too, although, stripped is more accurate. He's wearing only gym shorts and I can't help but smile.

Catching my smile, he says, "I usually sleep naked, but I figured that wasn't an option."

"Sorry to put you out."

He keeps his distance from me while I move to the sofa bed. I lift the covers and slide between the sheets. I expected to feel the bars going through my back like other pullout mattresses, but it feels like a real bed, comfier than my own. Maybe money can't buy happiness, but it sure can buy comfort.

Ben is watching with a curious grin from across the room. "I'll turn the lights off so you can sleep," he says, and a second later the room is dark, apart from the glow from the open bathroom. "I'm going to get ready for bed."

I nod, unsure if he can see me.

Darkness floods the room as he closes the door between us. I burrow into the blankets, close my eyes, and allow my mind to wander. I worry about Dad's trip, Patrick's accusations, and I'm nervous about work tomorrow. Will it be just another day, or will it be the day they find me?

By the time Ben comes out of the bathroom, I have myself so worked up; sleep is the last thing on my mind. He leaves the door cracked, providing a dim light to permeate the room. Ben climbs in his bed and I realize I should've stayed home. At least then I wouldn't be putting him in danger.

When I finally start to doze off, I see my mom's face with the trickle of blood dripping from her lips. My eyes fly open and once again sleep is a million miles away. The clock on Ben's nightstand tells me it's already two o'clock in the morning. I stare up at the dark ceiling as a few of the stupid commercial jingles pop into my head. At first, they remind me of Patrick, but soon I'm thinking of Ben. He was my secret weapon against Patrick. Maybe I wasn't so blind to him over the years. Perhaps these feelings were there the whole time. I used self-preservation as a shield to protect my already ravaged heart against everyone, including Ben.

"Ben?" I whisper into the silence.

"Yeah?"

"Patrick is just a friend," I say, wondering if I can qualify him as a friend.

"I know," he sighs.

It's silent for a while and I wonder if he's sleeping.

"Ignore Molly. She is a brat."

"A brat that's looking out for you."

"So she thinks."

"So, who's Natalia?" I ask.

"Nobody. I thought you were tired."

"I was."

"And now?" he probes.

"I have too much going through my head."

"You sure you don't wanna talk about it?"

"Yeah, I'm sure."

Silence ensues, so I go back to thinking about the commercial that Ben and I made fun of before everything changed. I remember laughing so hard my stomach hurt. I missed him so much while he was gone. Now he lies just a short distance away and I still miss him.

"Ben?" I whisper.

"Yeah?"

"Never mind," I mumble, chickening out.

"What?"

"Nothing, it's stupid."

"Tell me anyway."

"Umm, would you . . . Uh . . . mind if I uh, come lie with you?"

There's a brief pause before he says, "Of course not. Come over here."

I shuffle across the plush carpet. He lifts the comforter and I slip into bed beside him. He wraps his arms around me, pulling me into his warmth, and I let myself enjoy the solace of his touch. I bury my face in his chest feeling small in his big arms. Exhaustion washes over me as his fingers glide up and down my spine. It's soothing and the last thing I remember before drifting into a deep sleep.

nineteen ~

I have a vivid dream where I walk my pet panther on a leash like a dog. I can't understand why people are afraid. It's just a sweet little kitten until I realize it's not and the beast breaks its chain and pounces on a young girl with light brown hair. The panther disappears as a classroom manifests around us.

I find the girl unharmed and huddled in a ball on the floor. I comfort her, but when the girl looks up at me, I'm shocked to see my own face on the frightened younger version of myself.

Realizing I'm not seeing from my own eyes, I look to my hands, my arms, and down my body. I'm a boy, but not just any boy. I'm seeing from Ben's perspective. He was there when I collapsed in seventh grade. Ben watches the younger version of myself lying helpless on the floor. Commotion rises around him and Ben tells his neighbor to shut up. He stares at young Emily until she looks up at him with her pale green eyes. She cries out in excruciating pain, and Ben wants to help but doesn't know how.

The teacher covers part of his view before looking up at him, "Benjamin! Go get Mrs. Henson from next door!"

Not wasting time, he rushes through the crowd, pushing other students out of his way. He darts into the hall and barrels through the door into Mrs. Henson's classroom.

The classroom disappears and time skips forward. The paramedics roll twelve-year-old Emily out on a stretcher. Feeling anxious and worried, Ben lingers in the entrance wanting to follow the men wheeling her away.

Time passes until Ben stands outside in the cold breeze watching the ambulance at the curb. He hurts for the girl in the back of the vehicle. He watches tears flow down Emily's cheeks as she sits in the ambulance with the paramedics. When she notices Ben, she wipes the tears away, failing to look anything but miserable. The teacher puts her hand on Ben's shoulder and guides him back inside.

While sitting in class, Ben hears a rumor that Emily was released to the school nurse instead of being taken to the hospital. Asking permission to go to the restroom, he grabs the hall pass on his way out of class. A white door appears in front of Ben. He's nervous about opening it, and when he finally does, he finds Emily sitting in the nurse's office. She's holding her head down in her hands, her hair hiding her face. She looks up startled as she hears Ben's shoe scuff the floor.

"Hey," Ben says.

"Hey." Emily stares at him with bloodshot eyes and feeble distrust in her gaze. She looks frail and apprehensive about his presence.

"I heard they can't get a hold of your dad."

"Word travels fast," she says, wiping away another tear as it falls.

Ben looks to his feet. "I didn't want you to have to sit in here alone," he explains, remembering all the times he'd been alone, the times he needed his parents and they weren't there, how he waited for someone to show up and tell him everything would be okay, but it never happened. No one ever came.

"I'm sure the nurse will be back soon. She just went to call my dad again."

"Are you hurt?" Ben asks.

"I'm fine. They're just being stupid!"

"Should I leave?" he asks, seeing a glimpse of desperation before she pulls her poker face back together.

"Go ahead, leave. I'm fine!"

"Don't be an idiot," Ben counters.

"You're an idiot!"

"I'm just trying to help."

"I don't need help! I need to go home!" Unable to choke down her tears anymore, she looks pitiful. Her face plummets into her hands and she falls to pieces in front of him. Ben doesn't flinch at the uncomfortable sight of her raw and broken. He doesn't see her as pathetic like she sees herself.

"Go away," Emily snivels between tears.

Unfazed by her words, Ben sits down in the chair across from her as wet puffy eyes peer up at him.

He stays with her in silence for a few minutes until the nurse comes back and shoos him away. Even as the nurse escorts him out into the hall, he stares at Emily, ignoring the scolding he's receiving. Emily doesn't say anything, but she looks sad to see him go.

An hour passes without another Emily sighting. Ben stands facing his locker, dreading going to lunch because he knows the guys will be rehashing what happened to that freak, Emily. He rearranges his books to put off going to the cafeteria. The halls empty and eventually the bell rings. He closes his locker and turns to head to the lunch room, but Emily is standing there. He's surprised and delighted by her presence. She's no longer crying; instead, she's wearing a shy smile.

"Thank you," she says.

"I don't know what you're talking about." Ben smiles, knowing exactly what she's referring to.

"Are you going to lunch?"

He shrugs. "I'm supposed to."

"Skip it and come with me!" She grabs his hand, turning to lead the way.

Ben's anticipation builds as she leads him through the halls. Her touch is causing his thirteen-year-old mind to conjure naughty thoughts. She guides him to the basement where they reach an old door. She pulls a bobby pin from her pocket and fidgets with the lock until it snaps open.

"It's a trick I learned from my mom," she says, with a playful smile.

Ben is excited as he follows her through the door into the construction site where the school is being renovated. She takes his hand and they jog through the narrow halls scattered with tools but absent of workers. Ascending a narrow stairway, they pass decrepit windows at each landing. When they reach the top floor, they climb onto the wide ledge of a windowsill. Light pours in through the timeworn window and pools around them as they gaze out at the afternoon sun.

"Why were you so nice to me?" she asks, drawing his attention back to her.

"Do you remember last year when my mom went to rehab?"

"No." She shakes her head.

"Oh," he says, surprised she doesn't remember. "I was supposed to walk to the bus stop, but I walked to the park instead, missing the bus, so I didn't have to hear it from the guys at school. You saw me hiding like a coward and you came and sat with me. You made me laugh when I didn't think it was possible. I kinda thought it'd be cool if I could do that for you."

"You're not like the other guys at this school."

"And you're nothing like the other girls."

"I meant that as a compliment," she insists.

"So did I."

"I like you," Emily says, just before she leans forward to plant a kiss right on Ben's perfect lips.

The picture shifts again. Ben watches from his desk as his teacher opens the classroom door. Another teacher enters, and the adults whisper together before calling Emily somberly to the door. She gives Ben a nervous look as she heads out into the hall. She disappears as the door closes behind her, but the chattering whispers in the room have already begun.

The scene skips ahead to Ben standing at the front door of my house. Dad opens the door and tells him I'm not home and will not be receiving visitors any time soon. It doesn't stop Ben from coming back for the next two weeks, even though he's turned away or ignored every time.

Ben sits in class listening numbly to the rumors that have traveled the entire school. He knows my mom killed herself. She stabbed herself through the heart with a knife. At least that's the rumor, and now crazy Emily Burk is locked up in the loony bin just like her mother had been. He's pissed because he's not allowed to see me and frustrated that all he has to go on are rumors and gossip.

Weeks go by before Ben sees Emily walk into the classroom. He barely recognizes her. She's a walking shell of the person she used to be as if her spirit was crushed beneath the weight of burdens too heavy for a child to carry. Her eyes are grey and empty. Whispers buzz around the room like an annoying swarm of flies, multiplying faster than they can be killed. As Emily takes her seat, the classroom goes dark.

I feel myself lingering somewhere in limbo before finding my way out of the dream; at least it started as a dream. I know what I saw were Ben's memories, memories that should be my own. It's disorienting being in someone else's mind and I struggle to disconnect the accidental mental connection. I open my eyes and Ben's dark room unfolds before me. I wiggle away from him and sit up. The clock tells me it's seven in the morning. I should go back to sleep, but I feel eerie after witnessing Ben's recollection of events.

Ben was my first kiss! All these years spent as friends when he knew this all along. I kissed him, which is something I should have remembered, yet the memory remains absent from my mind. How many fractions of my life do I have yet to uncover?

I miss the girl I used to be. Ben fell in love with that girl and has been trying to hold on to her ever since. I watch him, peaceful as he sleeps. Things could've been so different if everything hadn't gone so wrong—if I didn't belong to a bloodline that's facing extinction.

I climb out of bed and shut myself in the bathroom. Leaning over the sink, I stare at myself in the mirror. It's weird to see the transformation between my twelve-year-old self and my current reflection. My brilliant emerald eyes show none of the grief I feel, yet they define me. I am Valla's descendant, hunted because they fear I may inflict misery and destruction on everyone around me.

I undress and climb in the shower, hoping to wash away the depressing thoughts. By the time I finish, my fingers are pruned, and every glass surface is foggy. I dry off and get dressed before leaving the bathroom with damp hair.

Ben is sitting up in bed as I walk into his room.

"Good morning, beautiful," he says sleepily.

"Did I wake you?"

He shakes his head with a yawn and shows me my phone. "Your dad called." He yawns again. "Why are you up so early?"

"Couldn't sleep," I say, setting my bag down and walking toward him. "I should've taken my phone with me. Did you answer?"

"No, I thought he'd be suspicious if I did."

"Good call," I say, as I take my phone and see three missed calls. "Sorry to wake you. I'll go to the bathroom to call him back. You go back to sleep."

"You can call him out here," Ben says, placing a hand on my arm. "Do you want breakfast?" He crawls out of bed looking tempting in only his gym shorts.

"I'm not really a breakfast person," I mumble, trying not to stare.

"It's the most important meal of the day."

I try not to be so distracted by him, but he's very distracting. Does he know what he's doing to me? He comes closer and kisses the top of my head pulling away with a smile.

"Maybe when you're done talking to your dad, you can catch me up on what I missed while I was gone."

The phone begins ringing in my hand.

"Go ahead," Ben says, as he strolls into the bathroom, his sensuality assaulting my senses.

"Hey, Dad. Sorry, I didn't hear my phone."

"It's okay, honey. I just wanted to let you know I'm on my way to the airport but won't be home in time to take you to work. Can you find a ride?"

"No problem, Dad, I'll find someone."

"Okay, I'll see you this evening. Love you, Emily."

"Love you, Dad."

When Ben comes out of the bathroom, I'm placing the cushions back on the folded-up sofa bed. He wraps his arms around me and pulls me down beside him on the sofa.

"I didn't know if you'd still be here in the morning," he confesses, without looking at me. "I'm happy you're still here."

"I'm not going to run away," I say, "at least not without saying goodbye first."

"Gotta say, that's not very comforting, Em." After a pause, he asks, "Will you tell me what's going on now?"

I sigh and nuzzle his bare chest. "I don't know what to say."

Silence ensues, so he leans forward to pick up the remote. "Another time then," he says, turning on the television.

I ask, "What about breakfast?"

"I thought you weren't hungry."

"Yeah, but you said it was the most important meal. I mean, how can I say no to that? What do the wealthy eat for breakfast anyway? Do you have a hen that lays golden eggs?" I give him a big smile.

He nods. "Of course, but I had that yesterday."

"Oh, my bad, just have the wait staff bring one of everything," I say sarcastically.

"Okay," he says, reaching for his phone.

"Seriously! Do you have your own wait staff? Who are you?"

He looks embarrassed and I know I'm not supposed to talk about his family's ridiculous wealth, but I'm at a loss. He was raised with everything at his fingertips.

"My parents hired a couple of people to help out, that's all," he says, attempting to be nonchalant.

"Help out? What do they do?"

"Cook, clean, you know, normal things. It's not like they wait on us hand and foot."

"Normal? Normal would be doing all of those things yourself. Ben, you're like royalty or something."

"Let's just go find some food," he says, pulling me off the couch. He slips a t-shirt over his head before we exit his room. I'm relieved the family room is empty as we make our way to the kitchenette.

With a smile, I point to the stove and ask, "Do you know what this is?"

"Shut it," he says. "I'm probably a better cook than you are."

"You mean you know how to use one of these contraptions. And don't doubt my skill, I make a mean grilled cheese," I brag.

"I can whip up some omelets," he offers, raising an eyebrow and pointing to the stove. "Prove to you I know how to use that shiny thing with the knobs."

"And go to all that trouble? How about some cereal?"

He opens a cabinet filled with cereal boxes. "You sure you don't want an omelet?"

"Thanks, but I'll stick with cereal. I wouldn't want you burning down this palace of yours," I tease as I grab a box.

"You have no faith in me, Em."

He places two bowls on the counter, and I pour the cereal while he gets the milk out of the fridge.

I wonder how the overwhelming wealth hasn't ruined him. He's still the same Ben that used to spit wads of paper through a straw at his friends when they fell asleep in class. He's the same guy that got suspended for fighting because he was sticking up for me. He's the same boy that sat in the nurse's office with me so I wouldn't be alone. He's still Ben, my Ben.

"What?" Ben asks, and I realize I haven't taken my eyes from him.

"Nothing." I shake my head and grab the milk. He slides our bowls down the counter and we sit on fancy high stools at the kitchen bar.

"So, why didn't your parents send you to a private school?" I ask, before digging into my cereal.

He chuckles under his breath. "They tried. Even though our high school was ranked third in the state, I guess they thought it'd look better on my transcript. I dropped out after a week, forged documents from my parents and went back to our school." He gives a sly grin. "It took my parents four months to realize it. They fired my favorite driver though. I still feel bad about that."

"Wait, driver, as in chauffeur? You had your own chauffeur?"

"Yeah, it's not as cool as it sounds. It's just something my parents did because they have lots of money and no interest in raising children. The next guy they hired was my punishment. He reported directly to my father. Not because Everett gave a shit, but because I made him look bad. So, my new driver would keep tabs on me all the time and inform my father of my whereabouts.

"Eventually, my dad stopped pretending to care, but this guy didn't. He was military, like my own personal prison guard yelling at me when I'd skip class even though my grades were perfect. He threatened to call the cops if I broke curfew. He even persuaded my parents to hire a tutor to teach me college courses, because he didn't think school was challenging me. When I got my driver's license, he was supposed to follow me, but I kept ditching him. Everett fired him too, probably realizing it was a waste of money."

"I thought that guy who drove you around in the black Lincoln was your dad."

A bitter laugh escapes him. "No, that was Frank."

"Sounds like Frank was good for you," I blurt, thinking Frank sounded like the closest thing to a parental figure Ben has ever had.

His forehead scrunches, and I'm glad he just took a bite so he can't respond right away.

"Maybe," he mumbles through a mouth full of cereal.

"Excuse me, sir," A female voice calls from the other end of the room. Ben and I turn in unison. Standing at the foot of the stairs is a tall young woman in a light pink knee-length dress with white trim. Her straight blond hair just barely brushes the collar of her uniform. Could she be the maid?

"Sorry to interrupt," she says with a faint accent, her expression guarded. "Your friends are in the garage."

"Thanks. I'll be up in a minute," Ben responds to the life-size Barbie Doll. I feel a hint of jealousy but ignore the irrational thought.

She nods and retreats up the stairs.

"I forgot I told the guys to come over today. We were gonna work on Alec's Camaro."

"That's okay. Go ahead. I have to go to work soon anyway."

"It's eight o'clock," he replies with a smirk. "You don't work until noon and how exactly are you planning to get to work without me?"

"I'll call an Uber. It's no big deal. Why are you guys meeting so early anyway?"

"Forget Uber. I already told you I'd take you. The guys only came this early because I work this afternoon. Don't worry about it. We'll reschedule for tomorrow."

"I don't want to be the reason you change your plans. And I thought your dad made you quit your job."

"I'm happy to change my plans. I'd rather spend my morning with you. Everett thinks I'm taking Taekwondo lessons instead of teaching them. I'll be back in a minute," he says, walking away.

He disappears through a door, and I sit at the bar alone, feeling incompatible with my surroundings. I don't have much alone time before another door opens.

"Oh goody, you're still here," Molly patronizes.

"Good morning to you too," I say.

"Yeah, whatever." She rolls her eyes. "Where's Ben?"

"The garage. Some friends stopped by."

"Why didn't you go with him? Are you already tired of each other after just one night?"

"They're here for Ben, not me."

"Do you even have friends? Or do you just float from one guy to the next?" she seethes.

"What's your problem with me?"

"Seriously?" She looks at me in disbelief. "Would you like the list? You've had Ben wrapped around your finger for years. You tell him you're too screwed up to date him and a week later you're seeing someone else. He was finally done with you! Free to move on and then you call, and he goes running."

My first reaction is anger, but soon I feel awful because even though it didn't play out quite like she thinks, I feel like a thief. I stole his heart years ago and have been robbing him of happiness ever since. "I know I'm bad for Ben. I just want so badly to be right for him, to be good for him."

"Yeah, well, you're not, and I'm tired of watching you torture him."

"I'm grateful he has someone to watch out for him," I say.

"I care about him a lot more than you do. Ben is the best!"

I admit, "I think he's the best thing that's ever happened to me."

With a sneer and a hand on her hip, Molly says, "Of course he's the best thing to happen to you."

A rattling of dishes from across the room brings both of our heads around. The Barbie of a woman is walking down the stairs carrying a tray. Immediately, Molly's mood brightens, and she skips toward the stairs.

"Yes!" Molly squeals. "Thank you so much!" She takes the silver breakfast tray and sets it on the counter.

"Be careful now, the plate is hot," life-size Barbie cautions with a faint accent, as she walks behind Molly. Her blond hair looks pale against her tan skin, and I wonder how old she is. She speaks nervously, "Now, I tried something new this time."

Molly throws herself in the seat next to me and removes the lid exposing a fluffy omelet and fresh fruit. "She's the best cook!" Molly brags to me as if we're good friends. Barbie stands beside Molly waiting as she takes a bite.

"Mmm," Molly moans with a mouthful. "It's dewishous." Molly dabs at her mouth with a napkin and turns to me. "I didn't introduce you two." She grabs Barbie's hand bringing her closer. "Natalia, this is Emily."

Natalia, as in the same Natalia she wants to be with Ben! I have to admit she's gorgeous, Molly-approved, and apparently, she makes delicious food. I can see why she would be better for Ben.

"Nice to meet you, Natalia," I say, as I get to my feet.

"I'm glad to have met you," she says with a polite smile as I begin to walk away.

"Where are you going?" Molly asks.

"I'll just wait in his room," I reply, wanting to free myself from the awkwardness.

"Whatever." She gives me a dismissive wave.

I enter his room and think seriously about escaping out the back door, but I told Ben I wouldn't run, so instead, I sit on the edge of his bed wishing I felt worthy of him.

twenty ~

The clock above the register—which is moving slower than usual—tells me it's two o'clock which means I've only been working for two hours. It seems like forever. I don't know whether it's the lack of sleep catching up with me or because Ben is picking me up from work and I'm anxious for my shift to be over, but time is dragging.

"Hey, daydreamer," Morgan chimes, standing at my register with a small container of fish food.

"Hey, Morgan."

"I was around the area and thought I'd stop by and see if you were working. I didn't see your car outside."

"It's in the shop."

"Oh no. Do you need a ride later? I'm meeting up with some old teammates, but I can swing by if you need me."

"Thanks, but Ben's picking me up."

"Ben?" She beams. "Everything good there?"

"Yeah, it's good. We're good." I can't keep from smiling. "And to be clear, nothing is going on between Patrick and me."

"Sounds like we need to catch up. Are you available this week?"

"Sure, I'll call you when I'm off."

She notices a guy waiting in line behind her, so she begins backing away from the counter. "Okay, I'll see you later."

"Bye," I say, before turning to the next customer.

"Hello, Emily, how are you today?" the stranger says, and fear punches me in the gut.

"Fine," I mumble, wondering how he knows me. A second later I feel stupid when I remember I'm wearing a name tag. "Did you find everything you need?" I stammer, trying to recover.

"I sure did," he says.

I'm relieved he was just a customer and not an Olvasho ready to discover and expose my identity. The rest of the day drags on until Ben picks me up from work.

As we approach my house, I spot Dad's truck in the open garage and wonder what I've gotten myself into. I want Ben here, but Dad and I still need to talk about Patrick, and we can't do that in front of Ben. I also need to ask Dad if he can help me fill in those missing parts of my memory.

All these things are swirling through my head as we make our way into the house. I'm surprised when Maggie growls at Ben. I thought she was over her aversion to him. While I give my attention to Maggie, Ben goes straight to the kitchen with the grocery bags he purchased before picking me up.

"Hey Ben, thanks for getting her to work and back," Dad says from the kitchen.

"No problem. Did they find out what's going on with her car?" Ben asks.

"I tried to jump it first, thought it might be the battery, but when it wouldn't start, I had it towed. It's probably the starter," he replies.

"Ah, I might be able to help with that," Ben offers.

"I doubt it'll be worth fixing. Sorry, Em," Dad says, as I join them in the kitchen. "It looks like you may have to say goodbye to your car. I don't like you driving something so unsafe. Your muffler has a hole in it, you need new tires and new struts, and it has two-hundred and fifty-thousand miles on it. And that's just the list of problems we know. I think it's time to move on."

"I knew this would happen eventually. I just didn't expect it so soon," I say.

"We'll find something better. We can go car shopping this weekend," Dad offers.

I nod, saying, "I have some money saved up."

"Keep saving it. Think of this as a belated graduation gift." He smiles, leaning against the kitchen counter.

"That's too much, Dad."

"No, it's overdue and don't argue with me. Samantha got a car when she graduated, so why wouldn't you?"

I don't think my dad has the money, but I don't want to have this conversation right now, so I change the subject. "How was your trip?"

"Uneventful. What're you two doing tonight?"

Without warning, Ben steps into me, wrapping his arm around my shoulder. My inherent reaction is to pull away, but I resist my initial reflex and relax into his side, saying, "We're gonna hang out here if you don't mind."

Dad looks to the arm wrapped around me, but doesn't comment; instead, he says, "I just finished installing the TV in the living room. It's an 8K ultra HD resolution with 4320 pixels. It blows the 1080p out of the water. Come look at the clarity." He appears entirely at ease talking to Ben about his newest electronic. He is excellent at pretending everything is fine, but I know he's pretending because I sense his tension as he leads Ben into the living room.

My feet stay planted in the kitchen feeling heavier now that I'm home. The weight of everything is a little more real when I'm here.

The splash of color on the wall next to the refrigerator draws my eye. Before Mom left, she tried out some paint samples. She wanted to brighten the place up like she brightened everything she touched. The splash of yellow only amplifies the drab brown walls. This house is filled with reminders of what's already been lost.

Unsolicited images of my mom lying on the floor in a widening pool of blood fill my mind, and I'm having trouble breathing. Plagued with panic, I bolt out the back door, hoping to find air more easily outside. Before the dizziness overcomes me, I sit on the edge of the back porch. Maggie comes and sits beside me, placing her head on my shoulder while I focus on my breathing. I should be excited my boyfriend and my dad are getting along so well, but I can't shake this uneasy feeling in the pit of my stomach.

"You okay?" I hear from behind me. I glance up to find Dad and Ben in the doorway, both looking concerned.

"Yeah, just a little dizzy. I think I need to eat something."

"I'll get started," Ben says, disappearing into the kitchen.

Dad's expression is one of confusion, and I can't help but smile despite myself. "Ben is trying to prove to me that he knows how to cook."

Dad shakes his head, looking somewhere between amused and impressed before settling on compassion. "Still having flashbacks?"

I nod, and he takes that as an invitation. He sits down next to me in silence for a while before he says, "You deserve to be happy, Emily."

"Do I? What if I don't know how?"

"Ben makes you happy. I never see you smile more than when you two are together. Just because you're different doesn't mean you can't care about people. It doesn't mean you can't love someone. Look at your mother and me."

"Yeah and look how that ended," I blurt, immediately regretting it.

"I don't regret it," he says with intent, drawing my eyes back to him. "Any of it. I know you worry about me, but you shouldn't. The moment I met your mother I knew there was no alternative for me. If I had the choice, I would do it all again. Your mother was worth every bit of sacrifice and so are you."

"Sacrifice? That's just it, Dad, I don't want anyone to have to sacrifice anything because of me."

"I might sound like a hopeless romantic, but I believe we were put on this earth to love and to be loved. And sweetheart, that boy in there loves you. I'm not trying to scare you, but I've seen the way he looks at you, and I've seen the way you look at him. He's more important to you than you let on."

There is a pause, giving me time to think. I'd never in my life considered Dad any kind of romantic until this moment and what's scary is how close his words are to the truth.

"That doesn't mean I'm endorsing sex by the way," he continues. "I will kill him."

I gawk at him.

He's smiling, thoroughly enjoying my horror. "I thought that'd get you out of your trance. Now come on; let's go see if your boyfriend can cook." He stands and offers his hand to help me up.

twenty-one ~

Days begin to pass with an unusual amount of normalcy, and I start believing one day I might be able to live this happy life instead of just pretending. As it turns out, Ben can cook, and Dad has a sense of humor.

Monday, I spend time doing laundry, cleaning, homework and talking to my boyfriend on the phone. Telling Ben not to come over is hard because I really want to see him, but in my experience, too much of a good thing can lead to trouble. Caring about him the way I do is a vulnerability that however much I try, I can't seem to abandon.

After class on Tuesday, I'm sitting in my living room with a thick book propped on my lap. Absently, I tap my pencil against my knee as I try to read the grueling humanities assignment. My thoughts keep floating back to Ben. When did I become this feeble-minded girl? Shaking my head as if I can shake free of my thoughts, I go back to reading. I scan the same paragraph I've already read three times with no idea what I've just read. Frustrated, I stick the pencil in the binding and close the book.

The rumble of an engine dies followed by a truck door slamming. I look out the window catching sight of Dad just before he enters the house. It's two o'clock, way too early for him to be home.

"Studying?" he asks unnecessarily.

"I'm trying."

"Go get dressed. You're going to take a break. I'm taking you to the mall," he says.

"Why? You're the only person I know who hates shopping more than I do."

"Go get ready, I'll explain in the truck."

Once we're on our way, I notice Dad's emotions are all over the place. Sadness, regret, and resolve are entangled in an angry cocoon of protection drifting heavily in the cab of the truck. It takes effort for me to stay locked out of his psyche. I've vowed I'd never go into his mind again because I know there are things he's keeping from me that will haunt me more than my own memories.

"Are you going to tell me what's going on?" I ask.

"We're working on honing your skills today. The mall always has crowds of people. Where better to practice?"

I sigh. Sneaking into the mind of others and taking a gander at their deepest secrets is definitely not what I wanted to do today, but I keep my mouth shut because it does no good to complain. Besides, this is something I need to learn to control.

"I know you don't like this, Em, but it could save your life one day, and you can't ignore your gifts."

"So I've been told."

"This is non-negotiable. I'm sorry, but I need you to learn how to make the best of it. It's the best way to protect yourself."

We don't speak another word, and the dread hangs like a boulder waiting to drop. We enter the sliding glass doors of the mall and walk around. I wonder how he expects me to dive into this. Focusing on the task at hand, I look at the crowd around us.

It isn't packed full of shoppers this time of day, but there are plenty of people milling around.

"Where should I begin?"

He points to a vacant bench in the middle of the atrium. It's a vantage point that will allow us to blend in while we observe strangers ambling by.

As soon as we're seated, Dad directs his gaze to a middle-aged woman inside a nearby store. "Try reading her."

I focus on the woman as I shift my mind into hers. It's strange being outside of my body but still remaining in total control. I concentrate on the woman, amazed at how quickly I'm in—in the store, sorting through a rack of over-priced clothing. Inside her mind she is . . . Bored. That can't be all, but it's the first thing I notice. She's completely disinterested in what she's doing. She's keeping herself busy with things she used to love but now have become tedious tasks. I feel despair seeping through her. This distraction isn't working for her, and I get the distinct feeling she's very ill. Her heart, saturated with so much despair, oozes sadness like puss from an open wound. The intensity builds until I have to bail. I break the connection as sorrow rocks my body, solidifying the fact I will never consider this particular skill of mine a gift.

I don't meet my Dad's gaze; afraid he'll ask about the unshed tears forming in my eyes. Persevering or perhaps running from the grief, I jump head first into the psyche of the next person I see. It happens to be the twenty-something guy behind the juice bar.

Perfect! Absolutely perfect to balance out my downward spiral into despair. His mind is merely happy with a mellowness suggesting a drug-induced calm. He doesn't feel worried or guilty for taking the extra unscheduled breaks to smoke his joints or for skimming from the tip jar. He's uncomplicated and content. I feel the pull to stay in his brain because the bliss is wholly sincere and relaxing. The simplicity of his mind is addicting. He possesses the "whatever" vibe I wish I could feel on my own.

I force my way back into my own mind. Dad's trying to hide his grin, but I feel his pride as he watches me. I don't understand the look because there's no way for him to tell if what I'm doing is successful.

"Why the prideful look?"

His grin grows. "Because I'm proud of you. I forced you to practice something you hate, and instead of fighting me you're soldiering through."

His praise makes me shift uncomfortably, so I bring my eyes back to the pursuit of finding my next subject.

After hours of honing my new skill, it begins to feel normal. That's what worries me the most. Reading other's thoughts isn't right in my book. Not only is it an invasion of privacy, but it is also hard to be in someone else's head and in my own. It's exhausting to feel all those emotions and stay unattached. What's worse, I haven't completely convinced myself that I'm not crazy.

Because my car is out of commission, Dad takes me to work on Wednesday. Once I'm there, I'm free to pretend my life is what it was before I learned the truth. Of course, Ashley bombards me with questions about my Friday evening with Patrick. To halt her interrogation, I give her a version of the truth.

"Ben and I are kind of together now, so stop worrying about Patrick."

"Ben!" she chimes. "You mean tall, dark, and yummy. That Ben?"

I tilt my head as I look at her. "Tall, dark, and yummy?"

"Yeah and rich and he has those sculpted biceps. I'm so incredibly jealous. Like, seriously, I would kill to be stuck in your perfect love triangle."

"Ashley, there is no love triangle."

"Oh please, they're both completely gone for you. You've gotta share your secrets with me. I mean, God, Emily, share the wealth! Sooo . . ." She nudges me.

"What?"

"Will you at least give Patrick my number?"

"No."

"You little tease. You're so not over him," she accuses.

"Over him? I was never into him!"

"Then why won't you give him my number?" She puts her hands on her hips like she's said something profound and she's waiting for it to sink in.

"Ashley," I respond calmly. "Patrick is not good for you."

"I think he's perfect." She smiles, eyes distant, perhaps staring into a make-believe future with Patrick. I let her have her moment and go back to work feeding the fish in the aquariums. I don't get far.

"So, does this mean I'll be seeing more of Ben around here? Because that's okay too."

"Maybe." I shrug.

"So what does 'kinda together' mean anyway? You're such a prude. Please tell me you've at least kissed him! Are you still a virgin? God, I know you must be dying for some good foreplay. I mean it's about freakin' time, Emily!"

I roll my eyes wishing she'd go back to daydreaming about Patrick.

I continue down the line of aquariums, hoping she'll drop the subject. I reach the last tank and turn to Ashley because there's nowhere else for me to go. I've backed myself into a corner, literally. From the gleam in her eyes, she knows she has me cornered. She crosses her arms over her chest and waits for me to give her something.

"Excuse me." A balding, middle-aged man comes to the end of the aisle behind Ashley. "I'm ready to check out."

Ashley glances at him. "Hold on, can't you see we're like in the middle of something here?"

He makes a frustrated noise at the back of his throat and stalks off toward the registers.

"Ashley!"

She glares at me. "You're selfish. You know that?" She turns to stroll down the aisle. "This is so not over by the way."

The afternoon becomes busy, and just as Ashley finishes with her row of customers, a man pushes a bag of dog food onto my counter. While I ring him up, Ashley says, "It's the single life for me, Emily." She pouts, as she sits up on the counter. "Why else would I ask about your nonexistent sex life?"

My customer pauses to glance at me. Embarrassed, I smile and hand him his receipt. As he picks up the dog food to leave, I catch him giving me a once over. Wanting to hide under the counter, I mumble, "Have a nice day."

He's not the only one who heard Ashley. We're getting side glances from shoppers, but that's what it's like working with Ashley. I never know what will come out of her mouth. She's a constant in that way, always saying whatever she's thinking. Even as I glare at her, I love that there is no pretense. She keeps it real, even if it makes me uncomfortable.

Ashley sighs, "You can have Patrick and Ben, but the next one is mine, okay?"

I make the promise, as another customer moves toward my counter.

"He'd better be hot!" Ashley picks at her nails while I continue working.

In the evening when Ben picks me up from work, Ashley insists on him coming inside. She skips over to give him a hug. A hug! I figure it's an excuse to feel him up, but then I hear her whisper, "I don't care how sexy you are. If you don't take care of my girl, I'll hunt you down." Ashley is a lot of things, but protective is not something I pegged her for.

Ashley locks the door after Ben enters. A customer approaches, but Ashley shrugs unsympathetically and turns away. Locking up a few minutes early is standard Ashley. She's not an ideal employee, but she knows her daddy will never fire her.

She saunters toward Ben with pouted lips. "Ben, do you have any single friends?"

"None good enough for you."

Ashley flips her hair and mumbles under her breath, "I hate you, Emily. You're a selfish bitch."

A tender grin plays on Ben's lips as his soft brown eyes find mine and he reaches for me. My next breath catches in my throat and butterflies dance in my stomach making him hard to resist. As he tucks me into his side, I hesitate to return his affection, feeling inept with Ashley's eyes on us.

Ashley lets out a snort. "Good God, Emily! Just kiss him!"

I must look as inept as I feel. I panic, pulling away from Ben to meander toward the exit. "We should go," I say.

I try to ignore Ashley's comment, but it becomes an echo in my ear, her laughter rings over and over in my mind. Oh God! What am I doing? She would know what to do with Ben. She would know how to kiss him—how to be half of a couple. She would know how to react to his touch like a woman should, and she wouldn't have to remind herself not to read his thoughts. Ashley would be a better option for him for so many obvious reasons.

Before my self-loathing becomes all-consuming, I reach the exit. As I unlock the door, Molly's voice rings through my thoughts. *"I'm tired of watching you torture him."*

I flip the lock, throw open the door, and head for the Corvette. I hate depending on someone else for a ride, and I hate having this reaction to such a small incident. After spending years in classrooms being analyzed and judged for every move I made, I thought I had a thicker hide, a stronger spine, an impenetrable forcefield between myself and everyone else. This is more than a leak in the roof of my defense. It's a fundamental problem because somewhere along the way I let down my protective walls and left myself vulnerable.

Ben doesn't speak, but I hear his footsteps following me. When I reach for the car door his hand lands on my shoulder. He pivots me around to face him. My first instinct is to fight, my true nature coming out in spades.

"I can't do this! I can't be your girlfriend!"

He spreads his feet, folds his arms, and settles in for my explanation.

"It's been all of what? Five days? Five days and I'm turning into this over-dramatic psycho. This person isn't me! I can't be what you want and for God's sake Ben, you deserve better. So much better! Molly's right. I'm not saying this to throw myself some kind of pity—what are you doing?"

His face is intense as he steps forward, closing the distance between us. I inch away until my back is against his car. He continues forward unfolding his tightly muscled arms and moving until his broad shoulders and chest are all I see. Still, he advances, pressing his weight into me. I feel myself warm from more than just the heat of his body. I lift my chin and search his face.

His lips press firmly into mine the second my chin ascends, disintegrating any hope of escape. He deepens the kiss as his arms wrap behind my back molding me to him. His tongue forces its way into my mouth, and I forget I shouldn't let it. He kisses me until I forget I'm upset, until I forget that my guard—which is imperative to my very survival—is crumbling. He kisses me until I forget I am supposed to be standing my ground. As my fingers claw into his back begging for more, I'm vaguely aware I'm standing at all.

I'm not sure when I wrapped my arms around him or when I molded my body to his, but I know I don't want to let go. He takes a step back, leaving his arms around me, so my quaking legs have time to recover. His gaze locks on my half-lidded eyes, and I try to straighten from my sated stupor feeling only a mild annoyance in the place of what would usually be a desperate need to escape. Before I get a chance to pull myself together, his fingers wrap around my arms, and his words begin.

"Don't for one damn second think you know better than I do, what I want. This doesn't have to be complicated. I know who I'm with, Emily. I know who you are and being together doesn't mean I expect you to become a different person. I love who you are. Get out of your head and stop thinking so much. You get that crazy look in your eye, and then you take off as if you can run away from everything that scares you. I'm done letting you run from me."

Speechless, all the words just . . . Poof.

"You got that?" he asks.

I nod as his hand caresses my jaw, tilting my face up to his. "Good," he whispers against my mouth. His perfect lips stroke mine until I'm pacified and lightheaded.

Ben sighs, stepping back so he can open the door for me. I'm in a daze as I climb in the car. As I put on my seat belt, I stare out the window. The pet store lights gleam through the floor to ceiling windows and right in the middle—front and center—stands Ashley, gawking at us. Her face is one of total shock and awe. She's going to stew over this for the next few days and will share her feedback with me on Friday, whether I want it or not.

twenty-two ~

Thursday morning I'm brooding. I sent Ben away after he brought me home last night because I couldn't trust myself. I tried to break up with him, but instead, I fell deeper into our relationship. It's as if he reached directly into my heart and planted himself there in a very permanent way.

And then there is Patrick, who isn't in my heart, but as I prepare for class this afternoon, he worms his way to the forefront of my mind. Skipping class is tempting, but I don't want him to think I'm avoiding him. Most importantly, I don't want him to know he's gotten so deep under my skin that I've spent half the day thinking about him. Therefore, I get ready and head to class.

I take my usual spot in the lecture hall and scope the room, but he is noticeably absent. I don't detect Patrick's presence at all as the elderly professor begins his slow step-cane-step hobble up to the podium. I turn in my seat, too curious to care if Patrick sees me looking for him, but he's nowhere. He didn't show. My heart races while the professor goes on with his lecture. I'm keenly focused on the lack of Patrick and begin to worry something has happened to him.

As the class comes to a close, I gather my things wondering if maybe he'll bombard me outside. After all the times I told him to leave me alone, I don't understand my disappointment at him not being here. I head out into the afternoon sun, feeling chilled by the lack of Patrick.

"Hey!" I feel a hand tap my shoulder from behind.

I spin toward the masculine voice, disappointed to find a dark-eyed stranger smiling at me. He opens his hand between us revealing my phone.

"You left this on your desk."

"Oh, thank you."

"No problem, I'd be lost without my phone. I couldn't let you walk away. Maybe I should've put my number in there before giving it back to you."

"I'm good," I say, already turning to walk away.

Ben and I run into Alec and his latest squeeze when we go out for pizza in the evening. Alec isn't surprised to see Ben and me together, and our reunion isn't awkward like I was expecting. Ben and I slide into the booth opposite Alec and his beautiful flavor-of-the-week named Reece. Between her long dark hair, flawless mocha skin, and delicately feminine features, she's a knockout. It's baffling how Alec continuously has gorgeous women connected to him. It's not that he isn't good looking or fun to be around, but there have been sooo many. I wonder how he manages to find them all. Reece seems sweet which means it takes a lot of effort on my part not to tell her to run.

Alec might be cool to hang with, but it never goes deeper for him. I've never had any interest in dating him, and he learned this early in our friendship; although, it took him a while to realize I wasn't playing hard to get. He lost interest soon enough and moved on like he does every other week, hence the beautiful girl plastered to his side with hopes of their future written in her eyes. If only he could focus his time and effort into one woman, he'd be a real catch, but Alec gets bored quickly. So, Reece will probably last a week or two, and sadly by week three, he will have a new piece of arm candy.

Ben takes my hand, and Alec curses under his breath drawing our attention to him. He glances at me before turning his hazel eyes to Ben. "How'd you get through?" Alec asks. "Blow torch?"

He glares at Alec for a moment then glances at Reece before threatening, "You wanna do this here?"

Alec's eyes narrow, then his expression dissolves. Choosing to let it go, for now, he changes the subject, saying, "We gonna do whiffle ball this weekend?"

"Yeah man, that'd be good." Ben looks to me. "You work until four on Sunday?" Ben asks.

"Yeah."

"Four thirty work for you?" he says to Alec.

"Yep."

"Gavin coming?" Ben asks.

Alec says, "Think so."

"Good."

"Good?" I question, thinking in no way is it good. I could avoid him until the day I die. That would be good.

"Yeah, good. The sooner he gets over it, the better," Ben says.

"Eh," I mumble.

"He's a big boy. He'll get over it." Alec cuts my protest short. "Heard Fletcher's back."

When I nod, he says, "You should invite her."

Fletcher is Morgan Fletcher. She also turned Alec down, but where he gave up on me, he still pursues her. Morgan doesn't mind his attention, and she gives it right back. It's harmless flirtation, but sometimes I wonder if there's more between them.

"You know she'll be merciless," I say, watching a grin spread across his face, showing off his amazing dimples.

"I'd expect nothin' else from Fletch."

"She might be working, but if she's not, you know it'll be game on," I warn.

Both he and Ben laugh. Morgan hasn't met a sport she wasn't good at and both guys know it. Even though they're threatened by her, they can't resist the challenge.

Ben takes me home after we leave the restaurant. I exit the Corvette and wait for Ben to round the car. His arm wraps around my waist and his lips brush against my temple. "You okay with seeing Gavin?" he whispers.

"I will be. I just thought you all hated me until I ran into you on campus that day."

He cups my cheeks, forcing me to face him. "Gavin needed time to lick his wounds, but none of us ever hated you, Em. You're the one who avoided us."

"I know what you and Alec were talking about and if I had to guess, I'd say it was a small ice pick. You chipped away piece by piece."

He stares at me for a moment, "What?"

"Not a blow torch," I say, and his eyes go hard. "It's okay. I know I'm not warm and fuzzy; although, I don't think I ever actually froze anyone's balls off like the rumors say."

He gives a small laugh but turns serious. Still cupping my cheeks, his eyes burn with sincerity. "It wasn't an ice pick. You know why? Because you're not an Ice queen and because every piece I have, you've given to me."

"I shut people out," I counter, pulling my face from his hands. "It's what I know."

"You're on fire, and you can't even see it," he says, confusing me as he takes a step away.

"What?"

"Emily, I don't mean to freak you out, but I've been trying to get through to you for years without any progress . . . Until last week. You shut down after your mom died and I don't know what happened while I was gone, but it's like you woke up out of a deep sleep. You're different now." He moves closer, eyes locked on mine. "You're back."

He's digging deeper into my heart, melting my ice fortress into big slushy piles.

"What happened last week?" he asks, shattering my warm thoughts.

I shake my head, pulling away from him, but he pulls me closer and holds tight, saying, "It's okay. I'll wait."

I didn't want the whole store hearing about the parking lot kiss, so I'm relieved to see that Ashley called off work. Of course, that means I have to work with Eric. He's an awkward man in his early thirties who has always given me the creeps.

"I worked with Ashley yesterday," he says, coming up behind me while I'm stocking the shelves in aisle two.

"Yeah," I acknowledge, as I fill a bin with rawhide bones.

"Yeah," he says, standing uncomfortably close. So close that I think he will help me lift the heavy bin back into place on the shelf, but instead, he watches me struggle to do it on my own.

When he just stands there staring at me, I ask, "Was she feeling okay yesterday?"

"Yeah, she was fine. You know, apart from being allergic to work." He laughs at his own joke and moves closer invading my personal space.

I take a step away, pulling down another bin and intentionally place it between us.

"I thought you were a lesbian," he says.

I pause what I'm doing. "Umm, nope."

"I thought you were."

"Okaaay . . ."

"Ashley told me she saw you making out with some high schooler in the parking lot."

I am going to kill Ashley! "It wasn't some high school guy. He's my boyfriend."

"You shouldn't settle for little high schoolers."

"He's not in high school. We both graduated this year."

"I wish I would've known you weren't a lesbian."

And like an idiot, I ask, "Why?"

"If I knew you were batting for my team, I would've thrown my name in."

His words make me shiver, and I want to laugh with disgust, but I keep my face neutral as I reply, "I'm only eighteen."

"So it'd be legal!"

My skin crawls. Even if he wasn't fifteen years older than me, there is no way it would ever happen, so I reply, "I have a boyfriend."

"I'm throwing my name in anyway," he says like it's a threat to Ben. He waits with anticipation, but I ignore him, and eventually, he gives up and walks away.

I'm standing in the middle of a bright white room. I try to walk for the door, but the closer I get, the farther away the door becomes and the more desperate I am to get out. I yell for help, but dark robed figures appear, reminding me of the grim reaper. Fear propels me forward and I run for the door. Grabbing the handle, I shove my weight into it and the door flies open. As I stumble through, I find myself standing in my bedroom. Maggie growls at me, drawing my attention to the bed, and I see myself lying asleep. A woman hovers over me, watching me doze. Her milky blue eyes pivot to me in the doorway. Her wild blond hair is streaked with white and snow boots peek out from underneath her silky white robe.

Her eyes become crystal blue as they focus on me. She lifts her hand, reaching out as she steps toward me. "You were bred to be orphaned, pursued but not found." She walks closer. "A victim, a killer, an innocent one."

Just before she touches me, I wake, sitting straight up in bed to find Maggie growling protectively at my feet. I look around the room, seeing nothing out of the ordinary. Maggie, done growling, climbs up on the bed to snuggle next to me.

twenty-three ~

Sunday morning Dad surprises me with a new silver Honda Civic. I have trouble accepting such a generous gift, but I love the car. I drive myself to work, enjoying the freedom of having my own vehicle again. I crank the air conditioning and blast the radio. The new car feels sleek and fancy after driving around in my old beater for so long.

A thunderstorm pops up out of nowhere around three o'clock. The clouds roll in swiftly, but once they come, they decide to stick around. At four o'clock it continues to pour buckets, effectively ruining our plans for whiffle ball. The boys decide it's a garage kind of day. While they work on all that *manly* stuff, Morgan and I make plans for dinner. Ben tells me he'll meet up with us at the restaurant later.

Morgan puts on a happy face as she meets me at the door to the Italian restaurant, but I can tell something's wrong. After the hostess shows us back to a booth, I can no longer hold my tongue. "Morgan, what's going on?"

Her forehead creases and she shields her mouth with a hand as she closes her eyes. She's trying desperately to keep it together, but she's falling apart at the seams.

"What's wrong?" I whisper as tears trickle down her face.

"I'm sorry." She wipes away the tears as they fall, looking embarrassed, and struggling to compose herself. She's trying to explain what's going on, but her shaking lips won't allow it. She moans, rests her head on the table, and begins to weep. I move onto the bench next to her, and my hand circles her back in hopes of soothing her suffering.

"I promised myself I wouldn't cry tonight." She sits up, wipes away a tear, and rolls her eyes. "So much for that."

"Happens to the best of us."

"No, it doesn't. I've never seen you with as much as a tear in your eye."

"I have my moments," I confess. "Just ask Ben." I pivot my body to shield her from curious eyes.

She smiles even as her tears continue to flow. Taking a calming breath, she confesses, "My patient died last night. I shouldn't be this upset. How am I supposed to be a good nurse if I can't handle death?"

She looks to me for support, but I keep quiet and continue rubbing her back, showing compassion the only way I know how.

"I cried all night last night. It was just so unexpected," she sniffles. "I was talking and joking with him, and then an hour later he was gone. Just like that. I knew he was sick, but I just. . ." She loses her words as the cloud of sorrow envelops her. Her loss is a reminder of how terribly fragile life is.

"I wish I could be strong like you," she confides.

Her words make me sad because no one should wish to be like me. "Compassion is not a flaw, Morgan."

"Look at me! I'm sniveling like a child in the middle of a restaurant. That has to be some kind of flaw!" The corners of her mouth curl up as she finds humor in the situation. "You must think I'm a basket case," she says, wiping the last of the tears away.

"No, I think you'll be a great nurse because you care so much."

251

"Thanks, Em."

The waitress comes by with our drink order. Reading the situation, she tells us she'll give us a few minutes to look over the menu. We don't get the few minutes because we're interrupted by Ashley. With her bleach blond tipsy attitude, she approaches our table, and unlike the waitress, she doesn't read the situation. Instead, she plops herself down in the booth across from us dragging her date in next to her.

"Emily, we spotted you from the bar. It's so good to see you, girl! You never wanna hang out with me outside of work, and you never respond to my texts. Don't think I haven't noticed," Ashley complains, beyond tipsy. "And Damn girl, that kiss!"

"Ash, come on," the guy with her says, trying to pull her out of the booth. "Focus for a second. We're interrupting here. Let's go."

Ashley strains to focus on Morgan. She leans across the table and grabs ahold of Morgan's hands. "Oh, honey, I'm sorry to interrupt. I'm Ashley. I work with Emily at the pet place."

Morgan responds with a genuine smile. "I'm Morgan. You're not interrupting. I'm okay. I'm done having my moment."

Ashley looks to me. "Why haven't I ever heard you talk about her before?"

"You have. You were only focused on—"

"I just came back to town," Morgan interjects.

"Well, it's good to know she has other girls in her life. I thought I was the only one aside from her sister. I was beginning to think she only surrounded herself with super-hot guys."

Morgan is still smiling, so Ashley continues, "Do you know all her man drama? First, there's Ben, who she claimed was just a friend! Then the blond hottie that came from nowhere, Patrick. Oh my God, I still can't believe you slapped him." She looks at Morgan and reiterates. "She slapped him, like, across the face because she's a crazy person." Ashley laughs, and in her drunkenness leans on the guy next to her. Then almost as an afterthought, realizing he's there, introduces him.

"OMG!" She strokes his chest. "This is my friend, Jeremy." I expect him to be irritated or impatient, but he looks to be enjoying the entertainment Ashley provides.

"Hi." Jeremy grins, giving us a small wave. His eyes are almost a silver blue, standing out against his mocha complexion. His black hair is trimmed short, helping with the sleek, sexy look he has going. His outfit is trendier than most men I know as if Ashley plucked him from the pages of a fashion magazine.

"Jeremy is my gay BFF." Ashley wraps her arms around him as if he were her boyfriend.

He doesn't mind; in fact, he seems used to it. "Someone has to keep you in line," he says.

"It's nice to meet you, Jeremy," Morgan says. Then turning to Ashley, she questions, "Will you go back to the slapping Patrick thing?"

Before I can think up a distraction, Ashley jumps back in. "He basically professed his undying love for her, and she slaps him! Have you seen him?"

"Ashley," I interrupt. "He did not profess his undying love! He kissed me."

"What!" Morgan screeches.

"My hand! He kissed my hand," I quickly concede.

Ashley adds, "I'm still not convinced nothing more happened over the Fourth."

"Oh, there was definitely something going on," Morgan agrees.

I turn to Morgan and say, "Are you kidding me? You were there!"

"Oh good," Ashley focuses on Morgan. "Tell me about this boat ride they went on! She claims it was totally innocent but come on. The chemistry between them is crazy intense!"

I shake my head and look to Jeremy who is silent, although he's paying close attention. He shrugs as if to apologize and then throws gasoline on the fire. "Ashley keeps talking about the make-out session in the parking lot."

"With Patrick?" Morgan shrieks.

I lower my face into my hands in defeat. Surely, they can't talk about this all evening.

"No, with Ben!" Ashley corrects, straightening from her slouch against Jeremy. "It was the hottest thing I've ever seen. She, of course, tried to push him away, but he pinned her against his Corvette with that perfect body of his and kissed her until she was wrapped around him. He had to, like, hold her up. Oh my God, it was so hot!"

Morgan looks at me to discredit Ashley's story, but this time Ashley is dead on. I do have a bone to pick with her though. "Ashley, what possessed you to tell Eric about it?"

"Eww, I so totally did not tell Eric anything. Eric's gross, I don't talk to him."

"Yeah, then how does he know?"

"I don't know. Maybe he was eavesdropping when I was on the phone." She flips an ultra-blond lock over her shoulder and leans across the table. "Sorry you had to work alone with him. I told him a long time ago that you were only into girls and thought boys were icky."

"You're the one who told him I'm a lesbian?" I ask, liking the idea she was trying to look out for me.

"Duh! He's a creep. He leaves me alone because he knows my dad will fire his ass if he messes with me. Why? What did he say to you?"

"He said I shouldn't settle for high schoolers and now that he knows I'm not a lesbian he's throwing his name into the running."

Ashley laughs so hard it draws attention from the tables around us. Tears of laughter escape her eyes just as the waitress picks this opportune moment to check on us. Luckily, Morgan and I know what we want without looking at the menu. Ashley and Jeremy don't order anything, insisting they already ate.

Ashley pulls herself together before the waitress leaves. "I think it's hilarious! Eric is delusional if he thinks there's any chance. He totally must not realize he put himself in a lineup with Patrick and Ben. He'd crap himself!"

"Humanities," Jeremy says out of nowhere.

"What?" Ashley's face twists with confusion.

Jeremy looks at me. "I thought you looked familiar. Do you have humanities lecture on Thursdays?"

"Yeah."

"Ben or Patrick? Which one sits with you?"

"Patrick."

"He wasn't there last week."

"No, he wasn't."

Ashley laughs. "See! I'm not the only one to notice how gorgeous he is! What do you think Morgan? He's hot, right? You wouldn't slap him if he kissed you, right?"

"Yes, I would!" Morgan responds. "He's my cousin."

Ashley's smile disappears. She reaches for Morgan's hand and pleads, "Will you give him my number? Emily won't. She says he'll chop me up and leave me in a basement somewhere."

"He's eh—Hey Ben," Morgan says, and we all turn to see him approaching the table.

"Hey," Ben says to everyone, but his eyes lock with mine triggering the flutter of butterflies trapped in my stomach.

255

I'm tempted to say, "Hey there, Mr. Sexy-pants," but before I can say anything, Morgan slides me over so Ben can sit next to me.

"Hi Ben," Ashley swoons.

"Hey, Ashley."

"This is Jeremy," I introduce, motioning to him.

"Hey," Ben nods to him.

"So, when's the rematch?" Morgan asks Ben in her no-nonsense voice.

"We're thinking next weekend."

"Even with the extra practice, I'll still whoop you guys!" Sweet little Morgan is big on trash talk. She's competitive when it comes to sports, even if it's just a friendly game of whiffle ball.

"Oh, we don't need to practice to beat you, Fletcher." Ben's smile turns cocky. "We'll try to take it easy on you."

"Easy on me?" she says. "Please, a little rain and mud wouldn't stop me, but I get that you guys don't want to get your nails dirty."

"Uh oh," Ashley giggles.

Ben bites his lip. "You want to play right now?"

"There's no lightning," Morgan adds.

"Fine." He stands up. "I'll make some calls."

Just like that, he's gone. Our food comes a few minutes later. Morgan fills Ashley and Jeremy in on the whiffle ball game and extends an invitation to join us.

Ben doesn't reappear until we're almost finished. He slides in next to me wrapping his arm around my shoulder. I lean into him as he explains the game plan. "We're meeting at Winters' place in thirty minutes." He looks at Morgan. "You might wanna change out of your heels."

"I could still kick your ass in heels, but I'm not going to ruin my shoes just to prove a point."

Ben and I bounce along the half-mile country driveway leading to James Winters' house. Winters pulls up next to us on his four-wheeler and rides alongside until we reach the back of his house. Ben parks next to a row of cars while James speeds off to do another lap on his ATV. I'm impressed Ben could pull together a group of thirteen people within an hour's notice. I don't have those specific set of skills, but I'm glad he does.

Morgan parks next to Ben's Corvette and she, Ashley, and Jeremy pour out of her car to walk with us to the makeshift baseball diamond. The rain is only a drizzle now, but the field has standing water left from the hours of rain. Alec and Reece are huddled close under an umbrella. Next to them is Gavin. He stares at Ben's arm around my shoulder, and as if to make a statement Ben pulls me in tighter.

Morgan wraps Gavin in a hug and says, "I told you she liked him, Gavin, you just didn't listen."

"Yep, should'a listened," Gavin replies with amusement, and the awkward moment is over. Wow!

"Fletcher, it's been a while," Alec calls, severing his connection to his girlfriend or whatever she is. He breaks free from under the umbrella to hug Morgan.

After pulling away from Alec, Morgan introduces herself to Reece. "Hi, I'm Morgan."

"I'm Reece, Alec's girlfriend." Reece holds tight to the umbrella even though the rain has stopped. She's glowering between Alec and Morgan.

"It's good you're here," Morgan says, rubbing her hands together. "Cause he's gonna need a shoulder to cry on once I'm done wiping the floor with him."

"Ooo!" Ashley taunts.

Morgan turns to her. "He's a cry-baby when he loses."

"You wouldn't know since I've never lost to you," Alec returns.

"That's only because you're always on my team, but not this time!"

The rest of the guys come over to meet us. I've met them all before, and although they are pleasant to me, they all love Morgan. Ashley and Jeremy blend right in with the group and soon Ben and Winters are breaking us up into two teams. Ben's team consists of me, Morgan, Jeremy, and two other guys. Ashley ends up on the other team, but it's all the same to her. Not wanting to participate, Reece moves to watch by the cars.

The whiffle ball is made of plastic, but over the years the guys have added layer after layer of duct tape to both the ball and the cheap plastic bat. This makes them sturdier, but the surface is less predictable, making for an interesting game.

The other team is first up to bat, and Morgan strikes the first player out. The second batter hits the ball and slides through a puddle into first. Alec hits a line drive down center field where Jeremy dives to catch the ball.

"Whoa, Jeremy, good catch!" Morgan praises.

Jeremy smirks, tossing the ball to her. "I have two state championships under my belt."

"That's my best friend!" Ashley yells from behind home plate.

"Ashley, stop cheering for the other team," Alec complains, handing her the bat.

Ashley blows him a kiss and steps up to the plate. She bunts the ball, submerging it in a giant mud puddle. By the time Morgan finds it, the first player is rounding home while Ashley makes it to first.

Morgan, covered in mud smiles at Ashley. "Good play."

Ashley curtsies.

Ben catches the next fly ball, and it's our turn to bat. I'm up first. Gavin pitches and I take a swing and miss. Nervous about another strike, I bunt the ball into Ashley's mud puddle and run to second.

Jeremy hits a homer. Morgan knocks the ball into left field and runs to third. So when Ben hits a ball to the outfield and is rounding second, the game rules change. Alec tries to block Ben from third at the same time Winters comes from behind with the ball. Ben slides into third taking Alec down with him in the process.

From there the game turns into a full-contact sport becoming muddier and less civilized the longer we play. Easy plays become difficult. Running becomes more strenuous over the soggy uneven ground, and we keep losing our shoes in the mud. We're all covered in sludge by the time the sun slinks from the sky. We call it quits in the fourth inning after our team takes a sixteen-point lead.

"Told you I'd wipe the floor with you," Morgan says, wiping mud from her face to smear it on Alec's sleeve. In return, he throws his arm over her shoulder.

"Well, you're a girl. We had to go easy on you," he replies, jumping away when she jabs him in the stomach with her elbow.

The banter between them makes me think of Reece. She moved halfway through our game to sit inside Alec's car. She looked bored then; now, she looks pissed. Alec either doesn't notice or more likely; he doesn't care. When Morgan is around, he's all about her. Tonight is no exception.

Morgan might be competitive, but she also thinks ahead. So, when we're all left covered in mud and wondering how we're supposed to get in our cars, she brings out a heap of old towels she snagged when she went home to change.

Ben grabs two towels and throws them over the seats in his car. Before I get in, Ashley grabs my arm and pulls me close.

"I had a blast, and just so you know, I was totally right. Other than Morgan and me, you surround yourself with hot guys. No wonder other girls didn't like you in school." She kisses my cheek and skips off shouting, "See you Wednesday!"

Ben and I say our goodbyes to everyone before leaving.

"Good call to invite Jeremy," Ben says.

"I think they would've come anyway," I respond, using my fingers to wipe some of the drying mud from his face. He gives me a look that makes me want to crawl into his lap. "I wish I wasn't covered in mud right now."

"I wish I didn't have to take you home."

I lean across the console to kiss him and end up getting more than I bargained for. It's long and sweet and turns a little wild, but I pull away before I'm out of breath. "We should probably go."

As we pull out of the driveway, Ben says, "I work tomorrow evening, but I found a play for us to see on Tuesday," Ben informs me. When I had admitted to him that I fell asleep during the last one, he offered to take me to another.

"You don't have to go. You might get bored," I warn.

"I won't get bored if you're there," he insists.

"It's a date, and I won't fall asleep this time."

He lifts a brow. "I'm not above shooting spitballs at you."

I can't help but laugh.

twenty-four ~

We're back in the field playing ball when the grim reaper-like figures come up from the deep puddles. Shadowed faces glower at me from towering heights. They point in my direction and I know they're after me, but when I turn to run, they go after my friends.

I hear Morgan and Ashley scream, but when I turn around to help them, the blanket of night sky extends for miles, and I can't see a thing. Screams and sobs erupt reverberating in my mind, and it's the last thing I remember before waking up covered in sweat.

My body is sore all over and now that morning has come the bruises are showing. Perhaps there are a few downsides to playing a contact sport in the mud with guys twice my size. I get up to let Maggie out and find my dad at the kitchen table with coffee in one hand and a tablet in the other. I drag myself to the door feeling as old as dirt as an ache in my hip begins to throb.

"What happened to you?" Dad asks, peeking out from behind his computer screen.

"I think I slid over a rock during our game last night," I say, opening the door for Maggie.

"How are your arms?"

"They're okay."

"I thought we'd practice your skills today, then swing by the shooting range, if you're up for it?"

It's weird how at times I forget I'm different. Yesterday was a perfect tease of what I wish my life could be all the time.

"Sure, where did you want to go?" I say.

"The mall worked well the last time."

The mall isn't as awkward this time around. It's become second nature to block everyone out of my head, and at the same time, it's easier to get into their minds.

After the mall, we go to the shooting range at Mike's Guns. Dad has been bringing me here for years, and I've always found target practice to be enjoyable, almost therapeutic. Now, I realize he was being practical and training me so I could defend myself. It worked. I'm comfortable with a pistol tucked between my fingers. I have a steady hand and excellent aim.

Tuesday my life is back to normal. After class I go to *The Wizard of Oz* with Ben and not only do I not fall asleep, I enjoy myself. But that night, my dreams get worse.

We're in the field again, but this time there is nowhere to run as the ground drops out all around us, leaving Ben and me standing at the edge of a cliff. I cling to Ben, and he howls in pain. When I look up at him, I see undiluted terror directed at me. He's begging for his life. As soon as it registers that I'm hurting him, I let go. When I try to comfort him, he shrieks as if my words are causing him pain. I look down at myself wondering what I'm doing wrong and see I'm wearing one of the dark hooded cloaks.

Wednesday morning Ashley is sitting on the counter painting her fingernails as I walk in to work. She beams at me but doesn't move.

"Emily, my whole body has been like, so sore after that game. Totally worth it!" she chimes, finishing her last two nails.

"Yeah, I know what you mean. I have a bruise on my hip the size of a grapefruit," I complain.

"Yowza! It took me forever to get all the dirt from under my fingernails."

"We'll have to do it again sometime," I say, as I clock in.

"Totally!"

It's a hot day, and the air conditioning loses its fight to the afternoon sun shining in through the wall of windows. Ashley and I roll up our sleeves, but she takes it a step further by turning hers into a belly shirt.

"So, Gavin's the one you broke up with, right?"

"Yeah."

"Alec's cute. Did you ever date him?"

I shake my head. "He's cool, but he's a man-whore. I think he sees me more like a sister than a woman, which is why our friendship works."

"Does Morgan know he's a player?"

"He's different around her, but yeah, she knows how he is."

"Different?" Ashley curses. "He's gaga over her."

"Maybe, but he doesn't know how to be serious," I voice. "Morgan's smart enough to keep to harmless flirting."

"You're wrong. She's crazy about him," Ashley says, surprising me. "If you think he's bad news, you need to tell her because something's going on. After you left on Sunday, he walked her to her car and the way he was acting like totally freaked me out."

"What do you mean? What was he doing?"

"He was flirting with her, and she was totally like eating it up."

Ashley can be blind when it comes to hot guys, so I'm taken aback not only by her observations but by her need to protect Morgan, a girl she just met. She's cautious of Alec instead of assuming he would be perfect for Morgan just because he's hot.

"Morgan is smart," I say. "She knows Alec almost as well as I do."

"Yeah, but he doesn't treat you the way he treats her. I'm telling you; she's completely gone over him, and logic won't keep her grounded."

"When did you get so wise?" I question.

"Hey, I notice things. Like you, Miss Pessimistic Patty, always focusing on the negative and not trusting anything at face value. That's why I'm always reminding you of the good in people. Morgan sees all the positives in people—which is why people like her by the way—but she might need to be reminded of the bad in people sometimes."

"Point taken. I'll talk to Morgan."

I'm walking down the street of an abandoned city with six hooded figures walking next to me. The empty streets reek of troubling times. Merchandise bleeds out through shattered windows of ransacked stores. Broken doors swing on their hinges, and car doors stand open on the side of the road. Old pieces of newspaper drift in the wind. Even the animals have fled this place, leaving it void of any life except for the overgrown vegetation.

I push the hood off my head and almost don't recognize myself. Pristine blond waves fold around my shoulders framing the sinister expression on my face. One by one the figures walking with me let their hoods drop revealing blond hair, blue-eyed men with unnerving expressions.

As we approach an abandoned car, the men with me stop as I move forward. With a flick of my finger, the car splits down the middle. Patrick falls out of his hiding place and onto the street. His shoulders slump as he gets to his knees.

"It's too late," he says in a broken voice. He shakes his head as his bloodshot eyes lift to mine. "You've already killed them all."

"They were weak!" I shout.

The force of my anger knocks him back, and he lies helpless in the street. His face is pale and strained as he looks up at me. His bright eyes fade to pale blue as I drain the life from his body.

I wake in a cold sweat. I turn the lights on in my room to keep away the dark thoughts. There is no way I'm going back to sleep tonight. I'm tempted to call Patrick to make sure he's okay, but I talk myself out of it. It was just a dream. It didn't mean anything.

twenty-five ~

It's another hot afternoon. The sun reflects off the dark pavement baking the cars in the parking lot. I don't spot Patrick's car, but that's not unusual. I head into the lecture hall early; afraid Patrick won't be here again.

The room has only a few students, so my eyes find Patrick right away despite him not sitting in our usual spot. Either he's attempting to give me space, or he's avoiding me, but I go to him anyway.

"Hey," I say, as I draw near.

"Hello, love." With a sigh and a bored expression, he looks up. "I've done exactly as you've instructed and left you alone. Now, what else can I do for you?"

I take a deep breath and sit in the open seat next to him. His eyes crease, staring with suspicion, and I remember how his sapphire gaze can break even the strongest women.

"I want to apologize," I say before I change my mind.

He snorts. "Why?"

"Because. I've just been kind of unfair to you. I think . . . I mean . . . I've been a little harsh, you know, about everything."

He's looking more self-assured by the second. "Go on," he encourages.

I narrow my eyes. "That's all."

"Are you sure?"

"It's not all my fault, you know. You've been weird and irritating, and I'm not okay with you showing up in my bedroom unannounced and watching me take off my clothes. You," I poke a finger at him, "should know that's not okay."

"I'm confused, I thought you were apologizing, but this sounds as if you're berating me."

"I'm sorry, but I think maybe you deserve it."

"I'm afraid you've made this terribly unclear. Which is it? You're sorry, or I deserve it?"

"Both!"

A Cheshire grin stretches across his face. "So essentially, you're sorry it's my fault."

"Forget it," I sigh, turning in my seat in an attempt to ignore his mocking.

"I can't possibly forget it when you're trying to make amends here."

"Fine, I take it back!" I cross my arms in frustration.

"It's too late to take it back. You already apologized."

"Well, then I guess I'm *un*-apologizing right now."

He nudges my shoulder. "I've missed you."

I frown his way, but with his warm smile and quirked brow, I can no longer hold back my grin.

He nudges me again. "I think you missed me too," he whispers. "No worries, your secret's safe with me."

I don't want to admit it, but he might be right. He has been on my mind.

"And while we're telling secrets," he continues. "I thoroughly enjoyed watching you undress, but I will admit I went too far."

"Ya think!"

He holds his hands up in defense. "I had a good reason for being there."

"You mean aside from being a pervert with boundary issues?" I challenge.

"I had only honorable intentions."

"Oh, this ought to be good. Honorable intentions? I doubt it."

"I was showing you how easy it is to sneak up on you. You need to be vigilant."

"Oh, Patrick." I shake my head. "Not this again. I really don't need to be reminded."

He drags his hand through his hair. "I think you do."

"Trust me," I glare, hoping to get my point across, "I don't!"

"I know it's offensive to be told you're not taking this seriously enough, but it's worse to watch your family die knowing it's your fault." There's sadness in his eyes as he speaks. "Truly, I know all too well what you're going through."

"You know what it's like to be afraid of what's inside of you? Afraid to close your eyes because of what you'll see? Worried that at any moment a stranger could abduct or murder you? You think you know what that's like?"

"Yes," he answers without hesitation, and I get a glimpse of the pain he's hiding. "I'm trying to save you and your family from a fate I've already suffered."

My irritation and mistrust of him begin to melt away, replaced with a deeper acceptance. He blames himself for what happened to his family, and he knows I'll blame myself if anything happens to the people I love.

"I'm going to protect you whether you want me to or not," he vows.

My voice drops to a whisper. "Anyone who helps Valla blood *dies*, remember?"

"That's right because you're the biggest, baddest wolf around. They're afraid of you because you're the only one strong enough to stop them."

"But I'm not strong enough to stop them. I'm not even strong enough to stop you. And what if they're right about us? What if my mom was . . ." I can't say it. "I mean . . ." I lower my voice to a whisper, feeling vulnerable to verbalize fears I've been trying to deny. "She killed people. What if it's just part of who we are? What if it's just what we become? I don't want to kill people, Patrick." I avoid his eyes, looking around the room, knowing it's not safe to talk about this in such a public place.

Patrick's voice pulls my attention back to him. "In a few minutes, the staff are going to announce that class is canceled. Let's go somewhere we can talk."

"Why is class canceled?" I ask, wondering what he's done. "How do you know?"

"Always the skeptic. Professor Fickle had a heart attack this morning, and they haven't found anyone to cover the lecture. I know because the staff has been thinking about it for the last half-hour."

"Oh my god, is he okay?" I breathe, feeling my heart tighten with worry over the charming old man.

"They don't know. Come on, let's go."

We stand and, on our way, out I spot Jeremy sitting a few rows back talking to a group of girls. I smile and wave as our eyes meet. He blows me a kiss, or maybe he's blowing it to Patrick, either way, I smile bigger and feel a glimpse of Patrick's internal frown.

"I see you've been busy making friends," Patrick says, as I push open the door. "This way." He touches my back to guide me. It sends a volt of electricity through me which I'm sure he felt, but I pretend not to notice. Instead, I walk quickly in the direction he sends me.

The brick pathway leads to a shaded area surrounded by mature trees heavy with leaves. Patrick halts, gripping my arm, so I don't continue forward. Looking satisfied with the secluded area free of any spectators, Patrick sits down on a bench.

Dropping my bag next to Patrick, I hoist myself onto the brick wall behind the bench. Patrick gives me an exhausted look, sighs, and then joins me on the wall.

"Don't take this the wrong way, but I can't stop thinking about you." I continue to talk through his pleased smile. "It's just that sometimes I don't know how to pretend everything's okay. Now I'm having these dreams, and I'm lying to all of my friends and my sister. How do you do it?"

His gentle laugh takes me by surprise. "You were pretending to be normal long before we met."

"I wasn't pretending. I was just trying to live a normal life. That was before I knew what I am, what we are, and what I can do. That was before I knew what happened to my mom."

"Keeping secrets is something you'll become used to, and you won't always have to live your life afraid."

"What do you mean?"

"Do you hate the people who killed your mother?" he asks.

"I try not to think about the pain she went through, let alone the people who caused it all. I don't want to be ruled by my anger. Why? Do you hate the people who killed your mom?"

"Him," he corrects. "And yes, I hate him very much."

"You know him?"

"Yes." He's quiet and there are ghosts in his eyes. With a shudder, he pulls himself out of his trance, saying, "Emily, you will learn to hate. You will learn to control the emotions from consuming you. You'll have to learn, or you'll die. That is your only option."

My eyes widen and I lean away from him. "I'm pretty sure hate is not the answer."

"No, it's not the answer, but you need to know what it feels like, so you don't let the feelings consume you."

Shaking my head, I look to my feet. "Patrick, you're speaking in riddles again."

"Let me be very clear." His words bring my eyes back to him. "You don't think you're capable of killing anyone, I presume. That is a problem."

I want to believe he's joking, but his chastising glare warns me otherwise. My gaze turns introspective. I disentangle my thoughts and get stuck on a wistful memory, a vision of my mother. This time she's smiling as she sings happy birthday and presents me with my cake. The idea of my beautiful mother killing anyone is strangling. She's murdered people! My mind knows the truth, but my heart is reluctant to accept it.

Freeing myself from the memory before it becomes jaded, I question, "Have you ever killed anyone?"

His guilty eyes shift to avoid mine, telling me what he doesn't want to admit.

I lay a comforting hand on his forearm regaining his attention and say, "I really don't think I could kill anyone. I wouldn't know how to live with myself."

"Sometimes there is no choice," he says, meeting my eyes once more.

"There's always a choice," I counter and watch as he slips into his mask of cool confidence, indicating I must have struck a nerve. Witnessing the change in his demeanor is unnerving. "Every time you do that it makes me trust you less."

"Years of training, love." His voice is blithe but chilling. "The real trick is showing the emotion."

I attempt to hide my shiver by shifting on the wall. He gives me a cocky grin, and I wonder why he believes murder was his only choice.

"Emily, killing is different for an Olvasho. When you take the life of another Olvasho, you gain their strength; rather like what you experienced in the boat with me. That power you felt; it would've become yours if you had finished killing me. These men have killed to gain their power, and you must kill them in order to survive."

For a second, I feel torn, straddling the metaphorical fence between arguing with him and defending his flawed logic. I know he's strong, but did he gain his strength by killing others? It feels impossible to justify.

"How many have you killed?" I question, wanting to know what made him this way.

His grin fades, his gaze going distant. "One . . . ten, does it make a difference?"

"Of course, it does. They aren't just numbers, Patrick. They aren't power bars. They were people! They had names and lives, and they probably have people missing them!"

"Your reaction is exactly why I'll protect you with my life and train you until you can kill me with a thought."

That sends a lightning bolt of fear straight to my heart as I remember my dream where I did just that. Fear molds my resolve. "I won't kill you or anyone. I'm not going to be this thing you want me to be. It might make you feel better if I take a life, but it is not gonna happen."

"Make me feel better?" His cynical chuckle starts the nervous churning in my stomach. "Emily, love," he breathes against my neck, as he moves in seductively close. "If you annihilate the entire world, it would not change the way I feel."

His breath sends a chill through my body, and I slide off the wall to put much-needed distance between us.

"Guilt," I whisper. "That's what you should feel while you sit here relishing in your own power. People are dead because of you!"

"I don't need a reminder. I have to live with it every second of every day but don't try to pretend we aren't the same. You are just as cold and selfish—perhaps worse. While I genuinely don't give a damn what people think of me—unless I want something from them—you . . . you pretend to be this strong, standalone badass when actually you're just too scared to let anyone close."

"How dare you!"

"I'm not finished! You practically run everyone away. It would be a wonder you have any friends at all, except I know the irresistible pull you possess. You attach shackles to the people around you, and while you pull them along, you push them away; but they can't leave you unless you unlock their chains." He slips from the wall and takes a step forward. "You make them suffer until there is nothing left." He steps closer. "And you know! You know what you're doing, but you pretend to be a victim."

I clear my throat and push back the tears that will make me look weak. "Who hurt you so badly you have to hurt everyone around you?"

He gives me a wicked grin. "The man who raised me, love. He was a real bastard. You remind me of him sometimes."

I react without thinking. A thousand needles sting my palm as the heat warms my hand. A red outline is already forming across the white of his cheek, but I refuse to feel guilty. It's his fault. How dare him!

"Even as cruel as he is, he's never hit me. How juvenile," he says with his condescending smile, acting as though he's been hit by a child rather than an angry woman with Valla blood.

I waver on what to say. Everything that comes to mind sounds petty, but I can't rein in my anger. In a fluid motion, I swing my bag over my shoulder and glare at this devilishly stunning, infuriating man. "At least I'm adult enough to know when I'm wrong, and man was I wrong! I take back my apology! I want nothing to do with you."

He chuckles, as if unaffected.

"Go to hell, Patrick!" I turn and walk away, hoping and praying he doesn't follow.

"Call me when you realize I'm right," he yells after me.

I don't look back, going straight to my next class. Class doesn't help and by the time I'm walking to my car the acidic taste Patrick left me with is burning. This is when the cherry red Ferrari pulls up.

The dark passenger window rolls down, and a deep voice calls, "Emily?"

I'm too angry to talk to anyone, so I pretend not to hear him. I continue to walk away until a door opens, and I hear footsteps behind me. I turn to face the man.

"Emily, I just need a minute," he insists. "I believe you're dating my son. My name is Everett Cetrone." He extends his hand and we shake.

He's wearing a three-piece suit despite the ninety-five-degree weather. He tugs at his collar and says, "If you would join me in the car for a moment, I'd be grateful. It's a very warm day."

Even though he comes across as charismatic and charming, my insides warn me not to get in the car, but he's Ben's father, and I don't want to be rude, so I get in without resistance. We shut the doors and the coolness surrounds us. I've never been in such an extravagant vehicle, and it makes me nervous that I'm sweating on such overpriced leather.

Everett breaks the silence. "So Emily, you're dating Benjamin."

"Yes, sir."

"I suppose you know he's declined his acceptance into Duke and Yale, among others."

I rein in my surprise and act nonchalant. "I knew he declined a few schools."

"He declined them all!" he growls. "Do you know why?"

I try to respect my elders, but his tone is filled with icy condescension, making my retort a little sarcastic. "He wants to pursue other things."

"Other things? I guess slumming it with an opportunistic whore who has no future qualifies as other things," he seethes. "Now, here's what I'm willing to offer. You'll get one-hundred-thousand to walk away from him and one-hundred-thousand each year for the next five years as long as you stay away from him."

I'm shocked by his offer, horrified by his insults, but mostly I'm heartbroken for Ben. It takes a lot for me not to jump out and compel him to drive his precious car into a damn tree, but I take the high road . . . kind of. "You can keep your money, sir. This opportunistic whore doesn't want it or need it. But I would like to thank you for helping me to understand why Ben calls you Everett instead of Daddy. You should be proud of your son because, despite you, he turned out to be an amazing man. I suspect he doesn't want to go to those schools because *you* want him to go. He's terrified of becoming anything like you. He'll do anything to keep that from happening, even if it means he suffers because of it." I open the door.

"I see through you, you money grubbing bitch! I know what you're up to. You won't get any money out of Benjamin. I'll cut him off, and you won't see a dime!"

I climb out of the car and lean back in. "Your money means nothing to me, and Ben doesn't give a shit about his bank account. He would be happier with a father who valued him over money and reputation. If you keep this up, you're going to lose your son." I smile. "Personally, I don't give a shit about you, but I'd do anything for Ben." Standing straight, I slam the car door and turn away as the car speeds off. Ben is right, his father cares more about money than he does his children and it makes my heart bleed for them.

I'm driving down the road digesting Patrick's accusations and Everett's behavior when my sister calls. My new car is synced with my phone, so the ringing comes from the car's speakers.

"Hey Sam," I greet, grateful for the distraction.

"Emily Burk, you little bitch!" she shrieks from the speakers surrounding me. "I just left Dan's parent's house where I had to hear from Leah that you have a boyfriend!"

"Sorry I didn't tell you."

"Benjamin Cetrone!" she shouts, and I turn the volume down. "Are you kidding me? How could you!"

"Samantha, I had no idea this would upset you. We just started dating."

"You're joking, right? Please tell me you're joking. Emily, how could you! You're so selfish. You don't think about anyone but yourself!" Her voice is angrier than when she started. She curses, there's a shuffle, and a deep voice comes on the line.

"Hey Emily, it's Dan," he starts. "I think the reason Samantha's so upset is because my sister, Leah, has had a not-so-secret crush on Ben for years. Leah is not happy about the idea of you two together. She's refusing to be in the wedding. She thinks you're trying to ruin her life and won't stand next to you or your sister."

I pull my car to the side of the road to keep myself from driving straight to Leah's house and committing murder. Patrick thinks I'm capable of it and at this moment I'm pretty sure he's right.

"Dan," I manage through clenched teeth, "Leah is playing her, you've gotta know that."

"I know," he says, surprising me. I knew I liked Dan.

"Even if I weren't in the picture, Ben would never go for Leah. She's mean and manipulative, and he's seen what she's capable of. She slashed my tires, convinced the entire school I was a whore and filled my locker—books and all—with syrup. She hates me!"

"I didn't know the extent, but I knew the general vibe of what she thought of you. Does Samantha know any of this?"

"No!" I rage, "And I don't want her to know. I was hoping Leah would give it up when we graduated."

"I'll try to calm Sam down, but this is something she should know. I know how Leah is, but she's my sister, and in the eyes of our parents she can do no wrong. I'll try to talk to Leah, too."

"I'd appreciate anything you can do, but please don't tell Sam about the tires or the syrup."

We hang up, and I stay on the side of the road sitting in silence for a while before I weave back into traffic.

When I get home, I remember Dad's leaving on another business trip. This time he'll be in Colorado for two days.

"I'll have my phone on as soon as I land," he says in place of hello, as I enter the living room. "If you need anything at all, please call. I'll be back Saturday evening. I'll call between meetings to check in."

"I'll make sure to have wild, crazy parties the whole time you're gone."

His eyes search my face. "Don't worry, Samantha will calm down."

I blow out a breath. "She called you?"

"Dan did."

"Oh, shit."

"We're gonna talk about Leah when I get back," he says, voice low. "You lied to me, Emily."

"It was better if I just put up with it, Dad. If more people got involved, it would've become this big thing. I was protecting you and Sam. It didn't need to involve anyone else."

"Leah should have faced the consequences for her actions."

"Dad, you're not stupid. Leah's family is wealthy and well-respected. Who do you think people would believe?"

He hugs me, saying, "Wealthy and well-respected doesn't mean innocent."

"Don't you have a plane to catch?"

"I do." He pulls away. "In the future, don't keep stuff from me, and especially don't hide it because you think you're protecting me."

I nod.

"Promise me," he demands.

"I promise."

He gives me one last look and heads for the door, saying, "I'll see you soon."

"Have a safe trip, Dad."

I sit down to contemplate and realize I've done precisely what Patrick accused me of. I've tried and failed over and over to push Ben away, but I can't let go. I'm inadvertently hurting him, just like Molly said. And now his father is threatening to cut him out of the family fortune because of my involvement. As if that's not enough, Leah has lashed out at my sister, causing my dad to find out about my high school bully—all because I said too much. All because I let my walls down and allowed Ben to infiltrate my defense.

It's time to build the walls back up on my ice castle, so people stop getting hurt.

twenty-six ~

I sit in the backyard with Maggie staring out into the darkness. I've missed two calls from my sister, three from Ben, and I ignore the voicemails and text messages.

My phone vibrates and Morgan's face lights the screen. Before voicemail picks it up, I shove my emotions to the side and answer, "Hey."

"You okay?" Morgan asks.

"Yeah, I'm fine."

"Your sister and Ben called asking about you. What's going on?"

"Leah's still trying to destroy my life while I destroy everyone close to me."

"I'm not sure what you mean."

Of course, she doesn't. Since when did I start speaking in Patrick riddles?

"Sorry Morgan, everything will be okay. I'll call them," I reassure her. "Oh, and Morgan, Alec will break your heart if you let him. He doesn't know how to be serious, and I'm afraid he'll ruin your faith in people. And that sucks because I think you'd be good together."

"Uh . . . I'm umm . . . not sure what to say."

"I know. We'll talk soon."

"Call me later, Emily."

As I hang up, I hear Ben's car coming down the street. The purr of the engine dies in front of my house, so I walk around from the backyard. I know I'm about to break his heart, but what other choice do I have?

"Ben," I call.

He pauses halfway up the front walk, then changes his course to come toward me. He's careful to keep a watchful eye on Maggie as she stands between us growling a protective warning.

"No Maggie," I command. Her hair stays raised, but she retreats in silence.

"We were supposed to meet at my house at eight. It's almost ten, and I couldn't get a hold of you." The contention in Ben's voice is audible.

"I need to be alone," I mumble.

"No!"

"Excuse me?"

"No, you're not staying here alone tonight so you can spend all that time in your head. Who knows what'll happen to you! Leah is not coming between us!" His body is tight, jaw tense as he stands too close.

"How do you know about Leah?"

"The only reason it took me so long to get here is because I stopped over there first. Leah won't be bothering you anymore, and I called your sister to tell her all the things you wouldn't."

"Ben! What the . . . you . . ." I stutter, no longer numb, but furious. "How dare you!"

"Come here," he says, taking a step closer.

I step away. "You have no right!"

"The hell I don't!" His anger eclipses mine. "I just got you back. I'm not losing you again." He grabs me and pulls me into his arms.

I push at his solid chest, but he doesn't budge, so I plead with him, "Ben, please let me go."

"Screw that! I'm not letting go."

"Ben, damn it. Let me go!"

"Emily, if you can honestly tell me you don't want me here, then I'll go."

He releases me, and I look up into his fierce brown eyes. I tell myself to lie to him. "Ben, I don't . . . I don't want you to go," I say in a weak voice, stepping into him. His arms wrap around me and I surrender, my anguish turning to tears against his chest.

This is how I end up on Ben's couch with my head against his shoulder. We don't talk about Leah, and I don't tell him about the run-in I had with his dad. He patiently allows me to remain silent even when he has every right to demand more. Instead, we drown our thoughts by watching TV, and within an hour I fall asleep.

Water is dripping nearby. I open my eyes to search for the source of the noise and find myself lying in a warm puddle on a tile floor. I look up to find a steady drip coming from above. Blood falls from the body of a beautiful woman slumped in a chair. It hits the tile floor and pools around me warm and sticky. I stand from the puddle to look into the glazed blue eyes of the lifeless woman. What begins as another bad dream turns into much more when my mind identifies the woman slumped in the chair. Recognition has my synapses firing on overdrive, starting a chain reaction I have no control to stop.

Like a bolt of lightning, I'm struck by a flash of light so bright it rips through my flesh and bones. It tears into my brain and sends a shock of electricity to every nerve in my body. I'm very much awake and want to scream, but the current flowing through me doesn't allow for movement.

A burst of images plays like a motion picture inside my skull. Snapshots of my lost memories piece themselves back together in an array of movement. I hear snip-it's of my mother's voice. I smell the gel Ben used to wear in his hair. I feel my first kiss. I taste the bitter pill I'm forced to swallow in the hospital. I remember the pain of having my memories sucked away from me. It's very similar to the pain I feel now.

I try to focus on the memories, but I'm lost in pure sensation. I feel I've been thrown into a tornado; the wind lashes at my skin and the missing pieces of my life whirl around me like shrapnel. I cannot escape. I pray for the fire to burn out and the memories to stop. I'm struggling within myself, wanting and needing all of the memories, but at the same time, the pain is overwhelming.

The cascading memories finally slow until all I see are her bright blue eyes. Those eyes are forcing me to remember, the same way they forced me to forget. I remember the woman my mother trusted with my safety and I recognize her from Patrick's memory. His mother saved my life, yet she was unable to save her own. Along with regaining my memories, I get flashes of her last moments, like the two intertwine.

She's sitting in a white room with no windows as teenage Patrick is being hauled away. He's covered in her blood and is screaming and lashing out at the men who are forcefully dragging him from the room and down the hall. Patrick's agonizing sobs fade as another door slams. Patrick's mother looks down to the empty floor and says, "Tell Patrick I'll always love him and tell him it wasn't his fault. Emily, it's up to you now. You must fight."

I witness the life fade from her eyes. The sticky heat from her blood lingers on my skin. My burning pain comes to an end, and I'm left feeling raw and powerless. I'm unsure of how she was able to share her last moments with me, and it leaves me feeling unnerved.

I pull myself back to the present and remember I'm leaning against Ben. Did he experience all of those things along with me? I push away to better judge his expression, but when I open my eyes, I can't see anything. I hear the television, so I know I'm awake.

"Ben?" I ask into the darkness.

"Yeah."

"Why is it so dark in here?"

I feel him shift in his seat next to me. "It's . . . Em, look at me. Hold on," he says, as he jets off the couch. I hear footfalls on the carpet and then the click of a light switch.

"Ben, please say something."

"Your eyes," he breathes, "they're . . . Your pupils and irises are gone. Your eyes are all milky white. Can you see?"

"No," I whisper, terrified.

"Come on," he says, grabbing my hand. "I'll take you to the hospital."

"No!" I panic.

He stops. "Why not?"

"I'll be fine."

"Em, this is not fine!"

"Just give me a minute to think," I say, not understanding what's happening. Could this be normal for an Olvasho? What if I never see again?

"Come on, Em, you can think on the way."

"No!"

"Why?"

"Because!" I yell, showing just how scared I am.

The TV goes quiet as Ben settles next to me. It's silent except for the slow intake and exhale of his breath, then he patiently says, "I'm trying to understand. Why won't you tell me what's going on? Help me understand."

"It's comp—"

"Complicated, I know!" His patience is gone. "Tell me anyway!"

"I'm different, Ben, and some people want me dead because of it, but . . . you're not supposed to get involved."

He takes another breath. "I'm already involved. Who wants you dead, Emily?"

"Can we focus on one problem at a time, please?" I motion to my eyes. "Clearly, this isn't normal."

"Clearly, but just a second ago you told me you were fine."

"Yeah, well . . . we need to call my dad."

Ben gets up to walk across the room. I hear him ruffle through my bag before he comes back to sit next to me, saying, "It keeps going straight to voicemail."

"Then . . . you're not going to like this, but I need you to call Patrick."

"Em, you're gonna have to explain that to me."

I rest my hand on his bouncing knee attempting to calm him. "Ben," I soothe. "Please call Patrick. His number is in my phone. He might know what to do. He might be able to fix this." I motion to my eyes and then move my hands to feel for his face. My fingers graze his lips, and I lean in to kiss him.

"Your eyes are really spooky," he says, and then a moment later, "Here, it's ringing." He places the phone in my hand as he abandons the couch.

I put the phone to my ear just in time to hear Patrick's say, "Well, that didn't take long."

"I'm blind!"

"I don't doubt it after the kind of power you just used, love."

"How did you know?"

"I'd be surprised if any Olvasho within fifty miles didn't feel that surge of energy," he says, reminding me how little I know about this new part of me.

"But—"

"Don't worry, love. I'm already on my way."

"What do you mean you're already on your way? You don't even know where I am."

"Yes, I do. Just sit tight."

"Patrick?"

"Bye, love."

After disconnecting, I put the phone down. Ben is silent and I can't tell where he is. I reach out with my mind, not to read his thoughts but to sense him. I feel him several paces away, so I stand to reach for him.

"What's going on?" he asks pointedly, as he backs away. "Why does Patrick get to know more than I do?"

"It's only to protect you," I whisper.

"I don't need protection, Emily! I need you!" He's angry and he has every right to be.

"Ben, you have me." I reach for him again. He doesn't move away this time, but he doesn't offer anything in return. "This is me. I tried to warn you."

Silence ensues and I turn away closing my eyes. When I was a child I used to believe when I closed my eyes, I turned invisible. I've wished it to be true so many times, but right now all I want is to open my eyes and be seen. I don't want to hide from him, but my life demands secrecy.

"Are you ever going to trust me, Em?"

I turn around to face him, opening my milky blind eyes. "This isn't about trust, Ben. I've put you in danger because I'm stupid and selfish," The words roll off my tongue and it feels good to tell him the truth. "Some people want to kill me because of who I am. They murdered my mom, and now they're after me."

The long silence after my admission is agonizing.

"Ben?"

"But I thought . . . How do you know? How do you know she was murdered?"

"I watched her die."

"Em," his voice changes into that sympathetic tone. It means he doesn't believe me and worse, he's feeling sorry for me.

"I'm not crazy!"

"I know you're not crazy, but you're confused."

"I'm not confused, Ben. Things are different, but I can't explain without compromising your safety. The only reason Patrick is involved is because he's different too."

"Come here." He pulls me into him. "Em, I'm trying to understand, but—"

"But I sound crazy," I say into his chest.

There's a scratching sound coming from the wall of windows. Ben pulls away and I hear the sound of swooshing curtains.

"Umm . . . Em, your dog is here."

"What?" I hear the door open and a second later Maggie nuzzles her head under my hand. "How?" I ask, not expecting an answer.

"She could feel it too," Patrick's voice rings from the direction of the door.

I look up even though I know I won't see him, asking, "Did you bring her?"

"No, she beat me here. Now, that's a well-trained dog."

Ben wraps his arm protectively around my shoulder, oozing disapproval of Patrick. He's worried about my sanity, but he still cares, and my devastated heart leaps with hope.

"Yuck, you two," Patrick groans. "Watch out love, he's a bit possessive. Now, come on, let's fix this."

"How?" I ask, unwilling to move away from Ben.

"If you would come over here, I can show you."

I feel caught between the two of them. I might want Ben, but right now I need Patrick.

"I don't even know what happened. Patrick, has this happened to you before?"

"No," he laughs, "but it is so nice to be let in again."

His cryptic message isn't lost on me. My mind is left wide open for him because it's too raw and disconcerted to confine. My memories are still sorting themselves out in my subconscious.

"Only you could do this, love. Only Valla blood is capable of such things."

"Why did I lose my sight?"

"Side effect from the overload in your head, I suppose."

"Can you fix it?"

"Not if he's here," Patrick says, and Ben tightens his grip on me.

"He stays," I argue.

"No," Patrick disagrees. "Not if you want my help. This will take all of our concentration, and he'll be a distraction."

I turn toward Ben, pleading, "I need him to fix this."

"How is he going to fix you? Emily, you need a doctor, not an egotistical asshole."

Patrick laughs. "To be fair, many doctors are egotistical assholes."

"Ben, trust me," I plead, placing a hand on his chest.

"I don't trust him."

"I know, but I do," I say, stretching the truth. When Ben doesn't make any move to leave, I say, "Ben?"

He breaks our hold and moves a few steps. His feet are soft on the carpet, but it sounds as if he's moving closer to—

"I'm not leaving her alone with you," Ben warns Patrick.

"Yes, you will. Otherwise, you'll be the reason she won't be able to see your pretty little face again."

"God, Em, I can't believe you trust him."

Patrick speaks before I can, "Oh please, Benny Boy, Emily and I have a relationship you couldn't begin to understand."

The swift rustling of clothes, scuffing of shoes, and the growing levels of testosterone in the room are the first signs of what is sure to be a nasty fight.

"Enough!" I shout. "I think my current condition trumps the need to see who has the biggest balls! Ben, I know Patrick's an asshole. It's a hard fact to overlook, and if this were a less urgent situation, I wouldn't ask you to leave us. Patrick, stop with the head games. Blind or not, you provoke him again, and I will ask him to hit you square in your pretty little face."

It takes a moment before either of them moves.

"Emily," Ben whispers, standing before me. He pulls my chin up and places a soft kiss on my lips. "How long will this take?"

Patrick answers, "I've never done this before so I can't be sure, perhaps an hour, perhaps a day."

"Just call me when you're done or if you need anything. I won't be far." Ben places my phone in my palm and his bitterness emanates through the room as he walks out.

"Did you really need him to leave?" I question Patrick.

"Of course. He would get on my nerves hovering over you, marking his territory."

As if wading into the shallow end of a pool, I feel Patrick's soothing calm lapping at my skin, invoking his peaceful aura onto me.

"Come here." He takes my hand and walks me back to the sofa. "Sit."

I do as he says, and Maggie snuggles up next to me as I ask, "Why did this happen?"

"I don't know for sure. What were you doing right before this came about?"

"I had a dream, a nightmare. I've been having them, but this was more. She took my memories. And um . . ." I think of his mom and I'm not sure if I should bring it up, except, I remember too late because my mind is wide open for him.

"Yes, you've met my mother," he confirms in a casual tone that hides whatever he's feeling.

"You knew? Why didn't you tell me? Patrick, your mom was one of the only people my mom trusted. She saved my life!"

"Yes, well . . . while you're still alive, let's get your sight back."

"I saw what they did to her," I admit, trying to keep the image from my mind so he won't have to relive it as I have. "I'm sorry. We'll get them, Patrick. I swear." I squeeze his hand.

"I take it you got your memories back, as well as seeing my mother's last memory."

"Yes, but how?"

"Only a Valla can get back a full memory once it's been taken. Most Olvasho only get fragments—if anything at all—and only the very gifted can steal or alter memories."

"Your mother was exceptional. Though, I don't know why she took some of these memories. They have nothing to do with Valla blood."

"Yes, but they could tie you to something more perilous. Like, for instance, neglecting who you are so you can spend time with your boyfriend."

I ignore his blatant reprimand and start with another concern. "It hurt! When I got the memories back, it was excruciating."

"Yes, I imagine it would be. You still shouldn't have told Ben."

"Like I had a choice. Look at me!" I defend and go on to admit, "I'm relieved Ben knows even if he doesn't understand. It feels good to know he still accepts me."

"He accepts you because he has no idea what it means. Though, I agree with Ben on one thing. You do look spooky."

I glare at him through blind eyes. "You have no boundaries, do you?"

"I used to. They nearly got me killed. Now close your eyes." His warm hands brush against my face, and I worry he's going to kiss me, but his fingers close over my eyelids. "I felt you reaching out from miles away. I hope no Olvasho besides my uncle was close enough to feel it." He moves his hands to my temples, and I feel even more vulnerable.

My panic rises. "Do you think . . . What if they find us?"

"I don't sense anyone near. You are safe with me. Now try to relax. I need you to relax," Patrick soothes. "If you're tense, this is going to be more difficult than it needs to be."

"How do you know this is going to work?"

"I don't. Now stop talking. Take a deep breath."

"What if I hurt you?"

"Shh," he pacifies, "you won't hurt me. Just breathe."

I focus on my breathing and feel his peaceful aura merge with my thoughts. I wonder how he stays so calm all the time. I want to know his trick.

"Shh," he hushes my not-so-inner thoughts as he moves closer. "I'm going to move my hand to the back of your head." He shifts one hand to cover both eyes and the other wraps around the nape of my neck.

Healing warmth radiates through my body bringing relief to my skull. Before long I'm hot, too hot. My cheeks feel flushed and sweat trickles down my back. I feel like I'm standing inside an active volcano. It burns like being stung by a thousand bees at once while the venom pulsates through my veins. I endure the miserable sensations without complaint, feeling my mind meld back together.

After what feels like an eternity, Patrick drops his hands and falls away. The absence of his touch affects me like an arctic breeze coursing through my body, chilling even the marrow deep in my bones. When I open my eyes, my vision is perfectly restored, but I hate what I see. I've hurt him. Sweat glistens across his pale face while faint blue irises have taken the place of brilliant sapphire. His heavy-lidded eyes fall closed, and his shoulders slump as exhaustion pulls his body deeper into the sofa.

"Patrick?" I move to graze my fingers across his forehead. His skin is cool and damp.

He cracks open one eye. "Yes, love?"

"I've hurt you. I'm so sorry." Worry laces through my thoughts. "Are you gonna be okay?"

He gives a weak shrug. "Meh, these things happen. I enjoy dancing with you, love. It's just exhausting." He falls silent, and I wonder if he's fallen asleep. I start to move away, but he reaches for me.

"Don't go," he pleads. "Stay with me. Please."

The sight of him raw like this, makes me ache for him. His desperation reminds me of six-year-old Patrick from his memory. I take his hand in mine and lean back into the sofa, our shoulders touching. "I'll stay," I whisper.

His body relaxes in the silence. Not only minutes have passed, but hours. I think about calling Ben, but I don't want him to see us like this and I'm not ready to pull away.

Though my feelings for Patrick are different from what I feel for Ben, I have extremely strong feelings for both of them. Ben is my best friend. He feels like home. Patrick, on the other hand, feels like survival I dislike him the majority of the time, but reality has shown me how much I need him. Although I probably shouldn't, I feel safe with him.

I continue to hold his hand, watching him sleep, feeling grateful for his presence. I feel hopeful because maybe, just maybe, together we have a chance against those who hunt me. Feeling reassured, my body unwinds, and I allow myself to drift off to sleep.

twenty-seven ~

I'm woken slowly by the comforting stroke of fingers in my hair. Sunshine glares through the floor to ceiling windows along the back of Ben's room. I look up expecting to find Patrick, but it's Ben running his fingers through my hair.

"Ben?"

He looks down at me, his fingers stopping on my cheek. "Good morning, beautiful."

"Good morning," I smile, wishing every morning could start like this. "Did Patrick leave?"

"He's outside with Maggie."

I want to explain to Ben how my feelings for him were stolen from me years ago. Instead, I sit up, wrap my arms around him, and give him a kiss.

The ringtone I have set for Dad chimes from across the room. I break our kiss and hurry over to pick it up. The text is short and to the point. My blood runs cold. Hoping for a mistake, I dial his number. Upon hearing his voicemail, I hang up and dial again. It goes straight to voicemail the next four attempts.

"What's wrong? What happened?" Ben questions.

"He's not answering." How did I go so long without realizing I hadn't heard from him? It was too long. I never got a call telling me he made it to Colorado. I flip back to the text he sent me. Ben steps closer and takes the phone from my hand to read the text.

Get to base. Ask for Chris. Bring Patrick.

"Em, what does this mean?"

My phone chimes again in a different tone and Ben opens the message. After a quick inhale, Ben looks at me with fear in his eyes. I try to grab for my phone, but he pulls it away.

"Give me my phone!" I demand.

Worried eyes burrow into mine. "Emily, what is going on?"

"Give it to me!" I shout frantically.

He relents and hands me the phone. I gasp at the image. There is no message from the unknown number, only a picture of Dad tied to a chair with a gag in his mouth, his face bloody and swollen.

Patrick walks through the door with Maggie. He reaches for my phone without asking, our mental link providing him a clue to what's going on.

"We need to call the cops," Ben insists.

"The police cannot help," Patrick says to Ben, and looks to me. "We need to go."

I nod. "Ben, I'm sorry." I bend down to pick up my bag and brush a fresh tear from my eye. I take a deep breath before turning to say goodbye. I'm startled to find Ben so close.

"Em . . ." He reaches out and gathers me into him.

Despair inches its way into my heart as I see firsthand just how much danger I've potentially placed upon Ben. My dad willingly stepped into the position of my protector and the image of him on my phone will forever haunt me. I can't let that happen to Ben. I love him too much.

"Ben, remember when I promised I'd say goodbye before I ran away?" I say with a sad smile. "I'm breaking up with you. What I'm doing to you isn't fair. You saw my dad, Ben. That could just as easily be you, and this is not your fight."

"It is my fight! You are my fight!"

"I'm sorry. I shouldn't have gotten you involved. Please . . ."

He leans down and his lips find mine. His arms hold me tight while he kisses me as if his heart will break the moment he lets go. Everything fades to the background as love for this man consumes me.

"We need to go," Patrick's voice interrupts our moment. "My car is just outside."

Remembering my fear, anger, and guilt, I tear myself away from Ben and head toward the door.

"Why does he get to go?" Ben asks.

Patrick cuts in, "Because I'm not dead weight. I'm the best chance she has."

Ben steps forward. "What's your deal, man?"

"It's such a long list, but mostly, Emily is in danger, Mark is in danger, and we're wasting our time because of you."

Ben glances at me before turning to Patrick and acquainting his fist with Patrick's jaw in a mean right hook. My shock registers a millisecond before pride, but both are back burners to anger. I get between the two of them and with a shaky voice, I say, "My dad might be dying right now, and this is what you're doing!"

Patrick straightens, wiping blood from his lip. He looks at me with a raised eyebrow as if to say; it wasn't me. Ben, on the other hand, looks guilty.

"Patrick, wait outside! Take Maggie. I'll be out in a minute."

"Do you want me to wipe his memory first?" Patrick asks like it's a reasonable question.

"Go!" I shout.

He shrugs, his complete lack of emotion is unsettling as he saunters out the door with Maggie.

I look to Ben My anger and worry melt into sorrow over what I'm doing to him. "I'm sorry, but I have to go," I say looking the way of the door.

He steps forward, pleading, "Emily, what's happening?"

"I told you, some people want me dead. Patrick is an ass, but he's right about the cops. They can't help. Neither can you. These people . . . they have abilities, like Patrick and me. It's something we have to take care of, and you can't tell anyone."

Worry creases his brow. He doesn't promise me anything, but I know Ben will keep my secret. With a conspiratorial half grin, I say, "That was a nice right hook, and it's about time someone hit him, but how's your hand." I give it a slight squeeze and watch him wince.

"That's what I thought," I say, as I place his wounded hand inside of mine and apply gentle pressure. I'm not sure how this works, but if Patrick can do it then so can I. I close my eyes and say the word *heal* in my mind, feeling the heat instantly. I feel the pain in his hand; however, it's the heartache I find impossible to ignore. I did this to him.

"Emily, what are you doing?"

"Shh," I calm. It's hard to concentrate on his hand when I have his thoughts running through my head, along with his verbal questions. My hands feel like I've placed them directly on a hot stove, yet the intense heat is what keeps me focused. It takes maybe thirty-seconds for the whole incident, but once I open my eyes and release his hand, I feel as if I could fall from exhaustion. I remain upright as I watch Ben open and close his right fist. His gaze is one of confusion.

"Weird, huh?" My voice comes out a little raspy.

"I knew you were different but . . . but . . ." He leans his forehead on mine. "I would do anything for you, but I can't let you walk away knowing you're in danger."

"Don't," I whisper, turning away before it becomes too difficult.

"Emily, I love you."

"You can't."

"Emily," he pleads, reaching for me.

Mentally, I block his movements, freezing him in time. I ignore his shock at his sudden paralysis, as I walk to the door.

"I care about you too much, Ben," I whisper. "That's why I have to say goodbye." Without looking back, I slip out the sliding glass door, closing it behind me.

Leaning against a pillar down the way, Patrick is waiting expectantly with Maggie beside him. My phone is smashed into several pieces on the cement. I don't question him. I nod for him to lead the way and I follow, letting go of my mental hold on Ben. As we walk away, I hear something crash against the inside wall behind us. I turn and think about going back, but Patrick steers me away.

"He's upset," Patrick says. "Going back won't make it better."

We ascend a cement staircase and wind our way around the house to Patrick's car. He opens the passenger door for me, and I climb in. He lets Maggie in the back before taking his seat behind the steering wheel. As he drives, I sob quietly into my knees. I've lost track of time, but after a while, Patrick reaches over to caress my neck.

"Do you think my dad's okay?" I mutter into my knees.

"If he were okay, you wouldn't have received that text," Patrick responds without any sugar coating.

Being cautious, Dad set his phone to text me if he was ever in trouble.

Get to base. Ask for Chris. Bring Patrick.

Base means his office and Chris is his assistant. I'm not sure why Patrick received an invite, but I try not to think of the worst-case scenario; yet, my mind drifts without concession.

I lift my head to Patrick. "Why did you smash my phone? Did you get the number? They have my dad. God, Patrick, we have to get him back. We have to call them."

"I got the number. We'll trace it when we have a secure computer. I took the sim card out so they couldn't track your location. I smashed it and left it behind so Ben would know there is no way to contact you."

"But the last location will lead them to Ben!"

"Ben will be fine. Once we get to the office, we'll reroute the tracking device to a different location."

"They have my dad. They must know where he works."

"They won't find us," he says with confidence.

"How can you say that?"

"Emily, do you trust me?"

"No."

He sighs. "Yes, you do."

We turn into the parking lot and Patrick parks the car. He notices me watching him and raises an eyebrow as if to question what I'm thinking.

"They made us watch our mothers die," I whisper. "I don't want my dad to die because of me."

"Mark knew what he was getting himself into." He says with his natural calm facade.

While I'm thinking of all the ways these people have infected my life, I recall Patrick's question, and this time, I have an answer for him. "You asked me before if I hate them and yes. My answer is yes. I hate them."

"Good to hear," Patrick says, before exiting the car. Maggie and I follow.

The two-story brick structure embellished by dramatic floor to ceiling windows looms before us. It's been years since I've been to Dad's office. Our footsteps are the only noise as we cross the deserted foyer and approach the unoccupied front desk.

Maggie growls a warning just before Chris appears in an open doorway.

"Phones?" Chris requests with his hand out.

Patrick answers, "Out of commission. We left them behind."

"This way." Chris leads us down a hallway with glass-encased offices all around us. We enter an elevator at the end of the hall where Chris swipes a card through a slot where the elevator buttons should be. It's only a few seconds before the doors open on the second floor and we unload out of the small space.

The second floor is similar in color and style to the first except no walls separate the offices. I wonder again what exactly my father does. Something with computers, right? I look around to see if I can figure out which desk belongs to Dad.

Chris stops when we reach a set of solid oak doors. He puts his finger on a scanner and one of the doors open. We step into the room, and I'm immediately blown away by the size of the space. The entire wall to the right appears to be a computer screen displaying multiple surveillance images. I recognize the outside of the building we just entered and the elevator we just left, but the picture of the pool in Ben's backyard is disconcerting. I stare in amazement as the image is replaced with the front of Ben's house.

"What is this?"

"Your father's office," Chris says, as he closes the door behind Patrick.

"But what is this?" I ask again, pointing at the wall-sized display ahead of me. The giant screen is broken up into dozens of small screens, and the majority of them are showing various places around the Cetrone's mansion. I see a closeup image of the garage doors and another on an entrance I don't recognize. Chris takes a step toward the wall and taps on an image, expanding it. I suspect it's a live feed as I watch the wind blow the leaves outside Ben's house. It shows a perfect view of the pool in the Cetrone's backyard. Those giant glass doors slide open and out steps Ben. He begins picking up the shattered pieces of my phone. I turn away from the wall and glare at Chris who I realize still hasn't answered my question.

"Do you know what your dad does?" Chris asks, registering my bewilderment.

"He works with computers," I reply.

"His job requires computers because he runs a high-end security agency."

"No, he doesn't," I say, sounding every bit as angry as I feel. "Why do you have Ben's house under surveillance?"

"We installed their security system."

"But you . . . he . . ." I look around the room. "Is this really my dad's office?"

"Yes, he's the head of the company."

"But . . . but isn't this . . ." I point to the screen. "Isn't this against the law or an invasion of privacy?"

"Our clients are aware our business has access," he says in a professional manner.

I shake my head. "We don't even have a security system in our house."

"Yes, you do."

"I've never seen it."

"Only because Mark wanted it to be invisible." Chris pulls a remote from Dad's desk and hits a button. Images of my house replace all the pictures on the screen.

"But . . ." I'm confused how we could have a state-of-the-art security system. "But our house is so crappy!"

"All the more reason not to break in," Chris returns. "Besides, your dad is a very busy man."

"I guess so," I say with disbelief, staring at the view outside my bedroom window. You can't see into my room, but you would be able to see if anyone was trying to get in.

"There are motion sensors in all the windows and doorways," Chris continues.

He's trying to make me feel safe, but I feel stupid for being left in the dark for so long. I take a staggering breath and sit down on the edge of a black leather sofa as Maggie rests her head on my lap.

"Chris," Patrick says, "she's already overwhelmed. You may as well show her downstairs now."

Chris glares at him while Patrick returns an arrogant grin.

"How much did Mark tell you?" Chris asks.

"There's not much I don't know," Patrick responds.

Chris looks at me before he places the remote back on the desk and walks to a bookshelf. My attention is divided between him and the giant screen with pictures of our house. The image outside my bedroom window has me remembering Dad's warning to check my windows. It dawns on me that Patrick couldn't have gotten into the house without Dad knowing. I open my mouth to ask when I'm rendered speechless as the bookshelf turns away from the wall and a secret staircase appears behind it.

Judging by Patrick's expression, I'm alone in my surprise.

"Come on, I have something to show you," Chris says.

Patrick moves before I do. He walks to the edge of the staircase and waits for me. I stand and follow him with Maggie at my side. I peer down the skinny stairwell before I descend. Chris follows, closing the bookcase behind us. Nothing about the space is creepy or exciting like one might expect a secret passageway to be. In fact, I would think nothing of it aside from it hiding behind a bookcase.

At the bottom of the stairs, it opens into a large room looking similar to the office we just left. There appears to be no other way into or out of this room aside from the set of stairs. I look to Chris for an explanation, but he's not watching me. He's opened a panel in the wall, revealing a keypad and a screen surveilling the office above. Chris punches in a code, and the staircase we just climbed down begins to rise, revealing another stairwell below. I look to Patrick who appears amused. Without a word, he follows Chris down the new set of stairs.

As we go deeper underground, our surroundings change. The finished space looks like an average living area with a leather sectional that wraps around an ornate glass coffee table. A state-of-the-art television hangs on the far wall proving my dad had a hand in the decor. I wonder how long he has been working on this hidden space. I nudge open a door next to the staircase to find a domestic tiled bathroom. Beside the bathroom is a small kitchen with all the amenities. The artificial lighting overhead does a poor job compensating for the lack of natural light, but it is, after all, a basement.

Patrick walks into the kitchen with purpose and begins opening cabinets and drawers while I stare conspicuously at Chris.

"What is this?" I question.

Chris moves forward. "I told you. Your dad has been very busy. He built this as a safe house for you. He thought you might need it one day."

I look around the room again. "He thought I'd need a safe house?"

"Yes, he did. Do you know where he is?"

"No." My heart sinks and I feel dizzy on my feet. I lean against the sofa, attempting to look casual instead of feeble.

"Your dad told me someone is looking for you," Chris says, coming to my side.

I shake my head, trying to fight this nagging lightheaded feeling.

"Anything you know would be helpful. I can be more efficient if I know everything you know."

"She needs to eat," Patrick says from the kitchen.

Chris's worried eyes are on me. "When's the last time you ate?"

My head is foggy, but I recall my last meal from lunch yesterday. "Umm, I haven't been hungry."

Chris sits on the back of the couch next to me, gently wraps an arm around my shoulder, and squeezes me. "I know you're overwhelmed. We'll get you something to eat."

What's worse than feeling weak and pathetic and clueless is actually being weak and pathetic and clueless. I'm an adult. I shouldn't need someone else to take care of me, yet it seems I've acquired a team to do just that.

Patrick watches from the kitchen. His impatient look gives me strength. "Here," he says, tossing me a granola bar. It's the same kind of granola bar he saw me eating the first day we met, and I can't help but smirk. I'm about to comment on it, but Patrick turns away. He passes the stairs and enters a room full of computers I hadn't previously noticed.

"This is the compact version of your dad's security station," Chris explains. "It shows security footage from this building as well as all of the other properties we monitor."

"Is someone always monitoring my house?"

"That's normally your dad's job, but I help out when he's out of the office. If the motion sensors are tripped, we get an alert and we access the feed," Chris answers.

"So, you see when anyone comes and goes?"

"You mean does your dad know you're spending nights at the Cetrone's?"

Great, I hadn't even thought of that! My cheeks feel hot. "I mean, did he see Patrick break in?"

"Which time?" Chris asks.

My head spins toward Patrick. "Which time? How many times were you there?"

"I told you to be vigilant." Patrick shrugs. "I was checking on your progress."

"You said you stayed away!"

"I say a lot of things, love. Incidentally, you failed on being vigilant."

"Are you serious?"

Chris cuts in, "Emily, your dad trusts Patrick. I reported his movements, but your dad said he was taking care of it. As for the nights you stayed at the Cetrone's, I reported that you were safe, and he didn't ask your location."

"Coward," Patrick coughs.

"You try telling Mark his baby girl is staying at her boyfriend's," Chris says with irritation.

"First of all, I'm eighteen! Secondly, Patrick, you were with me last night."

"Nonetheless, he should've reported it to Mark."

As a vein in Chris's temple starts to throb in frustration, he counters, "I was in charge of her safety, not you."

"I can't believe you!" I interrupt, "Either of you! I'm not a child!"

"Emily, I know you're not a child, but nothing is more important to your father than your safety," Chris says. "Your father is obsessive about your protection."

"Well, guess what? Dad is missing! So how about we stop talking about my safety and start worrying about his!"

Chris gets down to business. "Mark dropped off the grid at seven-fifteen last night. His phone shut down and hasn't come back on."

"Did he get on the plane?" I ask.

"No, we believe he was abducted from the airport. It's the last location on his phone's GPS, and his truck is still in long-term parking."

"Can we track the number that sent me the picture?"

"I'm already on it. I started monitoring your phone after your dad's text. The number is a dead end, registered to a dead guy. I have men working a few leads."

"What do we do next? Can we go to the airport?" I ask Chris.

Patrick cuts in, "You're not going anywhere. You need food and rest. Chris and I will continue conversing upstairs while you open that granola bar and start eating."

"There is nothing more to discuss." Chris counters. "My men are on it. You guys get situated and we'll talk later."

Chris provides a quick tour of the basement. Aside from what we've already seen, he shows us two furnished bedrooms, a workout space, and a storage area. He provides us with an untraceable replacement phone for emergencies and gives us the codes to enter or exit.

"I'll check in every day." Chris instructs, "Patrick can take Maggie out for bathroom breaks, but Emily, you stay put. I've already notified your employer of your resignation and I informed the school you'd be dropping your summer classes."

He is stripping my entire life from me. I know he's not to blame, but his words make it real. No more work, no more school, no more whiffle ball with friends. I can't talk to my sister or Morgan or Ben. For my own protection, I'm stuck in this underground cage unable and unqualified to do anything to help my dad.

"Emily," I hear my name and look up, not realizing I looked away. "Emily, it's important for you to tell me what you know. Who are these people? Why are they after you? What do they want?" Chris is persistent in his questioning.

Before I can answer Patrick pins him with a glare, saying, "If Mark wanted you to know, he would have told you. If he knew you were pumping Emily for information, what do you think he'd do with you?"

Chris pales but remains professional. "The only number programmed in your phone is mine. Call if you need anything."

When he reaches the top of the staircase, the stairs above descend, closing us off from the rest of the world, trapping us here in this underground tomb.

Patrick comes to my side, opens the granola bar, and places it in my hand as his eyes level on mine. "You okay?"

"I'm fine," I say before walking away.

twenty-eight ~

Sleep eludes me, so I curl up in a blanket and sit on the swivel chair in front of the wall of monitors. I'm watching, waiting for movement, hoping to get a glimpse of Ben through the glass sliding doors. I know it's unlikely I'll see anything at two in the morning, yet here I am desperately watching the monitors in Dad's underground hideout.

While exploring the space earlier, I found closets equipped with clothes and a safe filled with guns. Dad included a workout area complete with videos on self-defense. Patrick thinks I should spend my time training my mind. He tells me they fight with their heads and it's futile to practice shooting or fighting because they'll just use it against me.

I watched the videos anyway, using them to distract me and to work off some of the growing tension. To appease Patrick, I also practiced reading his thoughts which proved to be mentally exhausting. By all rights, I should be sleeping, but worry consumes me. I'm afraid there is little chance of getting Dad or myself out of this alive.

Movement behind me has me spinning around to see Patrick leaning against the doorframe. He nods at the computer. "This is a productive way to spend your time."

"It beats lying in bed waiting for the ceiling to crash down and suffocate me."

"Being a bit dramatic, aren't we?"

I shrug, looking back at the monitors, too exhausted to care what he thinks of me.

"You know he's not right for you," Patrick speaks in a soft voice.

"Yeah, well, I'm not really right for anyone." I laugh without humor.

"You're misguided if that's what you believe." He steps closer, spinning my chair to face him. He kneels down to eye level and gives me a comforting look. He's trying to soothe me, but under the consoling I feel his heart longing for more, proving his feelings for me are more profound than he's let on.

Bringing two beautiful masculine men to their knees is a brutal reminder of the darkness I hold inside. It's not a good feeling knowing it's not me they are drawn to, it's my Valla blood. The tender caress of a curse called love is destroying everyone closest to me. Ben happily jumped in front of the freight train I call my life and I shoved him aside. Now Patrick is standing on the tracks trying to stop me from going over the fast-approaching cliff.

"Emily, you are wrong on both accounts. Ben loved you before your blood was awakened and me . . ." He gently captures my face between his palms. His voice is filled with tenderness as he says, "I don't love you. I care about you, and I need you, so I'll protect you until my dying breath, but I will never love anyone, especially you."

I can't tell if he's lying to himself or just me, but then the backs of his fingers caress the sides of my face, and I can barely breathe. His touch has me holding in a moan, and I lean into him, lured by his soft words and dazzling eyes. I bite my lower lip as I stare longingly at his perfect mouth, all the while attempting to judge the honesty of his statement. I place a hand on his sandpaper cheek, loving the scruff that has grown since the night before.

A breath away from his lips, I say, "Then why are you trying to seduce me, Patrick?"

"Mmm," he moans. "I may not love you, but I do love when you say my name."

"You're unbelievable," I growl, pushing his face away.

He winces and I remember it's the same spot where Ben punched him earlier. I guess Patrick can't heal himself. I feel pride in Ben, but soon enough that pride turns to heartache. I slump my head into my hands wishing I could be left alone to sulk in solitude.

"You're wallowing," Patrick says with disgust.

"So what! Leave me alone!"

"You're not ready." Patrick hovers above me, ignoring my comment. "You have to get yourself together, otherwise nothing I do will make a difference and they'll obliterate you. They will use whatever they can against you, Emily."

"Don't you think I know that?"

He straightens. "You certainly don't seem to understand since this is how you're spending your time."

"Go away!" I grab the desk and turn my chair away from him.

"I'm preparing you. I'm going to keep pushing you," he warns.

"I just want to go home!" The words spill out of my mouth, making me cringe.

He crosses his arms and leans against the door frame. "Emily, you know that's not safe."

"Maybe I don't want to be safe!" I say with anger, turning my chair back to him. "Maybe I just want to be eighteen without having to worry if I'm going to die today! Maybe I want to be normal! I don't want to be a hunted, murderous creature! I am sick to my stomach worrying whether or not my dad is dead and who might be next!" I stand, letting the blanket fall from my shoulders, but I have nowhere to go. I have nowhere to hide.

He's glaring at me like I'm an insolent child.

"I can't do this," I whisper in defeat. "I'm scared, Patrick. I'm scared, and I'm not supposed to be. I'm not strong, or brave, or anything. I'm nothing, I'm no one, but that sure as hell isn't stopping them."

Stepping closer, his hard eyes find mine. "Allow me to impart wisdom I wish I had known sooner. You're afraid, which means you might just be taking this seriously. You're capable of greatness, Emily, demon blood and all. You have the inner strength of a martyr, which can be quite obnoxious at times. You think you're broken, but with every new challenge, you bend and stretch, growing and proving you're stronger than you believe. Your strength may whither, but you will not fail, because you can't afford a failure and you know it. You'll continue to mature and find strength in the growing pains."

"I'm no martyr, Patrick. I'm not a hero, and I don't want to become the villain you think I am. I'm a coward who wants to run and hide, which is exactly what it feels like I'm doing!"

"There is a time to fight. And there is a time to prepare," he says in a gentle voice. "Don't ever let me hear you call yourself a coward again. We both know that is not true. Stop being so hard on yourself. Learn to trust and love yourself through the fears and imperfections."

I stare at him surprised to hear encouragement. "Who are you, Dr. Phil?"

A shadow of a grin plays on his lips. "You doubting yourself is a distraction that could get us both killed, and I don't feel like dying today."

"Now, that sounds more like the Patrick I know."

It's early on day three of my isolation. I move around the kitchen enjoying the quiet time before Patrick wakes up. Upon opening every cabinet, I find a lot of food, but the nauseating side effect of dread makes it hard to eat. I push a box of cereal to the side and spot a bag of coffee. It's Dad's favorite kind. I open it and inhale the rich aroma. I close the cabinet and go for the coffee maker.

I've been underground in this confining space for too long with no new information or hope in finding Dad. Maggie, Patrick, and daily visits from Chris are my only company. Patrick is taking his vow to protect me very seriously. He took time away from his internship to stay with me and help me with my mind-reading skills. I try not to focus on his motivation for staying, but instead focus on his help. Apart from the two accidental trips into Patrick's psyche, I'm finding Patrick's mind is locked up tight, so it takes a lot of effort for me to break through. I'm getting better with practice and stronger at controlling my own thoughts. I'm building my mental fortress which Patrick believes is making strides in the right direction.

I still haven't been sleeping well despite the mental exercises with Patrick and the physical workouts I've maintained. In the downtime between physical and mental exhaustion, I watch TV rather than staring at the live security feed from Ben's house.

"Are you making coffee?" Patrick startles me, as he walks into the kitchen.

"Yeah," I say, scooping coffee into the filter.

"You hate coffee."

"So," I respond, pushing the brew button.

"So? Why are you making it?"

"Because I want to." I circle around him to get out a bowl and spoon. I go back to the box of cereal I'd pushed aside and fill my bowl.

"Are you going to drink it?"

"Maybe," I respond, pulling the milk from the fridge.

"Maybe?"

"Patrick, why does it matter if I drink the coffee or not? Why are you up so early anyway?"

"Couldn't sleep. I'm only asking because if you don't drink it, I will."

"It's all yours," I say, placing the milk back in the fridge.

"So why are you up already?" he asks.

"Bad dreams." I pick up my bowl and take it into the living room.

"Still?"

I sit down on the oversized couch. "Yep."

"Want to tell me about it? Maybe I can help."

"Nope," I reply, before taking my first bite.

"Do you want—"

"Nope," I repeat through a full mouth.

"—me to leave you alone?" he finishes.

I nod my head in agreement and continue eating, enjoying the scent of brewing coffee filling the air. It's as if it's just waiting for my dad. I look toward the stairs aware he won't be coming down them but hoping anyway.

Patrick pours himself a cup of coffee. "How many scoops did you put in this? It's way too strong!"

I shrug, as a stealthy tear slides down my cheek.

I'm pacing on day five in the underground hideout. Still no news. Nothing different at all, except now I'm making coffee every day which Patrick criticizes. He doesn't know I'm not making it for him, and I don't correct his assumption.

"Would you please sit down?" Patrick requests from his spot on the couch.

"I'm not in your way," I point out. "You can still see the TV."

"Yes, but it's hard to focus with you burning a hole in the carpet."

"I can't help it. I can't just sit around doing nothing. Aren't you worried at all?"

"Of course, I'm worried, but we're hardly doing nothing. You're learning how to control your gifts which is very important, but traipsing around in circles isn't going to accomplish anything."

I throw my hands out. "How can you be so calm?"

"Regardless of what you believe, I'm not heartless, love."

"You're the one who said you'll never love anyone," I remind him.

"I try not to form bonds of any kind. Don't take it personally. I can't afford—"

"You already told me you'd protect me with your life. I'd say, that's a bond."

"That's different."

"Different how? You took time away from your life to stay with me. You may not love me. You may not even like me, but you can't deny we have a bond."

"You're cute when you get feisty."

"I get that you're afraid to lose anyone else. You may not be able to justify our bond, but you're protecting me because you can't afford to lose me. You think saving me is the closest thing to—"

"You're a Valla!" he interrupts, sounding angry. "With Valla's blood pumping through your veins, you're unstoppable. If anyone can beat them, it's you! I have my own motivations for wanting these people dead, so yeah, I care about you, but you're also a formidable weapon."

"A weapon? That's rich! You expect me to believe you did all of this to use me as a weapon? Geez, don't you know how to make a girl feel special."

"When I attempt to make you feel special, you lash out."

I shrug. "I don't need to feel special. Maybe I prefer someone else help me."

"What, you mean like Ben?"

"I was thinking along the lines of a different Olvasho. Surely, there have to be other Olvasho aside from the ones who are hunting me."

"Good luck! You'll be hard pressed finding a more competent teacher. Not to mention the only other Olvasho who know you exist want to see you dead."

"Aside from you not killing me, what makes you so qualified to help?"

"I didn't grow up in the world you know. I'm not accomplished with sports or video games like most young men. I don't have much insight when it comes to cars or Kung fu like Ben. I'm not good with relationships or trusting others, but I am skilled in survival."

"Survival?" I question, crossing my arms. "That's your secret weapon?"

"Not so secret, love." His smile shows a confidence his eyes contradict.

"Really?" I ask more gently. "So, tell me. What was your childhood like?"

With a bitter smile, he turns off the TV and leans back to stretch his arms on the back of the couch. "What would you like to know? You're already aware of my dad's disappearance and my mom's death."

"When did she die?"

"March the second marked five years."

I sit down on the far end of the couch while I count back the months. "Five months after my mom," I whisper. "You were fifteen?"

"Yes."

"What happened to you afterward?"

"I was emancipated at sixteen. I moved around a lot from there, at least for the first few years."

"Emancipated at sixteen?"

"My uncle was the only family I had left, but my mom and uncle were estranged. They hadn't talked since before I was born. I was on my own."

"So, you didn't know Morgan and her family at all?"

"No, I met them for the first time this summer," Patrick says, relaxing his arms down to his sides.

"Do you know what happened between them, your mom and uncle?" I lean back into the sectional, getting comfortable.

"My mom was a radical. She would get stuck on a cause, and I'm certain things were too intense for my uncle. He was married to a normal human with a little girl and a baby on the way. He couldn't get caught up in my mom's latest mess. My mom was in over her head with Olvasho friction, which as you know, can be deadly. I don't blame my uncle for protecting his family. Mom burned a lot of bridges along the way. After my dad disappeared, it was just her and me for ten years. Losing her was . . . difficult."

I move closer to him and reach out. My hand touches his, offering him comfort. It takes him by surprise, but he wraps his hand around mine anyway.

"Of course, telling you my depressing life story is what gets you to warm up."

"Stop talking while you're ahead," I warn, hoping he won't hide himself, but it's too late.

"I should've opened up sooner." He smirks, running a finger down my arm.

I pull away, but he catches my wrist.

He loses the smirk, returning to the genuine Patrick. "I know I'm not always easy to get along with, but I'm trying. I know what your dad means to you, perhaps better than anyone. I don't want you to lose him, but I'm not going to give you false hope. Real life doesn't usually end in happily-ever-after."

"You're wrong," I say. "You're never easy to get along with."

On day seven in this hell hole, I'm running. In an effort to stop my pacing, Patrick felt it was necessary for me to have a treadmill, so Chris brought one down this morning. After my usual eight hours of grueling mental practice with Patrick, I'm excited to work on my physical exercise. The treadmill is not the same as running outside, but at least I'm moving. My tired legs go from sore to numb as my feet hit the belt one after the other. My lungs burn, struggling to keep up with my pace. By mile five, I'm a burned-out sweaty mess, but as exhausted as I feel, I also feel great. I feel alive.

"Emily?" Chris interrupts.

It doesn't take special powers to see he's bringing bad news. "Yeah?" I turn off the treadmill and straddle the belt as it slows to a stop. "What is it?" I pant, trying to catch my breath.

"Your sister tried to file a missing persons report this morning. She's freaking out because she hasn't been able to contact you or your dad. She won't believe anything I tell her. She usually talks to your dad every day or two. I'm not sure how else to calm her down, except to have you call."

I grab my water as I step off the machine. "What do I say?"

"Tell her your dad is consulting on a government job and can't speak to anyone until it's over. Tell her you hitched a ride with him out to Colorado because you broke up with Ben and couldn't handle seeing him. You're putting yourself back together and will come back once you get it figured out. Tell her you disconnected your phone so you wouldn't be tempted to call Ben."

"That makes me sound pathetic."

"It will keep your sister safe," Chris says. "She needs to stop poking around in this."

"Do you think she'll believe I ran away because of a boy?"

"She'll believe it," Patrick intercedes, entering the room.

"You think you know her better than I do?"

"Probably, but that's beside the point. She's going to feel like it's her fault because of the fight the two of you had the day before you disappeared," he says, coming to my side.

"How do you know about that?"

"Please," Patrick snickers.

"So, you think she'll believe it because of our fight?"

"Guilt can blind people of the truth. She will feel responsible and blame herself."

"You don't know my sister."

"I'm guessing she feels pretty guilty about siding with Leah by now. Trust me; she'll give you space."

"It doesn't matter how she feels as long as she leaves it alone," Chris interjects. "I'm sure you don't want to see your sister dead."

As fear for my sister squeezes my heart, I hold out my hand. "Give me the phone. I'll take care of it."

On day ten I don't see the point in getting out of bed. The clock tells me it's noon, but I have no reason to get up, so I stay bundled under the covers.

Patrick taps at my door before entering.

"I'm sleeping," I grumble.

"Actually, love, you're not."

"I'm tired," I complain, as he rounds the bed.

"Yes, I bet you're sore from all that running."

"No, I mean I'm tired of hiding!"

"Emily, we've been through this," he says with a sigh. "There is nothing you can do right now."

"I can't stay down here forever."

He sits down next to me. "It's only been a week."

"Time moves in slow motion down here. The fluorescent lights are sucking the life out of me, and at night I feel like I'm in a coffin."

"Are you afraid of the dark?"

"Are monsters allowed to be afraid of the dark?"

"Do you want me to pity you? Is that it?" He stretches out on his back, lying next to me.

"No, but I'm going crazy down here," I say, watching as he makes himself comfortable.

"You do know I'm volunteering to be down here with you, right? I could leave any time."

"Then go!"

"Emily, calm down."

I sit up and glare down at him. "Oh, calm down, geez, why didn't I think of that? Calm down? It must be that easy, Patrick!" I throw my arms out in question. "Calm down?"

"I understand you're mad."

"Wow, Patrick, you must have used your sixth sense! I mean, what gave it away?"

He shakes his head, exasperated with me. "Just come here," he commands, pulling me into his arms.

Before I can pull myself away, a blissful calm envelops me. I become limp in his arms, feeding off his soothing aura. Patrick's way of calming me is comforting and reminds me of how my mom used to console me. After a few minutes, we roll to our backs, staring at the ceiling with only our shoulders touching.

"Patrick," I whisper after a while of silence. "What was your mom like?"

"What do you mean?"

"What do you remember most about her?" When he doesn't answer, I continue, "My mom smelled like vanilla. It was her perfume, but I didn't know that when I was little. I thought it was just her scent."

Patrick's silence keeps me talking, spilling my guts. "When I was sick and had to stay home from school, she'd make me chicken noodle soup, and we'd watch murder mystery shows. I didn't know how much I cherished those times until they were gone. It feels impossible to recognize a perfect memory in the making until it's too late and the moment is gone."

I have a lot more to say, but I rein it in. I think of all the simple things my mom did for me in the mundane everyday moments. They're monumental in the way I remember her. Even if she was a killer, she was my mother first. I was nine when she left. I had no idea my nurturing, loving mother was out killing any sign of a threat to our family. Maybe others are justified in fearing Valla blood, or perhaps they should fear anyone they back into a corner and force to defend their young.

"My mom smelled like lavender." Patrick's voice is soft as he interrupts my memories. "I think of her whenever I catch a hint of the scent. And I loved her hair." He squirms next to me. "That's weird isn't it?"

"No," I answer. "My mom used to French braid my hair like hers all the time. I loved it. After she left, I tried to braid it myself, but I never got the hang of it."

Silence flows over our admissions, and although the topic is heavy, the memories are beautiful. I hold onto them firmly, like the prized possessions they are.

"She sang to me," Patrick whispers. "She was beautiful. There wasn't anything about her that wasn't lovely, and her voice was no exception." Unshed tears glisten in his eyes.

"My mom would build snowmen with me when my sister decided she was too cool to play in the snow," I say, revealing more of myself so he won't feel so vulnerable.

Patrick continues, "I had trouble making friends because we moved around so much. I remember wondering why anyone would want to settle in one place for their whole life. I wasn't into the things normal boys were into, and girls would follow me around like puppies. My mom was the only person I was close to and in a way, she was my best friend. That sounds so lame."

"It sounds lonely."

"I'm used to lonely."

"That's sad."

"Says the girl who pushes everyone away."

"Aren't we a joyful pair?" I sigh.

"What if this is one of those moments?" Patrick offers, "A perfect memory in the making. We don't know what tomorrow will bring so we should cherish the time we have."

I push up onto an elbow. "Patrick, why are you doing this?"

The light drains from his face and his long lashes frame beautiful telling eyes, giving me a glimpse inside his mind where love and pain are one and the same. He gently cups my cheek, sending a shiver through me as he says, "You're asking what you already know and hearing my answer will only make it more difficult for you to deny what's between us."

Averting my eyes, I whisper, "Patrick, you know how I feel about Ben."

"I'm well aware of your feelings," he says, covering his emotions behind an easy smile. "Even those feelings you pretend aren't there. Now, come on. Get up so we can practice."

"Again? I feel like that's all we do."

"Yes, and we'll continue until you are the most powerful Olvasho alive."

"I thought I already was."

"Yes, but it's all for nothing if you don't know how to wield your power."

"Yeah, yeah, I'm getting up."

Day eleven underground, I'm looking for a steak knife.

"Patrick, where are all the knives?"

From his spot on the couch, he turns to look at me standing in the kitchen. "Did you look in the dishwasher?"

"There are only three in there and they're dirty. What happened to the rest of them?"

He shrugs and turns back to the television. "Just wash one from the dishwasher."

I glare at the back of his head. "But what happened to the rest of them? There are six slots for knives. What happened to the other three?"

"I don't know, Nancy Drew," he says to the TV. "Let me know if you find any clues."

I retrieve a dirty knife from the dishwasher and begin washing it under the faucet. "Are you hoarding knives? It's just the two of us, where else could they go?"

"You forgot to include Maggie."

What would Patrick be doing with knives? My inner Ms. Drew is indeed very curious, so I drop the knife on the counter and head to Patrick's room. His door is closed, but I enter anyway.

"Hey," I hear Patrick complain, chasing after me.

I haven't been in his room since our first day. Unlike mine, his room is incredibly neat, like folded corners and bounce a quarter off the bed neat. Nothing is on the dresser but a lamp and a clock. The room is spotless. I throw open his closet doors sure to find his mess stashed inside.

"Holy Crap!" I exclaim, finding perfect order in the closet with shirts on one side, pants on the other, and he's color-coded his entire wardrobe with shoes sitting below. "It looks like a closet in a showroom for closets."

"What are you doing in my room?"

I wave my hand toward the closet. "OCD much?"

"I like organization."

"I'll say! For someone who likes order so much, it must be killing you not to know where the knives are."

"Nope," he smirks, before walking to his dresser. "I know where the knives are."

"Care to enlighten me?"

"One is in your room among the dirty dishes from your dinner last night."

"And the other two?"

"Are here," he says, opening the top drawer of his dresser.

"So, you are hoarding knives!"

"I've been using them to practice."

"Practice what? Knife throwing?"

"You are aware that Olvasho have healing abilities, and in remarkably rare cases there are some who can heal themselves." He pulls out a knife. "I was practicing."

"Practicing! Patrick, what do you mean you were practicing? How exactly have you been practicing?"

He pulls his long sleeve shirt up over his head and drops it on the dresser.

I wince when I see the varying degrees of healing to the cuts on his left arm. "Patrick, instead of maiming yourself, don't you think it'd be better to start with, I don't know, a paper cut or something small?"

"I concluded something as insignificant as a paper cut wouldn't be enough incentive for the self-healing to surface."

"So, you thought self-mutilation was the way to go?"

"My progress has been disappointing thus far, but I wanted to see if I could do it before I suggested you try."

"It was a struggle for me to heal Ben's hand, so you can try all you want, but I'm not about to cut holes in my body in the off chance I'll be able to heal myself."

"Even though your gifts far outweigh mine, I would advise against you harming yourself to test my theory."

"You should take your own advice. Do you want me to try to heal you?"

Patrick holds his arm out to me, palm up. "Yes, however, I expect you to do more than just try. Allow me to provide some incentive."

I gasp as he slides the blade deep across his upper arm, far deeper than the other varying wounds. His eyebrow is raised in challenge as he holds his open wound out to me. Bright crimson flows like a fountain down his arm, dripping through his fingers onto the white carpet.

"Patrick! What the hell!" I move forward grabbing his discarded shirt to hold it against the gaping wound.

"As you can see, I've been pretty unsuccessful, so you would be smart to heal this promptly unless you really do want to see me dead." His face pales as he staggers to the corner of the bed, emphasizing the magnitude of what he's just done.

"Patrick, you know I don't know how to heal something like this!"

"I trust you'll figure it out."

I help lower him to the bed before he collapses on the floor. Blood is pooling on the white covers, the shirt completely useless. I yank the blanket over and press it against the wound to suppress the blood flow. Remaining calm is impossible when there is so much blood, but I know my next move is critical.

"I need to call 911."

"The blood you see is coming from my brachial artery. Paramedics aren't going to get here in time. It's up to you, love." His eyes lose focus before he slips into unconsciousness.

I can't breathe! I can't think! I can't believe he did this! Closing my eyes, I center myself before fear and panic consume me. A deep breath through my nose fills my head with the metallic smell of blood. My thoughts spin out of control. Something nudges my arm, and I open my eyes to find Maggie sitting at my side.

"Maggie, I don't know what to do."

She whimpers, nudging me toward Patrick. His lips are turning blue against his now ghostly skin. He looks like a corpse and that image is what clears my head. Determined to keep him alive, I push aside my fear and panic, unwrap his bloody arm, and lay my hands directly over the wound. Sticky warmth fills my palms as I zero in on its source. He said it was his artery, so I visualize mending the most critical laceration.

My hands feel like I submerged them in boiling water as the warmth of his blood turns to lava against my touch. I suppress a scream, pushing through the pain. His unconscious state works in my favor because I don't have to filter through his thoughts as I'm racing to heal his body.

The bleeding slows considerably, and I know I've successfully mended his brachial artery; however, the incision in his flesh is still gaping. Fatigue slows my progress. Intense pain engulfs me. Minutes pass like hours. When the gash is sealed and the process complete, we're still not out of the woods. His heartbeat has dwindled to a thready pulse, and his chest barely rises with each shallow breath. Even after successfully healing his injury, there is no way for me to replace his depleted blood supply.

"You can't die, Patrick!"

I jump off the bed and run to the kitchen to get the emergency phone. Before I dial Chris's number, I wipe the blood from my shaking fingers.

"At your service," Chris grumbles, his tone incongruent with his words.

"I need blood! Can you get me blood?"

"What the hell do you mean, you need blood?"

"Patrick lost a lot of blood. I got the bleeding to stop, but he's lost too much! Chris, I don't know what blood type he is, but this is time sensitive! The sooner, the better!"

"I'm on my way," he says, before hanging up.

I go back to Patrick. The scene before me looks like something out of a horror film, but I take comfort in the way Patrick's chest rises and falls. Maggie lies in the darkening pool of blood on the bed next to him with her head nuzzled into his side. I sit on the other side and rest my head on his chest. I listen for each thump of his heartbeat, treasuring the sound it makes.

I wrap my arms around his cool torso and create a healing warmth with my mind. His body responds well to the heat, so I relax, knowing reinforcements are on the way. Relief is why I close my eyes, but exhaustion is how I fall asleep.

"Emily!" I wake to Chris's eyes wild with worry. "Are you hurt?" he says, doing a visual once over.

I shake my head, sitting up on the bed next to Patrick. "Did you bring the blood?"

"Yes, everything is in the hall. What happened here?" Chris moves to Patrick. Maggie growls a warning, but Chris ignores her. His hands frantically run along Patrick's body searching for a wound that could produce such a gory scene.

"I told you I stopped the bleeding," I say, as he continues to look for the injury I've already closed. "You're wasting time, Chris!"

Finally realizing there is no open wound, he turns to me with accusing eyes. "Where did all this blood come from?" He shakes his head. "Never mind. Your dad's preparations will come in handy," he says, moving into the hall. "We keep blood stored for you and lucky for Patrick, you're the same blood type."

"How do you know?" I say, following him out of the room.

"Because I do my research." He gives me a serious look, loading up my arms with equipment. "Now maybe you can tell me how you closed an arterial bleed?"

"What makes you think it was an arterial bleed?" I ask as we head back into Patrick's room.

"The amount of blood," he says, motioning to Patrick. "I need you to clean his arm so I can start an IV."

Dumping the supplies onto the dresser, I run to the bathroom for water and towels before rushing back to Patrick. Maggie whimpers when I move her away. Scrubbing the drying blood from his skin isn't as easy as I anticipated, but he's looking less like a murder victim. I'm laying clean towels under Patrick when Chris instructs me to get out of the way so he can start an IV.

After an entire bag of blood has dripped into Patrick, he's still looking pale. Chris says he's doing remarkably well considering the amount of blood loss. After Chris is done checking Patrick's blood pressure for the fourth time, I can no longer hold my tongue.

"How did you know how to do all of this?"

"I used to be a paramedic, but it turns out security pays better. It doesn't mean I forgot my medical training. So, do you care to explain to me what happened here?"

"Not knowing all the details may help keep you alive, Chris. My dad had his reasons for keeping certain things from you. He clearly trusts you, and you should give him the same courtesy."

"Okay, I'll let it go for now."

Nearly six hours and four units of blood later, Chris unhooks the last bag and pulls the IV from Patrick's arm. The improvement in his color is reassuring. Chris says his vitals have improved, which is excellent news since we've depleted my dad's emergency stash. Patrick hasn't woken, and I can't reach his thoughts when he's unconscious, but his heartbeat is strong, and his breathing is steady.

Staring at him these last few hours has given me time to think. Over the last week and a half, Patrick has become irreplaceable. Regardless of his motivations, he's taught me the things he felt were important. He's devoted himself to protecting me, helping me cope with the drastic changes in my life. Sure, he can be insensitive and arrogant, but he's proven to have a depth I've only begun to understand. Patrick said he doesn't form bonds of any kind, but the friendship we have built in this underground prison would be a hard one to break.

"You've helped me bear a weight that alone would have crushed me," I whisper, stroking my hand through his hair.

Patrick's eyes remain closed, but the smirk that stretches across his face has never looked so good. His lips open to speak, "To awaken the devilishly handsome prince, the princess must give truelove's kiss. Assuming, of course, you still want me alive, love."

Relief floods through me, choking me up. I blink away the tears. "I was so scared you wouldn't wake up."

Patrick opens his eyes, saying, "You thought I would die that easily?"

I continue to slide my hand through his hair, holding back the need to throw my arms around him.

"I knew you had it in you," he says.

"How could you do that to me? What were you thinking?"

"I thought I would wake to a kiss, like a proper greeting when someone beats death."

I slap his chest. "Don't you ever do that to me again!"

He smiles against my assault. "I make no promises."

twenty-nine ~

Fourteen days is what it takes for me to reach my limit. I haven't heard from Dad in two long weeks. The hope of finding him alive is all but gone. Each day brings agony from waiting to hear bad news. I need to get fresh air. Today! It's a matter of my sanity.

When Patrick mentions he's going out to drop research papers off to a coworker, I tell him I'm going along. He laughs at my insistence which turns me into a raving madwoman, ranting in run-on sentences until he changes his mind. I want to think I'm just that persuasive in my reasoning, but I know he just wants to shut me up.

"Hold on, I have to grab my contacts to disguise my eyes," I say before we leave.

He laughs at me, again. "Contacts won't help. They'll know you when they see you, but they'll feel your presence before that."

"Fine." I march past him and start up the stairs. "Let's go."

"Just so we're clear, you're staying in the car," he says from behind me.

"Fine!"

We leave Maggie in the underground lair while Patrick and I go on our errand. The sun feels like heaven, and I inhale the fresh air hoping it will last me a while. I look through the car windows watching the buildings pass by. I didn't realize how much I treasured normal everyday freedoms until they were taken away.

"Patrick, what exactly do you do for your internship?"

"I assist in head hunting. I do background checks on people to see if they're the right fit, but mostly I get stuck with the research that no one else can find." He taps the side of his head. "I have a secret weapon to get the information I need."

We pull up to a luxury hotel wedged between apartment buildings and Patrick parks his BMW.

"I'm just going to drop this off. Lay low. I'll be back in two minutes." He opens his door, taking his briefcase with him.

I doubt anyone would be able to see me through the deep tint in the windows, but I keep my head down honoring our agreement. After a few minutes pass and Patrick doesn't return, I begin to worry. I reach out with my mind and feel him on the second floor. Something feels wrong. Fear and foreboding loom in Patrick's mind so heavily it chokes my rationale. My need to protect him overrides my logic, so I jet out of the car without a second thought. Hurrying into the lobby, I track him. I feel him coming down the stairs and meet him just outside the stairwell door.

Fresh panic floods his face as he spots me. "What are you doing?"

"It's been ten minutes and I could feel something was wrong!"

"Yeah, the guy is an asshole. It doesn't mean you come find me. Let's go!" He grabs my arm and propels me toward the door but immediately switches direction and pins me up against the wall with his body. He leans in with a serious look and whispers, "Don't panic, but they're here."

"What? Where?" I turn my head to survey the lobby, trying to shove him away, but he doesn't budge.

"By the entrance." His voice is steady as he allows me to peek around his shoulder. The lobby is crowded with strangers, and I can't tell who he's talking about. There are no men dressed in black as I had imagined.

"I don't see them."

"The two men to the right of the doors," he responds with his mouth at my ear.

I look where he says and see the two middle-aged men he's referring to, but they don't seem threatening dressed casually in jeans and t-shirts. The most unusual thing about them is they look too much like male models, squeezing all their ridiculously toned muscles into tight shirts.

"They look like they belong in a cologne ad."

He presses tighter into me, obstructing my view. "Listen, when I pull away, follow me. Don't walk too quickly and don't use your abilities. We'll go downstairs and out the back entrance. Got it?"

I give a slight nod, adrenaline pulsing through my veins.

"Let's go." He backs away from me, taking my hand. We walk through the lobby slow enough to look casual, but once we turn the corner entering the stairwell, we move much faster. We skip down several steps at a time and almost knock someone down. I mumble an apology but doubt they hear it over their own cursing. We reach the bottom, and I dash ahead, unsure of when I stopped holding Patrick's hand. The exit is in view, so I reach out to push the single steel door open. Before I get all the way through the opening, Patrick catches me around the middle with both arms, picks me up, and brings me back inside. He warns, "There are more of them out there!"

I make eye contact with a blue-eyed stranger just before the door closes between us. "He saw me!" I shout, even though Patrick is still holding me.

He drops me to my feet, flips the lock at the top of the steel door, and drags me back up the stairs. We continue up the next three flights, but I've watched enough scary movies to know we're moving the wrong direction.

The stairs come to an end on the fourth floor, and we sprint down the long corridor. On the way, Patrick grabs a red baseball cap off an unsuspecting stranger. Too frightened by Patrick's intensity, the guy doesn't say a word. We turn the corner and Patrick pulls me into an unlocked room. He flips the deadbolt while I scan the dark hotel room. Patrick moves to the windows and lifts the shades.

"The roof connects to the next building," he says.

"Whoa! Seriously, that's your plan? Scaling rooftops?"

"I'll go first. We can get into the apartment building next door. There's a fire escape on the far side that's right next to the parking lot. We need to get to my car. If we can't get to my car, then we get to the bus stop two blocks south and take the bus downtown. We hail a cab or steal a car and get to safety."

"Did you know this was going to happen?"

"I knew it could. I try to plan for every scenario. Thinking ahead is the reason I've survived as long as I have."

"What if we can't get away?"

He grabs my shoulders. "No matter what happens, you have to trust me. I will get you out of here."

"But . . ."

"Come on."

He opens the window, and we climb out, hurrying across the rooftop. The windows to the adjacent building are locked, so Patrick breaks one with his elbow. Careful to watch for broken glass, we crawl inside. We run through the vacant apartment and exit into a hallway. At the end of the hall, the window leads to the fire escape, just like Patrick said. I'm crawling through the window when I hear someone shout from down the hall.

"Got them! They're headed down the fire escape!"

Patrick is right behind me, but he doesn't follow me through the window. He shoves the red cap on my head and hands me the keys.

"Car or bus! Go!" Patrick shuts and locks the window between us. He turns to face the two daunting men rushing down the hall.

My heartbeat races, but time stands still. If I stay any longer, Patrick's sacrifice will be for nothing. I can't bear to leave him, but my feet take over, scurrying down the ladder and jumping off the fire escape. When I get to the parking lot, a man is standing next to Patrick's car. I duck behind a dumpster to regroup and tuck my hair under the hat. I lock down my mind so they cannot track me and sprint the two blocks to the bus stop.

The bus stop is out in the open, so I hang back between a gas station and a dumpster until I see the bus coming. There's no sign of Patrick, but I can't think about him right now. I have to get out of here or confront them. Patrick doesn't think I'm ready, and I don't know if I ever will be.

The bus rounds the corner and I rush to climb on. I take a seat near the front while I scope for any blond bodybuilders. For the moment, I'm in the clear. The bus moves and I take a deep breath which lasts for exactly three-seconds.

A strange man takes the seat next to me. In a cheerfully dangerous tone that reminds me of Patrick, he says, "Beautiful summer day we're having."

Dread makes my movements slow as I turn to look at him. The tall, slender man sharing my seat is wearing a bright purple fitted suit, accented with white cotton gloves and a black cane. His shiny white hair hangs straight past his shoulders. He's smiling, but his features are too sharp to be attractive. His sky-blue eyes explode with excitement.

The place deep inside where I bottle my fear opens wide and swallows me whole. I'm paralyzed, unable to respond to the deceptively cheerful man who wears a tiger's grin.

"Such a beautiful day to meet such a beautiful girl." He reaches out and pulls off my hat. He strokes a lock of my hair and I can do nothing. I'm frozen, caught staring into the eyes of a predator.

"It's been so long my dear, but I've finally found you," he purrs. I struggle to move myself an inch away. "Don't fight darling. I'm going to take you home where you belong."

I attempt to leap from my seat, but a blast of energy engulfs my body. My fight turns into a pathetic struggle and within seconds everything fades to black.

thirty ~

I wake up shivering with my wrists chained behind my back and my ankles shackled to the legs of the steel chair I'm occupying. I have no idea how long I've been unconscious, but it's enough time for my body to ache with stiffness. The room is entirely white with bright lights covering the ceiling and a drain in the center of the tiled floor. My nightmares align with my reality as I recognize the room from the memory of Patrick's mother—only now I'm the one in the chair. Someone has dressed me in a white sleeveless dress covered with delicate lace fabric that hangs in shear waves to the floor, spilling over my shackles. I can't help but feel like a helpless lamb before the slaughter.

I struggle to find a comfortable position on the cold steel chair as time stretches into what feels like hours. The handcuffs dig into my wrists as I reposition myself, yet again. I'm trapped, completely at my captor's mercy, but I'm determined to keep my mind locked up tight.

After all this time waiting and wondering, the door finally opens, and the sound of footsteps surround me. I refuse to acknowledge their presence, but when the man in the ridiculous purple suit saunters into the room, I can't help but look up at him.

There is not an ounce of danger in his appearance, but menace radiates from his harrowing aura. It's the unease in the room, the way his gracious grin makes my feet itch to move, and the threat behind those sky-blue eyes. The men surrounding keep the fear from their faces, but not their minds. For his own men to fear him, indicates how dangerous he is. His stride is confident, his insatiable smile holds an allure, and his eyes possess a certain magnetism. He is a deceptive poison drowning out my ability to rationalize. My skin prickles making me feel insignificant and incompetent against this harmless looking man in purple.

He's still wearing those white cotton gloves making him appear old-fashioned and suggesting he never gets his hands dirty. Why would he? He doesn't have to touch anyone to torture them. He knocked me out cold with a single thought. My rationale escapes my mental hold, and it's a struggle to regain control. I'm the last of the Valla blood, and I'm going to die here just like Patrick's mother.

"Throwing in the towel already, are we?" His musical voice captures my attention, and I lock down the fortress I built to hide my thoughts.

The man in purple moves closer. "Intriguing!" He tosses his arms out with great enthusiasm. "That's brilliant! Do you have any idea of the untapped potential inside of you, darling? What you've learned in such a short time is simply astonishing. Patrick has taught you well."

Anger flares inside me at his mention of Patrick. I'm wondering how he knows Patrick taught me and if he's torturing him for information. What if he's killed Patrick? I couldn't live with myself if I'm the reason for his death. I keep the emotions from my face, but the villainous leader's face turns mischievous.

"How sweet, my darling." He folds his hand over his heart. "Truly, there's no reason to worry about Patrick. His fate is already sealed. Sad you didn't get a proper goodbye."

His words hit me like a physical blow crushing the breath from my lungs. Patrick is dead. The man's devious chuckle fills the room and my devastation turns into rage.

"Oh, you poor girl, letting love—the most fickle of emotions— compromise you so completely. I'd be ashamed if I were you. Not to worry, we'll work on those weaknesses."

I want to shout obscenities, but I hold my tongue.

"Sorry about those restraints. Can't say I didn't warn you not to fight. Now, where are my manners? Introductions are in order. I'm Sky Vallor from the Leona bloodline. I'm delighted to meet you Emily, daughter of Selma Konig from the Valla bloodline."

When he says my mother's name, my mind jolts with the mental images he places in my head. Her death is on replay, messing up my psyche. The next glimpse he forces into my mind is of Patrick's mother in this very room.

"She bled out, you know," he says casually, while I glare at him. "No need for such hatred. I'm just giving you the facts. I wonder . . ." Sky taps his chin, "after everything he taught you, do you think Patrick was a brave little soldier or do you think he begged for his life?"

He waits for me to answer, but I'd rather die than play into his cruelty. I keep my eyes level as I remind myself to breathe. Just breathe.

His lips curl wider, showing delight at my reluctance. "No worries, I can show you," he says, rounding my chair. "Bring Patrick in."

I brace myself for the trauma.

"So much death has occurred in this very room. Patrick's mother, Alessandra, was just one of many, although her death was a delightfully bloody mess," Sky brags, as he strolls lazy circles around the room. "Patrick learned to be more sophisticated as time went on." He removes a white cotton glove, but I'm distracted as Patrick enters the room. I gasp at the sight of him, as Sky continues, "I believe you are well acquainted with Patrick Glenn from the Isa bloodline. Forgot to amend my little fib earlier. As you can see, Patrick is alive and well."

Relief floods through me as he appears unscathed. In fact, he looks stunning in his tailored suit. He moves forward without anyone guiding him, without handcuffs or restraints of any kind. I don't get a chance to question him because Sky taps a bare fingertip to my temple sending a burst of images through my mind.

Teenage Patrick plunges a knife into his mother's chest. He releases a tormented howl and pulls the knife out, only to thrust it back in again. It takes several large men to haul Patrick off of his mother. They pry the knife from his hand and drag him from the room, leaving his mother to die alone.

I return to the present and my mind struggles to keep up with what my eyes are telling me.

"You see, my dear Emily, my second in command would be useless to me dead," Sky boasts. "Instead, he brought you home to me."

I'm disoriented, blindsided as the world tips on its axis to dump me into space. I fade into emptiness, feeling nothing. I find strength in the numbness, which soon dissolves when a wicked grin plays on Patrick's lips. The sting of betrayal sends ice searing through my veins. Patrick—my friend, my ally—is my enemy!

"Surprised to see me, love?" Patrick taunts, coming closer. "Let me guess, there was a man by my car at the hotel, so you did just as I instructed and ran to the bus stop where Sky was conveniently awaiting your arrival." He smiles. "You didn't suspect a thing. You were so compliant. It was almost too easy."

I recoil, burning with the violation of trust. Patrick set me up! He conspired against me and I trusted him. Unguarded, I let him into my head, into my house, and into my heart. I look around the room and cannot deny the fear I feel radiating from the other men. They fear Patrick just as much as they fear Sky. I've never felt so alone and defeated, my trust so misplaced that my heart plots to give up. At the same time, my mind races to conceive a plan to save myself.

Sky chimes in, "I was skeptical that you would find a way to get her into a red hat as we'd discussed, but I should've known better, Patrick. You never disappoint."

"She was like soft butter in my hands."

Sky gives me a look of disgust. "Sounds messy."

"It was a sweet victory," Patrick coos, running the backs of his fingers down my jaw. "But the most exciting part is yet to come. Brace yourself, love. We have another surprise up our sleeve."

I watch men drag an unconscious body through the doorway. His limp feet scrape across the tile floor before they throw the beaten man at my feet. I stare at the barely recognizable features of my dad.

Hope can be calamitous. I'd almost given up hope to find Dad alive and here he is, beaten and in ruins, but alive. Alive, but why? He's not a gift. They're using him to taunt me, dangling hope in front of me only to rip it away, breaking me further and further until I crack. I can no longer hold back the angry tears. I tug on my restraints, hoping the physical pain will become my ally and keep me from collapsing.

Patrick backs up as Sky steps forward, drawing all eyes back to him. "Now, Emily." He pauses dramatically to slide his glove back on. "We have a nice room for you down the hall—a luxury suite filled with anything you desire. Or . . ." he tilts his head to the side and shrugs, lowering his voice, ". . . you can sleep on the concrete floor in the cell across from *that* thing." He points to my dad.

I look at the floor, watching the shallow breaths shudder out of him, wishing I could take his pain away. My gaze shifts back through the room. Anger runs through my blood as I spot Patrick standing amongst the men. He's wearing a superior smirk, and I promise myself I will not say a word. I will get out of here and I will destroy them ALL!

"I'm so glad you and Patrick could really get to know each other, because you two are going to give me grandchildren," Sky announces.

Grandchildren? How can that be? Sky can't be Patrick's father, because I've seen Patrick's father in his memories unless the bastard just manipulated me into seeing what he wanted me to see. So, this is Sky's plan. It's why he hasn't killed me yet. He wants my DNA.

"I know you may not be happy about it right now, my dear." He runs his fingers down my bare arm causing me to cringe. "You will get used to it over time. Just think of how powerful your children will be."

He's lost his damn mind if he thinks that'll ever happen. I will die before I let Patrick lay a hand on me.

"How does it feel, Patrick, to finally get revenge on the one who killed your mother?" Sky says as he runs his fingers through my hair.

I jerk away, unable to hold my tongue any longer, I shout, "He killed her!"

Sky claps. "Oh goody, she talks. He killed her only because she helped you, dearie. It's your fault she's dead."

My mouth falls open, furious at the lies he's spewing. "You. Are. Poison!" I say through clenched teeth.

"No, love, he's right," Patrick says, and I sink deeper in the betrayal I'm already drowning in. "By helping you, my mother committed treason to our people. Like I told you before, no one who wants to live will help a Valla. Her death was necessary because you allowed her to help you."

"You can't be serious!" I spit, shaking, hot with fury.

"Oh, don't be upset with him, darling. I do believe he has great feelings for you," Sky mock-whispers as if sharing a friendly little secret. "But don't be too comforted by that fact. He loved his mother and he murdered her. Because of you, of course. Now don't get me wrong, he's certainly not heartless. He cried over her death for days until I sat him down and explained he was useless to me when he wept like a coward. If he didn't pull his shit together and become a man, he would end up the same way as his dear old mum."

I feel like I'm falling further down the rabbit hole. I glare at Patrick across the room, but he has no expression on his face as he stares back. He's a murderer and a liar, and yet I can't help but blame Sky. He made Patrick into what he is.

"Oh, my dear, I'm joyful to know you're fond of him!" Sky bellows. "You see, this is all part of my plan; to find my daughter a proper husband."

"Daughter?"

"No," Dad utters, conscious, but too weak to move. Despair crashes over me. My dad is dying before me just as my mom had, and once again there is nothing I can do.

"Oh, but you are wrong! That weak, pathetic pile on the floor is not your father. Do you really think that impostor is capable of making something so magnificent, something so special, so strong?" Sky pauses, looking delighted in himself. "Dear, you belong to me! I only regret your mother and I couldn't make it work."

The thought of Sky being my father makes me sick. It can't be true! I know my dad. He raised me, giving up everything to protect me, and now he's lying on the floor, broken and unable to fight. He's watching me through swollen eyes.

"Don't look at him!" The despicable man yells. "I am your father. Me!" Sky's polished shoe lands on Dad's chest. "He stole you! He raised you in filth, teaching you nothing!"

"He taught me everything."

"Everything, huh?" he says, with a malicious grin. "Like, who you are? Did he teach you that? Did he teach you how to use those powers you hold? Did he teach you who to trust? Let me tell you who he is. He is an insignificant thief who couldn't begin to understand the magnitude of what we are!"

"You are poison!" I shout.

A wicked chuckle vibrates his chest as he moves closer. "I may be poison, but you are part of me, darling. Don't ever forget that."

I spit in his face. A collective gasp sucks the air from the room and my heart leaps into my throat, anticipating the punishment to come. I glare at him and wait, watching his cold expression frozen on me. My breathing is thunderous in the lethal silence that ensues.

Sky moves and from the corner of my eye, I see his men flinch. Patrick raises an eyebrow, but Sky doesn't strike me. He wipes the spittle away with his pristine white glove. Maybe that's their purpose. Perhaps people spit on this man frequently. I certainly hope so.

His expression tells me he's listening to my thoughts and I can't help but smile because he knows my level of hatred for him. Even if it's true, even if this monster is my biological father, he will never be my dad and I will never succumb to him.

"I love your spirit, sweetheart; however, never is a promise you cannot make or keep."

Sky raises a hand in the air, and with a curt gesture, everyone moves toward the door, everyone except for Patrick.

Sky moves back into my line of vision. "He's pretty resistant," he says, nudging my dad with the toe of his shoe. "Your mother must have done a number on him. Did you know Patrick's mother was protecting your so-called dad? She cleverly made it impossible for anyone to access his thoughts without him being alerted. However, she created a back door into his mind that only she and Patrick knew how to access. So, you see, Patrick could slip into Mark's mind undetected anytime he chose. We didn't have to capture or harm him, but we couldn't pass up the opportunity to get even."

I find no sympathy in Patrick's expression, the bastard. He smirks with a wicked glint in his eye, and my rage boils just beneath the surface.

"You might as well give up this fight, Emily." Sky cups my chin delicately. "You cannot win."

"Win?" Patrick snickers from across the room. "She'll be lucky to survive."

"Yes, it'd be such a pity losing my daughter so soon after finding her. I'll give you some time to think it over, darling. Come, Patrick." With his arm wrapped around Patrick's shoulder, Sky leads his favorite protege through the doorway.

Before I can get closer to my dad, two men come back into the room. They unhook me from the chair but keep me shackled. They guide me down the hall into a place with two small holding cells. They remove my restraints and shove me into a cell. A few minutes later they drag Dad into the opposite cell five feet away. Without regard, they drop his mangled body onto the cement floor. He lets out a painful moan before unconsciousness consumes him.

The chill of the floor seeps into my body as I watch the

unsteady rise and fall of my dad's chest. He kept the truth from me. The men who initially abducted my mom didn't take her because she was pregnant; they took her so Sky could impregnate her. The thought makes me dry heave. Sky might be my biological father, but my dad is the man face down in the cell across from mine, and because he raised me, loved me, and protected me, he's suffering and may lose his life.

Hours later when the cold has thoroughly permeated my bones, I notice a movement from Dad's cell. He turns his face toward me and his cracked lips part, attempting to speak.

Tears fall from my eyes. "I'm sorry," I breathe. "I'm so sorry."

"Mm' always yer' dad," he struggles through broken breaths. "Mm' proud 'a you . . ."

Proud? How can he be proud?

"Don't talk," I whisper, even though I suspect he's telling me this because he believes he's going to die. He tries to look at me through the eye that isn't swollen shut. I wish I could reach him. If only I could touch him, I might be able to heal him. I might be able to give him a chance.

"Love you," he moans, wincing and clutching his side. His breathing is loud and fast.

Tears continue to flood my cheeks. "I love you, Dad."

I stretch my arms through the bars. I push until the bars dig into my skin, and then I push harder, enduring the pain in my shoulder. I can't reach him. I don't even come close, but I have to try.

"I'm so sorry."

"Noh yer fault," he slurs, "Should 'a protected you . . . Sor . . . Sorry. T . . . Tell Sam . . . Love . . ." he slurs and falls silent. His mind is blank when I reach out to him. His rapid breathing is shallow, and I suspect he's lost consciousness again.

My lips quiver and I hit the bars between us. Crying, though it resolves nothing, is my only option. Guilt consumes my heart. Because of me, Sam will likely lose the last member of her family, and I'll lose the only dad I've ever known.

My hopes are dwindling. It doesn't help that I haven't eaten or slept in what feels like days. There are no windows to give me a clue to the day or time, but my captors continue to bring meals that I refuse to eat.

The hours tick by giving me time to reflect on my many mistakes. Patrick, the manipulative jerk, told me all along it was stupid to trust anyone, yet, foolishly I trusted him.

A breeze against the back of my neck has me spinning around. There is a woman inside my cell, the same woman who keeps showing up at random. Though I no longer feel the breeze, I see it winding through her wild hair as her crystal blue eyes focus on me. I reach out to her, but my hand catches nothing but air.

I ask, "What do you want?"

Her careful voice reverberates through the room. "Rising from nothing to fight for a cause. A victim, a killer, an innocent one."

"Why do you keep saying that?"

A mournful expression clouds her beautiful features and she continues, "Finding freedom for souls we believe to be lost, by crossing lines that cannot be crossed."

I shout, "Who are you?"

She vocalizes, "Fear breeds allegiance that is easily broken, while love builds loyalties that remain unspoken." Her image fades and I'm left alone in my cell.

thirty-one ~

I hear someone enter. I keep my head down, hugging my knees to my chest as I sit huddled on the cold cement. With my eyes trained on the floor, I try to rein in enough strength through my exhaustion to hold my world together. Footsteps come closer as nausea rocks my body. I am the last Valla. The last demon blood with abilities beyond my comprehension, yet I'm trapped and powerless. The footsteps stop on the other side of the bars.

"This isn't exactly what I had planned."

Betrayal stings my eyes, but I force myself to glare up at Patrick through the dimly lit cell. Anger swells in my veins and my blood runs like molten rage, filling my body with a hatred I once thought unfathomable. I've thought of a thousand ways to tell him off. I want to make him understand what he's done. I want him to feel remorse; to feel the same impossible pain I feel, yet it's clear to me that nothing I say, no matter how articulate, will make a difference. He's here to gloat. At least now I'm smart enough to know anything I say will be used against me.

As he crouches before me, I notice the gun holstered at his side. Bile rises in my throat as I conjure a grin, saying, "Did you miss me?"

"Just when I think I've figured you out, you baffle me."

ANNA REZES

I force a condescending laugh. "Little insight, Patrick, I'm a person, not a riddle."

His charming smile stabs through me like a hot knife. "Is that where I've been going wrong?"

He's mocking me to see if he can get a reaction. I look at my dad in the next cell and close my eyes. He hasn't moved in hours and I stopped hearing his splintered breathing minutes before Patrick entered.

I clear my throat and swallow my tears. "Patrick, is there a point to this little visit?"

"There is a room for you just down the hall if you'd like—"

"I'd rather die," I interrupt.

"And you're doing a fine job of that by refusing the food and water they bring you. You gave up so easily, didn't you?"

"I don't trust any of you. Why would I eat the food?"

He sighs, "For starters, you'll starve."

"I'd rather starve than be poisoned."

He shrugs as he stands and spins away from me. "I expected more from you."

"I could say the same. You knew all along, didn't you? It wasn't the theater or the boat. You knew who I was the moment you first saw me, and you were laughing at me the whole time." My nails cut into my palms.

"I knew you were special the moment I heard your thoughts in my head that first day on campus. I figured out you were Valla blood the night I ran into you and Ben at the theater," he says, turning to face me. "You could hear my voice in your head which told me you were an Olvasho, but then those terrified green eyes landed on me and it all clicked together. That's the reason Sky wanted you, the reason he sent me, his second in command, out to find some unimportant girl. So, yes, I knew what you were, but I was never laughing at you."

348

I glare at him through the bars thinking back over all of his lies that led me here. "Well, congratulations, Patrick. Do you want a pat on the back or maybe a medal? No, no, a trophy that reads, world's biggest jackass!"

He says, "You should know your eyes tell me what you're feeling."

I shrug. "So, you know I'm pissed."

Leaning forward, he whispers, "They tell me you're afraid."

"Then you're focusing on the wrong thing," I growl, but he turns and walks away.

"I am surprised Mark has lasted this long." He takes the few steps to the door of Dad's cell where he pulls a key from his pocket. "Perhaps you need a wakeup call." Patrick faces me, leaning against the bars of Dad's prison cell. "When he's dead they will bring in your sister, then Benjamin, I suppose. It can all stop if you just have a little sit down with Sky. He is your father, after all."

I look away, unable to bear what he's saying.

He pushes off the bars, saying, "Fine, sit back and watch everyone wither away. Slow, painful deaths, Emily. Is that what you want?"

I say nothing.

"Giving up so soon?" he shouts, hitting the bars to my cell. "What's wrong with you? This is what I trained you for!"

I flinch and glare at him, seeing nothing but lifeless blue eyes staring back. His pull on me has been unequivocally severed. "You trained me for him! And I hate you for it." Spittle escapes my mouth as my voice quakes. "I hate you!"

"That makes two of us, but remember not to let that hate consume you, love."

"Ha," I say without humor. "Am I supposed to believe that? That you hate yourself? No, I don't believe that for a second. Since I met you, I've wondered what you've been hiding beneath that charming smirk and those hypnotizing eyes. Now, I know you're incapable of emotion. Your soul died the day you murdered your mother. I'd rather be cold and miserable than feel nothing. I'd rather die than be like you."

He grips the bars of my cell. "You go ahead and watch your family die and you'll become exactly like me. You'll build a callous around your heart and eventually it won't feel so bad."

He shifts to the other cell. With a click of a latch, the bars swing open. "Time to check on Mark."

"Don't touch him!" I shout, jumping to my feet. I squeeze the bars feeling like a rabid dog in a cage.

Patrick places a gentle hand on the side of my dad's face and Dad gulps in a rejuvenating breath. He's not dead! I was so afraid. He groans, cringing in pain, while deliriously swinging a weak arm at Patrick.

"Get your hands off of him!" I demand, a tear escaping the rim of my eye.

Blue eyes meet mine through the bars as Patrick easily deflects my dad's feeble attack.

"You're hurting him," I sob. "Please. Stop!"

"Is that what you think I'm doing?" His eyes begin to pale.

When Patrick taps a finger to Dad's temple, he ceases his struggle and lies limp on the cement floor. Only now his chest is moving up and down in a steady rhythm. Patrick straightens to leave my dad's prison cell. He locks the chamber door behind him, pocketing the keys before sauntering over to stand before me. He appears vulnerable with his misty-blue eyes.

"You've got it wrong," he says. "I'm keeping him alive. If for nothing else, to give you more time. He's going to die because apparently you've given up, but at least his extended suffering might save your sister's life."

"I don't believe your lies, Patrick."

"I'm not lying," he promises, moving closer. He is close enough to touch, but I have to plan carefully before I strike.

"I trusted you," I say with a shaky voice.

"I'm still on your side."

"Prove it." I flick the bar. "Let me out of here."

"You should've been able to do that already," he condescends, stepping even closer. "You're too busy starving yourself and wallowing in your own demise. We're not playing a game here, Emily. You can't just give up!"

"Careful Patrick, your seams are showing."

I reach through the bars at the same time I attack his mind. His physical movements lag as he focuses on defending himself against my mental assault. I pull his body against the bars, one arm around his neck, the other reaching for the gun cradled at his side. I unhook the holster and flip the safety as I place the barrel of the gun to his temple.

"Go ahead," Patrick mumbles.

"You don't think I will?"

"No, I wish you would. You were supposed to kill me in the boat. That was the plan. I was counting on your Valla blood to take over. It would have been a perfect death."

"Do you think I'm buying any of this, Patrick?"

"Emily, I've been ready to die for a long time. If you would've killed me on the boat, you could've inherited my strengths, just the edge you would need to kill Sky. You weren't supposed to have the control to stop yourself. You weren't supposed to have the conscience to keep from killing me."

He's putting up no resistance. I don't understand, so I ask, "Have you given up?"

"It's too late for me to give up. Killing me is the easiest solution, but your morals won't allow it. I know because I've given you ample opportunity."

"You're a liar."

"See for yourself." The tumultuous eruption of emotion escapes from Patrick like a tsunami crashing over me, leaving me to suffocate in his disturbing thoughts. He tore away the veil protecting his mind, destroying his best defense, at the same time inviting me in to look through his darkest secrets. I thought I knew him before, but I was wrong. Dead wrong. Infinite grief and venomous anger threaten to drown me before I put up a defensive barrier to block it.

"You want to know who I am?" he whispers. "Take a look."

Even if it's a trap, I have the upper hand. And this time I won't hesitate to kill him. I ease up on my resistance and hear his thoughts filter through my mind. I feel how difficult it is for him to keep his barriers down, to let anyone see beyond his masterful exterior.

"If you so much as flinch, I will kill you," I threaten, easing into his tortured mind, careful to avoid a fatal mistake.

I feel the angry ocean brewing as I dive in. I choke on the heavy aura of despair, disgust, and self-loathing. Fifteen-year-old Patrick is hunched on the floor of a dimly lit cement cell. His bloodshot eyes and tear-streaked face show me he's distraught. His dirty torn clothes and oily blond hair tell me he hasn't showered in a while. Purple bruises stain the skin around his neck and jaw. His knuckles are swollen, cracked, and caked with dried blood. He's a picture of hopelessness, and I wish I could do something, say something to this younger, uncorrupted Patrick, but I'm a fly on the wall watching events unfold, unable to change them.

Terror bolts red-hot up Patrick's spine as the heavy wooden doors to the cell chamber are thrown open. Sky saunters into the room dressed in a white pinstriped suit with black velvet accents. He looks like an albino tiger on the prowl: proud, distinguished, and most of all, deadly. He's wearing those ridiculous white gloves and I'm rooting for Patrick to spit on him, so they have a purpose.

"Who are you?" Patrick's voice vibrates with fear, as he rises to his feet.

Sky bows. "My name is Sky Vallor of the prestigious Leona bloodline."

"Where is she? Where's my mom?"

"She's safe," Sky says, as he sticks the key in Patrick's cell door. "My dear boy, you should not be kept in this hole. I apologize. You are Patrick Glenn of the prominent Isa ancestry, are you not?" He opens the door to release Patrick, but the shaken teen doesn't respond.

"Are you not?" Sky asks again with an edge of impatience. Patrick nods and Sky smiles his deceptive smile. "Come, my dear boy. We are allies in this war. I'm sure we can resolve whatever it is that led you here. Let's get you cleaned and dressed. We can't have the future of the Isa lineage rotting in a cell, now can we?" Sky offers his gloved hand to Patrick. "Forgive this miscommunication."

Patrick is apprehensive about taking his hand.

"This could be the beginning of a beautiful relationship," Sky announces, making my stomach churn. "You have such potential."

"What about my mom?" Patrick pulls his hand away.

"She's just down the hall getting cleaned up. I thought we could discuss it over dinner," he says, inviting Patrick to walk with him down a brightly lit hallway.

At the edge of a spacious dining hall, a plethora of potted lilac's scent the air with a lovely aroma. The three-story room surrounded by grand marble pillars supporting impressive balconies from the floors above. From the towering ceiling hangs a cascading crystal chandelier sparkling like diamonds. Under the glittering light is an elegant dining table with seating for twelve.

"This way," Sky says. "I'll show you to your private room." They ascend the winding staircase to the second floor. Sky opens a door to reveal an opulent room to rival an upscale hotel.

"Suitable dinner attire will be waiting for you when you complete your shower. I'll meet you in the dining hall at six o'clock. That gives you one hour." Sky leaves Patrick overwhelmingly alone.

Time skips ahead to Patrick looking in a mirror. He's freshly showered, wearing a stylish grey suit. He looks handsome and powerful but lacks the composure that's so typical of Patrick. There is a brief rap on the door before Sky bursts into the room with his unwelcome enthusiasm.

"Don't you look nice! Oh, but those won't do." Sky reaches his hand out to touch Patrick's jaw.

Patrick moves away. "It doesn't hurt."

"But it looks awful. Besides, I feel terrible about what's happened. Won't you allow this one kindness?"

Patrick is speechless, hypnotized by those evil blue eyes. When Sky reaches out, Patrick stiffens but doesn't move away. As the bruises disappear, an aura shifts between them. Sky is doing more than healing; he's getting into Patrick's psyche.

"That's better, my dear boy," Sky says, stepping back.

Patrick snaps out of his trance and touches a hand to his face. "Umm, thanks."

"It's the least I can do." Sky pats him on the back guiding him out of the room.

They descend the winding stairs into the open dining area with the colossal chandelier. The men seated around the table stand when Sky approaches.

"Come sit at the end by me," Sky invites.

"Where's my mom?"

"She'll be here soon, I'm sure. Women always take so long getting dolled up." The men at the table sit after Sky is seated, and Patrick nervously fiddles with the bottom of his jacket.

"Eat. Please," Sky encourages. "I know you must be starving. I'll go check on your mother." Sky stands and the other men at the table stand with him. Patrick begins to get to his feet, taking the cue from the others, but Sky stops him with a hand on his shoulder.

"Please, sit, enjoy the food. I'll be right back."

Patrick looks at the other men as they take their seats. "Hi," he murmurs.

The men don't acknowledge him. Patrick grabs a roll from a tray to occupy his fidgeting hands. He didn't realize how hungry he was until he finds himself reaching for another. After the second roll, he piles mounds of food on his plate. He gorges himself and by the time he's finished, he looks downright giddy.

Sky re-enters the room escorting Patrick's mother. Her long blond hair is curled and styled in a low chignon with tendrils artfully hanging loose. Her light makeup accentuates her angelic features. She's wearing a form-fitting white gown accented with silver, if you can count chains as accents. Her hands and ankles are shackled like a prisoner in transport. Her face contorts as she spots her son and the anguish is evident in her stilted movements.

Patrick sees them approaching and smiles as if nothing is out of place. "Mom, you've gotta try these mashed potatoes," he says, his pupils so dilated only a rim of blue remains.

"Don't do this, Sky!" She grabs Sky's wrist pleading with him. "I beg of you, don't do this!"

"It's already done, Alessandra! You take my daughter from me; it's only fair I take your son from you."

"He's innocent."

"Not for long!" Sky sneers, wrenching out of her grip.

As if nothing is amiss, Patrick piles another helping of chicken on his plate. "Mom, seriously, this chicken is amazing."

Alessandra sits down across from her son and watches him eat. Patrick doesn't notice her silent tears. He doesn't feel the tension in the room. He finishes eating and leans back in his seat, full and content.

Sky turns to Patrick. "Son, I'm afraid we need to talk about your mother's situation."

"Her situation?" Patrick questions, having a difficult time focusing.

Sky places a hand on the back of Patrick's neck forcing his mental influence. Alessandra moans and it's obvious Sky is mentally restraining her.

"Your mother stole my daughter from me." Sky's theatrics are at play, as he clears his throat like he's choked up.

"She did?" Patrick's addled eyes try to focus on his mom.

"Yes, you see, my daughter is not well. She has this condition that without my assistance, she may kill dozens, even hundreds. She must be contained, but your mother helped her escape. My daughter needs me, Patrick. Without my guidance, who knows what she will do."

"Mom, why did you let her escape?" His innocent confusion paints him younger than his years.

Alessandra cannot speak. She tries to fight Sky's dominance over her, but she can only submit.

"You see, Son," Sky says, hiding his contempt, "your mother enjoys watching other people suffer. She must reap the consequences of her actions and because you are her son, how do we know you are not an accomplice?"

"What?" Patrick breathes, reverting to the mental state of a five-year-old as the narcotics from the tainted food hit Patrick's bloodstream. He's too drugged to see the situations for what it is.

Sky simplifies. "Your mother is bad. You must punish her to prove you are not also bad."

"What do I have to do?"

An evil grin stretches across Sky's face. "We'll think of something, my boy. Come, let's go to a more private space down the hall."

Patrick is oblivious to the severity of the situation. He obeys and escorts his mother toward the door. She smiles and looks to him lovingly, cherishing his touch, perhaps because she knows it will be the last opportunity she'll have.

They enter the empty white room. Two men follow shutting the door behind them. Sky drags a cold steel chair to the middle of the room. "Patrick, help your mother to the chair. Those stilettos must be killing her feet."

Patrick guides Alessandra to sit down, gently wiping away her tears.

"Come here, Patrick," Sky says, opening a small cabinet built into the wall.

Patrick follows and peers into the storage cabinet filled with knives and guns. Sky removes an eight-inch dagger and hands it to Patrick who embraces the knife like it's the most natural thing in the world.

"Now Patrick, this is where you prove to me, you're someone I can trust. That woman over there is a bad person. If you don't take care of her, she might kill us both."

"Oh!" Patrick looks at his mom. He doesn't appear to recognize her.

"You must kill her, Patrick. With this knife." Sky nudges the hand gripping the blade.

"Now!" Sky shouts. "Patrick, kill her now!"

Patrick moves swiftly across the room and plunges the knife into his mother's chest. She screams as the hold Sky has on her breaks. Patrick blinks and shakes his head as he begins to understand what's happening. His hold on the knife hesitates while his eyes focus, but his mind is not his own, and he shouts in agony. Tears stream down his face as he thrusts the dagger into her heart again, unable to regain control.

Sky motions for his men to intervene. They grab Patrick and drag him away. He's wearing her blood on his hands and howls his grief, realizing what he's done. He kicks at the men holding him, lashing out as rage consumes him. His mother slumps in the chair, bleeding out. Her gaze, twisted with grief, is soft and loving as she watches him for as long as her eyes will allow. Patrick cries out for her as the door closes between them.

The energy in the room shifts, and before Alessandra dies, Sky steals a part of her, pillaging her vitality. He extracts what's left of her life force by consuming her soul, feeding his power. Sky killed Alessandra. Patrick was merely the weapon he chose to carry out the deed.

Realization dawns on me. Emancipated at sixteen, Patrick has never been free. Sky beat him down one twisted lie at a time and eventually and inevitably it consumed Patrick with darkness. Every time Patrick tried to escape Sky's hold, he was ambushed or manipulated, molding him into the monster he never chose to be. Patrick was forced to become a loyal accomplice to an evil man and thus became evil by default.

He was sent to find the girl with Valla blood five months ago with no idea what he was getting himself into. He was taught to believe Valla descendants were demons and must be eradicated or controlled. He proceeded to comb the Midwest for an eighteen-year-old girl who fit the description of a Valla. He never expected to find me.

His orders were to report back immediately if he found Valla blood, but Patrick found a purpose in me. He was captivated from the moment we first met. It took him time to convince himself that I was actually Valla blood because I was nothing like the demon Sky had made me out to be.

My presence took away some of the torment that had been consuming him. He spent hours near me without my knowledge to reassure himself there was hope. Patrick had to give up my father to appease Sky, so he would have time to train, prepare, and equip me with the skills needed for the imminent fight. He believed together we could defeat Sky.

Patrick was sure I was ready to face Sky when he felt the strength of my power the night my memories returned. He realized his mistake when I went blind. Even though the trip to the hotel was a setup, the emotions I felt from Patrick were real. And at the compound, the betrayal I felt had to be genuine to convince Sky. It was the only way we had a chance of surviving.

Easing out of Patrick's mind, I realize I'm still holding him against the bars. I release him and stumble back. I flip the safety, before letting the gun slide from my grip to clatter against the cement floor.

Consumed with guilt, Patrick keeps his head down. "I learned how to adapt and do what I needed to do in order to survive. You'll never know how deeply I wish I could take it all back."

Sky used him as a weapon, the same way he plans to use me, the same way he wants to use our children. It happened to Patrick slowly. He became what he is by losing one hope at a time. Now he's left with only one hope — me.

"Emily, say something."

"He nearly destroyed you," I breathe.

ANNA REZES

He shakes his head in disagreement. "Emily, he did destroy me. It wasn't until I met you that I started to piece myself back together."

His flawless beauty is covering something so mangled and scarred he's barely recognizable as human on the inside. The terrible things he's seen and done and the horrendous acts that have been done to him break my heart. I blink the tears away, but more continue to trickle down my face. He touches my cheek, his pale irises imploring forgiveness.

"Together we can stop him," Patrick pleads.

It finally registers in my brain that my pedigree makes me nearly impossible to kill. I just needed a wake-up call and a key out of this cell. Patrick provided both. Most Olvasho wouldn't dare come near me because of the power I inherited from my mother. And even though my biological father traditionally should not be able to pass on the Olvasho traits, there is nothing traditional about him. I have the strength of both, making me more powerful and dangerous than any other. I would be unstoppable if I knew what I was doing. My mom's letter comes to mind: *"You have abilities that others can't begin to comprehend. You will be the one to stop this feud. It only makes sense it would be you."*

Me.

"I knew you were trouble the moment I laid eyes on you," I whisper.

Before Patrick can blink, I create the illusion he's suffocating. It's only in his mind, but his body reacts all the same. His eyes bulge with surprise and he chokes. His face contorts with betrayal. His protest only lasts a moment before he passes out. I reach through the bars and guide him to the floor knowing he'll be out for a while.

A tremble takes my body and I'm relieved no one is here to watch me fall apart. My world shifts in front of me, forcing me to make black and white decisions on issues that are very grey. The responsibility is on my shoulders alone. I'm determined to do whatever it takes to save others from Patrick's fate, even if it leaves me corrupt.

Of one thing I'm absolutely certain, I will find a way to stop Sky.

thirty-two ~

I don't let myself wallow for long. No one is going to rescue me, and I just knocked out the only person who was willing to help. I get to my feet, straighten my shoulders, and wipe my tears aside. I leave the gun behind because I'm my own greatest weapon. I reach through the bars to retrieve the keys from Patrick's unconscious body and unlock my cell door. Dad appears comatose, but he's breathing better than he was before Patrick helped him. He looks peaceful as I walk away from his cell feeling resolute and hoping to return to him soon. I pound three steady thumps on the main door, signaling for the guard to open it from the outside.

The door opens without delay. When the guard realizes it's me instead of Patrick, one hand reaches for his handcuffs while the other palms his gun.

"If those handcuffs come anywhere near me, I'll use them to strangle you to death," I warn.

As the guard shoves the handcuffs back into his pocket, he identifies Patrick lying on the floor behind me. His eyes sharpen on me while he tightens the grip on his gun.

"Sky has big plans for me. He'll be pissed if you do anything to harm his long-lost daughter and spoil his fun."

His finger moves to hover over the trigger. "Wrong move!" I say, as I barrel into his psyche and he shifts the muzzle beneath his own chin. His terrified eyes plead with me as he tries to fight for control, but his fight is useless. Patrick was right; controlling him is no challenge for me. Once I locked down my emotions, I could've broken out at any time. Either Sky severely underestimated me, or he wanted me to break free.

The guard mumbles some gibberish about being sorry, and I release my hold over him. His gun falls to the floor and I turn away assuming he isn't dumb enough to pick it back up.

"Take me to my father!" I demand.

The guard takes the lead, but I pause when we pass a fruit bowl. "Are these safe?" I ask.

"Safe?" The man looks puzzled.

I grab an apple, practically salivating over the possibility of food. I hand it to the guard and give him a cunning smile. "Taste it for me, will you?"

He takes the apple and puts it to his lips. His hesitation is fractional, but I smack the apple away. It's laced, yet he was going to eat it anyway, willing to sacrifice his cognitive skills in order to keep me from escaping.

"Take me to him," I demand.

"This way," he says, placing a hand on my arm to direct me.

I rip my arm away and step back. "The last man to touch me is dead in my prison cell," I fib. "And he was a friend. Imagine what I'd do to you!"

The guard leaves distance between us as he directs me turn for turn down the hall. We come to a stop outside a guarded door.

"I presume you know who I am," I say to the guard standing in my way. "You'd be smart to step aside."

He opens the door for me and both guards follow. It's the enormous dining room from Patrick's memory. While the guards wait by the door, I pull back the throne-like seat at the head of the elegant dining table. I slouch into Sky's chair, plop my sandal-clad feet up onto the table, and cross my ankles. The layers of flowing material keep me from showing more than I intend to show.

Sky loves drama so sitting on his throne with my feet resting near his plate is my idea of setting the scene. The men are watching me intently. "Well?" I say. "What are you waiting for? Go get him!"

They look up to the second story balcony just as Sky approaches the railing adorned in a black pinstriped suit which looks dramatic, fitting his ego as well as his lean body.

"Bossing my men around?" Sky raises an eyebrow, looking down from his balcony perch.

"Aren't they my men too . . . Daddy?"

A lion's grin curves his mouth as he saunters the length of the balcony. He is the devil, but instead of horns and a pointy tail, he has snow white gloves and a coal-black cane. "All this can be ours, Daughter!" He waves his arms with theatrical flair, his voice echoing as he starts down the winding staircase. "But darling, why the change of heart? Of course, I had a feeling you might, but why so soon?"

"Perhaps I find a bed more fitting than a dungeon, or maybe I find being on the winning side a bit more fun. On the other hand, it could be I want to inherit the full ability of my powers. You might be strong, but together we'd be unstoppable."

"Cunning, you are not," Sky says, reaching the bottom step. "What is it you truly want?"

"He's dead!" I swing my legs to the floor.

"Who? The impostor you call your father?"

"No." I shake my head and feel him itching at the confines of my mind. "Patrick."

He laughs. "Yeah right, you are capable of a lot, but—"

"Reach for him," I interrupt. "You won't feel him because he's dead. If you want to work together then you should know, I do not take betrayal lightly."

Trepidation radiates from the men in the room, but I feel only disbelief from Sky. Sometimes I'm able to feel a person's mind when they are sleeping but being unconscious is entirely different. I can't sense Patrick, and I hope this monster can't either.

"You bluff well, my dear, but I can sense a lie."

"Why would I lie just to be discounted?"

"Why, indeed?" He taps a finger to his chin.

"If you don't believe me then let's go check on him." I stride toward the door. "Shall we?"

"You didn't kill him because I don't sense him in you," he says, unmoving.

Ignoring him, I open the door. "I don't need to consume souls for strength. I am strength. I'm my parent's daughter, after all, half evil and half Valla," I remark, gaining me his laughter.

"Do you want to know how I know you're lying? Once you got a taste of Patrick, you would not be able to stop yourself from consuming his power!"

He is so wrong. I recall the boat ride when I didn't even know what I was taking, and I stopped myself. "Shows how little you know about me, Daddy." The door falls closed between us as I make my way into the hall.

"You are weak!" Sky demands, pushing open the door and striding through.

I turn to face him, crossing my arms over my chest. "Is that so?"

"You value things like love and loyalty, but you're longing for things that are beneath you, darling. You are a born killer! You are not half evil, Emily. The devil herself lives in your veins; such is the nature of Valla blood! The sooner you accept this fact, the sooner we can plan our future!"

"Our future?"

"I built my strength up over the last two-hundred-years and now need only one life a year to maintain my youth. Becoming so powerful, I sought to build my legacy. Together we'll make an army and become immortal," Sky monologues like a cliché supervillain. "You'd be a fool to deny any power, especially Patrick's. I lived two lifetimes feeding off the weak before I killed my first Valla. That's when I felt true power. Lucky for me, Valla's descendants kept breeding, and once I tasted that power, I had to have more. I consumed them mother and daughter—the last of which was your mother. Tragic, there was such potential if your mother and I had joined forces, but she escaped to hide from me. As you discovered, no one can hide from me for long."

"You mean like my human father hid me for eighteen years."

His fingers stroke my cheek. "I found you, didn't I?"

I push his hand away. "Patrick found me and brought me here as a weapon to destroy you."

"Tell me buttercup, is it just your love for him that is blinding you or are you always this naive? You've already allowed him to manipulate you once. And now look, you fell for his trickery again," he coos. "It's so like Patrick to get someone else to do his dirty work."

"That sounds more like your style, but what can I say, I guess he learned from the best," I say, staring him in the eye. "What do you think it says about you, that your second in command has betrayed you? If you believe any of your men are loyal to you, then you're the one who is blind. Your men only comply because they're afraid, but there are limits to fear. What happens when they find out I'm more powerful than you?"

He grips my upper arm and tows me alongside him like a disobedient child. "You don't know who you're talking to!"

I pull at his grip, but it's unyielding. "I know exactly who I'm talking to and if you think you can control me, you must not know who you're dealing with."

"I can crush you!" he sneers, opening a door. He shoves me inside releasing me to stumble over my feet.

Before I right myself, I recognize the drain in the tile floor and realize he brought me to the white room of death.

"I will crush you," he says, standing in the doorway.

"Apparently you don't know who I am." I right my stance. "I cannot be crushed."

"Powerfully big words for such a little girl. But can you back them up?" he goads.

"I'm not fighting for power or immortality. You have two-hundred years on me, but you still don't see what you're fighting for is meaningless. You are alone even as you stand surrounded by your puppets. They don't need you. To them, you are a virus."

"I am omnipotent!" he shouts, prowling into the room. "You will bow before me!"

He throws his arms into the air with a flourish and his hair floats around him, standing on end like a thousand tiny bolts of lightning. We enter a new level of eerie as the door slams shut behind him without either of us moving. I struggle to remember who I am as I feel his mind fighting to penetrate my barriers.

"I have no desire to be immortal," I say, while I mentally push him away, enjoying his frustration. "Live or die makes no difference, as long as I protect the world from you."

His features twist with disgust. "Now you sound just like a human."

367

"That's the nicest thing you've said to me, yet."

"I've seen it time and again." He shakes his head. "You deny it, but once you feel the power, the excitement, the pure ecstasy, I guarantee you will give in!"

"You are so wrong!"

A mysterious wind whips the back of my knees like a physical kick. My legs give way and I fall forward, landing on my knees. It's unnerving. Olvasho have the ability to manipulate minds, but Sky is manipulating the air around us. His mental influences are manifesting into physical power. I didn't know that was possible, but here I am on my knees in front of him. I immediately pull myself up, refusing to submit or show subservience of any kind.

Sky is infuriated and growls his frustration, "This is a waste of time!"

"You're afraid of me."

"You are wrong, child. I am afraid of no one! You are insignificant. The only reason I haven't destroyed you is because you are my kin and the last of your bloodline. I've waited too long to end it by simply snapping that fragile little neck, but don't tempt me."

He's conflicted. I would already be dead if he weren't. I mean something to him. Not because we have a father-daughter bond, but because I'm his special pet project. He needs me alive to start building his army. My death would mean he would lose years of planning and an entire army of Valla blood.

"I'm all you have left," I say with an air of nonchalance.

"You," he jabs a finger toward me, "you fight for life and love because you don't understand true power. I will kill everyone you love! Then we will see how you cooperate."

Sky's pride causes him to deny he has any flaws, but he has one critical flaw. He views love as a weakness. He is not wrong. Love opens us up to vulnerability and can end in tragedy, but love is also profound, giving courage to even the greatest of cowards. I have my moments, but I am not a coward, yet he's incapable of understanding my courage as anything other than weakness. He will never comprehend who I am because he sees in shades of grey and my world is full of color. He may touch the surface of my emotions, but he'll never comprehend the depth of my soul.

With that thought, I penetrate the walls of his mind for the first time and find it's wide open. Too easy, it must be a trap, but I jump in anyway. This is war. I will do what needs to be done to stop this evil man.

There is a vast difference between Sky and Patrick. When I enter Patrick's mind, I get the distinct feeling of water, like I'm diving into an ocean. This is not the case with Sky.

Sharp winds lash at me, disorienting my thoughts. I peer out at the barren desert landscape shielding my eyes from the sandy current whipping violently through the air. I'm standing at the precipice of a plateau hundreds of feet in the air. Unusual for a desert, the breeze is frigid against my bare arms and the wind whips at the long layers of my dress.

Fear sits heavily on my shoulders sending warning chills down my spine. I sense looming danger hovering all around me. The atmosphere darkens and something silky grazes my shoulder. Fear whirls me around to face the imminent threat, but when I turn, I find myself alone on the plateau. Moving away from the steep ledge, I search for Sky. The gentle graze tickles my shoulder once more, raising the hairs on the back of my neck. Catching a glimpse of a shadow above me, I look to the sky. Terror grips me, digging its nail-like claws deep into my skin. It clings to me, making something as natural as breathing next to it impossible.

There are hundreds! If I had to put a name to them, I'd call them phantoms. They are vague apparitions of the people they used to be. The disembodied shadows float around and above me in a swarm.

The wind ceases, and in the silence, Sky speaks, "Admiring my collection?"

Spinning to face him, I gasp at his distorted features. Inside Sky's mind, he is easily eight feet tall making his already narrow frame painfully thin. Static in the air causes his straggly white hair to float haphazardly around his shoulders. His lips are pale in his elongated face. The whites of his eyes are black, contrasting the bright blue of his irises. Beneath cat-like pupils, dark streaks run like smudged mascara down to his chin. His skeletal structure protrudes beneath the pale skin of his naked chest and arms. White skin darkens to black at his elbows and extends down to taloned fingers. Below his waist, his legs are covered in fine black feathers resembling fur which fades into bony black ankles and taloned feet.

"You look . . . repulsive," I say, unable to hide my disgust.

"Yes, isn't it wonderful?" he says, revealing jagged teeth. He twirls in a circle to give me a full view of him.

His mind is not what I expected. It's different from anything I have experienced in my training with Patrick. The control and connection I have with my physical body is weakening as the strain between my mind and body intensifies. I attempt to retreat back into my body, but I get stuck in the periphery of his psyche. Like a slingshot, the barrier around his mind snaps me right back to the plateau. I was right. It was a trap. Sky's mind is not built to keep people out, but to hold them in.

"It's a prison," I breathe.

"Ding ding ding!" Sky mocks, gleefully. "You finally understand."

The connection to my physical body is weakening the longer I'm in his head. I feel his mind consuming my own, and I shout, "You're psychotic!"

"You have no idea," Sky remarks, then peering up, he calls, "Selma, come say hello to our daughter."

"No," I cry. I don't want to believe she's here. When she died, I had hoped she found peace.

An apparition floats before me, the blurry shadow melting into beautiful features. The longing to wrap my arms around my mother is all-consuming. Her vacant eyes come alive with recognition and her transparent hand tingles as it touches my cheek. "Emily." Her voice is an eerie sound, an echo of a memory.

"No touching!" Sky thunders, as he flicks his taloned fingers to knock her away.

I gasp, my emotions in my throat. Sky looks down, hearing my tell. A cunning smile plays on his lips showing off his sinister teeth. My mother hisses at Sky but keeps her distance.

"Meet my army." He circles his hand toward the sky. "They will rip your soul from your body at my command. Now, let's talk about your future since the only way back to your body is through me," he says, hovering closer with his creepy malformed body.

He believes he can contain me here, but I can't allow myself to fall for his deception. I search the sky, unable to find my mother amongst the sea of souls. And that's just what they are, souls that Sky imprisoned after he murdered them. My fingers curl into fists at the injustice as I glare at Sky. He's trying to manipulate me with fear and distract me with my own heartache.

"Delicate heart, wield your flames." Turning my head, I follow the voice. "Use the fire from within." My mother's voice is a rushed whisper. I barely make out her words before the freezing blast of wind hits her like an explosion and she vanishes.

Sky sucks air through his wicked teeth as his straggly white hair whips around him. His extreme reaction indicates my mother's words are important, but I don't understand what they mean.

I look to the lost souls who have been withering here for so long they have forgotten who the real enemy is. Since my mother is willing to risk the wrath of Sky, perhaps the others will follow her lead. I just need to wake them up to see me through clear eyes, so they know their fate does not have to end here.

My mother has disappeared, so I call out to the mass of shadows. "Alessandra? Patrick grieves for you every day."

"What do you think you're doing, child?" Sky chides.

"This monster," I point to Sky, "has destroyed enough lives! Patrick had lost all hope before he found me and brought me here to stop this evil man." My eyes slide across the apparitions. "Destroying Sky is the only way Patrick or any of the people you love will stay free of your fate. I cannot do this alone. I need your help!"

"They will not help you." With a wave of Sky's hand, the shadows make a ring and whirl around like they're caught in the stream of a tornado. "They are loyal only to me. Selma sometimes forgets her manners. I have yet to break your mother of her bad habits."

Ignoring his mocking comments, I address the phantoms floating above. "The Valla bloodline dies with me!" I shout. "This evil man is my blood but will never be my father or my captor. I come here willingly and will not leave until you are all free!"

Sky's atrocious laughter penetrates the air, as he shouts, "You are wasting your time!"

That's when they strike. Alessandra's translucent body dives through me, and splintering pain rakes my mind. Another spirit plunges through my torso. With the second impact, I fall to the ground in Sky's mind, and though it's distant, I feel my physical body react, falling to the floor in the white room.

At the sound of Sky's cruel laughter, I lift my head, but I cannot stand as my body is paralyzed with pain. When the initial shock subsides, I feel new energy. What I thought were attacks were just the opposite. After the spirits traveled through my body, the power of wind and water linger within me increasing my strength.

A blue flame bursts from the ground and my mother's features blur as she also dives through my body. Fire energy permeates my very being. I realize now, the spirits have come to my aid, awakening something within. Sky leaps toward us and I react on instinct. When I reach my hand out to stop Sky, white-hot flames burst from my palm.

Sky jumps away from my trajectory and the apparitions above halt their movement. Hundreds of misty transparent eyes peer down at me. Awakened by my flames, their eyes begin to focus.

"Darling, you are unsalvageable!" Sky spits with disdain, and then his eyes widen in shock as my mother's translucent hand solidifies in mine. My body glows as she transfers her strength to me.

"Go after her now!" Sky orders his army of floating soldiers, but they remain stagnant. "I said, kill her!"

They don't respond to his command.

My mother's voice echoes, "We take no more orders from you!"

"I am your master! You will do as I say!"

"You are not our only master," Alessandra attests, floating to my side. "She is your blood which gives her power over us."

"She is nothing!" Sky shouts.

Another figure rises next to Alessandra. When his features solidify, I recognize him as the burly man from Patrick's memory.

Patrick's father takes Alessandra's hand as he speaks, "Two hundred souls and she still has more power than you."

"Enough!" Sky commands. With exaggerated movements he throws his arms in the air, causing the wind to toss around us. "Emily, be gone from my mind! I grant you passage back to your body."

I feel the restraints on his mind releasing me and feel my physical body calling to me like a beacon. It's summoning me home, tempting me to return to my body, but I remember whose hand I'm holding. I remember my promise. I remember my mission.

I look at my mom. "Can I set you free?"

"We can become yours if you take us into your mind, into your body," she responds.

"And then I can set you free?" I implore.

"That has never been done."

Sky interrupts our conversation, howling, "You won't be able to let them go! The power will consume you!" I feel an intense force as Sky attempts to push me out of his mind, but my mother's presence keeps me anchored.

"But it can be done?" I ask my mom.

"The transfer, yes," she nods, "but even if you can't free us, we would rather be with you."

"How do I do this?" I ask.

"Imbecile! It will destroy you!" Sky's eyes glisten with rage and with a flick of his wrist, a cyclone roars up from the ground creating chaos as the apparitions above are tossed around like leaves in a windstorm.

Sky propels a second howling wind funnel in our direction. I launch flames that get caught up in the increasing speed of revolving air. Fire is drawn up into the cyclone, creating a massive flaming twister. My inferno devours the wind, consuming it until all that's left is a hovering cloud of black smoke.

I don't have time to relish in the small success, because Sky is a formidable opponent and is already launching his next attack. When I dodge the razor-like wind, his anger escalates. His advances grow increasingly haphazard. The temperature plummets as he continues lashing out with sharp currents.

"Mom, how do I get you out of here?" I shout to be heard through the pandemonium.

My mother's celestial voice at my ear startles me. I hadn't realized she was still so near. "Call to us and grant us passage through your mind into your physical body. Your mind will try to reject us, but hold strong and we can make it through."

"Spirits!" I bellow. "Enter my mind and free yourself from Sky!"

The phantoms rush at me one after the other, and I automatically throw up my defenses, protecting my mind from them. They ricochet off of me and my mom waves them away.

She turns to me. "Emily, you need to open your mind. You need to accept them."

"I'm sorry. I didn't know what to expect," I tell my mother.

"Simply believe in your capabilities, sweetheart." Her soothing words renew my strength.

I address the spirits, "Come back. Please, try again."

The phantoms seem hesitant which is uproarious to Sky as he bellows with laughter.

If Patrick could rip apart his walls for me, then I can do this for these lost souls. "Spirits," I call, "I will set you free. I'm ready now!"

One brave phantom rushes forward and dives into my mind. I fight my instincts and hold back my defenses. My mind absorbs the soul, and I feel her with all of my senses. I see her there in the confines of my mind. I taste her essence, hear her cries, smell her sadness, and feel her as my mind swells to make room for her. As soon as my mind assimilates, I shift her over to my physical body in the white room. Once she has passed over, I feel like myself again.

I don't have time to think because when the spirits see my success, they all rush forward, flying into my body. The pain is like nothing I've ever experienced. I collapse against the intrusion as my mind struggles to absorb the spirits. Seeing my affliction, my mom waves the remaining spirits off.

Sky advances while I'm defenseless, battling the agony in my head. The wind lashes my face like a whip, throwing me backward onto the ground as blood trickles from my temple.

"Emily, you must fight!" my mother yells.

Once I adjust to the feel of the spirits inside my mind, I get to my hands and knees. A steady stream of blood drips down my cheek and I'm momentarily dizzy. Seeing my struggle, Sky strikes again, but I don't go down this time. I force away the thoughts in my head that are not my own and allow the spirits to move from my mind into my physical body. Once they are out of my way, I rise to my feet and retaliate.

"This. Ends. Here!" I shout as flames burst from my hands forcing Sky to retreat.

Strong gusts of wind push against my flames, trying to extinguish my fire, but a new power awakens within me, adding strength and increasing force behind my flames. I hold my own against Sky as the spirits resume transferring into my body. Overcoming the pain of them melding into me, I begin to experience their power.

Wind lashes my back, ripping my dress as blood seeps through the delicate fabric. I encircle myself in a ring of fire allowing myself a moment to recover. Time slows to a crawl as I continue to fight

Sky, all the while absorbing the spirits as they come. The pain lessens with each new addition, and the accumulation of power is overwhelming. As my mind adapts to the spirits, Sky's wind diminishes, and my fire grows into an inferno guided by the air current I now control.

As the remaining spirits escape Sky's hold, he stumbles, collapsing to his knees, his voice filled with resignation. "All that power feels amazing, doesn't it?"

"Stopping you feels amazing."

"Do you plan to steal my soul as well?"

"I don't want any part of you."

"You are part of me, darling, and it seems as though you've inherited the gifts of the Leona bloodline as well. You are continuing my legacy, whether you realize it or not. You will not be able to give up those souls. The feeling is too magnificent! The power will rule you."

He's right, I do feel magnificent, but these are human souls. No matter how great they feel, they are not something to be owned or possessed.

"Once again, Father, you have no idea what I am capable of."

"Just you wait. Just you wait until you go back to your body."

My mother and Patrick's parents are the only spirits left in Sky's mind. Alessandra steps before me. "I made the right decision believing in you all those years ago. I would still choose you, even if you're unable to grant us freedom."

"I will. I will find a way to free you!"

She lowers her eyes. "In any event, please tell our son we love him. My death was never your fault or Patrick's. It lies solely with Sky, who you have bested." She lifts her eyes and her hand caresses my cheek. "I am forever grateful." Before I'm able to respond, she jumps into my subconscious. With a warm smile, her husband follows suit.

Sky is unable to transfer into my mind because he neither has the strength nor my permission. He begins decaying before me. He will be the only one to remain in the prison of his own making.

I face my mother. "Mom, why are they saying these things now? They're in my head. I can set them free!"

"Emily." She cages my cheeks in her hands. "My strong, beautiful daughter, I am so proud of you. Even when it's difficult, you value morals over temptation. Sometimes the right decisions are the hardest to make." She places a hand on my chest. "Listen to your heart." Her lips press into my forehead. "Now go before his mind collapses."

My mother dives into my body before I can say anything, ask anything, before I can wrap my arms around her and beg her to stay with me. The plateau shakes under my feet warning me of disaster. I escape back to my physical body just before Sky's mind implodes.

I'm back in the white room with Sky. His face contorts with anger. "You stupid bitch!" He raises his cane to strike me only to disintegrate before my very eyes. As his body turns to dust, his suit and gloves fall to the floor. His cane remains upright for a second longer before it clatters against the tile.

I have no time to assimilate because the cacophony inside my mind cripples me. An all-consuming power is blazing inside of me, a hundred times amplified now that I've returned to my own body. Euphoria encompasses me as supreme power circulates through my veins. It's building me stronger, making me indestructible, changing me into a God among humans. This is the power Sky bragged about. It's invading my being, clouding my judgment, but I'm helpless to fight against it. The omnipotent strength occupying my mind obliterates my weak human resolve.

Patrick's mind reaches for me, causing me to stutter in my thoughts. He's worried about me. The reminder of loyalty halts the overwhelming urge to consume. I am bound to Patrick, obligated to fulfill my promise to the broken child from his memories. I am bound to the promise to free the souls now trapped within my mind. Sky can't destroy any more lives. I defeated him, but will I become just like him? Will I continue his legacy just as he predicted?

As my thoughts drift to the man who raised me as his own flesh and blood, cracks begin to chip away the steel bars that greed is creating around my heart. I must release the souls before the overwhelming desire for power consumes me completely.

A blood-curdling scream escapes me. Like a wild vine grown untamed around a tree, the power strangles me, taking over my very essence. The splintering in my head is agony as the yearning for more absorbs my voice of reason. Now I understand why my mother and Alessandra said their goodbyes before they left Sky's mind. They knew I could defeat Sky, but they also knew the power would consume my being.

The agonizing pain continues. I have failed them. None of us are free.

thirty-three ~

"Tom, do you really need to wake her?" Julie whispers outside Morgan's bedroom door, but Tom is already opening the door. They enter the room and he calls Morgan's name.

She sits up and turns on the light. "Yeah, what's wrong, Dad?"

"Have you heard from Emily or Patrick?" he asks.

"No, Dad. For the twenty-fifth time, no."

"Do you have any idea where Emily might go?" he asks, walking further into the room.

"Dad, I already told you. Samantha said she went to Colorado with her dad."

"She's not in Colorado. Are you sure she hasn't tried to call you or reach out?"

"Tom, stop interrogating her," Julie scolds.

"Anything from Patrick? Have you talked to Ben?" he continues, ignoring his wife's request.

"I promise, Dad, I don't know anything." Morgan shakes her head exhausted and baffled. "All I know is Emily broke up with Ben and left with Patrick. Ashley told me Emily quit her job. I don't think she's coming back, Dad. What's going on? Why is it bothering you so much?"

"I need you to call Ben," Tom says with urgency. "Ask him to come over. He must know something!"

"Dad, it's five o'clock in the morning!"

"Something else is going on here. Trust me, Ben knows something, whether he realizes it or not."

"Dad, this is crazy. The police even said they're in Colorado."

"The police can be deceived," he says. "Now call Ben or I will!"

Morgan picks up her phone and dials Ben.

"Morgan?" Ben answers, voice heavy with sleep.

"Hey, sorry to call you so early."

"You okay?" Ben asks.

"Could you come over? It's important. I'll explain when you get here."

"On my way."

Morgan puts the phone down and glares at her dad. "Dad, whatever is going on, this better be worth it."

"Something's wrong. I . . . I . . . No!" Tom shrieks in agony, as blood trickles from his nose. His eyes roll back, and Julie catches him mid-collapse, softening his fall.

The power shift going on down the hall jolts Patrick from his unconscious state. He awakens, lying on the cold cement floor just outside of Emily's empty cell. Disoriented with a pounding headache, he moves his stiff neck around on his shoulders. He stumbles to his feet, and the sensation of terror engulfs him when he realizes Emily ditched him to face Sky on her own.

His thoughts are fuzzy, like static caused by faulty wiring between his mind and body. He stumbles to the door trying to mute the incessant struggle. His mind reaches for Emily and finds her amidst grave turmoil, pivoting on life and death. A blast of energy rolls through the building, permeating the minds of every Olvasho in its wake. A violence that is not his own seethes through Patrick's veins as devastation resonates through the air.

A muscular man smashes through the door. Rage consumes Patrick, and he lashes out, swinging fists and dodging blows, unsure of why he's fighting, except it's the only thing that feels right. Patrick lands more punches than the other guy, but he's thrown off his feet when a second man tackles him. He rolls to the floor narrowly avoiding the boot aimed for his ribs.

Gunshots echo from down the hall and bullets ricochet off the walls. The brawl turns into a bloodbath as another Olvasho holding a gun in each hand comes firing toward the fighting men.

Tom is sitting in a chair in his living room while Morgan wipes the blood from his face with a warm rag.

"Dad, you need to go to the hospital. Mom, can't you make him go? People don't collapse unless something is wrong!"

"I'm not going to the hospital," Tom refuses.

Morgan looks to her ashen, freaked-out mother, but Julie escapes by answering the knock at the front door.

Softening her voice, Morgan implores, "Dad, this isn't you. Please, for me, please let me take you to the emergency room. All the paranoia and insomnia in the last week could be linked to what's going on with you now."

His face softens. "No matter what happens, I want you to know I love you and I have valid reasons."

When Ben enters the room, Tom studies him with calculating intensity.

Morgan apologizes, "Ben, I'm sorry to drag you here, it's just—"

"What do you know of Patrick and Emily?" Tom interrupts.

Ben is frozen like he's caught in a trap, startled by the power in Tom's words.

"Ben, your hand, did she fix it?" Tom is insistent. "You know what she is, don't you?"

Ben covers his mended hand. "You're one of them, aren't you?" Eyes wary, he turns to study Morgan.

Tom confesses, "I am, but Morgan is not. Morgan is in the dark, and I only recently told her mother. Now, where is Emily?"

"She got a text from Mark. He was taken. She . . ." He stops short.

"Ben, I'm only trying to help her," Tom encourages. "That you're cautious in telling me shows you have her best interest at heart. Something is happening to her. I can feel it. I need to get to her before it's too late."

"Too late for what?" Morgan asks. "What's going on?"

"The current is getting stronger," Tom mumbles. "I don't know if I can fight . . ." His words turn into a growl. Tom closes his eyes, breathing against the building rage as a red haze blurs his vision. He roars an incoherent warning before launching at Ben.

Ben jumps aside, years of martial arts training coming in handy. Tom—no longer in control of his body—attacks Ben. Ben dodges the punches and kicks, holding his own.

"Dad! Stop it!" Morgan shouts.

Tom turns his fury toward Morgan who becomes his next target. She stares at the rage in her dad's eyes, and fear paralyzes her. Understanding what is about to happen, Ben grabs Tom from behind and neutralizes him before he attacks his own daughter.

"Don't . . . let . . . go," Tom croaks through clenched teeth, thrashing against Ben's hold. A guttural moan chokes his throat as he fights to speak. "She's fighting . . . she's doing this to us." A savage cry escapes Tom and Julie collapses into tears on the floor.

Morgan desperately wants to understand why her father's body appears to be taken over by a wild animal. "Who is doing this to you?"

"Emily." His cry is grief-stricken. "She's dying!"

Morgan's heart drops and she looks to Ben. "What the hell is going on?"

Bullets are flying in every direction, but miraculously Patrick remains unscathed. When the gun is empty, Patrick moves on instinct to tackle the shooter. A frenzied rage has a grip on both men as they engage in a brutal fight. Patrick gains the advantage with a stranglehold, and it takes every ounce of his restraint to keep from killing his opponent.

Clarity hits Patrick when he realizes this power is greater than his own. It's Valla blood at work, consuming every Olvasho with Emily's wrath as she fights Sky.

Patrick's body collapses as the all-consuming violence burns out as quickly as it began. He struggles to get to his feet as the need to find Emily overwhelms him.

Tom goes limp in Ben's arms as he lowers him to the floor. "He appears to be docile for the moment, but I'll keep an eye on him."

Morgan takes the opportunity to check on her mother who is falling to pieces. She does her best to offer comfort, and even though she doesn't know if everything will be okay, she mumbles the words anyway.

"Morgan, he's conscious and trying to say something," Ben says from where he's guarding Tom.

Tom's voice is weak from all the shouting. Morgan grabs a bottle of water and Ben supports his head while Morgan helps him drink.

"Dad, what happened?"

"It's done," he rasps, his forlorn eyes forming tears. "She . . . she lost. She's . . . dead. Emily is dead."

thirty-four ~

It's quiet, too quiet. And it's bright, so bright it should hurt my eyes, but it doesn't. It's a beautiful light, the kind people run to, but I don't need to run because it's surrounding me. All of the pain I felt is gone, and my soul is content here in this tranquil place. I don't have to wonder where I am. I know, because only one thing can end all suffering. There is peace and light in this place that cannot survive among the living.

"You have done it. You have set us free," my mother says, her face glowing with admiration and love.

A warm feeling fills the hole she left in my heart all those years ago. There is no sadness, only love replacing the hurt that once was. I wrap my arms around her. "Mom, I've missed you so much."

"I have missed you," she says, before pulling back. Her hands cup my cheeks. "I always knew you'd be the one to finish this. I'm sorry it's been your burden to carry."

"It's finished. It's not my burden anymore."

"I wish that was true. There is a great deal more for you, Emily. There are people counting on you."

"It's too late." I motion to our surroundings, wondering if this is heaven.

"If I could do it for you, I would," she whispers, sadness seeping into her bright eyes.

"Do what?"

"Fight. Suffer." She brushes the hair from my face. "Live."

"Mom?"

She hugs me again, whispering in my ear, "I love you. I will see you again someday."

The tranquil surroundings become cold; the feeling of peace turns to sorrow as my mother slips between my fingers. I open my eyes and my senses come screaming back. I am alone, lying on a cold tile floor surrounded by white walls. The illuminated ceiling tiles make everything agonizingly bright.

The emptiness I feel after holding two hundred souls is crushing. The silence is too silent and my mind echoes through the hollow space. As I forced the souls from my mind, my soul temporarily fled as well, escaping the undulating pain, but death would not accept me.

I gather myself from the floor and feel new aches in every part of me. I hear footsteps in the hall. They are coming closer and they're coming fast. I reach out with my mind, but pain incapacitates me. Moaning, I fall to my knees and grab my head.

The door bursts open and I look up, unready to face another opponent. Patrick enters the room looking like he's been through Hell. Blood drips from his mouth and his once crisp white shirt is torn and stained. He hurries toward me and kneels down. Gently, he touches his fingers to my cheek as if seeing a ghost.

"You're alive," he breathes.

"Of course." I give him a weak smile. "Sam would kill me if I died before her wedding."

A broken laugh escapes him, and he visibly relaxes, releasing the breath he'd been holding, but his smile fades as he looks around the empty room. "You beat Sky, but where is he?"

"Gone."

"Did you kill him? Is he dead?" He reaches out to help me up.

"I'm not a murderer, Patrick." I breathe, struggling to stand. "I don't kill people."

"What?" Patrick is frantic, terrified. He pulls away. "Where is he?"

"He's gone."

"We have to go after him now while he's weak. If we don't, he will kill us. He'll kill us all!" The relief I saw in his eyes a moment ago has vanished.

"No." Exhaustion is making my explanation unclear.

"What do you mean, no?" He looks at me crazed with anger. "He raised me, Emily! I think I'd know. First, he'll kill everyone you love, slowly, while you watch. Then he'll take your power away, along with your life!"

I point across the room to the pile of dust. "Patrick, that's all that's left of Sky. He can't hurt you anymore. He can't hurt anyone."

Sky's black cane stands out against the stark white floor, and Patrick stares at the crumpled suit covered in dust. "How's this possible? What happened?"

"He was feeding off the souls of those he killed. It gave him power and youth." My unstable body sways and Patrick catches me. "After I took the souls from Sky's mind, his body turned to dust."

"You took the souls?" He stares into my eyes as if searching for proof.

"Yeah," I breathe. "I have to find my dad." I take an unsteady step and fall back into him.

"Are the souls inside you now?" he asks.

"Of course not. If I held onto them, I'd feel a hell of a lot better than this, but then I'd be no better than Sky."

"How did you set them free?"

"He killed my mom. I wasn't going to let her spend eternity with him."

"That doesn't answer my question. How did you let them go? The power—"

"Nearly consumed me," I finish for him. "I don't know how I did it. I just did. Now let's go find my dad."

Patrick wraps his arm around me and guides me to the door. "We need to get you both out of here. Your dad is in terrible shape, Emily."

We move forward, but I'm barely able to make it out of the room, so Patrick sweeps me up into his arms and rushes us down the hall.

It looks like a tornado ripped through the building. Broken furniture and unidentifiable wreckage scatter the halls while bodies litter the floor and blood spatter stains the walls.

"Patrick, what exactly happened here?"

"I'll explain when we have more time," he says, as we reach the prison cells.

He sits me down as he gathers up my dad, and I ask, "Can you fix him?"

"No, Emily. If I tried, I could kill him. His injuries are too complex. I bought him extra time, but there's too much internal damage. We must get him to a hospital, and we need to get you to a safe place."

"Where are we, Patrick?"

"We're at compound seventeen, just outside of Columbus, only twenty miles from home. We'll drop him off at the trauma center on our way to my uncles. I'll be right back for you," he says, before rushing out of the room with Dad's limp body in his arms.

I push forward on my hands and knees, crawling out into the hall to examine the three men lying on the floor. Only one of them is breathing so I move toward him. Somewhere in the recesses of my mind, I register the sting of broken glass under my hands, so I drop to my forearms. I continue moving forward army crawling across the littered floor until stars swirl dizzying circles around my head, forcing me to lie down.

The cold tile is a relief for my overheated body. I rest my forehead on the floor as a thundering eruption blasts through my skull. Wrestling with nausea and a throbbing in my head, I look up when I hear footsteps. Stabbing pain behind my eyes pushes me over the edge and I lose consciousness.

I wake up to a jostling movement and know by the sweet aroma, I'm in Patrick's arms. I rest my head against his chest until he sits me on a cool leather seat. I hear the click of a seatbelt and my head bobs like a rag doll.

A car door slams, vibrating through my brain, launching shrapnel to the parts of me that didn't ache before. My neck remembers its job, and I turn to focus on Patrick. He's got blood and stains and . . . oh no . . . I put my hand to my chin. I feel nothing, but I taste the lingering acid in my throat. I threw up on him.

Patrick's face is pale, and anxiety creases his forehead. "Hang on, Emily. We're going to the hospital and then to my uncles."

I don't argue. I'm too exhausted. A moan from the backseat confirms my dad is still alive. Despite my anxiety, I can't keep my eyes open. Sleep mixes with wakefulness, and I can't tell where reality ends and the nightmare begins. At one moment I'm in a car riding through dark alleys with Patrick by my side. The next moment I'm trapped in an empty room. I look out the window and see I'm several stories up. I scramble toward the door, but smoke begins billowing through the cracks.

Sirens blare. I open my eyes to see the emergency entrance to the hospital. Patrick pulls my dad from the back seat. Cradling his debilitated body, he rushes into the building. I unbuckle my seatbelt and reach for the door handle wanting to stay with my dad.

"Emily, stay in the car!" Patrick's intrusion in my mind causes me to crumple into myself. The pain is unbearable. I close my eyes and wait for the stabbing pain to cease, but instead, it burns. Fire licks at my skin as I lie crumpled on the floor of the burning room. I pick myself up and move to the window. I'm on the fourth floor and I hear the distant sound of sirens.

A door slams and I'm back in the car, hunched over and burning alive with the pain inside my head.

"I'm sorry, Emily. I needed to make sure you stayed in the car. If they saw you, they wouldn't let you leave, and they can't help you right now."

"Just make it stop," I whimper, holding my head in my hands, in too much pain to care how pathetic I sound.

"I'm sorry, I'm so sorry. Using our mental connection only seems to make it worse. I won't do it again," he whispers. His hand rests on mine, but the calm I usually feel from him feels like acid eating at my skin. I cringe away from his touch, shrieking in agony.

He snatches his arm back mumbling another apology as the car moves forward. "We'll be there soon. Just hang on."

I count to ten in my head over and over again until I get stuck on four. I'm on the fourth floor, wondering how I'm going to get out of this place alive. An explosion shakes the building, and the ceiling begins to cave in. I am distracted by the rumbling under my feet and the sound of gravel under . . . a car?

I look out the window and see the gravel driveway that leads to Morgan's house. The sun is just beginning to light the sky. The car stops with a jolt, and my door is ripped open. I'm out of the vehicle without any effort of my own.

"Oh my God! She's covered in blood!" Morgan shouts.

"Most of it isn't hers," I hear Patrick say. "Watch her arms. Be careful of the glass."

"Whose is it?" Morgan gasps.

"What happened?" Ben's chest rumbles as he talks. It's then I realize I'm in Ben's arms. That's nice. Patrick brought me home.

"Patrick?" Tom's tone encompasses so many questions.

"I don't know what to do! Everything I try seems to hurt her more!"

"What about Sky?" Tom says.

"She killed him."

I shake my head in dispute.

"He's dead," Patrick amends.

"But at what cost?" Tom questions.

"Emily? Can you hear me?" Morgan sounds so worried. "Patrick, why didn't you take her to a hospital?"

"Let's get her inside!" Tom's tone is insistent.

"Is there something wrong with hospitals?" says Morgan.

"We dropped Mark off at the ER, but they can't help Emily. I'm hoping Tom can."

"Can you help her?" Ben asks.

"I'm not sure."

"Somebody please tell me what's going on!" Morgan demands as we enter the house.

"Patrick has healed her before," Ben says to Tom. "Isn't this the same kind of thing?"

"Patrick doesn't have the skills to fix this, and I don't know if I can help."

"You'll try, won't you?" Patrick pleads. "You have to!"

"I don't have to do anything!" Tom is seething. "You're the one who did this to her! Don't blame me!"

Morgan instructs, "Lay her here."

"I was protecting her," Patrick defends, as Ben places my aching body on the couch.

"How the hell did you think you were protecting her by leading her straight to Sky?" Tom shouts.

At the same time, Morgan asks, "How did she get all this glass in her arms?"

"Face it, Patrick, you hurt everyone you care about!" Tom fumes.

The pain is all too familiar as those words sink in like a shadow covering my heart. I feel Patrick's agony as if it's my own—because it is.

"Dad!" Morgan scolds.

"I'll see what I can do," Tom says. "Patrick, you should leave!"

"Please, just save her." Patrick stands ready to leave. Using all my strength, I grab his hand pleading for him to stay.

"Emily, you're like a daughter to me, and I'm going to do everything I can to help, but Patrick did this to you."

I wish I could explain but pain explodes in my head and I black out with a scream. I awaken back to the blaze. Thick smoke rolls in quickly like dark clouds heavy with rain before a thunderstorm. The oppressive haze blocks my view, and I pull my shirt up over my nose to keep from choking. The smell of burning timber is pungent causing my eyes to water as another explosion shakes the building.

My body is jostled, and my leaden eyelids open just long enough to see Tom's head bowed in concentration, as he places his hands over my temples. His touch generates a searing heat that sends me right back into the fire.

The flames are greedy, stealing oxygen as it consumes the building around me. Smoke engulfs the room. The effort it takes for me to breathe is like gasping through a pillow.

"Emily, grab my hand," Tom says, his voice a faraway echo.

A crackling sound comes from the opposite side of the room where the flames consume the door, eagerly eating through it like a ravenous swarm of locusts. Through the door a female figure appears, strolling through the flames as if they are a part of her.

Tom shouts in the distance, "No Emily, don't look there. Come this way!"

I look back to Tom's figure and take a step toward him, away from the fire's soft caress. Tom's smoky image disappears, but I hear his voice, "Emily, you must wake up before it's too late."

"Stay," the feminine voice entices. I pause, captured by the woman in the flames, relishing in the comforting warmth. Her hand reaches out to touch my face. Fire coils around me, licking up my legs and around my body like a lover's kiss. I could get comfortable here.

"Emily, Wake Up!"

A loud thud startles me awake. A cold rag touches my forehead, and my eyes flutter open to see Morgan standing over me. Ben and Patrick pull a feeble looking Tom up from the floor.

"What happened?" I mumble unintelligibly, fighting the blanket of sleep from pulling me under again.

Her worried eyes soften, and she says something, but my eyes are too heavy and my mind too tired to make out her words. I mean to respond, but I've already drifted back into unconsciousness.

thirty-five ~

I lurk on the edge of sleep, hearing faint voices before my body fully awakens.

"Do you want me to stay with her for a while so you can get some sleep," Morgan whispers close by.

"No, it's okay. I want to be here when she wakes," Ben says from right next to me.

"If you change your mind, let me know," she offers.

"Will do."

I open my eyes, waking to find Ben slouched in an armchair next to the bed.

"I thought for sure I'd wake up to you playing your guitar," I rasp.

Ben bolts upright in surprise and then his face turns soft as he says, "I thought about it, but it's at home, and I didn't want to leave you."

"How long have I been sleeping?"

"You were in and out for a while, but you've been sleeping steadily for the last sixteen hours." He hands me a glass of water from the nightstand, and I drink greedily, clearing the cobwebs from my throat.

"You've been here this whole time?" I'm horrified at what he must have seen.

"Except when Morgan kicked me out so she could change your clothes."

"Is Tom okay?"

"He's fine. He'll be happy to know you're awake."

"He didn't want Morgan involved in this."

"I think he's relieved he doesn't have to keep it a secret anymore."

"And how do you feel?" I wonder what he thinks of me now that he knows who I really am.

"Emily?" I hear Morgan before she enters the room. "Is she awake?" She walks through the door, and her face lights up. "How are you feeling?"

"Umm, I'm okay."

"You're a dirty liar, but if that's how you want to play it, that's fine. Can I get you anything?" she asks. "More water, medicine, food? Never-mind, I'll get you all three." She comes closer and holds my hand. "I'm really glad you're back. You gave us a hell of a scare."

"I'm sorry for all of this."

"None of it was your fault," Ben says.

"The not asking for help part was your fault," Morgan argues. "But I'm happy you're safe now."

"There's nothing anyone could've done. Sky would've killed you all just to hurt me."

"Patrick is pissed about you ditching him to face Sky alone," Morgan warns. "Also, I just spoke with Samantha. Your dad just got out of surgery. He's in critical condition, but he made it through the worst of it. They expect another surgery in a few days, once his condition stabilizes."

"Stop overloading her with information," Ben says.

"That's good news," Morgan prompts, squeezing my hand. "She needs good news."

"How's Sam?" I ask.

Morgan's face scrunches, giving me the answer before her words can.

"She'll be fine," Ben answers. "Morgan's going to the hospital in a little while to check on her. She's just worried about you. We didn't tell her you were here. In a few days, things will get straightened out. Right now, you just need to rest."

"Speaking of," Morgan pulls away, "I'll be right back with some food and medicine."

"Thank you."

"Of course." Morgan nods, walking out the door.

"Emily Burk, who knew you'd have me beat when it came to dysfunctional families?" Ben jokes.

"What? Like you didn't believe that when you thought my mom was only crazy?"

His warm smile and consoling brown eyes give me the comfort I couldn't find anywhere else.

I confess, "I missed you."

"Ditto," he says, holding my hand. "Em, I hope you know, discovering this whole other side to you doesn't change how I feel about you. I know you're kind of a big deal now, but to be honest, I always knew you were."

"Ben, you've gotta stop putting your life on hold because of me." The words fall out of my mouth and I continue without holding back. "You need to go to one of those Ivy League schools, or become a musician, or I don't know . . . a Kung fu master, anything. You have too much talent to waste, and I won't be responsible for holding you back. Just make sure you get away from your dad, and I'm not just saying that because my biological father ended up being a mass murderer. I love you, and whatever happens, we'll figure it out, but don't deny yourself the life you deserve because of me. Look what I've already put you through. My life is unpredictable and messy. Ben, I still want you in it, but not if it's hurting you or clipping your wings."

"You love me?" he asks, and I realize I've never actually said it to him before.

"Well, yeah." I shift uncomfortably.

"Emily, I'm not sure what I want to do with my life or how I'm gonna get there. What I am sure about is you. All the other stuff will eventually come."

"It's not that easy. I don't know what my life is going to be like."

"We'll figure it out together."

"But, Ben—"

"You need to rest. We can talk about this later." Ben leans forward to place a sweet kiss on my lips. "I was so scared, Em. I know I'm probably not supposed to admit that, but damn . . . we thought you died. When the car pulled into the driveway, my first thought was just to get to you. When I opened the car door . . ." He falls silent, his eyes glistening with unshed tears. He shakes his head. "Your dress was ripped, and you were covered in blood. It was matted in your hair, and your arms were filled with shards of glass. You kept whimpering. I could tell you were conscious enough to feel the pain, but you couldn't focus. I was so afraid I'd lose you. I know you weren't really mine to lose, but I thought I'd lost you."

"I'll always be yours," I whisper. "I'm sorry you had to see me like that. I was careless. I should've listened to Patrick and waited for him to help me to the car. I wouldn't have looked so much like *Carrie*."

He's about to say something when my dog bounds into the room with her tail-nub wagging.

"Maggie!" I reach out for her and let out an oomph as her heavy body lands on mine. I ignore the discomfort as I relish in her affection.

Patrick trails behind Maggie and hangs back by the door. His averted gaze gives me the impression he's suffering. "I picked Maggie up from Chris. They were more than happy to part ways," he says, leaning against the doorframe with a bowl in one hand and a cup in the other.

Tension radiates from Ben the moment he sees Patrick. His aversion has only grown with recent events.

"Morgan asked me to bring your food and medicine up," he says, unmoving.

"I'll take it," Ben offers.

"Wait! Ben, can I have a minute alone with Patrick?"

Ben turns wary eyes to me. "I don't like him. And I don't trust him."

"I know, but he's the reason I'm here. He brought me back to you. Without him—"

"He's also the reason your dad is in critical condition and you almost died!" Ben interrupts.

"And if he were anyone else, I would be dead! He risked his life to save me and I'm not asking you to like him, but I need you to understand he's a part of my life."

Ben is silent for a moment. "Okay," he surrenders, leaning forward to kiss me. "I'll be back to check on you in a little bit."

"Thank you."

His fingers leave mine as he walks away. He maneuvers around Patrick, making firm eye contact on his way out. Patrick remains in the doorway, his eyes reflecting on a bitter memory.

"Patrick?" His shoulders jerk, startled by my voice. His eyes finally meet mine. "Come here."

He moves to the nightstand, hands shaking as he sets down the things Morgan promised. He pulls away, but I catch his arm, pleading, "Talk to me." I pull him in for a hug, and his body collapses onto mine.

"Emily," he breathes, the anguish overwhelming him.

"I'm okay. I'm right here."

"You weren't supposed to do it alone." He lifts his head. "What were you thinking?

"You! I was thinking about you! I was protecting you and all the other people I care about."

"How can you say that after what I did? Emily, why would anyone want to protect me? Especially you?"

"It was wrong what Sky did to you. And I couldn't let him hurt you again. I couldn't let him use you as a weapon against me, and that's exactly what he would've done."

"You could've died! It makes no sense you didn't."

"I wasn't alone. When I was in Sky's mind, I had help. He could've overpowered me if it wasn't for my mom's belief in me. With her strength and guidance, I was able to awaken the other spirits. They reminded me of the Olvasho powers and somehow awakened the fire energy inside of me. I wouldn't have been able to figure it out without the help of your mom and dad."

"My dad?"

I see the flash of disappointment before he hides the emotion, but I realize I just dashed his hopes of finding his father alive. "I'm sorry, Patrick."

"I'm sorry about Mark. I tried to keep him out of it, but Sky wanted him and I . . ." The anguish is clear in his voice. "You have to understand you were my top priority. You weren't ready to face Sky and your dad bought us more time. Had I asked Mark, he would've volunteered."

"My dad's going to be okay because of you. If it weren't for you, we would both be dead."

He pushes himself up to sit next to me on the bed. "I am far from a hero, Emily. My uncle and Ben are right to hate me. I'm the one who got you into this."

"My biological father got me into this. You suffered because of what Sky did to you. Your mom saved my life, and you got caught in the crossfire. Patrick, I don't blame you for what happened to me, and your mom wanted me to tell you she doesn't blame you for what happened to her. None of this was your fault. You need to stop torturing yourself for Sky's actions. He was planning to kill you when your usefulness ran out. He used you, Patrick, and you did what you had to do to survive. The others don't understand what you've been through. I've seen what happened to you, and I still can't comprehend it, but it's important you never let someone else decide who you are."

"I owe you my life," he vows.

"I don't want your life, just your friendship . . . and some answers. Patrick, when I was fighting with Sky . . . What happened in that building? Those men were dead."

He hesitates, and I know the answer.

"I killed them," I whisper with tears gathering in my eyes.

"They killed each other. Your Valla blood awakened while you were fighting. Remember the story I told you about Valla's sisters experiencing Valla's emotions? Everyone in that building believed they were fighting for their lives."

"I killed them," I breathe, horrified.

"You made us violent, but it was our choice on how we handled that violence."

"I'm a monster."

"Remember, Sky was the monster! He was the reason for all the hostility. We were fighting a war, and there are casualties in war."

I can't breathe. "It's my fault, Patrick."

"Just like you told me, Emily, none of this is your fault. Sky would've killed every person in there once they fulfilled their usefulness. By defeating Sky, you saved countless lives and freed all the souls he held captive. Emily, there is not an Olvasho alive who could fault you for the things you did."

"And what about Tom? What did he do to me? I thought you were more powerful than him. Why could he heal me when you couldn't?"

"As you know, all Olvasho have the ability to heal, but some have stronger healing capabilities than others. Tom and my mom were raised as healers. Because the Isa bloodline has a soothing aquatic feel, healers are more prominent in our lineage."

"Wait. You've already lost me. What do you mean by aquatic feel?"

"Haven't you noticed when you're in my mind. It feels like—"

"Like I'm diving into an ocean." I finish his thought.

"Yeah, kind of."

"Sky didn't feel like that."

"No, I suppose he wouldn't. The Leona bloodline feels like the summer breeze," he explains.

"Sky's mind was cold and windy."

"Sky was a sadistic bastard!"

"So, Valla feels like fire?" I ask.

"Yes, although, I'm curious. You have mixed blood. Sky seemed to think you may have inherited the gifts of wind from your Leona heritage along with the flames from Valla."

"I felt both in my fight with Sky."

"So, as I was saying, my mom and uncle were raised as healers. They have abilities I never learned. My mother was going to teach me when I was old enough, but she died too soon. When Sky took over my training, he had no interest in healing, so I don't fully understand what Tom did to make you better. He said you were nearly unreachable like you had cocooned your thoughts into the recesses of your mind. You were unconscious for hours before Tom could break through your psyche. It was taxing on him, but he brought you back to us."

"So where is he now and how is he?"

"He's resting. It took its toll on him mentally and physically. He should be back on his feet by morning. You should take your medicine, and I bet your soup is getting cold."

"What is today?" I ask as he hands me the medicine and a glass of water.

"It's really early, but technically it's Monday, August sixth."

"Happy birthday, Patrick! Sorry, this isn't how you should be spending your birthday."

"I'm alive for my twenty-first birthday. That in itself is a miracle." He stands up to leave. "Now eat, and I'll send Ben back in."

His eyes look less barren, his aura a tinge brighter as he walks out of the room. I stroke Maggie's head and grab the bowl of soup taking a tentative bite. I hear Ben arguing with Patrick downstairs. My heart feels warm knowing Ben still cares enough to fight and Patrick is strong enough to take what's thrown at him. Maybe my life can have some semblance of normal after all. I relax, knowing my world is going to be okay.

thirty-six ~

Fine hairs rise on the back of Lathe's neck, and a niggling in his head implores him to be more cautious today. She's agitated. She's been agitated a lot lately. The breeze traveling down the sealed corridor is a telltale sign something has happened to upset her.

Even in her craziest moments, there is some sanity begging to seep through the ramblings of a mad woman. She was sane once with the rare and exceptional gift of foreseeing the future. Held in the highest esteem among the Olvasho, she was strong and lovely without a care in the world before her innocence was ripped away from her. She was barely older than Lathe is now when Sky ruined her. Now she lashes out at the others. They would feel more comfortable with her dead, but Lathe won't allow any more harm to come to her. For as long as he can remember in his twenty-two years of life, it's always been his responsibility to watch over her.

He pulls the hood from his head and reaches to unlatch the intricate lock system. Tornado-like winds lash at him as he enters. Over the years he's managed to securely fasten everything to the floor and walls. It minimizes damage when she gets in one of her moods.

"Mother?" Lathe calls into the dark room. "Mother, it's too dark in here. May I have some light to see you?"

"I see it! I see it!" She jumps from the shadows and grabs his shoulders. Her glassy, unseeing eyes are fixed on him while her untamed hair lashes in the wind.

"What do you see?"

"There is so much darkness in the space we breathe. So much darkness!"

"Allow me to turn on the light, Mother."

"No! The darkness. We must hide in the darkness. We will stay in the shadows until it passes."

"Until what passes?"

"The oxygen will burn in her lungs and breathe new life, a new life no man can control. The fire will burn. And she will be stronger than the demon slain. The demon is dead, but the blood will rise again. The demon will come to life! We will suffocate in the darkness until she falls!"

"What are you talking about? Who is she?"

"She has defeated your father. And like a phoenix, she will rise from the ashes and be reborn stronger than before!"

"No one can defeat my father!"

"It is already done. The prisoners have been set free. Sky is dead."

"But how? No one is capable of conquering his power."

His mother spins away and the lights in the room flicker to life. The strong winds cease and Lathe notices she's wearing her snow boots with her nightgown again. She crouches in a ball on the floor appearing feeble despite her potential. Her body vibrates with fear. In a shaky voice, she says, "Come sit with me, my son. We will hide here in the light so the darkness cannot reach us."

"Mother, who did this? What did you see?"

Terrified eyes look up at him. "Your father's blood runs through her veins. She is your sister, but her demon blood reigns. She will fight it, but she cannot win. Valla will rise again!"

ACKNOWLEDGMENTS

Thank you to all of you who helped me complete this book. I am so grateful for your support throughout the whole process.

To my mom, thank you for always encouraging me to write and being my very biased number one fan. You are amazing.

A special thanks to Mary Catherine Kline. Without your incredible patience and your brilliant ideas, this book would never have reached its potential. Even through the difficult parts, you always remain so positive and encouraging. I cherish all the hours we spend working together.

A huge thank you to all the ladies who have been with me from the beginning, cheering me on. To Melissa Dirienzo, Heather Coates, Brenda Perkins, Sarah Ware, and Sara Wilson, I appreciate you more than you know! Thank you for enduring my endless questions and giving me your honest feedback. You ladies are awesome! To Melissa, sorry for all the exclamation points!

To my husband, thank you for supporting my passion for writing, putting up with my ridiculous writing habits, and patiently listening to me read you hundreds of pages out of order. Thank you for showing me love so powerful, it bleeds into every story I write.

Continue Emily's story in Descendant of Valla, the second book in the Valla Series.

For more from Anna Rezes visit:

www.annarezes.com

www.instagram.com/anna_rezes

www.facebook.com/annarezesauthor

www.twitter.com/annarezes

Made in the
USA
Monee, IL